P9-BYB-493

Bridge of Sand

BOOKS BY JANET BURROWAY

Descend Again

But to the Season

The Dancer from the Dance

Eyes

The Buzzards

Raw Silk

Material Goods

Writing Fiction: A Guide to Narrative Craft

Opening Nights

Cutting Stone

Embalming Mom: Essays in Life

Imaginative Writing: The Elements of Craft

From Where You Dream: The Process of Writing Fiction

Bridge of Sand

BOOKS FOR CHILDREN

The Truck on the Track

The Giant Jam Sandwich

Bridge of Sand

JANET BURROWAY

HOUGHTON MIFFLIN HARCOURT
BOSTON • NEW YORK • 2009

www.hmhbooks.com

Library of Congress Cataloging-in-Publication Data
Burroway, Janet.
Bridge of sand / Janet Burroway. — 1st ed.
p. cm.
ISBN 978-0-15-101543-6
1. Widows — Fiction. 2. Interracial dating — Fiction.
3. Gulf Coast (U.S.) — Fiction. I. Title.
PS3552.U76B75 2009
813'.54 — dc22 2008022758

Book design by Melissa Lotfy

Printed in the United States of America

DOC 10 9 8 7 6 5 4 3 2 1

For Peter *luceo non uro*

A handful of sand is an
anthology of the universe.

—DAVID McCORD

I

Storage

1

SMOKE HURLED ITSELF UP out of a field a couple of miles to the north, toward Shanksville. Up ahead was a white farmhouse with a crooked chimney and, nearer the road, a boy and a dog staring, the boy's hand on the dog's head like a piece of Americana hokum.

Phoebe said, "If that's a controlled burn, they've lost control of it."

Dana said, "It's the wrong color for a burn."

They were side-by-side on the backseat of the limo, both still stupefied by the fumes that poured from the collapsing towers on their TV screens not two hours ago. Dana thought of the crematorium where they were headed; and it also came to her that the smoke out the window—not mushroom shaped but rather like an oak in summer, thick trunked and burgeoning—was the color called *taupe* or *mole,* which is a good color for the upholstery of a mortuary limousine (her fingers splayed on the seat beside her) but not a good color for a burning field.

But the possibility did not occur to her that the ash was mixed with Pennsylvania dirt and limestone spewed from a thirty-foot crater made by the nose cone of a plane where another forty-four had been pulverized. It was only later, when she understood her place as an incidental widow—her experience, whatever it would have been, shunted aside by general catastrophe—that she thought how one thing follows on another, how nothing keeps something else from happening, how foolishly we suppose that we have earned respite, that Armageddon will not be followed by emergency, that because the car is totaled the pipes won't burst.

A mirror was mounted on the window between them and the driver—mourners need to check their mascara—and it gave back her blanched face, brown hair lopped at the chin, regular and unremarkable features except for a full, mobile mouth, out of which it would (and did) surprise anyone to hear an acerbic remark. A good face for a politician's wife. Whereas her friend Phoebe, a lawyer in her own right, had a glimmering black coif and high color, interesting bones. Wit fit her. It was Phoebe who wore the mascara.

Dana said, "What if I threw a funeral and nobody came?"

And Phoebe: "Do you want to cancel?"

At which Dana lifted her hands far enough off the upholstery to suggest the pointlessness; and Phoebe let out her disconsolate bark of a laugh, and the limo hit pothole after pothole on the weather-beaten turnpike west toward Somerset.

She had hated him, and then he died.

No, it was more complicated than that. They had met in college, bantered, flirted, become infatuated, married, and were disillusioned; then he slowly came to disregard her, and they lost a baby, and she came to dislike and then to scorn him, until shockingly before his fortieth birthday he was diagnosed with an already-metastasized colon cancer, and she nursed him gently, dutifully, until he died.

No, but it was more complicated. Graham Scott Ullman had in ways she could no longer remember reminded her of her father (who was also a Republican, though in midcentury mode). At Pitt he had financed himself by inventing a kind of dating service for potential roommates. His entrepreneurial enthusiasm was (like her father's) infectious. He got in on the business side of a nerd-rich software start-up, and when OmniOptions, Inc., went public he took his cut and his place on the board and went public also, into the Somerset County Council and then into the State Senate. He was still a banterer, and Dana only gradually realized that the banter was always at someone's expense, and that banter is not the same thing as conversation, and that the cleverness he most admired tended toward spin and scam.

She was not a bad politician's wife. Art history is a classy background with no threat attached. She'd spent most of her childhood in the backseat of a Chevy Malibu and knew how to be still while bored. She could cook, and liked to, and playing hostess kept her from having to talk too long to anyone. Through two campaigns and two terms in Harrisburg, she did volunteer things that were good for Graham's career without committing her to one of her own, mostly in libraries and children's wards; and she supposed she would be a stay-at-home mother when the time came to stay at home.

She got at last joyfully pregnant, but faltered in the third trimester with toxemia. Her calves and ankles swelled. She was hospitalized at thirty weeks and gave birth a week later to a girl—they named her Chloe—whose heart was faulty and who died at two days old.

Since she had known, held, watched Chloe for less than forty hours, people, including Graham, supposed the trauma was of a generic nature. But for Dana the little girl was so uniquely formed, so particularly her infant self—the broad translucent toenails, the fully articulated lifeline in her palm, the feathery blue burst of iris, the kidney-shaped mole under her left ear—that though she and Graham had always agreed about cremation, Dana could not commit her baby to the flames. They buried her in a country graveyard near Somerset.

Dana had long ago given up both her father's hope of paradise and her mother's promise of reincarnation. The heaven she most admired was tempera on Renaissance ceiling plaster. Nothing in her experience suggested that the personality would cohere beyond the body. On the contrary, recycling seemed the fundamental principle: nothing blooms but through decay. She believed only and absolutely in immortality at the subatomic level, and considered the nitrogen cycle sufficient marvel, sufficient glory.

But that had not been put to the test, and now it was. Tentatively, and then fiercely, she embraced Chloe's dispersal into the universe. She lay awake at night allowing herself to contemplate the little body in its batiste dress in its maple coffin, welcoming the insects and the ooze, not flinching from the translucent larvae, the self-generating maggots. She gathered this corruption in her arms and crooned to it. She held it to her heart. She lived the teeming, and then the subsiding, and then the still, ashen entropy of the beloved matter. Toenails, palms, iris, mole. Dust to dust. And then she slept.

Dust motes danced in the morning sun when she woke.

Night after night she did this. She did not speak of it.

Their friends were very kind, and appropriately promised healing and acceptance. But for Dana it was not the baby but her marriage that had died. Chloe rotting seemed supremely vital, whereas the inert weight of her days with Graham was revealed to her, the mechanical eroticism of their sex, the rote moral disconnect of their conversation, none of which could be raised again to semblance of a life.

So it is perhaps an enigma that, eight months later, as she was gathering herself to leave Graham and found that he was leaving her instead, she felt no hesitation in devoting herself wholly, for the first time, to her husband. He was her patient. She was patient. Quiescence again came easily to her, and she lived in postponement as in a cushioned space. She listened to his long denial and his scattershot anger and his surprisingly brief fears. When there was no further treatment, she brought him home, where he lay for two months on a rose-colored sofa decreasingly coherent and then decreasingly conscious while she patiently, arduously, unresentfully took care of him.

He had been apparently comatose for a week or so when she came in from an omelet supper in the kitchen, to find him, eyes closed, one index finger raised from the blanket.

Smiling, he said, "Mushrooms."

And at this evidence of continuing appetite, the mystery of the persistence of the pleasure of the senses, for the first time she wept, and perhaps for the first time truly loved him.

One finger on the limo door, the driver handed her out, looked down past Dana's elbow and away. He was no more than a kid, color drained behind a black spot on his chin where he had avoided shaving around a zit. This same drained look was on the faces of those who came toward her, Harriet Honeycutt with a smear of foundation on her jaw, Ben Honeycutt with his glasses fogged and his tie askew, Tom Bradshaw nodding like a puppet. She was surprised and a little impressed to see Tom here. He was only a financial adviser; you wouldn't have thought he'd bother.

"Oh, sweetie, it's so awful."

"I'm so sorry, Dana—and just now . . ."

"Oh, my god. Oh, my god."

The condolences had naturally an apocalyptic cast. Thirty or forty gathered in the chapel that had been set up for two hundred. Graham's Senate colleagues would have had to start from Harrisburg at just about the time the Pentagon got hit, so most had not, and A. L. Moran, or his sons, had pulled out a felt board to pin up the regrets that came in by e-mail, phone, and even, in a couple of instances, Western Union. Those who had made it hugged and clung. You could have thought it was the death of Graham Ullman that had forever changed their world, except that people kept disappearing into an alcove, a restroom, the veranda, muffling their chins into their cell phones. *Terrorists? Invasion? War?*

Two of the eulogizers did arrive: Representative Harvey "Rex" Snyder, who never missed a chance to make a speech, and Lee Terriman, a hunting and fishing buddy who had loved Graham for the qualities that made Dana queasy. A few more locals hurried in, everyone determined to go ahead with the rite, like people on a lurching plane who stave off fear by staring at their paperbacks.

A. L. Moran & Sons was a plain-Jane chapel with a stained-glass window so nondenominational it might have been a pile of balloons, and the gorgeous morning sun tossed triangles and parabolas of bright color on their faces. There was a simple podium, a low, gray-carpeted dais, and the coffin on a conveyor belt whose curtained access to the crematorium suggested an airport screening. Reverend Parkhacker, who had in fact known Graham and could have salted his sermon with a few reminiscences, felt compelled instead to commend our souls to Jesus. Several times. He spoke heavily of forgiveness, and gingerly of Revelations. Rex Snyder began by saying it was a blessing that Graham had not seen this tragic day, but then slid into stumpspeak, unable to avoid *mission* and *outcomes, influx* and *saturation,* and even, she thought, once, *appropriations*—though probably he'd in fact said *appropriate.* Lee Terriman had prepared a series of anecdotes to do with camping mishaps and fumbled technology, and being unable to speak extempore, he struggled doggedly through them, the mourners urging him on with forced laughs. Then they flung themselves to their feet and into "Amazing Grace." A. L. Moran, a balding, suited presence with a walk like wheels, came to whisper Rex out of the room. By the time the coffin slid away, everyone down the rows of pews knew that that smoke in Shanksville was from another plane. *Here? Invasion? Chemicals?*

Most furtively dispersed. Rex hurried off to a photo op as Johnny-on-the-spot, and for the next two weeks would be given credit as the only legislator with the prescience to come home to his constituency when he was needed. Only fourteen went on to Harriet and Ben Honeycutt's house for the catered lunch. They filed past white damask with white roses, delphiniums, and Noritake platters bearing two hundred servings of skewered pork, cold crab cakes, Brie, *asperges en croute,* and Godiva-dipped strawberries. They bore their plates to the rec room and stood munching in front of replay after replay of the second plane going into the tower like a needle into a silo. Tom Bradshaw came back to the dining room, and again Dana was surprised that he, just the guy who looked after the portfolio, had felt either obliged or friendship enough to come for canapés. He set his half-empty plate on the table and turned to embrace her again. He breathed into her neck. She wondered briefly if this was the beginning of a come-on.

She said, "I'll get in to see you this week."

Tom held her yet a moment, stubble against her jaw. "No hurry. No." He stepped back and gave her a watery-blue blink with his nod. "You just take your time, get your bearings. Plenty of time." And she saw—from the way his eyes slid, like the limo driver's, past her elbow and into the middle distance of the Kurdistan rug, the way his hand bounced as he turned awkwardly away—that Graham had not been wise to take his pension out of the state plan and put it into tech stock; that there were debts still riding from the last campaign; that the insurance and the annuities might not be inviolate.

Tom retreated. Phoebe joined her, indicating the loaded table and the dwindling crowd. She said sotto voce, "I had an aunt who gave birth the afternoon JFK was killed. She said the birth was stolen from her. She named him Jack—in the heat of the moment I suppose—but she always called him Eli."

It was true, of course, that babies were being born right now all over the USA. It had to happen to somebody. Other people than Graham were being buried, and others incidentally or accidentally dying. Approximately one out of 365 people were celebrating birthdays. Halve the number for poverty or indifference, that would be something short of three million birthday cakes. A few hundred parents would have hired donkey rides or clowns.

Harriet Honeycutt's catered arugula drooped onto the tablecloth, Brie oozing toward gilt paisley on the porcelain.

Dana said, "What if we took all the party food that isn't going to get eaten today, tie it up in the tablecloth, and ship it to the Middle East?"

Phoebe said, "I don't think we'll be sending asparagus."

2

WHAT NEXT?

Even the most immobilizing loss rests on a substratum of possibility. America felt the tectonic slippage and called it *moving on*. Love surged from the epicenter and rigidified. The anthrax paranoia peaked and subsided. The Guardian Angels took to the subways, the Senate sang "God Bless America" on the steps of the Capitol, the President threw out the first pitch of the World Series at Yankee Stadium and the first missiles of the war at Kabul and Kandahar.

But Dana in those first months seemed both unstable and stuck. Her fits of organization were canceled out by stretches of indifferent exhaustion—a symmetry reflected in her financial situation, where the maxed credit cards absorbed the savings, and the loans against Philadelphia Life and ING wiped out the usual windfalls of widowhood.

Phoebe urged her not to make any drastic changes—*Don't sell the house or fall in love*—but it wasn't that she was reckless, but that she couldn't seem to reconnect with her own life. She wandered through the house all day, CNN on the TV in the family room where she could tune it in and out at will—the news channel as imaginary friend. She folded Graham's shirts into plastic bags. She spent one afternoon gathering whimsical kitchenware into a whiskey carton, wondering who it was who had thumbed through catalogs and made phone calls to acquire these things. Catalogs and condolences still poured through the mail slot daily. She taped the whiskey carton closed, biting the tape with her teeth.

What, exactly, is a box cutter anyway?

You are reading your magazine, aware of only a slight disturbance —the drinks cart rattling?—and look up to see a flight attendant bleeding from the throat; she staggers toward you and collapses in the aisle. And then there are—how many minutes?—half an hour by all reports, to sit needing to pee and with some small part of your mind determined to guard against that humiliation, assessing the set of their mouths as they go about their business in the aisle. You sit rigid, the magazine still open on your lap with its bronzed blond beckoning to some island paradise, a dull undercurrent of acceptance running in you; you say, This is it, now we are gone; *and things become violently slow in the suddenly augmented light, the drops streaming almost horizontal on the little oval of light beside you . . .*

Dana had argued for a country house, so what she and Graham had ended up with was in a gated suburb of the turnpike called Bobbindale Heights, handsome neocolonials gabled and vaulted and too big for their lots, where the smokeless gas fire nevertheless blackened its limestone surround, and the heat trapped itself against the upper reaches of the plaster. Dana had annoyed her husband by referring to this living room as the "vault."

In what he had called the "turret," she went through his papers, wondering in a desultory way whether she would turn up evidence of infidelity (as had happened to Julie Messinger, to Lydia Perlewitz), but all the betrayals were of a monetary kind, and the only thing suggesting a secret life was a folder of line drawings and overexcited prose concerning something called a "BLU-114/B Soft Bomb," which was "highly classified" and about which "very little was known" except that "the Nighthawk stealth fighter carried it against Serbia in 1999." As neither Graham nor the Pennsylvania legislature had any connection with bomb manufacture or Serbia, this probably represented some boy-fantasy of prowess.

You have achieved the cockpit, the captain with his throat cut sagging into the cramped space between the seats, the copilot still breathing bubbles of blood where he slumps against the window; you have trained seven months for this; you are primed as an athlete, humming with exhilaration, honed. There is no more fear in you than in a runner with the hurdle in front of him, the hunter with the gun raised at the elephant, only a concentration so fine it is like the moment just before coitus, Allah in a fireball—get there, get there, yes!

Through the autumn all hundred and sixty souls (or so it seemed) who hadn't made it to the funeral came to call on her. They parked on the circular drive and got out bearing pecks of apples or pounds of chocolates and varying proportions of kindness and melodrama. They sat on the edges of the chairs worrying keys and handbag clasps and wads of Kleenex damp or dry. They brought their angst and dumped it in the space that Graham had remortgaged to eighty percent of appraisal and was, in fact, no longer hers.

These were their friends. They drank coffee or tea or Scotch according to the hour and spoke of Graham in terms that heroically blurred his edges, as if the timing of his death made him a policeman or a firefighter.

Jerry Wiegler, for example, affable, paunchy, twiddling his watch band, saying, "You wouldn't find a more generous or loyal guy. Not many of his kind!" His jowls wobbled with emotion. He pulled at the placket of his golf shirt. He roused himself to rhetoric. "We need his kind to fight these devils."

The trouble with this was that it trampled on the affection she'd felt for Graham in his last days and the self-esteem she'd earned by being a good nurse. It reminded her that she'd been saved from the mess of divorce by the closed shop of mortality. It reminded her that Graham thought the job of government was to put itself out of business. It reminded her that a campaign kickoff always meant campaign kickbacks from pharmaceuticals and coal, and that Graham would have rented out the capitol building for heft enough on the bottom line. As for generosity, Jerry himself would stand and grill fifty filets mignons at a backyard barbecue, though he was almost certainly skimming from his company pension fund. In fact, he was probably a crook *in order* to bestow sirloin with an open hand.

After he left she cleaned out the mudroom, loaded her hatchback, and made a trip to the Salvation Army. When the Waldefords had come and gone, she went through the bedroom closets and called Goodwill. After the Harts, she carted trash to the curb and took an armload of cocktail dresses down to the Caring Connection for Disadvantaged Girls. She slept badly, waked at 1:28 or 3:14 or 5:07 by the digital clock and twisted among the images of the second tower going down, the implosion like a feathered flower being pulled into the ground by its stem.

You are sitting at your desk absorbed by some glitch in a paragraph of policy initiatives. Glance up to see an airplane at an unfamiliar angle—nose foremost—but you don't have time to make sense of this before—what? The noise registers? Or does not? Death comes as a thunder that does not quite reach your brain: the window glass, the paperweight from the third desk over, a crown of Bic pens imbedded in your torso?

Once she had cleared away the skis, the files, the squash rackets, the mason jars, she was seized with a spiritual paralysis. She carted objects from one room to the next and back again like a prisoner assigned a rock pile. One afternoon in a dusty corner of the garage she found a turn-of-the-century kitchen dresser, and she circled it mindlessly, fingering its broken varnish, testing its rusty hinges. She had bought it years ago at a flea market in Johnstown, brought it home roped on top of the car, and then forgotten it. It was solid oak, strongly built, intricately fitted (by someone who had wanted to answer every whim of his wife or bride?) with flour and sugar bins, sliding shelves, a bread board, spice rack, cutlery and linen drawers. The glass of the upper cabinets was warped and bubbled—original, then—but the knobs had in some middle decade been replaced with cheap handles now corroded, and the wood overlaid with coats of darkened lacquer.

She pulled it out into the center of the garage and attacked it with potent-smelling stripper, a putty knife, and rubber gloves. And what she accomplished in the months from October to March was, approximately, to strip this hutch. By Halloween, when it got cold, she dragged it into the house and cleared the dining room. Afraid to use the chemicals with the windows closed, she bought an electric heat stripper, and when that didn't work she wrapped number 3 fiberglass paper around a scrap of two-by-four and sanded in long strokes along the grain. She leaned over to work on the sideboard surface, and when her back tired she bent at the waist, sanding from the floor to the lip of the top shelf at the limit of her reach.

The patterns of the harder and softer wood rose toward her, warm out of ordinary oak, as if honey, caramel, and molasses had been poured and solidified. No, it was more complicated. The grain contained the world—stippled and burled along one plank and watermarked like moiré silk in the next; here zebra stripes, here the lidless eye of a peacock tail, jagged lightning bolts, dark knots circled like stones dropped in a pond. She floated on the intricate behavior of the grain, the news channel subliminal in the background while her eyes followed her hand, her ears keen to the steady scratching of the sandpaper, and the smell of sawdust making her breathe belly deep. Was this what they meant by disassociation? Denial? It was a kind of peace.

You are three floors above the smoking hole; the flames are at your back, below you the cascade of paper like some monstrous ticker-tape parade; the heat comes hugely at you and you know you will either burn or leap into that shower. The pieces of it flutter, waft. Choice seizes you.

For one whole afternoon this fact of the paper held her mind, the wonder of the survival of the fragile; and on the phone she pointed out to Phoebe that you might read this meaning in it: people die but their stories stay. "Rock, scissors, paper," she recalled. "One chance in three. The first few days, people said, 'It's only a game,' 'It's only a movie,' but nobody ever said, 'It's only a newspaper article.'"

Phoebe said, "Yeah, but you know, that paper in the towers was ninety percent financial crap. Accounts, debts. If it tells a story, it's *Das Kapital.*"

"Oh," said Dana, disheartened. She thought of the neglected forms in the "turret," the detritus of bureaucracy in death's wake.

She went back to sanding.

Or you are falling with the rubble, inward, downward, arms above your head because that is some peculiarity of reaction to gravity; hit and hurt on all sides but only dimly aware of this because you can take nothing in but the elemental sensation of falling, the way you've dreamed it a few dozen times in your life, but this time it does not end, you do not wake, it keeps going on, on, until the breath is all sucked out of you and your feet touch something, are broken on something, that is not the ground but is now the ground, the mountain of mortar and mortality where you finally lose consciousness . . .

She asked Phoebe, "Do you think everybody imagines what it was like?"

"More or less," Phoebe said.

"More? Or less?"

"More, I guess."

"Then why do we have so little imagination that we're bombing caves? They're *guerillas.* You can get that in any high-school history book—the redcoats always lose."

"Oh well," said Phoebe. "Now we wear camouflage."

"Maybe we brought it on ourselves. Our hypocrisy, our arrogance."

"It could be argued."

Dana said, "Nineteen guys and less than half a million dollars. It's the most cost-effective military operation in the history of the world."

"Yeah," said Phoebe, and Dana could hear her flicking an ash on the edge of a saucer. "But I don't know as I'd say that in, you know, your average social situation."

When the surfaces were done she brought a half inch of stripper inside in a jelly jar and began to scrub the right angles with a toothbrush. Since there were a total of thirty-two doors, drawers, shelves, and racks, this was dispiriting Zen work, apt to raise the question of what she was doing it *for.* It was time to jump-start her life. But she had no juice. She was scooped dry, scarcely energy to move her voided husk across the room. With stripper on a Q-tip she chafed the mitered joins of molding.

At the back of one of the drawers she found a scrap of newspaper from 1924, an ad for a doll with a Kewpie face and a price tag of a dollar twenty-five. This sparked a memory of the first time she met her grandmother Hoffstetter, who had an agglomeration of such dolls in a glass-fronted case in Brunswick, Georgia. Later, when she spent two years in that house, it had seemed faintly *weird* for a grown woman to own this collection. But on that first meeting she had furtively coveted a miniature Red Riding Hood, and she remembered being distracted from her greed by chasing fireflies in the humid night.

She thought there was a snapshot from that trip. She dug behind the linens in the hall cupboard and pulled out a Kinko's box into which at some point she had emptied the contents of an earlier and scruffier box. Including the cockroach shit. She thumbed through: her mother in vintage thrift-shop crepe and lace-up boots, her father in a Bogart hat in front of a barber pole (there was ten years between them but it might have been a generation), herself gawky in denim bell-bottoms, nose screwed up against the sun. And here it was in square, fading Polaroid: the imposing, purse-mouthed grandmother and herself no older than eight or nine, holding triumphantly up to the camera a mayo jar that looked empty in the light of the flash but that had contained a couple of dozen slowly perishing fireflies. Meticulously recorded on the back in her father's hand: *June 1973, Dana and Mother Hoffstetter, 431 Tippet St., Brunswick, GA.*

She asked Phoebe, "Do you think behavior is metaphoric?"

"Such as."

"This hutch, for instance. My grandmother had one and kept dolls in it. I wondered if I'm—trying to reconnect. As if I went off track when I left high school, and I'm trying to tell myself . . ." This embarrassed her. ". . . trying to *restore* . . . see what I mean?"

"You're not restoring that thing. You're renovating it."

"What's the difference?"

"Restoring means taking it back to what it was—pegs and linseed oil. You're going to polyurethane, no?"

"Oh, god, it sounds tacky."

"No, it's fine. Renovation is moving forward; restoration is looking back. Anyway, it's a handsome piece; you don't have to make it into some *objet.*"

Phoebe was overworked in her Somerset office (marital and family law), but she came sometimes for a late snack or a Sunday afternoon. Sometimes she ran interference with the callers, but more often the two of them tucked up at the kitchen table in that impotent conspiracy of the divorced and widowed, like buddies in a foxhole whose loyalty to each other grows with the bleakness of their prospects.

"I've forgotten: which side is it that kills the women and children in a war?"

"Here's what I don't get. If you have a family cutting each other up, some shrink sits them down and says: *'Guys, this doesn't work, you have to learn to get along.'* But if the whole world is dysfunctional, everybody says: *'Hang tough, kick butt!'*"

"You're an innocent, Dana. In my line of work I see what people do to each other."

"But then they get divorced, they get restraining orders. Nobody hands them a machine gun and says, *Go for it.* What makes nations so different? — is what I'm asking."

"Because it's *territory.* They killed us on our land, so we have to go after them on theirs. It's wired into the bottom brain, the lizard part."

Phoebe had got herself a new shorter do, sleeked to a point along her jaw. She claimed she was giving up smoking, but Dana saw no sign of it. On the contrary — the fume hung between them anyway — Dana reached across the table to filch a Virginia Slim. She made a moue to mean: *I'll give it up again when you do.* Phoebe stilled Dana's hand for a second on the pack, then shrugged and reached across with her flat brass lighter.

Dana said, "You know what I realized? I have six digital clocks in here. Microwave, oven, radio, bread maker, coffeemaker, cappuccino maker."

"Yeah . . . ?"

"There are no off buttons. They can be wrong, but they can't be off."

Phoebe laughed, effortful. "What we need in this country is a good five-cent dose of *off*."

"A little can't-do."

"A twenty-four-hour moratorium on decision making."

"A Society for the Prevention of Cruelty to Pessimists."

"Make democracy safe for atheism!"

This was a comfort. But sometimes Dana saw her own reflection in Phoebe's non sequiturs, and wondered if she was slightly off the rails. She said to Phoebe, "Here's what I think about when I wake at five. You're an Afghan woman. Pregnant. The well's been bombed so you have to walk two miles to water and carry it home on your head. This is just ordinary daily stuff, okay? Going-to-the-supermarket stuff. You have three kids. The ten-year-old carries the baby, but you have the toddler by the hand. You're nearly home when you hear the planes. You can't look up because the pot is balanced on your head. You have to decide in a split second, just by the sound, whether to pick up the kid and run, let the water pot fall and break, or take a chance you're not in their sights and you'll get the water home. Every day this happens."

Phoebe blew the smoke carefully out of a keyhole at the side of her mouth. "Let's do a weekend at Hamilton Spa, okay? Buy some tchotchkes, get a facial and a pedicure."

"I can't afford it," Dana said.

She upended the drawers and the doors on a plastic tarp and gave everything three coats of semigloss Spar urethane. She spent an afternoon in Home Depot picking porcelain knobs, brass plates, and hinges; another with a drill and screwdriver, positioning and tightening. In the wavering glass of the cupboard doors, polished to mirror shine, her face was gently distorted, like a miniature version of a funhouse or an ineptly repaired bisque doll.

Reassembled, the oak piece was beautiful. It shone with her squandered care. But there was no place to put it. In the dining room it looked like a country cousin to the mahogany. The kitchen was too high-tech. What she had thought of as an eclectic batch of household furniture turned out to be altogether too spindly, too neopatrician for a hunkered-down plain oak kitchen hutch.

She stood in the family room and tried to imagine it among the Scandinavian credenzas and repro end tables and the oil copy of a Miró. She tried to imagine herself purchasing these things, which she surely had. There was no family in the family room except the one on the TV, a model mom in a Liz Claiborne mock neck who, in the thirty seconds Dana watched, successfully passed off a frozen corned beef as her own concoction, sliced up seconds for her adoring husband, son, and daughter, and turned to wink at America.

Dana went back to the "turret" and stared at the statements, policies, forms, and fine print that formed the smoke screen to Graham Scott Ullman's posthumous worth.

Then she went into Somerset, to the Gothic Revival mansion that had been refurbished on a conservation grant into the offices of Donald Hunter, CPA. She signed Form 1040 for the year 2001 and wrote a check for $13,846 taxes due.

Then she went to the clapboard Queen Anne lodge that had been remodeled at taxpayer expense into the offices of Tom Bradshaw Financial Services and demanded, for the first time in her life, to know the bottom line.

Then—it was happy hour—she drew up at the Folk Victorian bungalow restored on a loan from the Historical Preservation Society into the law offices of Phoebe Sternberg, P.A., Family and Marital, and waited in the parlor with Phoebe's cold-nosed sheltie until the last client and the receptionist had gone. Then Phoebe took her back to the office and poured out what she called "a stiff Shiraz."

"I have to put the house on the market. Otherwise the mortgage is going to wipe me out."

"Rent the house and live on the rent."

"Phoebe, you're not getting it. The payment is three thousand a month."

"You'll have to get a job."

"I'll have to get a job *and* sell the house. I think I can clear about fifty thousand, which will give me time to figure out what I want to do."

"Go back to school, maybe."

"When I was gearing up to leave Graham, I used to see myself on the road, going from place to place, looking for the right one to settle down. I spent my whole childhood on the move; I know how to move. I think maybe I have to go back down to Georgia, where my mother came from, pick up the threads."

"Looking for your roots."

"There were no roots in the backseat of the Malibu. My mom always wanted to move on, and my dad always wanted to give her what she wanted."

"It doesn't sound like it worked out too well."

"No. But I was thinking about the first time we stopped off at my grandmother's. The only thing she said that I remember—I suppose because it insulted us both—she asked if my mom approved of my outfit, which was 'unbecoming.'"

"A bitch."

"Yeah. I was thinking that my mom married to get away from her, and then later I came up north for the same reason. All this time I've been trying out suburbia: yuppiedom, Republicans, Presbyterians. Pennsylvania's unbecoming to me. This is where I *unbecame.*"

"I don't know, Dana. You might be after some pastoral fantasy, you know? Some nostalgic golden age that wasn't."

"Actually my childhood was a drag. But it was my drag."

Phoebe smelled of Red Door. The sheltie smelled of fish and dog. Phoebe twisted the stem of her wineglass and frowned, part sympathy, part pained. "Sweetie, lots of people end up in the wrong place. I can understand you wanting to get away from hawks and brimstone. But if that's what you're after, it doesn't seem too smart to head down *south.*"

"I can't think of anything I'd miss, except you."

"You might end up missing your, I don't know, your favorite frying pan."

"Come with me. Bring Roscoe. We'll take the camcorder and do a buddy flick."

"Believe me, I've seen it happen over and over in divorce. You get rid of all your clutter thinking you're dumping the pain along with it, and then you end up grieving for the Le Creuset."

"I'll store some things."

"I don't know."

You must make a choice, although there is no choice. The green far beneath you is dotted with barns, a field of ruminating cows like ants on a flannel board. Where or how you land doesn't matter, only that you should take control. And it is time to rise. It is time to rise. You take up such weapons as there are: a bottle for blunt instrument, a pillow and a blanket for a shield . . .

"Shit, Phoebe, nobody *knows.* But at some point you've gotta—you gotta, you know, *Let's roll.*"

Phoebe pulled the dagger points of her black bob along her chin. She bounced out her Slim. She said, "I don't . . . think that ended so well either."

3

SHE SOLD THE TROOPER and took the Celica, nervous because it was ten years old and she might miss the four-wheel drive; stuffed the trunk with linens and the rudiments of a kitchen (because who knew where she might end up?); tacked southeast on I-70 and back west on 81 to give wide berth to beltway traffic, the pavement falling under her wheels with a grainy feel just short of hangover. Disappointing weather went south with her, fading from drizzle to a fine mild haze.

She'd carried on through spring on the impetus of paring down and selling up—the house to a couple who agreed to her price, so she figured she'd asked too little; the Trooper to a hunting buddy of Graham's, who already knew about the frazzled clutch; most of the furniture to a job-lot secondhand grifter—what can you do? She put the rest in storage. Not much: the fake Miró, the clumsy desktop PC, the few genuine antiques, but mostly just stuff that was sentimental-old. She found the only books she couldn't part with were the dogeared art folios she'd bought as an undergraduate at Pitt. She kept the kitchen hutch. In all, what she left behind took up less than a single crate at the Stor-&-Mor.

It was gray for June, grassy meridian and a scrim of trees, punctuated at intervals by kiddie colors offering the same half dozen brands of burger, brands of gas. That last week, bunking with Phoebe, she'd been claustrophobic, irritated with the tag ends of paperwork, straining at the leash. The feeling had been growing in her — even though she'd been hot and half-alive for most of her two adolescent years in Georgia — that if she once stood on the front lawn of her grandmother's house she could recast the dice and start again: *Advance to Go.* She had not confessed to Phoebe this symbolic turn of mind.

Not that she expected anyone but strangers to answer the door. Her grandfather had died before Dana went to live with Grandma Hoffstetter, and Grandma herself while Dana was at Pitt. That was more than fifteen years ago. At most there might be a neighbor or two who remembered the dour, big-boned matriarch of Tippet Street, or the shadowy grandfather of whom she had no recollection whatsoever, or even their whey-haired daughter with her skin as thin as milk glass who had disappeared into the blue.

Now cutting south on U.S. 17 she passed a church marquee reading God Is Our Refugee. Her laugh flattened against the window glass, and all of a sudden (on a powerful impulse that she ought to *point it out* to someone) she was twelve again, a mix of primed and bored and scared, shunting between whichever of these United States had proved a disappointment to her mother and whichever next glowed with promise. Conifers blurred by between Motels 6 and Arby's. Dana remembered how fervently, on such pilgrimages, she'd looked forward to playing Monopoly with her parents in the dank motel they'd fetch up in. It was an infatuation, an addiction. She remembered how she egg-walked until she saw that they were in that mood; how her father moved cautiously, holding back enough cash to pay the rent on Boardwalk while her mother bought utilities and railroads, hotels on New York, two-hundred-dollar houses on Pennsylvania Avenue. Dana had tried, veering wildly, to steer a course between risk and caution. But it was Mom the chancer, the high roller, who always won. And always afterward there was a sour sense of letdown. Which would not prevent Dana from building hope the next day, mile after dreary mile, that they would play again.

Just after the road crossed I-66, she came up on a bulldozer and a steaming tar truck, a sign tipped on its corner saying SHOULDER WORK. The traffic clogged and slowed, then stopped. Every third car displayed a tattered American flag on its antenna, or a flag decal in the window, or a patriotic bumper sticker. Beside the idle 'dozer, a shirtless black man lifted a pointed spade to the reach of his arms and drove it into the edge of the tarmac, shoulders working. Dana leaned to position him in the lower corner of the tinted window on the passenger side. She remembered (mile after mile, state after state) lying in the backseat of the Malibu flopping one foot against the ceiling curve, watching the treetops speed past, the roofs and billboards and blasted rock walls, while she pretended that the window was a television set. Mostly it was a dull sort of reality show, but every once in a while they would come to a stop and a *composition* would be revealed. Like this, for instance: black-dirt road and grayish trees, the dark man with sweat on his forehead catching light, up ahead a slight girl in an orange vest holding a stop sign, the yellow truck and its wisp of steam that suddenly waked the tang of tar. In an art history lecture once, the instructor had told them that eighteenth-century picnickers took along a frame to help them "see" the landscape. She'd laughed like everybody else, but she recognized her childhood, whipping back and forth across America trying to fix one image in the window frame.

Somebody up the line honked. The figure in the orange vest made a girlish gesture of admonition, flapping from the elbow. But a second later she twirled her sign, and the line of cars crept forward.

The backseat of that Malibu had smelled slightly sour, an *eau de* spilled milkshake and mildewed fries. On the passenger side up front, Mom would splay her fingers to unfurl her hair—luxuriant in the slanted light, multihued blond, naturally crimped so that it stood almost as wide as long; the hair of the seventies. As often as not a half-smoked cigarette would lodge deep between index and middle fingers. Now and then it would catch a strand at her crown and the car would fill with the stink of animal burn. Mom would pull the visor down, smear her lips together, check her teeth for stains. She would be blaming someone, the dentist who wanted to lance her gum, or that last boss who withheld Dad's paycheck. "All you have to do is stand up to him. *Assert* yourself."

And he, mirroring her gesture with thick fingers through thinning hair, would nod. "I expect that's a fact." Capitulation as strategy.

Even then, even at fourteen, even at twelve, Dana had known that her mother was a torn person, torn between the small-town belle she'd been bred to be and the free spirit she aspired to. (It was a phrase she used: "I'm torn between the pilaf and the fries, I'm torn between the paisley and the batik . . .") Nights in the motel—or in the two-bed apartment they would take for a few months in Kansas or Colorado or Idaho or Wyoming—Mom would swipe an Afro comb through her thick mane, shed the hair out of the teeth, and let it drift into a metal basket. She would be smoothing some kind of unguent over her neck and down her arms, touting the attributes of Havasupai cornmeal or the healing properties of certain ferns; smoothing, smoothing, smelling of grease and flowers.

"Shoulder work," Dana said aloud. She shifted into fifth and set the cruise control for seventy. She thought of Atlas with the weight of the globe between his wing blades. She remembered Pollaiuolo's painting of Hercules strangling Antaeus, the hero bulking muscle from biceps to chin; or a flamenco dancer with her elbows thrust forward and her eyes strained back; the whack and crunch of football pads when they connect. Shoulder work.

Dad's shrug the day Mom disappeared.

He'd twiddled with a nightstand drawer. He wore some kind of tweed jacket and looked too fragile for it, as if it would rough up his skin. Long face, long bones, an arm that would put its whole length into a hammer blow or a hug. She was fifteen by then. The little table was glossy, spindly. Dana said, "She's taken the money, hasn't she?" His eyelids dropped, but his mouth made an uncomplaining grin. He shrugged his hunched shoulders; a labor of Hercules.

The weather came in chunks: counties' worth of cloudlessness, then a cataclysm of rain and thunder that after twenty minutes was swiped out of the sky to leave gleaming heat on the damp road. Miles of stately pine were succeeded by acres of outlet stores succeeded by construction and bulldozed dust. A tape of Leonard Cohen played on an endless loop: *Everybody knows the dice are loaded,* and *First we take Manhattan, then we take Berlin.* By noon of the second day, all Dana saw was the asphalt wheeling underneath her eyes.

She sped past turnoffs to the places that promised leisure, pleasure—Myrtle Beach and Charleston, Hilton Head—left the interstate at Savannah and took the coastal route, which was overbuilt now, a gauntlet of gas and fries. When she hit the outskirts of Brunswick, the refurbished storefronts looked familiar only because they resembled every town she'd already passed. But she checked in at a Hampton Inn, fortified herself with a BLT, bathed and put on fresh underwear, and got back in the car, feeling momentous with her quest.

And when she turned at the corner by the old Food Lion—still here, still a huge excrescence on the asphalt, a faded awning and a stiff blue lion on a cartoon crest—her heart beat hard because this was where, weekends and summers of those two high school years, she had punched in the codes of crackers and cabbages, oatmeal and hot dog buns, and where without knowing it, without ever touching her, the shy, sly boy had cracked open for her a universe of which he himself was surely ignorant. Cassius Huston. She remembered his name. She could not be sure whether, then or now, he was aware of hers.

She drove slowly past the post office, the little park, a half-remembered clapboard house turned into Mrs. O'Meany's Cafeteria. The four hundred block had on its even-numbered side a vacant lot and a new animal hospital, Puppy Love, and across from these a strip mall, which she drove on past.

But the next house after the intersection was 501. Disoriented, she turned back to the mall and pulled into its parking lot. The string of shops was slant-roofed, stucco-fronted, and scrofulous, as if built in a burst of enthusiasm that then seeped away. There was a Shoe Repair, a Salon and Pedicure, The Christian Bookstore, Heidi's Flowers, the Smokehouse, Gun Shop, and Grasshopper Gifts. A section of wall perpendicular to the street read: Miracle Plaza, 401 W. Tippet.

Then this was it. She dug the snapshot out of her bag and peered at its faded blues and yellows, her grandmother's pinched, for-the-camera smile, her own toothy look of triumph—but even the fireflies had to be assumed, let alone the house, the garden, the garage. She got out and turned uncertainly in place. The site would have been a third of the way down, about where the Smokehouse stood. The houses had sat closer to the street than the shops were now—here in the parking lot—and the strip built on what were once the deep backyards, the rabbit haunts, and the copses from which every tree had been expunged. She stepped into a space next to a rusty Taurus and posited room for a sidewalk, a front porch, an entrance hall. The kitchen must have sat on this patch of tarmac, the swinging door into the dining room would have crossed into the handicapped space. And here, she decided, just here, the doll-filled hutch had stood.

The smudged brass plate of the Smokehouse gave with heft and a whoosh. Inside there was brick-patterned linoleum, square tables under checkered cloths, an open hatch from which poured the scent of fresh-charred flesh. There were café curtains and framed photos of baseball teams and brass sconces with hurricane globes. But there was also, on the far wall—too far to read the print—a poster she recognized as a painting by Magritte, the one with the locomotive coming out of the fireplace, the smoke sucked back up the chimney, and the mantel clock with its back to the mirror. Which seemed an arresting—a bizarre—choice of decor for a steak house in Brunswick, Georgia. She thought the place was empty, but then her eye snagged on movement in the window seat behind her, and she turned to a ham-sized forearm resting on a gingham mountain. The mountain quivered as it stood, levering up with massive knuckles on the checkered cloth so that a glass of shaved ice also shivered.

"One?" he said.

"I'm sorry, no, I've eaten. I was just wondering if you could tell me something about this place."

He had paunches under his eyes and a defeated air. Something had happened to his life that was no business of hers. He swiveled his belly over the corner of the table to face her. "Ma'am?"

"I used to live here when it was houses, twenty years ago."

"There's no houses here."

"Right. But I mean before the mall was built?"

"I don't remember before the mall."

"Oh. Have you lived in Brunswick long?"

The man's eyes narrowed, retracting into flesh. "I was born here, lady."

This confused her. She half raised the snapshot, as if to present him with the evidence.

"Joey!" he called, and a grizzled, bullet-headed cook materialized from somewhere beyond the hatch. "This lady's looking for somebody used to live here."

She had not said that.

The cook, in a T-shirt emblazoned Grill 'Em and an apron streaked with sauce or blood, came forward and rubbed at his forehead with a scrap of blue cloth. "How do, ma'am. What's the name you're looking for?" He had the sallow, Middle Eastern look of a cop-show villain, though he spoke with a drawl.

"Hoffstetter, but I don't really expect to find them, I was just looking for the house." He shook his head, ruminating. "Old times' sake," she added with an apologetic laugh.

"Nobody-a that name," he said.

"No, I was just wondering, you know, if you remember when there were houses here."

He discreetly rubbed his Adam's apple. His face assumed a defensive look. Where he stood, the fireplace in the poster made a square hat for him, his face obscuring the locomotive. Maybe it was more of a mystery, more interesting, how a Magritte painting came to be in this place than how she came to be.

"That's a long time ago," he said.

She could recognize impasse. She had barged into their territory and insulted them. She should have sat and ordered a steak; that would have honored their purpose here. The big man—the owner, he must have been—was cradling his belly, and the littler man was knuckling, now, the stubble on the underside of his jaw. It made no sense to stand her ground, forwarding her puny claim to the tired site of a razed house belonging to people long since dead. "Well. Thank you," she said. And thought: *the South,* although there was no shortage of strip malls or pendulous flesh in Pennsylvania. She backed up, bowing her way out, at which the cook lifted an eyebrow at the mountain, and the other smiled, a crack across his pudding face that made it shudder, the two of them tolerating a woman, and she was seized with an impulse to dig in.

"This was the first time I was here," she said, and panned the snapshot face-foremost, as if before the jury, first to the big man and then the cook. "Visiting my grandmother when I was a little girl. The address is on the back—my dad wrote it, he's dead now, they're all dead, but that's his handwriting, and this is me, and I remember the day because it's the first time I ever met my grandmother."

She had their attention. The big man's jowls settled and stilled. A surge of something—self-pity?—engorged her vocal cords. "After my mother left us, I had to come back and live with Grandma, and I worked part-time at the Food Lion down the street."

The cook's face slackened, and he wiped a hand across a stain on his apron. "Aw," he said, or "Ah."

"Anyway my grandmother had a cupboard full of dolls, and I only saw her that once when I was a little girl because she and my mother quarreled." It was too late to stop. She was emotionally revved, freewheeling. An intake of oxygen burned. "I never knew exactly what the quarrel was except that she always put my mother down . . ." More than once when Graham had been deliberately dense or cold she had done this, used the wounded and tentative as a method of attack. *Your waif attack,* he'd called it. ". . . but I remember she smelled of talcum powder and had these dolls. And outside . . ." There appeared in her mind, a gift of this argumentative free fall, the genuine memory of a willow tree that had stood in the backyard beside a shed of knotted, graying wood. ". . . that first time I caught fireflies under a willow tree."

The cook pinched a corner of the Polaroid. "Aw," he said again.

"There was a water oak or a horse chestnut tree, and a swing made out of a two-by-four"—for these had also magically appeared, together with her mother's voice haranguing: *I told you it was a cockamamie idea to come here, there's nothing here but spit and scratch . . .*

"You might check up at the post office or the county seat," said the cook.

"I'm real sorry we can't help," said the mountainous proprietor.

Her eyes were hot because sympathy always triggered tears, and because the air was heavy with stale ash. She could have gone on and on now. She had to will herself to stop, take a burning breath and clamp her tongue. Because it's the first law of thermodynamics: self-justification in motion tends to remain in motion.

"Your *grandmother,*" the cook commiserated.

At the motel she watched two murders and a documentary on poltergeists. She checked the phone directory for Hoffstetters, expecting none, and there were none. She decided to call Phoebe. She would say: *the famous grandmother's house is a strip mall,* and they would have a laugh. She would say: *and they told us irony is dead.*

But she did not call and in fact turned her cell phone off. She pulled out the Rand McNally and forced herself to invent an itinerary. She would drive straight south on 95 to I-10 and then head west fast. This is what you do on the American highway, you make time. This is what stands for accomplishment, production. She would cross Texas in a single bound, to the places that held the best memories for her—Santa Fe and Tucson, Sacramento, Malibu—places hot or balmy, where the schoolkids had been nonchalant about arrivals in the middle of term, and where Dad had found salaried work that was called "construction" and not "handyman."

She took a swim in the motel pool but the water stank of chlorine and whatever the chlorine was meant to kill. She showered for a long time in the stingy spray, soaping her shoulders, scrubbing at a film of chemicals and bad faith. When she stood at the window to towel her hair, looking out on asphalt, panic jolted her diaphragm, the earth tipped, and she saw herself pitching forward all the way to Florida. *What have I done?* she asked herself, and the phrase took on the rhythm of the falling: *What have I done? What have I done? What have I done?*

4

SHE WOKE TO A PARKING LOT, an odor of diesel fuel. She knew she was in Georgia, but all she could remember of getting there was the rolling road. She had squandered two days and six states, and she had a feeling this was not the way to conduct a life, but she did not know what else to do.

She made a cup of weak motel-room coffee and dawdled over it, dreading to get back behind the wheel. She was not afraid of an accident, still less of what "might happen to a woman alone," but of pointlessness itself, the existential fear, that old *nausée.* And of the absolute quality of her solitude. Why had it not occurred to her that on all those childhood trips she had been one of a trio—the one with license to be bored, to be petulant, the one not responsible? Nor can you arrive at the age of thirty-eight without experiencing the death of someone you know. But she had not so far counted her own dead, and now she did: grandmother, grandmother, grandfather, grandfather, father, mother, husband, child. What had made her suppose she could drive America alone?

The phone book still lay splayed on the superfluous bed. Was there maybe an old classmate she might call, might meet for coffee? Marilyn with the outsized earrings, horsy Harriet, Sally who floated gardenias in her pool? No. They would be listed under unfamiliar names, gone, divorced, surrounded by children, they would pity her for her widowhood. They would neither assuage nor distract her from this hollowness.

She closed the phone book. Among the towns listed on its cover she caught sight of *St. Boniface.* A mill ghetto, she remembered. She remembered Cassius Huston came from there.

For those two years she had split her time among the glaring classroom, the Food Lion checkout, and the hot, heavy darkness of "home." Grandma Hoffstetter was fastidious to the point of combing fringes on her rugs. She polished with a cloying oil. She kept the house dark in the illusion that it would be cooler. There was no action that a reasonably tall teenager could perform that did not threaten Grandma's draconian order.

At first Dana escaped into art classes. But Miss Kapanke gave crushingly dull assignments: *Draw this apple and this bottle. Today we will add a bowl.* When it came time to view the students' work she would say, "Hmm," or "Uh-huh," or "Interesting—is that what you see?" As far as telling them how to improve—actually *teaching* them—Miss Kapanke paced the classroom in her muslin smock, tucking a strand behind her ear, making maddeningly enigmatic pronouncements. "Art is simply a form of light used to illuminate life," or "Art is not difficult because it wishes to be difficult but because it wishes to be art," or "You can never have the use of the inside of a cup without the outside." Then she would say a name, meaning that the riddle wasn't even in her own words. The names never meant anything either, to the dogged class.

The still lifes gathered drearily around the picture rail. *Bowl of oranges in charcoal. Watercolor of banana and vase.* Miss Kapanke paced the room. "Some one or two of you will get it," she predicted.

And then it all changed in an afternoon, in an instant, because of Cassius Huston, who stocked the shelves at Food Lion. A bag boy. A black bag boy who came up from St. Boniface, somewhere south of town between the suburbs and the mill, on a rickety old bicycle that he locked carefully inside the stockroom.

He was younger than she, tall early, ghetto cool. He moved with a conscious, gangly grace. He affected a little fuzz on his chin, pointed into a goatee. His hair was cropped as close as a layer of moss, as close as the karakul fur on the collar of Grandma Hoffstetter's old cloth coat. The shape of the head (did he know it?) was high domed, perfectly formed, like the head of a Pharaoh in an Egyptian frieze.

Maybe she had a crush on him, which was so unthinkable in Grandma Hoffsetter's context that she did not think it. She only watched him lobbing cat-food cans to the shelf or hoisting bags to carry to a car—careless, self-contained, self-entertaining.

Then she was standing at the cash register five hours into a Saturday afternoon, facing the vegetable bins where Cassius Huston sought to liven his own boredom by clowning as he stacked the eggplants. *Aubergines,* Dana had learned to call them from the name on her acrylic-paint tube. Cassius lifted one elongated purple globe in the spread of his hand and brought it up to his face like another head. He stroked the leaf end with his spare hand, making it a goatee. She laughed. He addressed it in words she could not at this distance hear. The black boy and the fat plant faced each other against a backdrop of stacked greens, the ugly glare of the strip lighting glancing on the flesh of each, stabbing a white pinpoint on their mirrored domes, sliding along the jaws, the two forms matched in darkness though the undertone of the one was smoky and the other umber, a moment of comedy from which into her dull state there came: *enlightenment.* It roused and rooted her at a stroke: *It's about light. It's all about light. Let there be light.*

She had no particular talent as an artist and her drawing did not improve. What improved was her way of seeing. She got it. Art opened to her, she opened to art. That moment's perception attached itself to Caravaggio, and then to Leonardo, and then Vermeer. From thence to Rodin, Moore, Seurat, and so on, even to *Guernica.* Even to the dull, receding streets of Brunswick, the high, tight windows of her grandmother's house. Color, form, space, perspective—all as a function of light. She had shed her adolescent stupor and looked beyond herself for purpose.

If only she could be jolted from her lethargy again.

In the phone book the little towns were alphabetically arranged, and St. Boniface was the last of them. There was one listing for Huston without an *o*. She remembered from the work roster at Food Lion that there was no *o*. *Huston, Margaret*. What the hell. One wrong number more or less . . .

"Hello?" The voice was male, deep, black. Already she regretted her rashness.

"Hi. I was wondering if I have the right number for Cassius Huston."

"This' Cassius."

"Oh, hi. This is Dana . . ." Her face burned like a schoolgirl's. She fumbled for her own maiden name. ". . . Cleveland. We used to work at the Food Lion together, back a million years ago. I don't know if you remember me. I was just passing through . . ."

You could hear the uncertainty in the silence. *Discombobulation,* Grandma H. would have called it. She opened her mouth to plunge on when he said, "I remember. You back here, then?"

"Just for the day, and I thought I'd call a few old friends, and I thought of you . . ." Such baloney. They were never friends.

"How long you here for?"

"Not long. Just long enough for a swim and a bite. I'm on my way to California."

"California!" This seemed to impress him. "Where you going to swim?"

"I hadn't thought." She hadn't. The swim was an invention. She cast clumsily around her memory for a likely beach. "Maybe Jekyll, what do you think?"

This silence was deliberative, not discombobulated. "You going to be at the public beach at Jekyll, I might could come by there and say hello."

His offhand tone was as phony as hers. Well, what would he think? They had known each other only because they'd worked the same after-school hours. What legitimate purpose could he think she had in calling him?

"I'll have to see . . . how my schedule works out." God. Stupid. "Um, I could probably be there in an hour or so."

Her jaunty new bathing suit was still damp from the pool, one of the few things she had bought for the trip, a racer back with a geometric pattern in greens and blues. She hung it on the hook in the backseat—for a flag, she told herself—and started off again. At least it got her on the road. Either she would turn off at the island or she would not. On the radio, Saddam Hussein and the U.N. haggled over sanctions. The conundrum: how do you know when a liar is telling the truth? Thinking at least to smell the sea, she turned onto the intracoastal waterway. But almost at once she caught from the direction of the Atlantic a whiff of sulfur, a smell with a texture to it, a stench that would coat your lungs. When she crested high ground the stacks of a paper mill appeared, belching smoke into the cloudless sky, and some sort of giant conveyor belt carried whole trees up an incline to dump them beyond her sight in a sound of cavernous grinding and chewing.

She was in that charged frame of mind in which every coincidence seems providential, so that when a billboard rose up out of the hill ahead advertising a summer stock production of *The King and I* (Jekyll Island—Seven Miles on Your Left!), she filled with the memory of Dad taking her to musical comedies in shabby small-town theaters (Mom's preference was for muddy fields of rock bands with no place to pee). Yul Brynner's shaved head appeared in her mind's eye, thirty feet high on the screen. She turned off the radio and belted out, surprised to find every word of the lyrics at her command:

Whenever I feel afraid
I hold my head erect
And whistle a happy tune,
So no one will suspect I'm afraid.

A side road and a gated arch appeared toward the ocean on her left, and Dana took the turnoff, remembering that Jekyll Island was a playground of senators and banking wizards early in the last century. She passed down a winding pavement and wandered through lackadaisical mansions sprawled out among the monkey puzzle trees, the careless grace of stone patios and bougainvillea, moss hanging like crochet from the wrists and elbows of ancient oaks.

She stopped at a 7-Eleven for a soda but, finding wine, bought that instead. She parked at the public cabanas and changed into her now-dry suit, took her beach bag, and headed toward the water that was laid out to infinity in either direction. Either he would show up or he would not. In any case she could manage a swim before she went on to Florida.

There were very few people on the beach, mainly families, spaced thirty yards apart, as if the shore had been divided into plots. On one side two parents and a boy, on the other a mother and two gender-unspecific toddlers. The sea was flat and shallow near the shore, but farther out the waves hiccupped hugely out of nowhere, crested, and crashed. Dana dropped her things and ran into the water, expecting it to be cold, but it was not, in June in Georgia. It was refreshingly, kindly cool on her ankles, her knees. She dared herself in up to her breasts, ducked under and came up streaming. The surface of the water dazzled. The sky was almost white. A pair of flying bluefish broke from the waves and soared into the horizon. They took her breath away. She felt a sudden surge of energy as if it came from the ocean floor, and she plunged defiantly in and out, saying to herself: I can *do* this. I can *be* alone.

After a while she went back up to the beach towel and poured a paper cup of wine. There was no sign of Cassius Huston. So much the better. She opened the Joan Didion paperback that Phoebe had tucked in her bag and determined to concentrate, but the sun on the page scattered the sentences. She stared into the sea that was a deep midday blue, and the water resolved itself into the memory of a shallow fountain, somewhere in the Northwest, Idaho perhaps, in the central square of a county seat in summer. She was seven or eight, and she and Dad were waiting for her mother, who had some faintly embarrassing errand, a palmist or an acupuncturist. The fountain wasn't running but its basin was full, a bright blue doughnut above the painted bottom. Dad had taken out the little notebook he always carried in his pocket, and he tore off page after page, making a few magic creases, securing the folds with toothpicks, setting little ships afloat. One, two, three, four—every one seaworthy around the blue rim of the plaster pond. She was awed almost to disbelief, because she had once been reprimanded for dropping a book in the bath. She had spilled milk on her paper dolls. She knew the stuff went soggy. How did Dad make paper float?

"'Scuse me, do you have a light?"

She started, and looked up and laughed, although—she did not have the same apparatus for recognizing a black face as a white—not certain for the moment that it was he. Flared nostrils, fringed eyes, dense hair not close-cropped, but cut square and matte. His face had a gravitas she did not associate with the boy. But he grinned and she remembered the sly smile. A light, eh? But what was he going to do in the middle of the afternoon with families at thirty paces either side? She rooted in her bag for the flat brass lighter Phoebe had given her, chattering as she did when she was ill at ease.

"Yes, it happens I do. I gave up smoking, but I've hit a kind of rough patch and I've taken it up again just for the duration. I thought I should cut myself some slack." Something like that, and handed him the lighter.

"I'm sorry to hear that. You doing okay?"

"Pretty well, pretty well."

He squatted on the sand a little ways away. He was empty-handed except for the one cigarette, dressed in a pair of cutoffs and a denim vest—powerful arms that she had to notice—but he couldn't get the flame to catch in the wind.

"Let me. It's temperamental." She put a hand out for the lighter and the other for the cigarette. He took the cigarette out of his mouth and handed it to her and she put it in her mouth and lit it, and it was only later she understood what a complicated thing was already going on, that she had said she was not afraid to put in her mouth what had been in his mouth, and that he had accepted this. That he had admitted to a failure of competence and she had both showed him up and shrugged it off. The moment was sexual, but not mainly sexual. He thanked her. He squatted in the sand a few feet away, smoking. She lit one, too.

"The old Food Lion is still there, I see."

"Yeah, still there."

"Some other poor bunch of kids on minimum wage."

"You know that's right."

"I was remembering how you used to clown around with the vegetables."

"Did I?"

"Yeah, you used to talk to the eggplants, stuff like that."

"Some shit. I don't remember that. You remember that?"

"Uh-huh."

Any attempt to explain would only make it worse. The aubergine would make it worse. Nor did she want to spoil a memory he didn't share. So she carried on brightly about the one experience they had in common (not home, not school): *Remember old Mr. Chapin? And that geek in the front office, what was his name?* The pickings were slim. She asked, "How come you came so far to work?"

"Wa'dn't zip for part-time in Boniface!"

"Oh." She felt obscurely chastised. Not wanting to ask family, marital-status questions, she floundered forward about herself. "I lived right around the corner with my Grandma. It was the first time I'd been at the same school for two years running."

"I remember you traveled all over."

"You remember that?"

"Yeah. I remember your hair was long, all shiny and shit."

She shook her head, denying, pleased, and something else. Short of breath. "What do you do now?"

"I do security down at Atlantic Mills. Every day they chew up fifty-sixty ton of pine trees to make cardboard boxes, and I go make sure nobody hijacks their 'zalea bushes." He glanced sideways to see whether she could do irony, then belted laughter when Dana laughed. Straight on, his face was fuller than it had been, the beard a very little fuller, the eyes both softer and warier than she remembered, amber in the midday glare.

She looked away, to the bleached sky. She said, "I feel sorry for people who have to stay in on a day like this."

"Uh-huh. Mostly I do day shift, but I traded with a friend, his mother's in the hospital, so I don't go on till six o'clock."

That put her more at ease—was it said to put her at her ease? She said, "I want to make I-10 tonight, but I thought it would be a pity not to stop for a swim." Then, having established that neither of them would be available after dark, she risked: "How did you get the name of Cassius? Were you named for Cassius Clay?"

"Now, how come you don't ask was I named for the guy that offed Julius Caesar?"

She felt her sunburn flush. "Sorry! Too ignorant, I guess."

But he belted a laugh; self-irony seemed his natural habitat. "No, I was named for Clay. Cassius Marcellus Huston."

"Your daddy named you," she guessed.

Soberly: "No, my mama named me." He fingered the sand. "My daddy didn't stick around too long."

His fingers plowing forward let her know that he might later regret saying this. She pressed on. "Me, it was my mom that left us. Then I stayed with my dad for a year or so, but he got a job offer in Alaska, and he couldn't haul me up there."

"Alaska!"

"I didn't want to go either. I wanted to stay in school. Everybody said what good luck I could keep Grandma company. I said it, too."

"But, after, you got out."

"Yeah, and then I married straight out of college and never did anything with my degree. And then my husband died last year and left me needing to get a job." She was conscious these sentences were edited downward on the social scale.

"So you just up and going to California."

"Sure. I don't know what I'm looking for, I might as well look there."

He shook his head, eyebrows raised, and she had the brief pleasure of seeing herself as adventurous. Then hard on the heels of this moment came the knowledge that, apart from Cassius Huston, there was no witness on the horizon, no person remotely familiar to her from here to the far edge of America.

"I was going to leave my husband," she blurted. "I thought about it a long time, and it felt necessary, even, you know, positive. But then that was taken away because he was dying, and how could it be brave to leave him dying? So I took care of him till he died. And then I buried him the morning of nine-eleven."

"Damn."

"Nine-eleven was nothing to do with me; I didn't know anybody in the towers or the planes. But when my husband died, his death was one more thing that got wiped away. He disappeared in the smoke." It occurred to her that this was precisely the purpose of cremation, but she would not stop for paradox.

"Terrible." He wagged his head.

"Those attacks changed all kinds of things we don't know about. Funny off-center stuff, like a bone that knits wrong. Did you know there's a seed business in California that went bankrupt? Because now they're x-raying packages in the post, and this business sends out their seeds, and the x-ray kills them."

He looked at this oddity, looked out to sea. "We got new rules at the plant, 'beefing up security.'"

"Code orange?"

"Some shit like that. They didn't hire any extra, mind, just set more rounds to a guard. Mostly it's bosses at the monitors, and us humpers turn a key in a lock to prove we been there—two miles, twenty-six locks to a round. You think those terrorists interested in a paper mill?"

"Who knows? It's a big enterprise."

"Anyways, most folks don't worry about it here. Everybody just trying to get through to payday."

She offered him a cup of wine and another cigarette, and they smoked and listened to the surf, the gulls, a mother calling to a child out in the water. With the hand that did not hold the cigarette he poured sand through a loose fist. He grabbed at a little hump in which the shape of his fist was made and then unmade by the sand falling down its sides, and then he turned his hand and loosed it enough to let the sand pour into the cavity it had come from, making and unmaking the same little pile, half an hourglass half measuring the time.

He took a breath. "I'm separated," he declared, and the word hung there on its own for long enough to seem like a state of being. They both saw this, and both laughed.

"I mean, not divorced by law. I haven't clarified my mind on that."

"No. It takes time."

And as it turned out, his state was so far from "separated" that she might have said *ensnared*. He was thirty-five, the sixth of seven siblings. His wife was a schoolteacher, his one child a daughter, three. His wife was named Isobel and his daughter Kenisha, an African name though he did not know in which language. He came from three generations at the paper mill, all the family, to a density of cousins and in-laws. They were "stokers," "beaters," they worked on "chippers" and "digesters"—these words unknown to her but falling from his tongue as casually as she would say *gouache, bas-relief.* He himself was considered a maverick because although he could make much more inside the plant than as a guard, he would not confine himself in that heat and noise.

"My whole family think I'm mule headed. I say, mule head this: I don't need no furnace in the summertime."

Her beach towel was huge and lush, and he had no towel. But he took off his vest and spread it on the sand. For the next couple of hours as the tide came in they had to keep moving up the beach. Each time the vest got nearer, but never touched her towel. Dana saw that he would not intrude on her territory. Of course such behavior might bespeak passivity. But what she heard in the depth of his deep voice, the formal consideration before he spoke, was a male restraint at once familiar and exotic, a reluctance to reveal himself that made each revelation a risk, a gift.

The marriage had fallen apart because of the baby, which was not planned, but which he wanted—"You know, some pride"—while his mother-in-law insisted that he couldn't support it. His wife, torn between them, had waited too late to decide. But the fight had soured the marriage, and when he left he moved back in with his family (good; then there was no question of "his place") because he wanted to put away money so he could travel. All he knew he wanted to do was travel. It was family tradition that his grandmother's grandmother, freed in North Carolina, had come from Cameroon, and he dreamed of tracing his roots back to Africa.

"Meantime I got myself a old Grand Am, and what I like to do, I cruise around just thinking."

"What do you think about?"

"Dreaming, you might say. Listen up, did I startle you when I asked for a light? I'm sorry . . ."

"No, I jumped because I got caught talking to myself."

He had straight, strong teeth and a supple laugh. "That's what I do when I'm cruising, I talk to myself, making things up."

They talked about cars and car travel (he had been no farther north than Savannah, no farther west than Panama City), his plethora of family and the paucity of hers (how he had lived with six brothers and sisters in a two-bedroom madhouse and she had lived alone with her grandma in the dark). He had a flick of a glance that was both daring and assessing, a quick focus, a face on which everything registered, including a reflection of Dana's own.

And he came back and back to what clearly never left his mind, brought out a snapshot of his wife, Isobel—Dana was surprised that she was not beautiful, but pleasantly severe, her straightened hair arranged in waves around her face—and then a studio portrait of the little girl, organdy and cornrows against a fake sky, chin atilt, mischief in her eyes.

Cassius said, "We had terrible fights. Terrible. I swore I wouldn't let Kenisha hear, and then I did."

"What will you do?"

He held his jaw in both hands, pressing at his temples. "I don't *know.* The marriage ain't worth patching. But no *way* I'm going to let Kenisha be raised up by her."

"You can get joint custody. Lots of people do."

"Those people ain't met Isobel." He rubbed at his hairline,

scattering grains of sand. He patted the sand at his feet and swept it in an arc.

Dana still held the photo: the carefully ironed dress, the standard-order sky, the little girl's expression of brass and sass. She tried to imagine what Chloe would have looked like at the age of three. She was not prepared to mention Chloe.

"It will work out. Whatever you decide, she'll always know how much you love her." This was an inadequate banality, and at the same time seemed to mean more than she intended. Quickly, she recounted the memory of her dad's paper boats. "Just a couple of folds in the paper, one toothpick, magic."

"I can do that. But it's no good in this ocean here."

She imagined him making paper boats for his three-year-old, setting them in a plastic pool. He had eyelashes as dense and tight curled as his hair. Nappy lashes, around irises the color of old brass. She could not take her eyes from them. She said, "I don't suppose it ever entered my father's head, that's what I'd remember thirty years later on a beach in Georgia." She also meant: *Thirty years from now I will remember this afternoon.*

She pulled out another cigarette for each of them, handed him the lighter, and showed him how to cup it while wheeling the stiff flint. She said, "My best friend Phoebe lent it to me. When I'm ready to give up smoking again, I'll send it back. It'll be a symbol of my independence, do you know what I mean?

"You'll have to run that one by me."

"Like the flag is supposed to show your patriotism."

"Like fireworks on the Fourth of July."

"Exactly."

"Your independence."

"That's it exactly."

They sat pleased with each other while he looked away and fisted another quantity of sand. She was not so slow that she didn't realize there was some asymmetry in their talk, that she was setting the pace. But it seemed to her that this amounted to a leveling. She felt enlivened in his presence; he had the power of sex and size and turf. They acknowledged the balance with extreme deference.

The only time he bridged the barrier between his vest and her towel, the shadows of the houses had begun to cross the sand. He reached then to her basket for her pen and her paperback. "Let me tell you when you get to Florida, this place you should stay. My mama's sister lives nearby there. It's on the coast, clean, just a little plain rent cabin behind a store." He wrote *Sollys Corner, Pelican Bay* and the number of the highway. He looked up under his coiled lashes, held her eyes. "I would know where you are."

She took the book and pen. "I hear you," she said, and, sensing that permission had to come from her, lightly touched his arm for emphasis. But it was nearly five. They'd killed the wine and most of her cigarettes, while he kept apologizing for accepting them. She would have liked to tell him, now, about the aubergine and the light, but she had no meaningful way to do this. It would have been trivialized, sexualized in the telling. She said, "I have to get on the road if I'm going to make any distance yet tonight."

"I know. And I got to work." He gazed at her. "But I'm off tomorrow." He swallowed, dragged a finger in the sand. "Do you have to go?"

"I thought of that. No, not really, I could get a room."

"I'll pay half."

Her breath came short. "No, but. Look. Let me think about it a little while. You go on to work. I'll either call you or not, okay?" As she said this she felt herself to be honoring his restraint. A stab of virtue, perhaps. Or a failure of imagination.

"Okay, but call me one way or the other, let me know. I'll be waiting to get your call."

She wrote his work and home numbers on the inside cover of her book, underneath the aunt's address. She gathered her things. He asked permission to put his arm around her. Powerful and light, his arm. She put hers around his waist. Over the belt of his cutoffs, a pouch of dark flesh in her palm, undulating as he walked. It stopped her breath again. He asked her again to call him, whatever she decided, so he would know. He walked her to the car and kissed her, powerful and light.

"Oh, Jesus, that would work," she said.

"Oh, yeah."

He stood on the sidewalk and watched while she drove across the beach road and back among the stately homes. After a while she parked and sat trying to find calm again. But what use was calm? What was the point of thinking about it? Thinking about what? Who was waiting for her? Who was there to judge her? Who would care whether she made good time to Florida?

5

THE FIRST HOTEL she came to along the coast was a Sheraton, not a high-rise but a cluster of cedar-shingled minimansions spread out over a grassy beachfront. The desk clerk was a slender youth with the air of middle age, gracious to the edge of superciliousness, an eyebrow permanently arched. It struck Dana that he was wearing a wig, though she wasn't sure how she knew this, since its blond shag was brushed expertly around a long, rather handsome face. His skin had the yellow underlight of a fake tan.

"Just let me see if we can accommodate you. Oh, dear."

There were no vacancies among the ordinary rooms (he regretted with a hand against his clavicle), but they had a few suites left, "on special" at two hundred and twenty-eight dollars a night. He smoothed the air between himself and Dana with the palms of both hands. "You'll be *very* comfortable there."

This was a price that as Mrs. Graham Scott Ullman she would scarcely have noticed. But in the past couple of months she had so thoroughly indoctrinated herself to her new poverty that it registered with a shock. Nevertheless she donned the mantle of a senator's wife, said, *"Fine,"* with some hauteur, and handed over her credit card.

It was a cedar villa with living room, kitchen, two balconies off the upstairs bedroom, a view of plank walks reaching into the sea. It was as spacious as a house, laid out in sand-colored bourgeois luxury. Only later did it occur to her that if she was slightly daunted, to Cassius it must signal *trespass.*

She shopped for breakfast groceries, bourbon, wine (what would he drink?), stopped at the dining room for a salad dinner she did not eat, went back and settled in. When she turned on her cell phone, there was a message from Phoebe: "Hey, sweetie, I'm sure you're having great adventures, but don't forget to check in with the stay-at-homes. No news here, just the standard custody and alimony wars. Love you. Bye." Dana swallowed a tickle of guilt. It was not the time to return the call, she reasoned, in this interim of adventure, with its uncertain outcome. She saved the message and put it out of mind.

Then the wait began. She dialed Cassius's home number, not thinking that at midnight this was any worse than a nuisance. Hadn't he said to call? It did not occur to her that she had given him an ultimatum: don't-call-me-I'll-call-you. The male voice was sleepy and sour. "Who this calling Cassius?"

"My name is Dana," she said. "A friend." Sleepy and sour, the man said he would deliver the message.

She called the work number, where the guard on duty seemed never to have heard of a Cassius Huston. "He doesn't usually work at night," she said, "but he traded with a friend . . ." She kept her voice cultivated and brisk—a benefactor of some sort. "It's not an emergency, but it is of some importance." Two hours later she called again and went through this rigmarole to another white voice with greater indifference than the first.

And so through the night. She kept seeing the crown of his head as she had known it in that earlier time, and she longed to trace its outline with her fingertips. The thought of it washed through her as delicious fear. She was so unused to desire that it took her as the shakes; it shook her. She slept three hours but mostly sat—couch, bed, floor—muscles deliberately lax but nerves erect, waiting as she had perhaps waited three or four times in her life, but had not expected to wait again. Not at thirty-eight, not the ingrown, skeptical person she had become.

Sunday. At seven she bathed, washed her hair, shaved, pumiced and filed, perfumed her shoulders. At eight she breakfasted on peaches. At nine she called his home again — fearful, doubtful. If he had changed his mind she would handle it. But it would be hard.

The same male voice answered, surly, but called Cassius to the phone. He was asleep, of course; he'd been at work all night. His voice sounded offhand, almost cold. "Where you at?"

"Well, I think I'm crazy."

"Don't say that."

"But I'm at the Sheraton on Jekyll. Are you still game?"

"Sure."

"Okay. It's Villa Starfish at the Sheraton. It's just past registration on the downhill side."

"I might not find it. Why don't you meet me at the same beach as yesterday?"

This put her off. He could find the Sheraton, couldn't he? A feeling surfaced out of a younger and more vulnerable time, of having trapped herself into playing out a fleeting infatuation. "All right. What time?"

"I'll be there ten or ten-thirty."

"Can't you make it sooner? Checkout time is noon." She heard the petulance in her voice, but having herself driven an hour to Jekyll Island yesterday, it did not occur to her that St. Boniface would be forty-five minutes away.

She chose her blue shorts and the new eggshell top that hugged her rib cage. Slipped her creamed heels into new sandals and drove to the public beach. He would be there at ten, she thought; no, at 10:10. She turned off the AC so she could lay her arm along the sill, smoked a cigarette, watched families drag their gear out onto the sand.

Ten-twenty. His Pontiac was older than she expected, weathered and a faded Wedgwood blue. Cutoffs and denim vest, around his neck a bright orange towel with a spiky border in brilliant white. Once more the sight of him — shoulders the darkest color in the grain of oak, poured molasses—took her breath away. He didn't touch her, only indicated with a brusque gesture that they would go in her car, and her heart sank. He got in, and she drove and began to chatter, said she was nervous and that she chattered when she was nervous, she was sorry. But chattered. Told him of the supercilious desk clerk and the extravagance of the villa. He slumped sullen, and she thought: it's he who feels trapped. He's changed his mind. He'll screw me and go and I'll check out at noon. Can I handle it?

Inside he stared at the carpets, the plate-glass doors onto the balcony. She led him around downstairs; she showed him the TV and the freezer and the barbecue. He followed, nodded, mumbled, "Uh-*huh*" and *"fine."* He cast his eyes around, caged, impatient. She desperately laughed and chattered. Finally he leaned against the kitchen island and put his arms around her, expelled a hurting breath. "I been thinking about you all night."

Oh. It would be all right then. "So have I." And she shut up, gave up, leaned into him. The tension of a sleepless night pooled from her.

"All night I been wondering would I be here."

"Be here, be here."

All permission had to come from her. She led him upstairs and they sat on the bed, stunned, and, all-permission-had-to-come-from-her, she fumbled at her clothes and shed them to the floor. Below the sea sponge of his hair, almost no hair: minutest mustache, merest brush of beard on point of chin, a few harsh curls of pubic hair. For the rest, dark shining; thick dark rolling over muscles polished like moving wood. On one shoulder a cauliflower mole the size of a thumbnail.

"You're proud of your mole," she accused, and he acknowledged it.

"My beauty mark!"

"I like a man who likes his moles." She touched it lightly, and he began to touch her face, one fingertip width at a time, plane and crevice and point of bone. She closed her eyes and experienced herself through the medium of his hand, as if he were drawing her into being. "Dana, Cassius," he said. He lay her down and painted her into the daylight, stroke by stroke, her body made palpable in the filtered light off the sea beyond the curtains. When they turned, finally, the length of their bodies together, it was as if reluctant, holding back before the rush of luminous dark.

Afterward, she passed him a cigarette, settled herself under his arm, pulled his free hand over her and studied its lifeline, dark creases in a palm that was pinker than her own Pennsylvania-pale hand.

"Cassius and Dana," he said.

"Tell me anything."

"What you want to know?"

"Anything about you. Tell me why your mama named you Cassius."

"Oh, well, once upon a time . . ."

"Really."

"This is really. Once upon a time my daddy was a pretty ace boxer, had a trainer down in Jax named Toes Lefkin, trained these boys for the Olympics and said my daddy had a shot at it. This was before I was born, when Cassius Clay was just coming up to the title, so my mama thought to make up to my daddy, naming me Cassius, you see?"

"I see."

"My mama's idea was, a man with a little Cassius would stick around. Only this Toes, *his* idea for my daddy was, he would train up just so far and then lose. That was his deal. My daddy would knock out two, three other black rookies, and then he would throw to a white man. What Toes had in mind, that was his specialty."

"That's awful."

"Yeah. You want awful, break a brother's face, fall down in front of the whites."

"What happened to him?"

"He fell down too many times."

"He got hurt?"

"Shit, that *was* the hurt. You listening, girl? Mama say he got hit too many times, but everybody knows it was hitting the bottle got him. That was his ropes."

"I'm sorry."

"He hung around awhile going down. Then he went off, left me with the name, and Mama picked up with Uncle Raymond."

His arm was damp around her shoulder, and Dana, tracing his palm, understood again that, later, he might resent the telling. She cast around for a way to lighten the mood. "Tell me about 'the guy who offed Julius Caesar.'"

She still meant, *Tell me about you,* which he seemed to know, because he said, "I had some trouble 'long about seventh, eighth grade, before I knew you."

"What kind of trouble?" She expected larceny, a gang.

"I was fat. It did me no favors to be called Cassius."

"Fat? Were you?" She laughed and reached for the pouch below his ribs to verify this possibility. *Be here, be here.* "You look like you could defend yourself."

"Not back then. Anyway, Clay turned to calling himself Muhammad Ali, which the brothers thought was way-gone too cool for me. They started in 'Mu-ham-*mud*' and 'Look here at Ali-ass Cassius.'"

"Poor Cassius."

"'Sting like a butterfly, float like a bee,' they'd say sometime. But Mr. Samuels, he was auto shop, but smart, he showed me about all these other Cassiuses back in Roman time, badass politicos and generals, speechifying mothers. Shit. There was at least a dozen of 'em."

"And that gave you confidence."

He pulled her to him. "Naw, it just kept me inside at recess."

She did not check out at noon. He didn't have to be at work now till Monday morning, so she called and extended her reservation, suggested that she'd pay the motel and he could buy dinner. He accepted this.

They slept together, he wrapped entirely over and around her, powerful and light. She slept as deep as darkness, and when she woke left him asleep and walked out into the light. She swam, she swam. The tide was up to the rocks that bordered the hotel property, so that you waded straight into it from a cedar dock and stairs. She grinned oafishly at the sky and watched the fish leap.

Later she made an omelet that he solemnly praised, though he neatly expunged the bits of bell pepper. *Make a note: He doesn't like bell peppers.* They cleared the table together. She said, "You're a helpful sort. Who trained you so well?"

"My mama trained me good."

"You're fond of your mama?"

"Oh, I *love* my mama!" (And she misunderstood. She thought if he loved her they must see eye to eye, though why she should have supposed this in the face of universal evidence to the contrary she could not later say.)

When she went back upstairs it was to find that he had taken her flung clothes and folded them neatly on the bureau. For a while she stood and looked at the symmetrical stack—this orderliness that underlay his power. She had expected him to be a good lover. She had not expected him to fold her clothes.

She wanted to swim again but couldn't get him to go with her. He would not, in fact, venture out on the balcony, and she wondered briefly if he had some reason to fear being recognized. They made love again, and again she offered him a drink, which he refused.

"You don't want me to have one either, do you?"

"No." Impatient.

"But you can't stop me." Flirting.

He took her two wrists, pinned them lightly behind her, shifted both into the grip of a single enormous hand, and holding them without any pressure in the circle of thumb and finger: "What you gonna do now?"

"Oh, you can *physically* prevent me from having a drink. But if you do, that's it, kid. 'Cause ain't *nobody* gonna tell me what to do."

He let go her wrists, laughed, shook his head. "You are something else."

And she was. Something else than yesterday, than a week ago, something else entirely than the do-gooder wife of a minor politician or the dazed automaton who had spent four months stripping a kitchen dresser. She made the drink and drank it while they smoked, she tempting him now out onto the balcony, where twilight and the slanted rays from the other side of the world made the water black and blazing. (Did his eyes check left and right? Perhaps for dolphins.)

Around ten-thirty they got back in the car. He wanted to drive to Brunswick, to a place he knew. They tooled along for half an hour, rap on the radio, he driving easy, windows open and seats back, her bare foot on the dashboard. "How do you like my mellow Celica?"

"She cruise so fine."

But it was Sunday, the restaurant wasn't open, which upset him. "I could *take* you *there*." (She thought he meant it was cheap enough, and didn't care.) They spotted a McDonald's on the other side of the road and careened across. It was three or four minutes to eleven, but they got hamburgers, fries, and a couple of sugar-dripping, deep-fried apple pies. They drove to the dock and pulled up at the picnic tables, deserted except for three hulking white youths at the nearest table. Cassius was checking lights as she got out, so she preceded him by a few seconds, and therefore heard one of three say, "Them damn niggers."

She rounded the front of the car. "Cassius, wait a second. I just heard one of those guys say, 'Them damn niggers.'"

"Well, what you want to do?"

"What do you want to do?"

"I want to have my supper."

"Then I want to put my arm around you."

They passed the three self-consciously entwined and strolled to the farthest table, where she sat with her back to them, he facing them (had he arranged this?), and they tried to eat.

She spread her hands. "Cassius. 2002? You still get this?" He flapped a pair of French fries, rolled his eyes and snorted. She said, "I think I'm such a knee-jerk, and I haven't imagined it at all. I haven't thought it through, what it would be like, to live that every minute of your life."

"I don't let it bother me."

But while they sat, mouthing cardboard burgers, she chattered again, finding nothing better to talk about than the boondoggles of Pennsylvania education. He couldn't listen, who had hung on her words all day. She rambled brightly. He hemmed and nodded.

His eyes kept flicking past her shoulder—at one point, she thought, alarmed.

"Cassius, are they getting up?"

He turned to face her. "Listen. Don't nobody mess with you when I'm with you."

She was amazed. It hadn't crossed her mind that they'd come after *her.* But of course; punish the bitch who's out with the nigger. She hadn't been frightened and was not now. She felt recklessly strong. He could waste the three of them if necessary, and she'd help.

"But I don't see why you should have to mess with them. Wouldn't we be more comfortable somewhere else?"

"I guess we would."

So they gathered up the burger rinds and shoved them in the garbage bin, walked back past the table (but not entwined), got in the car and drove. He headed for another part of the beach but almost immediately got lost and had to circle past the picnic tables. It occurred to her that there was a tonguing-the-toothache purpose in this mistake, a need to confirm what and where the danger was.

They found the stretch of beach he wanted, a patch of rocks and a narrow walkway of hard sand, summer houses on the rise behind. He picked a boulder and sat. "I was thinking you set on my lap about now."

"I'll be too heavy; the rock's too hard." She sat sideways on his thighs. She was too heavy, the rock too hard, so she stood again and straddled him.

"You just know how to do everything, don't you?"

Straddling him, she fed him pie, and when the filling ran down his chin she licked it off and felt him harden under her. When the pie was gone they walked and ran a little on the beach. She lifted her arms and stretched, sandals dangling from her hand. The stars were astoundingly many in a blue-black sky.

Looking at the stars, she insisted, "You have a huge family, and I have none." She didn't know what she intended by this except, perhaps, a sentimental longing that she should share his family.

"My little brother Antwan, he's all right. I could show you off to him. But Luther is a *hard* Christian, and they most take after him."

"Will you be in trouble with them?"

"Ain't no thing."

After that he fell silent (*in a brown study* was the phrase) until they were back at the Sheraton, sitting barefoot on the rug.

Then he said, tentatively, "I got four days' sick leave coming."

She ran her hands over the carpet nap, palms tingling. "You could call."

"Or you."

"Me?"

"Say you the emergency nurse, I got something."

"What, like a gunshot?"

"Gunshot! No, shit, something I can get over by Friday. Bronchitis. Strep."

"I don't know if I can pull that off."

"Oh, you can pull it off." With the clear challenge that she could do so if she cared to. Which she could, surely. She knew how a nurse would talk. She knew how to say *adenoids, bronchial crisis, influenza.*

6

FOUR DAYS! was a disorienting stretch of freedom. The first few hours of Monday they were numb, like people who walk away from an accident with all their expectations and intentions shattered. He led her upstairs and, having no other plan, they made love again by default.

When he took off his vest she remembered the shirtless worker framed in the window of the Celica, shovel above his head, then slicing straight into the earth; and she thought she would explain to Cassius about *shoulder work*. But it was complicated, too somehow personal to be explained, not like the flag, the Fourth of July, her independence. And what was it that made her think again of that scene on the road except that the two bare torsos were black and muscled, so how would she explain, even to herself, how she came to speak of it? She would insult him comparing him to a man with a shovel, although her father had many times in her childhood appeared as a man with a shovel and proud of it, both himself and her. This is the "white man's burden" circa the twenty-first century: too many tangles in such a train of thought, too many possible detours and dead ends. Better to respond directly to the sight and smell of him, to palm those shoulders with creamed hands, feel him roused and rising to envelop her where she straddled him on the bed. Even though it felt a bit of a failure, too, a little cheapening, to pursue only the desire, and not the convoluted minefield of conversation.

When she bent to go down on him he laid three fingers on her shoulder (*shoulder work?*) and said "I don't ask that."

"What?"

"You don't have to do that."

His face in the midmorning light, dimmed by expensive commercial curtaining, was closed, eyes closed, mouth closed, a dark shadow possibly grimacing? "No," she said—there was a sense in him that this would demean her, then? A sense personal, to do with prim Isobel, or cultural, to do with power and subjugation? "No, I don't have to do that," she said, and deliberately lay her cheek along his thigh, caressing his thigh with her cheek as he groaned and she brought him to her mouth.

Afterward they drove—or he drove, in her car, while his sat on the beach where he had left it. She saw that he would not bring a scabrous Pontiac onto the hotel grounds among the SUVs and Audis. He retrieved from the trunk a paper bag with a change of underwear, a T-shirt, a pair of chinos. Which, then, he always kept there in case? Or had put there the first day with her, in hope of needing it?

Over the next three days they drove to public beaches from Fort Frederica up the Intracoastal Waterway to Harris Neck. They wandered through the Brunswick mall and along a street of secondhand stores and ice-cream shops. They ate at a bar in a Brunswick ghetto that served red beans and rice, where she was greeted by the proprietor with elaborate courtesy, and where there was one other white woman, in a frilled blouse and fishnet stockings.

Here Cassius was at ease, joking with the barman, steering her by the elbow to show her off. In more public space, on the hotel grounds, even driving through a suburb, he became alert as a cat. He had degrees of wariness she couldn't anticipate. In the Brunswick supermarket he reached for boxes, suggested, chose; but if she needed something from the village store on Jekyll he sent her off alone. On sand he walked loose and easy. Where the sidewalks started he pitched just slightly forward on the balls of his feet, eyes darting. It was not significantly different from her caution in certain Philadelphia neighborhoods, but the social map he carried in his head was more nuanced, convoluted, ever present—and partially—code yellow, code orange—surely imaginary?

With each other they settled into a kind of charged comfort. Sometimes they sat over food too sick with desire to eat, and would laugh at themselves and scrape the dishes in the sink. In talk, he moved in and out of black English, a set of signals involving play, self-parody, machismo, and conscious pride. Sometimes he had the rhythm of a preacher: "My mama raised five boys and two girls, and she didn't lose one to drugs, and she didn't lose one to jail, and Luther may be a righteous dick, but there ain't no law 'gainst that!" Sometimes he spoke school English, all the *g*s carefully in place: "I can't say what Isobel is thinking most of the time, what she's intending." Sometimes he slipped into a hip Ebonics meant to taunt her: "Yeah, you go, girl, shake it like a sistah." This last tone was in its irony vaguely familiar; and one afternoon at the island store when the ponytailed checkout girl called her "Sugah" it came to her that her mother had used her Southern accent this same way—"Y'all don't carry on and raise a ruckus, hear?"—exaggerating the drawl to make clear she knew better if she chose.

Dana was confident enough by now to spool out this train of thought to Cassius. He was interested. But when she was done imitating her mother, he observed, "You—you say, *What?*"

"What?"

"Lot o' time you don't understand me, and you say, *What.*"

"I don't. Do I?"

"Ahn-huh. And if you ask me why is that, I can tell you: you didn't have to understand my talk but I had to learn yours. It's always the same."

"With us honkies."

"Ahn-huh." He was teasing, but it stung.

Nevertheless little by daily little they learned each other, dipping into dissimilar memories, daring similar confessions. He astonished her with bursts of tenderness, even romance. Once he skidded to a stop beside a churchyard in the kind of neighborhood that made him nervous, leaped out to steal a rose and brought it back to the car, folding his pocketknife with one hand and holding out the blossom with the other, singing in a mock baritone, "This bud's for you."

He was interested in insects. He called her attention to weirdly horned beetles and crickets hard as plastic hidden in the grass on the beach verges. He stopped once at a bush in the otherwise bald lot of a Burger King, pointing out a banana spider she would not have seen, though once the web came into focus it loomed three feet wide between the viburnum and a power pole. The mother spider was as big as a hand, ripe with yellow and brown striations. She had just given birth. The web pulsed under the feet of a hundred, two hundred newborn spiders, each no bigger than the head of a tack.

"Is that the buzz?" he whispered. "Is that some cool mothering?"

Later, in the dark, he described taking down a mud-dauber nest near the sandbox where Kenisha played. "There's the eggs in the little holes, and right beside each one is a maggot the mother put there, little white egg, white maggot. See, maybe she goes away but she leaves food for the chirrun." He fell silent. He worried her hip with the palm of his hand, kneading. At last he said, "I don't mean she don't feed Kenisha, but it's not taking *care.* How I married somebody doesn't have that mother thing?"

She knew he was running out of money. Surreptitiously he counted through his wallet. She had reserved the villa through the weekend, and at $228 a day she, too, was overspending, though for the time being she could afford the luxury. One afternoon he told her he would have to "go get some cash" and asked to be dropped at his car on the beach. He didn't say "to the bank." She knew he could not be seen at the mill when he was supposed to be off sick, and she worried that he would go to one of those gouging cash shops. She would have offered to pay for everything, but that would wound his precious manhood. Nor did she want him to think her rich, which would widen the space between them. Would she fret this way if he were white? *Yes,* she decided.

Meanwhile she washed his clothes, the chinos, the underwear, the vest. Would he be offended that she washed his clothes? *No,* because he folded hers. She dialed the domestic ritual onto the machine: Small Load, Permanent Press, Low Heat, and waited for it, staring out over the balcony to the sea. The brief solitude was welcome — erotic, even. She stood taking in the erotic hot perfume of the dryer.

He came back energized and proposed that they should drive all the way to Savannah, which they did, so she found herself a passenger retracing her route north. In Savannah he chose for the first time a restaurant with a view — a fish chain with a noisy dining room and beyond it a deck on pylons over the Savannah. They threaded through and sat on plastic chairs, Cassius picking at shrimp and hush puppies while she dealt inexpertly with a plate of snow-crab legs. She saw: in the city, in chinos, a well-brought-up black man could make a raid on the middle class, supposing he had the money, which tonight he did. Nevertheless he was ill at ease, tentacles out to sound and movement, almost sullen behind the deep bronze of his eyes. She probed him about his work. "How many guards are there?"

"Three shifts, you got the supervisors on the monitors, parking lot, the roundsmen, maybe ten, twelve to a shift."

"Do you carry a gun?"

"At the plant I do. You mean am I packing now?" He laughed at her. "Girl, no *way.*"

"Have you ever used it?"

"On a copperhead one time."

She laughed and made limpid eyes at him. "My homeland security."

"Ain't no such thing. At Atlantic, they got forty thousand acres of pine. You think you can control a fence around forty thousand acres? Anybody with a mind to get in there will get in."

"Let alone a *homeland.*"

"They don't care anyway. It's the inside jobs make 'em all worry."

"What would people steal?"

"Computers, machine tools, copper. They've got some expensive pictures, whole head office is full of them, up and down the walls."

"What kind of pictures?"

"I don't know. Pictures. Paintings. Real pretty, some of them. Some of them monster, like in a museum."

She imagined the murky landscapes of motel decor.

"Insured up the ass," he said, "but all the same, we play pig for them." Saying *pig* made him reckless. He waved his palms in the air. "Really we fo' *show.* We doing a little see-curity soft-shoe."

She laughed and offered him a forkful of crab. "I had a neighbor in Bobbindale who paid hundreds a year for a system they never connected, just so they could put the little sign in the yard: Protected By."

"That's what I'm saying. We nothing but scarecrow." He paused, washed the crab down with his beer. "You heard the one about the wheelbarrow?"

"No," she lied, delighted, because this was one of her father's jokes.

"Nigger in the African diamond mines." In her father's version it was a laborer in Colorado gold. "Every day he wheels out a wheelbarrow full of straw, every day the guard picks through it, looking for what he stealing, and never finds a thing. Finally the guard retires. When he's on his way out, he says, 'Tell me for true, what are you bagging?'"

And the guy says: Wheelbarrows. She laughed along with Cassius, hearing her father's guffaw.

"They got no diamonds at Atlantic. Ass-expensive pictures, though."

He paid with a flourish, not so much largesse as relief, and they headed back to I-95 (tracking up and down the highway just as she had done as a girl), her bare foot on the dash, the fingers of his right hand combing through her hair at the nape. Even near midnight the wind was hot through the open windows. Because of the wheelbarrow joke she was thinking of her father. She saw him, hangdog, hanging around day after day in that crappy little Nebraska town, losing weight, not able to leave in case Mom showed up. Dana had been an angry, exasperated teenager then, whereas now she remembered her dad's wan vigil, even the desolate "efficiency apartment" with an aching fondness. Why is it that nostalgia attaches to the hardest times?

Cassius was looking out his window at the bleached mansions along the beach, hulks against the night sky. They had not mentioned that he would have to go back to work tomorrow. After a time she asked, "What are you thinking?"

"Me? If I was a terrorist, know what I'd do? I'd go low next time. I'd get fifty guys . . ."

"Fifty is a lot."

"Doesn't have to be suicides, just fifty guys sympathetic to the mother *cause,* know what I'm saying? They rent them some rental cars, check into fifty fat-cat high-rises on the beach. Savannah, Jacksonville—Miami would be even better. It'd cost what? A few thousand for fertilizer and the rentals? They just register for the night, park in the garage, take a cab to the bus depot or the airport—they're miles in every direction by the time the bombs go off. Some serious chunk of coastline is flat-down *trashed.*"

"That would work, all right."

"I make you nervous?"

"No."

"I tell you what. I'm just fooling around, but it makes you nervous, because you thinking about yourself being in those hotels."

"I'm not."

"You thinking room service, where, me, I come out the caves down here."

"No, you've got me wrong. I came out of the caves myself."

They rode in silence for a while. Cassius dimmed his lights passing an eighteen-wheeler, flipped on the brights again. He relented. "What you thinking, then?"

"I was thinking about my dad. When my mother left us, we were in Nebraska. We stayed there maybe four months in a little town called Sable Creek and my dad worked odd jobs. I'd come from school and find him sitting on the porch—not a porch, a little strip of cement, on a metal chair with pipe legs. He'd bounce on it like a rocker, pretending he wasn't waiting for her."

"She never come back."

"She never did."

"I know what you're saying, girl."

"She didn't have that mother thing."

She tucked her fingers under his thigh. He pressed the button to close the windows—to hide inside the tinted glass, to eliminate the wind? He wiped his mouth in the way that means the words are jammed. He said, "I can't walk away like she did or my daddy did."

"I know. It's one of the things I admire about you."

"Yeah, black daddy always walks away. Isn't that what you think?"

"No. It's what the statistics say. It's not what . . ."

"What the statistics say about a art-ass white girl takes up with the bag boy?"

"Don't do this. There's no reason we have to fit the numbers, okay? I understand you can't leave Kenisha." But this was disingenuous to a degree. Hadn't she just said she admired him because he defied her expectations?

"I don't think you can understand, girl."

"Don't you? Well, I can. I had a daughter, too." She must have mumbled this, because he shook his head, leaned toward her frowning. "I had a daughter!" she said again.

"You walked away?"

"No, she died just two days old."

"You never told me that. How come you didn't tell me that?"

"What is there to say? She was two days old. She had a bad heart. She was very small and lived two days. If I'd had her three years it would be worse, but it was bad enough." She resented naming Chloe in this defensive mood, presenting her to win a point. *The waif attack.* "If I'd had a choice, I'd have done anything to keep her."

"Ah, girl."

"Don't think I expect you to run off with me!"

"Hush, now. Look like I been running off with you a *while.*"

Friday. At dawn she fed him, held him, drank in his smell to last her through the day. She said, "Now, listen up!" and he laughed at her using his expression. "Last Saturday you had a pack of cigarettes and some matches in your car, and you left the matches and only took out one cigarette to come looking for me, in case you wanted to get away real fast. So don't you *never* try to put nothing over on me, you hear?"

"Never, never!" Laughing, he threw up his hands.

She tore a page off the memo pad and under the Sheraton logo added the name of her suite and her cell-phone number. She tucked this in the pocket of his vest.

"But anyhow," he said, "you be here tonight." It was a question disguised as swagger.

"Oh, yes. What time do you get off work?"

"Around six. But I have to be home some. I'll see you nine, maybe ten."

"And you can stay the night." Also a question.

"I can do pretty much what you want me to."

She spent the day in febrile calm. It was as if she moved in soothing water. She had nothing to do but to honor her body with preparations and ointments, frankincense and myrrh. She stood in the steaming bath surrounded with cultured marble and beveled mirrors, taking stock, trying coolly to appraise her body. What she discovered was that she had not observed herself for many months—or was it years?—and that less had changed about her than she might have expected. Not that she was not older, but that she recognized herself. She had aged mainly in the eyes, which were hazel, wide set, and faintly lined. She did not like her mouth, also wide, nor the plain brown hair that she had decided to grow again, and that now fell feathery on her neck. Her father's hair. Why hadn't she inherited her mother's glorious multicolored mane, that straw-and-cornsilk Afro? She was a little heavy in the haunch (is that a virtue in a black man's eyes?). She was still flat bellied and slim ankled, she had pale full breasts below a flush of sunburn on shoulders that were square and bony like her mother's, though like her father's her arms were strong. She couldn't tell if she was good to look at, but looking roused her, or melted her.

You are something else. She was. Something that existed in its own right, in a state of discovery rather than regret and apprehension. She put on the bright blue-and-green bathing suit, her flag. She swam and slept, swam, bathed, daydreamed and remembered. Reading was out of the question, television offered a choice of incest in Missouri or mayhem in Kandahar. She snapped off the set and lay on the carpet, felt its texture scintillate against her skin. She touched her throat, her thigh. The cool of the countertops was likewise sensual, like chilled flesh. She drank half a bottle of wine and then, feeling that this dulled the delicious state of waiting, washed it out with glass after glass of water, sitting on the steaming deck looking out over the steel-blue sea.

The day was long. By four her calm became jagged around the edges, and she thought she needed something concrete to do. She drove to the little ragtag row of shops, where she bought half a dozen candles and the makings of a superior pie: Granny Smiths, flour, butter, brown sugar, lemons, cornstarch, cinnamon, nutmeg, ginger, cloves. The villa kitchen was sparsely equipped so she also bought a pie pan, a rolling pin, a roll of waxed paper, a good paring knife. The thought that it was the most expensive pie she'd ever made delighted her. She went back to the villa and pared the apples to paper-thin perfection, the evening news droning on in the living room. She ate the parings for dinner while she sliced the apples in see-through slivers. She smeared the flour and butter across her fingers with her thumbs, flicking air into the crumbs as they fell into the bowl. She rolled the dough between sheets of wax paper and lay the scented apples in. When the air filled with the smell of hot cinnamon and cloves, she stretched on the carpet again and drifted in the keenness of her senses. *I attend,* she thought. *I wait, I listen, I am present at, I heed and serve.*

He did not come. Nine came, and ten. The darkness shuttered over the Atlantic. A bird set up a crooning she had never heard before. She took it to be a heron or a loon, but this was only because of the hollowness of the sound; because "hollow" and "loon" and "heron" make that sort of sound together. She turned off the television so as to listen more carefully. The few cars and the little laughter in the grounds died down, and by midnight everything was still.

Had she been meant to meet him at the beach? Could there have been so drastic and so simple a misunderstanding? He had left his car there all week, had not wanted to bring it on the grounds. Now that she thought of this, it seemed obvious. Yet surely if that was his intention he would have given her a more exact time. If she left now, and he came here, she would have missed him just the same. If he didn't see her car, he would think it was she who had run out on him. She could not call his house, not a second time at midnight when his surly brother Luther would be the likely one to answer. Could she? Or call and hang up? What purpose would that serve? Cassius had had an accident! Or he had simply lost her number. But the Sheraton was listed in any phone book, and he knew her name. So, then, he had changed his mind. He had thought better of it. Worse: he had been lying all along, all week. She was a conquest like any other, and this was his revenge, on the honky who didn't know what he encountered every day. But that was not possible, was a traitor fantasy. He folded her clothes. He held her wrists to keep her from a drink. He said, "You just know how to do everything." *No.* He was hurt somewhere on the road. He was still at the beach, believing it was she who had changed her mind.

If you fed all that onto a Möbius strip and looped it through a tape recorder, and played it once around every four minutes from ten P.M. to dawn, with the grinding gaps made by a quarter bottle of bourbon between midnight and three, followed by a percussive head to keep the beat—that would not equal by half the night she waited. After dawn sometime she slept. She dreamed only raucous, jolting sounds. When she woke it was blazing midmorning and she lay on the fake leather couch in her sticky skin, the smell of apple pie mocking the muggy air.

A meal of alcohol and apple parings makes for an unstable gut. She forced down a wad of toast and stood for a long time in the shower. The only sensible thing was to head on down the coast and continue her intended trip. She could not do this sensible thing. She should call Phoebe, who could always be counted on for the light touch and sound advice. But she did not want to admit to an affair and abandonment barely a week out of Pennsylvania.

She sat stymied. Somewhere between midnight and sleep she had entered into a bargain with herself, that she would not risk dialing his number until he got off work at six o'clock. Now she determined she would swim in the meantime, tour the island, search the beach for clues. Perhaps she would let herself drive to the mill. Instantly the image flashed itself: Cassius running over the grass to meet her.

She drank coffee, stuffed her beach bag with paraphernalia, drove to the public beach, and parked, searching the tire marks in the laughable pretense that she might tell one from another. But this reminded her that she did know what his car looked like, so she headed back to the mainland and down the coast to Atlantic Mills.

The mill road wound toward the sea and then straightened parallel to the shore. The sulfur smell was overwhelming, the air vibrated with an underbeat like a timpani in the roots of things. A chain-link fence stood between her and a lawn that ran for a quarter mile to an imposing office building. It was a plain, creamy structure several stories tall, Georgian perhaps, or Deco—it was hard to tell at this distance. Beyond a farther fence, the plant straddled a brackish channel, two mountains of logs on one side and several of chips and slag on the other, the giant chain conveyor grinding upward with its load of trees, and then the five stacks, cock-erect to the blue sky. They puffed a staggering quantity of cumulus smoke, below which the air was clear to the glittering horizon.

Twenty feet in front of her a white-haired black man was tying a magnolia sapling to a stake. He had strips of cloth tucked into a rubber band on his wrist, and he slipped them out one by one, knotted each loosely below a node and around the stake.

She stood for a long time breathing the heavy paper stench, willing Cassius to come striding across the lawn, doing his "rounds." But when the old man eyed her for the third or fourth time, she got back in the car and doubled back toward the parking lot.

Lots, rather. South toward the mill itself were another several acres of parked cars, and three roads to them forking behind a security hut, where a sign declared AUTHORIZED PERSONNEL ONLY / VISITORS MUST HAVE PRIOR AUTHORIZATION. She hesitated, idling in the dusty heat, then started when an executive-looking sedan of some sort pulled around her and was saluted by the guard. He leaned out of his hut, a round white face, a uniform. The barrier rose. She stayed as she was, safe behind sunglasses and tinted windows, but when the guard leaned out again, his attention on her, it was fight or flight.

She rolled slowly forward, lowering one layer of the protective glass.

"He'p you ma'am?"

"Yes. Thank you. I was wondering if one is allowed to tour the mill." She said "if one is" like an academic or a Brit. But she was dressed wrong, tank and shorts, sandals. Nobody would go looking for industrial tourism in that outfit. So she smiled with conscious naiveté, hoping for indulgence.

And he smiled indulgently. A plump young fellow, pink-cheeked and sky-blue eyed, a Kewpie cop. He had a minor dribble of mayo at the corner of his mouth. "Yes, ma'am," he said, and touched it off with his little finger. "But you need an appointment in advance. You just call up the office and they'll put your name on my list here."

"Oh. You can't arrange it on the spur of the moment?"

"No, ma'am. You need to call. It's" — he gave her an important look — "they've tightened up security since nine-eleven."

She returned the look. "Of course." A parking lot guard is a kind of bureaucrat. *Just trying to get to payday.* "I'll make an appointment, then."

"It's best if you call a couple days ahead."

"Thank you. You've been very kind." She may have said this pretentiously. He may have smirked. She backed and turned.

She drove to the beach again and swam again, but the air was humid, the surf like oil. She moved her towel up the beach away from the tide, a petulant and self-punishing reenactment.

When she got back to the Villa Starfish, the message button on her phone was flashing. Her heart soared and the whole world righted itself. She fumbled at the receiver. "You have a *hand-delivered* letter here," the unctuous voice intoned. She ran down the road to reception, where the clerk with the perfect wig and the bottle tan made a show of searching the mailboxes, then flourished a square envelope like a greeting card, addressed in pencil: *Miss Dana, Villa Starfish.* His eyebrow signaled curiosity. "I *hope* everything is all right."

"Oh, quite," she said, with that tic of defensive hauteur that belonged to her repudiated life. "You live in a *lovely* corner of the world." And ran, heart pounding, back to her living room.

Dear Miss Dana,

I hope these few words find you OK because when I get thru with you, you are going to wish you never knew Cassius, because when I come on the Island I am going to kick your white ass back to the stone age. And I mean your own father won't know you. You better find you a fucking white man and leave black mens alone. I know you have been calling to his mothers house but I am only going to tell you once leave my husband alone. And by the way I have got your tag numbers so you better think about what you are doing before I put a whipping on your bony ass. I don't need to sign this cause you know whom this letter is from.

She sat back with her hands on the arms of the plush chair and stared at the black screen of the television set and the bright water in the window beyond, where there were no disasters in progress although her breath had stopped and her focus skittered between the black glass and the bright glass. She had expected a love note, an apology, a plan. She had even registered the round, careful handwriting and felt a flush of tenderness for it before the words registered and this flash of hate came at her. She read it through again. She saw the poignancy of "whom." She did not for the moment understand what "tag numbers" meant. The distance between what she expected and what she read left her momentarily blind with shock. Except that she was not blind because she saw the blank TV screen, that there was no disaster on it, that she must simply be sensible now and go.

She checked all the windows on every side of the villa. There was no one there — a tangled white couple wandering laughing toward the dock, a kid in the road with a soccer ball. Someone, one person bolder than Cassius who was not afraid to face a hotel clerk, had walked this envelope in to the front desk and gone away again, forty-five minutes back inland where black people could afford to live.

She flung her clothes in the suitcase, gathered her towel, her rolling pin, the pie. She rummaged in her basket for the paperback where Cassius had written not only his phone numbers but the address of his aunt in Florida. *The White Album,* she now realized her book was called. He had said, "I would know where you are." He had held her eyes as he said it, not the ironic look but the locked and earnest one. He had known, then, that there might be trouble. He had told her in code what she must do.

She felt no compunction to explain herself to the Duke of the Front Desk, who had in any case imprinted her credit card. She left the keys on the kitchen counter, flung the suitcase in the trunk, set the apple pie on the front seat of the Celica, and took off toward Florida with the visor blocking, on her right, a gorgeous bloodred sun.

II

Steerage

7

JACKSONVILLE AT DAWN sits askew to everybody's image of Florida: more discount than Deco, more hospital than high-rise, Miami cut off at the knees. But when you leave the ring road and head west on I-10 you are in another country altogether, flanked by eighty-foot pines on either side, driving a gray carpet down a green corridor. This is what the natives call "the other Florida." It is really Georgia by a different name, rolling red earth, pecans and cattle, a scattering of water oak and sweet gum—though unlike Georgia shabbily edged with sea.

Any turn left tracks down the panhandle to the Gulf. The main highway is 319, which cuts through the capital in ten minutes, goes two-lane, meets 98 at the coast in a half hour more, curves right again and, dipping in and out of sea view, follows groves of palmetto, salt water on the left, swamp on the right, mounds of shucked oyster shell, and the occasional great blue heron balancing on one skinny stilt.

It is the character of this segment of the coast that the best real estate lies off of it. Down the west side of Florida the beaches are deep and white and the water earns its Spanish name, *azul.* But here in the armpit of the Gulf the underlying land is shallow. If you sucked all the water out you would have mere meadows and mere hills. So the pale sand and blue water lie offshore on islands, capes, and finger-thin peninsulas. Along the coast itself the sea is cypress stained and marshy. You need a long dock to reach water deep enough to swim, and even then you're tickled and poked by vegetation you can't see; your feet touch silt that is river-dirt-fine and a little slimy. People do build houses on the narrow strip of land between the highway and the sea, but these tend toward bungalows, painted pine or vinyl sided, propped on creosoted pylons. And the owners tend to live in them. People who can afford weekend mansions want to walk out onto beach.

Pelican Bay lies along this coast. It is not really a bay (though there are squadrons of pelicans), but a scoop of sea within a shallow stub like a bone spur broken off in some forgotten hurricane. It has a few dozen of the modest seaside houses, owned in this case by retirees, proprietors of local restaurants and shops, and several who inherited a fraction of original Coca-Cola stock from their great-grandfathers. The inhabitants across the highway on the landward side are mainly fisher families, or serve the islands' tourist trade, or belong to the workforce of Lhamon Paper, whose mill lies on a more valuable peninsula fifteen miles west. A packed dirt track perpendicular to the shore leads back into a tangle of sweet gum and palmetto, ranch-styles, cottages, and trailers, and is called Sink Street because it ends three miles inland at a brackish pond. Though the street runs north and south, it represents a social boundary of sorts, so the locals refer to West Sink and East Sink. Solly's Corner lies at the juncture of 98 and Sink.

At first Dana didn't see it. The store was badly marked, set back on fifty yards of scrappy lawn, a wind-torqued cypress obscuring its peeling sign. Nor did it appear to be a store, but a ramshackle house of grayed cedar siding—two stories and an attic, it looked like—under a dramatically steep shingle roof, with two red gas pumps in a sandy forecourt.

The old man who came out to meet her was a cartoon of a cracker, splay footed below greasy work trousers, a lurid blue

Hawaiian shirt, white wisps floating around a glowing pate that showed only when he lifted his mesh-sided cap. Since she didn't know the name of Cassius's aunt or how to ask for her, Dana started in the passive. "I was told you have a cottage for rent."

"Yes, ma'am." The old fellow removed the cap by its brim and resettled it. "Up behind the store here if you want to take a look." He walked her up the drive, a hirsute forearm on her window ledge as if to guide or push her, chewing on a jawful and keeping up an energetic palaver while she tried to creep at his old man's pace. "It's two hunderd and fifty a week, two weeks minimum, two weeks advance. You got lucky there. Canadian family just pulled out yes-tidday, otherwise this is our prime time. I like May and October my-self, mostly locals do—there's less bugs—but Nor'easterners like yourself are starved for heat. Am I right?"

"Absolutely," Dana said, wary though a little charmed.

"We see a lot of Nor'easterners around here. Don't think we don't."

"I'm sure."

"The place is plain but clean."

Her stomach skipped because that was what Cassius had said, plain and clean; because she was fool enough to feel a surge of hope at those words. "That's what I heard," she said.

He stuck a hand through the window. "John Solomon, but ev-erybody calls me Solly."

"Ah." She took his hand. She was disappointed. She'd hoped Solly was the aunt (had she been thinking *Sally*? Aunt Sally in mammy kerchief?) and that this old fellow was the handyman who pumped the gas. "Dana," she said, and hesitated. "Cleveland," her maiden name. "Dana Cleveland. How d'you do?"

He sniffed and gave the pie on the passenger seat a glance. He startled her by leaning in, shouting fluently, "Fine, thank y', except I'm a touch deaf on that side. Bovine spongiform encephalopathy!" And guffawed. "Fresh sheets Fridays, utilities included. If you want the beds made that's an extra."

"No, that's all right."

"Up to you. You'll want to keep a brick on the trash can though. Coupla college kids last spring, not three licks of sense between 'em, had half the possums in the county set up under the porch."

The cabin itself was a rough-paneled rectangle with a screen porch overlooking a needle-covered slope, a smell of juniper siding, a tiny sitting room and bedroom flanking a kitchen mostly cheap Formica and pressboard, clean as a whistle. She said it would do fine and offered to walk back to the shop with him.

"Naw, that's all right, settle in, you can come down later on and pay me. You'll prob'ly want to have a look at the bay before it gets to sundown. There's good oysters and bay scallops down at Henry's on the dock."

She hesitated, seized with minor inspiration. She had been over this many times on the road. If Isobel Huston had the name of her villa at the Sheraton and the number of her license tag, she also had her cell phone number. She might very well guess that Dana would go to the aunt's place in Florida. But Dana did not think that any of Cassius's family would tack after her six hours to the Gulf. Whereas Cassius might have lost her number in whatever marital or family skirmish took place, but he would know how to call Solly's Corner. *I would know where you are.*

She asked, "Do you have a telephone?"

"Not in the cabin here, but up at the shop, yes, ma'am. Most people have their cells."

"I do have a cell phone, but it's been acting up," she lied. "Would it be all right if someone left me a message at the store?"

"You give 'em the number, that'd be all right. Long as it's not rush hour, I don't mind coming to get you."

"That'd be very kind. I won't make a habit of it."

He flipped on the window air conditioner and a pair of ceiling fans, selected a key from an overburdened chain and set it on the pine stand by the bed. "How long you fixin' to be here?"

"I'm not sure," Dana said. "My husband died last fall . . ."

"I'm sorry to hear that."

"Thank you. I just need a little R & R."

"Now what do they stand for, them *Rs*? It ain't *religion and redemption.*"

He laughed again, and she with him. "I'm not sure I know myself. *Rest, relaxation,* I suppose?" *Recreation? Rehabilitation? Restoration?*

"All's we got here is S and S. Sun and sea. You got to get on the island to even get to the sand."

"Or the surf, is my guess."

"That's right, that's right." He gave her an appraising look. "You've showed up to the right place I can tell." The look held for an awkward moment, and she wondered what he was appraising. Stability? Solvency? Gullibility?

She unpacked, minimally nesting, her clothes in the closet that was a bar behind a curtain, her coffeepot in the kitchen, in the living room a familiar cushion and the candles she had bought on Jekyll Island. She checked that the little TV worked—yes, a network rerun of a hung jury—brought in the collapsed pie and ate a wedge standing at the kitchen counter. It was ninety degrees and sticky; the fans stirred a barely lukewarm breeze from the window unit. All the windows showed pine trees, needles for ground cover, a dappling of hot sky. Sink Street ran wide and rutted out her kitchen window. Between the back of the store and the cabin a rope hammock had been slung between two pines. She showered and set up a few books on the windowsill above the wicker love seat. Then she headed down to the store.

It was closed. A sign on the door said Open Daily 7–7 and it was not yet six, but she knocked and called and no one came. She pulled the screen open and peered through the mullioned panes. In the half light she could see racks of candy, shelves of bread and cans, a counter with a wall of cigarettes behind it. The lights were off and the brass knob didn't give. In the forecourt she lifted a pump handle—it twirled its numbers and flipped up a row of zeros like she'd hit the jackpot—then put the nozzle back in its cradle. That the pump was on with nobody home seemed odd and wrong.

Over the smell of diesel it came to her that the wind had shifted, and that what her nostrils picked up now was paper mill, overwhelming as soon as she recognized it, a penetrating dry stench of bad egg, pitch, and rot. *Ugh.* Ah! That was why a one-bedroom cabin, utilities included, could be had for two hundred and fifty a week. The air reeked. But either the wind would take it away again, she reasoned, or she would get used to it, or at worst she would move on.

She got in the car and backed bumpily over roots to the highway. She headed along the coast until she saw the sign for Henry's, where the old man had said she could get dinner. But here, too, the lights were off, the screen door wedged closed with a piece of doweling through the handle. She headed farther west, past an antiques store, a gas station, and a bait shop. In pretwilight the waterfront looked rolled up, the Dairy Queen dark (Dairy Queen? At not quite six-thirty?), the bay of Mercer's Garage padlocked and chained. There was no one on the road except three young blacks in T-shirts and flip-flops going west at a controlled lope.

A mile farther on she found a 7-Eleven with a bare bulb lit above the counter, so she went in and poured herself a cup of boiled-down coffee, picked out a loaf of bread and a canned ham, eggs, jelly, coffee, and butter. Went back for milk and a can of mushrooms. A mouse-colored hound dog followed her with eyes only, its long face prone on its paws. She tumbled her stuff onto the counter in front of a weedy, cadaverously pale teenage boy who looked at it all in a despairing way, as if he didn't have any idea what to do next. Then he began reading the prices and picking them out on the cash register with his middle finger.

"The town's real quiet," Dana observed. She noticed that "real quiet" was her version of Southernspeak, a bigotry. "Very quiet," she amended.

"Yeah," said the boy, and swiped his head sideways mournfully and mouthed the price of the jelly as he rung it up.

"Would there be any place for me to get some supper?"

The boy looked at her now. Sizing her up? Or was that innate bewilderment? "I don't *think* so," he said. "Y'know there's been an accident up't the mill."

"Oh, I'm sorry. Somebody hurt?"

He stared at her. "*Doh!* One of the men fell in the digester?"

The question part of this was meant to ask whether she knew what a digester was, which she didn't, but she nodded (why? unable to admit ignorance to an ignorant boy?). "Someone from here?"

"Over the island. But he was old Solly's nephew. So you see."

She saw—past tense. "Solly? Mr. Solomon that owns the store?"

"Yeah, Solly's Corner Solly."

"That's terrible. Just this afternoon? Just now?" The boy shrugged but looked at her sidelong. He jabbed at the machine with a tattooed forearm, and the dog raised its head sharply, then set it down again.

A digester? A vat, the brimstone smell? Digesting wood, presumably, to make pulp for the paper process? A man falling into the acid and being—digested?

"I'm so sorry," she said again, and the boy said, "Yeah," satisfied this time, that he had impressed her.

You try to make order in one direction and things shoot off in another. Why should someone die here the moment she arrived? It's the residue of nine-eleven; there's not more death but you're more aware of it, you take it more personally. She went back to the cabin and put her groceries away. She made herself an omelet. The mushrooms made her think of Graham lying, dying, on the couch at home. The paper stench seemed to have abated (she was already used to it?) but she felt sick. She wanted air, and since there was no one around to ask permission, she assumed hammock rights, took a cigarette and her cell phone out with her and lowered herself into the ropes.

The pines were limbless for fifty feet over her head, their trunks braided around with ivy. Above that, some of the lower branches were scorched and broken, dangling precariously, though at the tops a hundred feet above her each twig ended in a green explosion, tinged with orange as the sun went down. The trees soughed slowly back and forth. A wind chime sounded from the eaves. She let her head loll toward the road and imagined that Cassius's aunt would come walking by. They would speak of him. *I met a relative of yours in Georgia, he told me this would be a good place to stay.* But how would she know it was the aunt? No, that isn't how it would happen. Cassius would call. Or he'd arrive—his ancient Pontiac pulling up the dusty road she had just come. She would explain to Mr. Solomon . . . what? But a digester. What a gruesome thing. Why did death follow her around? No, that was magic-think, as Phoebe would point out—a form of egotism. She had come here because Cassius had sent her, and Mr. Solomon's nephew had nothing to do with her. She sighed, picked up the cell phone and dialed Phoebe.

"Dana, where've you been? I didn't want to pester you, but I was worried."

"I've been having an adventure, as you said."

It took her half an hour to catch up, from the strip mall in Brunswick to Jekyll Island to Solly's Corner. Even so she edited. She omitted. She slapped at mosquitoes and did not think it necessary to dilute her story with a local accident. She wanted not to conceal but to convince, put the best face on it, to foreground Cassius, his sweetness, his brightness, his irony. (*Irony is dead . . .*)

Phoebe listened. She said very little. A girl or a very young woman passed up Sink Street with a stroller, flapping a hand at Dana, who waved back. She strained to hear whether the telephone might be ringing in the store, but all she heard was the wind chime, and then an owl somewhere. A couple of cars threaded back into the woods. She imagined Cassius pulling up beside the hammock.

Be here, be here.

He would open the door and a chestnut-dark foot, shin, knee would emerge. He would stand in his sandals and cutoffs and denim vest with an orange towel over his shoulder and his arms polished by sunset. Dana was looking at the swaying treetops and telling Phoebe about Cassius's arrival at Jekyll Island and so remembering him there, and so imagining him here, and also seeing Phoebe as she listened, tousled from the shower in her terry robe, phone tucked against the collar while she lit a cigarette. And of these four images the least present in her mind, the least substantial, was the vast tree-brushed sky she could actually see.

"Jesus, sweetie, did you use condoms?"

"Phoebe! Of course. I'm telling you, he's a sweet, thoughtful person."

The owl called somewhere up there, invisible in the branches. She told Phoebe, adjusting her tone toward flippancy, about the schoolteacherly demeanor and the eloquent threats of Mrs. Isobel Huston. But what she mainly wanted to convey and was failing to convey was her sense of enlargement, wonderment. The vast space between her belly and the tops of the trees. The susurrating pines. The distance to the pinpoint stars. That she was *something else.*

Phoebe said, "You know, Dana, infatuation . . . you worship an illusion. You project what you need onto somebody else."

"I agree with you."

"Good."

"But that's not the case here. This is a good, kind man in a trap. I'd like to help him out of it."

"Be careful, sweetie. You may not know what you're getting into."

"Well, I do know *that,* Phoebe. This is new ground."

"Then step carefully."

She may have dreamed the wind chime, but what waked her next morning was the peal and clangor of children on the road. They were coming by in clots of threes and fours, some black, some white, from which one would roll off to another group, steam ahead, hang back examining a root or spot of ground, melt into the batch and be absorbed again. The older ones came behind, more decorous and more guarded, mostly paired. She counted twenty-one altogether. She was intensely interested in whether they segregated themselves, and was disappointed that she couldn't tell. Certainly there was traffic among the groups, especially the younger ones. But were they talking or taunting? Was that foursome really together, or was it the angle of her vision that made it seem they walked abreast? She watched till they disappeared beyond the cypress toward the highway—where, she supposed, a yellow bus would scoop them toward some town big enough to have a summer school.

She breakfasted, pulled on her shorts and top, and climbed the sagging steps of Solly's Corner. It was already hot. Flies the size of plug tobacco banged at the screen. The old fellow sat behind his rack of chewing gum and plastic worms, coughing a phlegmy cough but as willing to chatter as before.

"I got to charge you tax on your cabin, some goldurned regulations. They change 'em every fortnight, seems like. At least we got the garbage service now—that's just started up this year. Used to have to cart the trash to the dump at Winona Crossing, but there was a councilman from Tallahassee got a place across the road, and it wasn't two months later we had collection."

Dana thanked him and picked out more crackers and soda than she needed. "I'm sorry to hear about your nephew."

"Well." Solly raised his cap and wiped his head with an ironed plaid handkerchief. "Things change all at once. It was the same in Korea. People were there beside you and then they weren't." He nodded at this grim assessment. "*You* had your experience of that."

"Yes," she said, impressed that he had remembered her widowhood. But when she went to the refrigerator to pick up a quart of orange juice, the old man followed her, fixed her with a flinty glare and, wiping his hat back off his head and fanning himself with it so the white hairs lifted in the wind, barked "Don't forget to sweep up back there when you're done."

Dana leaned into the cold compartment and carefully checked the date on the orange juice (it was fresh). By the time she turned again Solly had padded back to the cash register and replaced his cap. When Dana came up he was thumbing the pages of an ancient *Field & Stream,* sniffing softly. She set her basket on the counter.

"You've got a great place here."

"You think so?" He looked up, tapping a ballpoint on the magazine, freckling its margin.

"My family moved around a lot when I was a kid, and this is the kind of place my dad always picked to stop. He liked to find out how business was."

"Izzat so."

"It is. He liked gadgets and slogans and vending machines. If he got a conversation going, I could wander around for half an hour picking out a comic or a candy bar."

"What was your favorite?"

"I liked—*mm,* I liked Mounds, the bitter outside and the coconut between my teeth."

The old man totted up her bill on the big brass register. "Tell you what. Bet you a Mounds you can't name a dozen candy bars."

"Bet I could."

"Go on, then. It's like a test."

"Okay," she said, humoring him, and counted on her fingers, "Mounds, Mentos, Snickers, Starburst, M&M's, Hershey, Milky Way . . ." In fact she knew the names of more nuts and chocolate sitting aslant these racks than she knew of the trees and plants outside. "Reese's, Tic Tac, Red Hots, Butterfinger, Almond Joy—isn't that a dozen?"

"Yah, yah." He gestured satisfaction, shoved her bag across, and dropped the candy bar in it, then was taken with a coughing fit. Dana stood awkward while he subsided, wiping his eyes. He blew his nose on the handkerchief.

"He was the last," he said. "His dad—my brother—and the wife is both gone. The wife and I weren't blessed with kids, so the name dies out with him, and the paper mill being in the family, too. He was the last of the lot."

"I'm sorry. That must be hard."

He pushed his nose back and forth with the plaid cloth. "He has a daughter. But that don't count, does it? You can't track where your genes has gone."

"Oh," Dana protested, "that's not necessarily the case these days. Lots of girls keep their maiden names."

"Well, but it don't count, does it? All that is, is just complications. Complications."

"*I* use both," Dana pointed out. "On my credit card, that's my married name. But you ask me, I give you the one I grew up with."

"Why is that?"

She considered. Why was that? She and Graham had agreed, exactly, that it was less *complicated* for a politician's wife to identify herself by her husband's name. She hadn't made a thing of it. She found the *Ms./Mrs.* battle tedious. *Ms. for miserable,* Phoebe said of her clients—but then Phoebe had letters *after* her name. Solly was peering at her, a sort of wise old cracker look with challenge in it and also, without any apparent reason, sly. When people look at you that way it means they are trying to read some sign in you, trying to figure out what your look gives back. Dana had no idea what he wanted.

"I suppose," she said with some sharpness, "it's because I liked my daddy better than my husband."

She thought the old man would be shocked, but she had touched some other nerve. He eyed her. Closed his ledger and capped his pen. Looked up again and wiped his cap off his head. "I expect you did."

8

IT IS POSSIBLE — just — to balance discipline and daydream, and that is what she tried to do. It was true she needed rest and relaxation (*recuperation, renovation, redemption . . . ?*), so she set herself the task of not hanging around the store waiting for the phone to ring, but indulging herself in what the Gulf had to offer. She would not doubt him because she had spent a night doubting him and in the morning he was there. Then she had spent a night not doubting but simply numb with his not being there — numb with her hunger, if that is possible — and after all had found that he was *prevented,* which is more full of longing than desire itself. Now he would arrive, or call, whether or not she put all her energy into wishing it. So she would wait. She would be a tourist, allowed to take him with her in her mind. She imagined him doing the same on the road, talking to himself, "making things up" about how it would be when he could get to her.

She was taking a calculated risk (Mom bent over the Monopoly board, madly mortgaging to buy Park Place) that Isobel Huston was not coming after her. She kept the threatening note as her bookmark; she read it over again and again. The more she read it the less ruinous it seemed. *Kick your white ass. Put a whipping on your bony ass.* The kids along Sink Street said, "I'm'a kick butt, man." A mother she'd overheard on the Island said, "I'm gonna whup you upside the head." This was the South. Just because she and Graham had battled each other with frostbite was no reason to panic at a little heat.

At first reading, she'd seen Isobel long legged in a miniskirt, huge haired, red fingernails like claws. But now she remembered she'd seen a picture of her, that Isobel wore square glasses and rather a prim expression, had a compact, sturdy body. And it occurred to her the letter projected destruction *because it was well written;* it projected *sass.* Dana tried to imagine Isobel sitting at a desk in her glasses and her sass. What would she feel (apart from the things she wanted Dana to know she felt)? Bitterness toward him certainly. Glee at the chance to scare the bony ass? Pleasure in her prose?

She tried to see herself in the third person, as the other woman, *her.* She looked in the mirror trying to see her face as it would be seen by someone for whom the generic face is black: *Her skin is like skim milk, or whey with little flecks of rust. Her nose is a scissor blade, her hair is wispy, her ass is flat.* She had thought of *whey.* But would Isobel Huston have any whey in her frame of reference, something out of a Victorian nursery rhyme? Or suppose Isobel came from somewhere that the cow was really milked, the butter churned, so that whey was part of her everyday experience?

We can't imagine each other, Dana thought. We can hardly imagine a landscape we haven't seen, a face twenty years older, the texture of the moon—let alone the triune, bihemispheric intricacies of a human brain. But we have to try. It's a dirty job but somebody's got to do it. Because the human race is growing and living longer and the land is shrinking and dying faster, and the brain does not keep up with its own inventions so we go to war for the same reasons that lizards do, *because there are more juicy flies in your patch of desert than in mine and because my eggs are more precious than your eggs and because this ur-lizard is the holy highest king or president or CEO among the lizards.* And if there were a God, that's the purpose She/He would have put us here for, that exercise: human beings are the two-legged creatures that have to imagine each other.

Meanwhile, however, she took the precaution of getting Florida insurance and license plates—in her maiden name—the latter accomplished in about half an hour at a one-story cement-block courthouse at a place called Winona Crossing.

After Graham's death she had been listless and heavy. After Cassius's lust she was energetic and accomplished, valuable, worth treating well. So she went to Henry's on the dock and ate broiled scamp and snapper. At the fish shed next day she bought shrimp as big as pirates' hooks and a serious pot to boil them in, and ate them on her screen porch listening to owls and shushing pines. The stink of Lhamon Mill came and went according to the prevailing winds, breathing inferno and then backing off only so long as to hit with force when it returned. The offshore beaches were out of range of such fronts, so she drove to Sag Island across one of those feats of unimaginable human engineering, where pylons sunk deep in the sandy bottom of the bay held up a slender seven-mile bridge along which cars and boats and house trailers and tons of delivery trucks rumbled day after day, year after year. On the island she walked on sand like pulverized pearls, dug coquinas up with her toes and saw them tip and bury themselves after the retreating wave. Dogs, huge or minuscule, pedigreed or mutts, dug for sand fleas and ran yelping after fiddler crabs. She ate pistachio ice-cream cones. She swam in sucking surf. Dolphins played not a football field away, and she imitated them, arching in and out of the water, surfacing to watch the pelicans that flew in communities but fed singly. One by one, each bird would peel off from the V formation, fold its wings, and plummet like a blunt-bodied bomb. There would be a calm. The water would recompose its surface. Then the pelican would bounce out juggling its prey and clamber clumsily skyward. Dana, too, would plummet under and shoot from the water. Under her breath: *I can do this. I can be alone.* That was her mantra—or rather, a spell, because it was whispered with the hope that Cassius would materialize when she got back to shore, as he had at Jekyll.

One afternoon she emboldened herself to walk onto the pool deck of the Swashbuckler Inn, and not being accosted, made a habit of rinsing there after her swim, first under the shower pipe and then in the sparkling pool. One day the hotel parking lot was full of bellicose motorcycles and the pool crammed with beefy bikers and their girls in fringed bikinis. The next day she drove to Sea Oat Dunes, where a thousand horseshoe crabs copulated on the shore, the size and shape of biker helmets thrown down in pairs on the damp sand.

She bought a second bathing suit, a two-piece that would let her belly tan. She was careful of her body, slathered it with number forty-five sunscreen, and then number fifteen, and then number eight as she bronzed. Her hair lightened in the sun and she fed it expensive protein-enzyme concoctions. For her thirty-ninth birthday she bought herself a sundress with a pattern of silk-screened sea horses at one of the island boutiques, and then on Cape St. Just a floor-length split skirt and wedge-heeled sandals strung with shells and bells.

Cape St. Just and Sea Oat Dunes and Sag Island were all several notches upscale of Pelican Bay. At the end of the island with the highest dunes and the best angle on the sunset stood a gated tract that, although the mansions tended to Spanish style and heavy tile, blatantly called itself Confederate Cove. Along the central shore lay a necklace of more modest villas, the older ones flat to the sand and the newer thrust up on pylons, sometimes balancing three stories above that. Where the bridge road met the beach the houses were interrupted by a smattering of hotels and real estate agents, souvenir shops, boutiques, restaurants, and piers from which land buggies and sea skimmers and paraphernalia of every nautical sort could be had for rent.

It was clear that tourism brought some melting-pot—as opposed to material—advances. She didn't brave the gate at Confederate Cove, but the public beaches were a global soup of Old South accents and glottal languages, extended Latino families, a British couple whose alabaster skin became daily redder and more septic looking. Another Englishwoman—Scottish, possibly—buried her giggling Asian toddler every afternoon in the sand. Dana saw—she collected—a Japanese girl caressing the thigh of a boy whose drawl was pure Alabama, an East Indian or light-skinned black with his arm around a petite platinum blond, an Arab man with a distinctly unoppressed bikini-wearing woman. Even the bikers, the second time they congregated at the Swashbuckler Inn, brought along with them a mulatto beauty who cleaved the water with her glamorous breasts.

On the mainland the demographic was more covert and more complicated. Dana spent an afternoon at the far end of her street, at Devil's Sink, which was no more than a large pond encircled and canopied by water oak and live oak so that it lay entirely in deep shade. Cypress knees jutted out of a black silt surround. A handful of water scooped up clear and dark as brewed tea. There was a floating dock on the near bank, and on the other side one of the live oaks sent a limb perilously out into space. A rope hung from this branch, and here under curtains of parasite moss the children dared each other to swing to the darkest water and let go. There were taunts and competitions, courage tested and humiliations dealt, but it seemed that in this context the blacks and whites played together, even the teenagers, even the parents kibitzing from the bank.

Likewise at Solly's Corner. Mornings the women from both West and East Sink neighborhoods came for milk and bread, for tomatoes when Solly stocked them, lemons and okra when they were to be had. They were cordial to each other and to her, and in the afternoon when the bus dumped its cargo of summer schoolers, the kids crowded into the store unearthing nickels and quarters from wrist wallets and socks and pockets, bargaining with Solly for an extra Tootsie Roll, trading Pokémon cards, shy or sly or cheeky with each other without reference to skin.

But between the pond and Solly's, down Sink Street, West was for white and East for black. Nobody crossed the road to borrow a cup of sugar or to join a Saturday barbecue. East Sink went inland to the AME on Sunday morning, West Sink went along to the Baptists at Apalachicola or the Catholics at Panama City. The kids not in summer school stuck to their neighborhoods, except for a few teenagers who mowed lawns or bused dishes on the island. The walk to the school bus was a sort of no-man's land. The black kids poured out of East Sink and the white from West. They grouped and regrouped, but warily, weaving the road in a pattern in which, however, there was no doubt which thread led where.

This much she picked up in two weeks. She wakened to children's voices, she shopped at Solly's, she swam at the island or the cove or the sinkhole, and every evening before the store closed at seven she reassured herself that no one had left a message for her, and that the old man nevertheless remembered someone might.

"You immigrating, I see," he said one day, wagging a finger at her.

"Excuse me?"

"I see you got your Florida tags."

"Oh. No . . . no, I just didn't want to be caught, you know . . . with them out-of-date."

"Ah-huh," he said—sly, not believing.

She learned sideways, from what she overheard, that her guess about the death of Solly's nephew was more or less accurate, and from raised eyebrows and unfinished sentences, that there was some question how accidental it had been. She had a kind of provisional membership in the neighborhood. Everyone was friendly to her, black and white. They gossiped of weather, prices, prospects for employment. They clucked and murmured, solacing each other's aches and blues. No one except the old man showed particular curiosity about her. When she praised the local friendliness he agreed, "Salt o' the earth, and some pepper, too." She hadn't a clue which of the women from East Sink might be Cassius's aunt.

It was ten at night when the pounding came at her door. She was settled not too comfortably on the wicker love seat, head on her cushion at one end, feet on the other, knees in the air. Open facedown on her stomach lay a paperback of *The Accidental Tourist* she had picked up on the island. The title had caught her attention, but the book had less to say about her own situation than she'd hoped, and the story had lost out to daydream.

Daydreaming—evening dreaming—had led her to a memory. It was in the same town as that plaster pond where Dad made the paper boats. So she was—seven? eight? And it must have been, then,

Logan, Utah? A hotel was under construction and Dad had landed a contract to plaster the inside. He got a regular paycheck, which meant unusual treats—she remembered a restaurant where she'd been served Italian dressing and discovered the taste of raw crushed garlic. They rented a house in that town, with a yard, and a black maid who came once a week. Her name was—not Clara, something more elaborate, Clotilda or Camilla. This woman had a daughter who stayed with the grandmother when Clotilda came to clean.

But one day the grandmother was ill or away, and the girl came, too. Like Dana seven or eight, she was missing a molar—mesmerizingly, her tongue tip appeared in the empty space—and she had a mischievous grin and braids, not the multiple cornrows of Cassius's toddler, but two tight plaits with a single part down the back of her head.

The garage of that house had shelves maybe four feet deep, three tiers of them to the rafters, like the open side of a dollhouse. Dana and the girl climbed into the shelves and played at being ladies. They brushed imaginary poodles, draped themselves in dishcloth furs, poured tea from a flowerpot into jar-lid cups. Then Dana thought of and furtively borrowed from her mother's kitchen a teapot shaped like a kneeling camel. You poured the tea (water with grass clippings) into the blanket on the camel's back and out its open mouth. This was a squeal-inducing find. The girl (her name?—entirely gone) was a gifted mimic, and inventive, too, of domestic scenarios. The two of them took tea, switched roles, whined as children, scolded as parents, made pompous plans as man and wife. Where had that girl learned with such confidence the tone, the tilted head, the drawn-out speech of the idle rich? Was it her mother's mimicry of her bosses? Television? Where, when it comes to that, had Dana learned to recognize it?

In any case they had elaborate games, and afterward Dana pointed out to her mother that there was no need for Camilla or Clotilda to have a babysitter. The girl could come every week.

Mom's behavior was perplexing. She smiled, she nodded, she gave Dana a pat or hug. She was so glad the two had had fun together. But it probably wouldn't be a good idea to repeat. It might cause complications. Well, with the cleaning, the scheduling. Mom and Dana might have errands on cleaning day, mightn't they?

The reasoning was so thin, the facial expressions so contorted, that Dana knew she was being lied to, but had no idea why. The intimation of a secret so adult it could not be explained came to her together with the possibility that she, Dana, had done something gauche or even wicked, from the consequences of which she needed shielding.

Yet this was the end of the sixties. Mom preached universal brotherhood. She praised Martin Luther King. Aretha Franklin was her particular heroine. What struck Dana now—a moth circling around the paper lantern, the book rising and falling with her breath—was that her mother, who was born of Emma Hoffstetter into South Carolina in the forties, had *advanced* to hypocrisy. Daughter of that mother, she nevertheless saw what was right, even if she couldn't act on it. It represented progress of substantial kind that she was ashamed of her own spurious reasoning.

Dana shifted on the couch. She watched the translucent, beating belly of a tree frog sucked against the windowpane above her. Then the door banged, a hard repeated pounding, which her heart answered because the first thing that came to mind was that Isobel Huston had followed her after all and meant to put a whipping on her bony ass.

The woman was white—though creamy tan, with an artful tousle of ash-blond waves tied off her forehead with a paisley scarf. She was small featured, pretty, rather dolled up in a white halter neck and capri pants, and she was exuding anxiety as thick as sweat. She wrung her slender hands. Her speech was clipped but its vowels broad, a drawl under pressure. "I'm so sorry! I need help. Solly—Mr. Solomon—has fallen. I don't know how bad it is. Could you possibly . . . ?"

"Of course. I'll just grab some shoes. What happened?"

"He's cut his head. I don't know how bad it is." Her face convulsed. "But I can't get him up, and I've *got* to get him to the clinic."

"I'm with you. I'll go with you," Dana said.

She scrambled over the pine needles after the smaller woman, who was more agile in spite of her stack-heeled sandals. They leaped the steps. Inside, John Solomon was lying at the end of the counter on the splintery floorboards, his head pillowed on a five-pound plastic bag of Mahatma rice. There was blood sunk deep into the boards and dried into his hair, a glistening gash on his forehead already crusted at the edges.

"All right, all right," he said irritably.

"Here's help, Solly. We'll take you down to Winona Crossing and check you out."

"I just went to reach the grinder."

"Never mind, we'll have you checked." The woman knelt on the floor beside him and tried to lift his head. Behind the counter a split bag lay in a scatter of coffee beans, a metal scoop and broken mug.

"How long have you been lying here?" Dana asked.

"He isn't sure. A couple of hours, I think. Solly. Solly! Help me now." The woman tugged and patted at his shoulders. She cooed, she lifted. Her tone, her gestures, were affectionate and familiar and proprietary. Dana guessed she was either a relative or else one of those public-spirited women that are born out of need in every community, who make it their hobby to look after the old and the damaged.

Not helping, Solly sagged back. "Damn nigger in here. I told him to call you."

"Was that one of the Adams boys?"

"One of 'em. Not the moped, the other one. I hadn't locked up yet, and he came in." Solly grunted and rolled against her effort.

"What do you mean?" Dana asked. "Were you mugged?"

The woman looked at her and shoved at her hair. "No, he *said:* he slipped when he climbed up for the grinder. You can see where he hit his head on the counter there."

"What does he mean about the boy?"

"One of the locals. Solly asked him to call me, but he wouldn't."

"Why not?"

"Be-cause," she explained carefully, "somebody would say: *was he mugged?*"

Stung, Dana reached to help tug at Solly's overalls. The old man lay unwilling, but with a combination of their lifting and cajoling, and Solly's begrudging use of his own leg power, they got him onto the flatbed of the woman's smart little SUV, where for want of a better pillow they propped him on the rice again.

"Adena Dern. Thanks."

"Dana Cleveland. You're welcome. Where are we headed?"

"There's a clinic at Winona Crossing."

Dana sat sideways in the welcome blast of air-conditioning, a hand back on Solly's arm while Adena drove. Adena tooled expertly—well above the speed limit—back along the coast road that had brought Dana to Pelican Bay, black silk water on the right, black shag marsh on the left, black velvet sky overhead, prattling in her nervousness (just as I do, Dana thought), mostly in complaint of Solly, mostly in the third person.

"He drives me crazy. You drive me crazy, don't you, Solly? There's not a reason in the world he needs to be wearing himself out grinding coffee after hours. Climbing around on ladders. A man ought to rest at his age, do some fishing, watch TV."

"I *been* fishing," Solly muttered. "Didn't care for it."

"Grinding the coffee every night for fifty years, and sweeping and mopping while the place falls down around him. That store . . . !"

"I got help."

"Oh, he's got help, for all the help Trudy is, the blind leading the blind, I swear to gawd . . ."

"Who's Trudy?" Dana asked, but all the answer she got was "Good question," from Adena, and from Solly, "Nothing wrong with Trudy."

Then the old man was quiet. Maybe he slept, while the trees toward the water thinned and a crescent moon appeared over the Gulf behind a strip of cirrus cloud. Adena drove and grumbled. "The place needs a ton of work. Really it needs tearing down, which he ought to do now Bucky is gone. You know about his nephew?"

"I do. I heard."

"Bucky was my husband."

"Oh, I'm sorry."

"Was—we've been divorced four years. But thanks." This was real news. Dana tried to recollate the relationships. "I'm just worried about Solly now. He doesn't look it, but he took it hard. And he's borderline senile, you may not have noticed."

Dana glanced back hoping the old man was asleep, but she couldn't be sure. She lowered her voice. "There was one day, I think he thought I was someone else."

Adena did not lower hers. "Set in his ways, my gawd. That store—he caters to the locals, and they're all broke as sin, the whole bunch them. He could make a good living if he'd open himself up to the tourist trade. You know, it's the last store before the bridge. Half the people headed over there would think it was their one chance to get a raft or a pair of flip-flops if they could just notice the damn store, but, *nooo,* he won't cut down that little corkscrew of a tree so you could see the sign."

"He could have a new sign closer to the road."

"Yes he could, for a coupla thousand dollars. They've got to root them in the ground because of hurricanes. Two swipes of a saw and a lick of paint, he could have it for nothing and put the money in fishing gear."

They left the coast and turned north over a bay, past pockets of deep woods with side roads plunging through them, closed shrimp shops, and darkened cottages. The clinic was lit up, though, out in the middle of nowhere, a flat one-story building with a single corner of curved brick like a fifties burger stand, sharing a bare patch among the trees with a small supermarket. A brisk white nylon nurse directed an orderly to slide Solly onto a gurney. Adena and the nurse knew each other; they both knew Solly. The paperwork was minimal and fast, though they were told it would take the doctor on call half an hour to make it in. Meanwhile the nurse rolled Solly down the hall to wash his wound. Dana and Adena drank tepid coffee on hard plastic chairs.

"You must think you've dropped into some horror movie, all the accidents and drama. It's not like this, I promise. It's been a terrible two weeks around here."

Adena had the creamy, tended look of someone who was high school prom queen and had moved effortlessly on to golf. Dana was not surprised to learn that she sold real estate on Sag Island. Yet her animated features and her tumbled locks expressed that everything was right out there, everything open and available. She used her eyes, her hands, the whole circumference of her mouth. She had a habit of leaning in close to make a point, a gesture of confidentiality without the attendant lowering of her voice. This would be a natural maven of hospitality, a woman who gave everything away out of sheer guilelessness. *The South,* thought Dana. And thought that, though Adena Dern had none of the sidelong humor of her closest friend, maybe she had found a Florida Phoebe.

Dana said, "My husband died as well. We weren't divorced, but it was in the offing."

"Well, then you know. It's a crazy mixed-up feeling. It should be guilt."

"Maybe not."

"But when Hancock came in to tell me — she owns the agency — I could see more or less what it was before she opened her mouth. That twisted kind of smile — you know? — that's an apology for bad news. Not knowing how to say it. I've done it, too. But when she said Bucky'd fallen from the catwalk and then — I've done it, too — trying to let me down easy, said he was *bad hurt,* and then *probably terminal,* and then *well, already dead . . .* I'd have to say it was a shock. But. It's a terrible thing to say: it was like a weight off my shoulders, like my whole body bounced, you know? And I thought: *I remember this. It's joy.* I know it's a terrible thing to say. But . . ." She leaned within inches of Dana's face. "He was a terrible man."

There was more of this energetic confessional. Bucky had been her high school sweetheart. Bucky was football, she was pom-poms, Bucky was cool, she was brains. There were not that many guys to choose from if you didn't go up to the university in Tallahassee, which there wasn't the money for. She and Bucky sort of wandered into marriage — boredom, lack of options, too much pot and too many promises to back out on. Bucky went to work at the mill as a matter of course, and got shit-faced every other day as a matter of

God-given rights. She'd got her real estate license and gone to work because she couldn't count on his paycheck. One week in the bank and the next week blown on booze. Terrible fights, terrible sex, a long slog and a drag, who needs it? Their daughter Bernadette had kept them together for a dozen years. But Bernadette was sixteen now, gorgeous, troubled, a handful, honest to gawd, and Bucky hadn't done a goddam thing for her since they split.

"He was a world-class jerk, every which-a-way. Shows up at two in the morning singing, ranting, a kid trying to sleep. Stingy, pissed, pissed off—a temper!—could dish it out but couldn't get it up, know what I mean? He was the kind of guy, I'd ask him for something, underwear for Bernadette, a lawn-chair cushion, he'd go, 'Let's go get it now. Let's go right now. I've got the car keys in my hand, I'll buy it and bring it home and burn it, yeah?' He didn't hit anybody, he was afraid to, and then despised himself for that and then felt sorry for himself because he despised himself. One time he pulled that bring-it-home-and-burn-it number, I threw a dozen eggs at him, one at a time. *Wham! Wham!* He just stood there. You ever seen one of those kid shows where they pour the goo? That was him, a second grader dripping goo. What a jerk."

Dana listened, admiring. The resilience. The blatancy. There was not a scintilla of self-protection in the woman. She'd lay out her wounds, her scars, and cheerfully describe the slashing. Every once in a while Dana would say, "I know. I understand." Which she did, approximately, although she would never have volunteered such feelings to a stranger.

Nor did she, apart from the few murmured assents that referred to her own marriage, return the confidence. She would have been hard-pressed to say why—though it would in a way have relieved her—she did not mention Cassius. There seemed no need to explain what she was doing here. Adena was, conversationally speaking, all give and no demand.

The doctor came trotting up the hall, a small balding man with a manner more glad hand than bedside. He greeted Adena by name, acknowledged Dana with a bow, and launched into a series of laid-back assurances. Solly was fine (*"fi-uhn"*), a bruise here and there, just the one contusion. Possibly a hairline fracture, and that shoulder'd sustained a jolt.

"I'd like to send him up to Tallahassee General. Not that Solly'd sue me, hah, but if you've got scanners, you might as well scan, eh?" He tapped his head to indicate the logic, then, very casually, lowered his voice. "Some tingling in the left hand. Always a possibility. These old fellows, you think they've fallen and that's how they hurt themselves. Fact, is, they've had a tiny stroke and that's why they fell."

"Stroke?"

"Not to worry. Just wanna be sure, Mizz Dern."

"What does Solly say?"

"I'll give him a shot of Pentothal, he'd agree to a triple bypass. Come on back."

They followed to the corner room with the curve of glass brick. Solly was hooked up to a monitor, his head bandaged and his hair slicked back, one hand stuttering over the boiled-wool blanket. He nodded to them both but it was Dana's hand he reached for—confused no doubt.

"The meat fellow and the Cokes both comes on Tuesdays," Solly said. He peered at Dana. His fingers agitated at the blanket.

Adena said, "That's right, Solly. Both on Tuesday."

"I may git there and I may not."

"Tuesday's tomorrow." Dana meant to humor him.

Adena said, "Tuesday is tomorrow, Solly."

"It's a plain old cash register. Pick it up in no time."

"Oh," said Adena. "He's asking would you mind the store."

"Would you?" said Solly, and squeezed her hand hard. No evidence of stroke in that grip.

Adena leaned over the old man and straightened the neckline of his gown. "Solly, now. Mizz—Cleveland, is it?—Mizz Cleveland's come down for a vacation. You don't want to ask her that."

"I do," said Solly, and his rheumy blue eyes looked straight into Dana's, pleading. "Just a coupla hours in the morning and a couple in the afternoon. There's the key right there in my pants pocket, the one with the plastic top. And the dairy stuff needs checking. The sell-by dates is on the front. You know what I'm talking about?"

"I know what a sell-by date is. The only trouble . . ."

"Oh, and the Al-Anon folks come Wednesdays. Could you give 'em a pound of the Folger's wholesale? It's marked on the can."

"On the coffee can," Dana said stupidly. The last thing she wanted was to mind a country store. She looked to Adena for help.

Who, sighing, conveying somehow with her eyebrows that she was giving in to Dana, said, "I guess . . . I *could* bring Bernadette over afternoons to help."

9

It was nearly two in the morning when Adena dropped her at the cabin. She meant to go straight to bed, but she was wired with late coffee and the hodgepodge of the unexpected. And she was curious. She had the key, after all. There was no reason she shouldn't have a look.

The screen door creaked in a suitably eerie way, the key turned against grating rust. She reached for and found a switch with one sweep of her hand, as if she'd known exactly where it was. The metal shade over the counter threw a shallow cone of light. She'd seen this room many times: high ceiling, shelves around three sides, half a dozen aisles of shorter racks in the center, candy and cat food, toilet paper, laundry soap. A potbellied stove now cold stood in a corner behind the counter. The back wall held the refrigerator cases and a door to whatever lay beyond.

But this low-light view of it was suffused with some emotion, too, part stealth—the sense of license in somebody else's space—part jitters, knowing she'd obligated herself, and that the blood was still there on the floor. Also a rush from childhood: the smells of Juicy Fruit and tobacco in close air, a release from the tedium of those long drives. Dad always avoided the franchises and the chains for places like this, the odd little mom-and-pops—the Gas and Gulp, the Dew Drop Inn, Ye Olde Trading Post—where Mom dallied in the ladies' or paced outside wiping her neck with a damp paper towel, and Dana walked between the aisles with quarters in her fist, liking the dust on things, the creak of the floorboards, rust and mold, the settledness, the sense of its having been like this for a long, long time.

She walked through the aisles now, patting the candy bars, passed the refrigerator wall, and pushed into the room beyond. As she reached for the light she remembered an afternoon in one of those Last-Chance-Gas-and-Reptile places strung along the Mojave Desert, when she had entered a shop back looking for the john and found herself surrounded to the ceiling on every side by snakes in cages. The memory raised hair on her arms, and in the second before she found the switch, activated heart and sweat glands, stung the surface of her skin hot and then cold.

Here there were only cardboard cartons, canned goods, and potato chips, a rather fine old cracked-leather sofa, some potted plants, and a sleek new Sony TV. It had been a porch once, from the look of it, closed in with jalousie windows to make a warehouse-cum-living-room, with a kitchenette beyond the boxes. The couch was generously laden with cushions made out of afghan squares. Blankets pieced together out of the same bright stuff hung over the back of the couch, and on the floor near one end a stack of orange and yellow squares were skewered into a deep handled basket with foot-long needles and a crochet hook. So. Either the old man was a closet knitter or he had company. On the wall behind the couch—also possibly a woman's touch—hung a print in murky blues and browns, three contorted figures under an arch or the mouth of a cave. She recognized it, maybe; maybe William Blake. Outside the jalousies she could just make out the hammock to the right, beyond which would be her cabin; and on the left an ancient and venerable live oak with a tire hung from it on a rope. The tree was floodlit from two sides, its raddled trunk hugely branching in the upshaft of the light, which struck Dana as touchingly bourgeois, to floodlight a tree in the backyard. She retreated to the shop.

The refrigerator case was stuffed to the gills with beer, and in one section sat those cheese and lunch-meat packs on which she was supposed to check the dates. Not tonight. Behind the counter a door led back to a narrow hall with a half bath: cracked linoleum under a scrubbed old pedestal sink and cistern toilet. Beside that, a stairway led up to the living quarters. Not in her charge. She moved behind the counter and spread her hands across its top, a proprietary gesture she must have learned from the movies. She pressed No Sale on the old-fashioned cash register, and it dinged loud and sudden in the silence and flung a drawer at her, full of coins and bills, the ones stuffed in tight, a smaller stack of fives, tens, twenties. Jesus. It raised her hackles. It must be some kind of fluke Solly *wasn't* mugged.

The black phone sat beside the register, an early punch-button shaped like the old rotaries. She fingered its buttons so lightly that she felt her fingerprints, as lightly as she had touched Cassius's skin. This thought set her torso tingling. She imagined the electricity reaching through the line to Georgia, vibrating in his mother's house, the ringtone as recognizable as a voice. But if she was going to call Cassius she could have done it on her cell phone before now. There'd be no advantage in calling him from Solly's store. If they guessed where she was she would be that much more vulnerable. Still. This was where he sent her. This was the phone she had been praying would ring. The sight, the feel of it, the possibility, threatened to sap her willpower.

She cupped her hands over the receiver. It was three in the morning. She must not call. But what if Cassius himself answered? Would he be gladder than sleepy, or sleepier than glad? *Be here, be here.*

She reached under the counter and swept her hand along the shelf, half expecting to find a gun. What she pulled up instead was a ledger in which was recorded, in neat black ballpoint, the dates and prices of deliveries. You could figure out from it, if you took the time, just when and how everything arrived. You could guess at how much to order. On the front-inside cover was a list of phone numbers, most of them the 800 lines of distributors, but also a few attached to local names, including *Adena D.* and *Trudy L.* Those two names were in the expenses column of the ledger, too. It looked like he gave each of them $500 a month. Curiouser and curiouser.

She found a broom in the little hall and a bucket under the counter, swept up the coffee beans and filled the bucket awkwardly at the bathroom sink. Broke open a new packet of scrubbing sponges and attacked the blood on the floor. It had started as a puddle and sunk into the wood as a stain about the size and shape of her sandaled foot. The boards were splintered oak in serious need of sanding. She rubbed and dipped her sponge. The blood diluted and sank deeper in. Nevertheless the grain revealed itself as the thin stain spread, just as it had when she sanded the hutch, but these wide planks were brittle, stippled with little knots like ostrich hide. Really it was a waste of such fine old wood to let it go like that. She agreed with Adena, there was more to do here than one old man could handle. She shoved hard forward on the sponge, and a splinter stabbed deep in at the base of her thumb. The pain made her gasp. She gritted her teeth and yanked, let the shard fall, needle sized and needle shaped. And there appeared in the black flash of that pain the ugly idea that Cassius did not want to hear from her. Did not expect to contact her. Would not come here. It would not be worth it, whether he cared for her or not, the family anger, the turmoil, the danger to his visitation rights.

She was sponging drops of her own blood into the floorboards now. Fiercely, she put the thought out of her mind. She would not doubt him. Would not. Doubt was just another form of pain, a metaphysical spillage.

But the impulse to call had been successfully quashed. She rinsed her sponge, put the bucket back, and picked up the key.

As she locked up and turned, she saw, silhouetted in the light from the road, that the gas pumps had grown a lumpy connection, a body almost as square as they were, one thick arm resting on each, a round head between. Dana caught her breath and checked her flanks in case she would need to run. The woman—she knew it was a woman—lowered one arm and settled her chin in the hand of the other, leaning on the pump. A couple of small bats flapped in their frantic way overhead, zapping insects.

"Can I help you?" Dana thought she had better say. She listened, but there was no other sound of humans, just crickets and frogs, a hum of electric power from the highway. The flesh at the base of her thumb thumped with pain.

"You folk to Mr. Solly?"

"No, I'm just helping him out."

"You the one renting his cabin."

"That's right."

"Where he at?"

As Dana's eyes adjusted she could see that the woman was not particularly large, but solid, her eyes gleaming out of blue-black skin; and could also see suspicion in the slant of her head and the possessive weight of her arm on the pump.

"He had an accident. He fell, and Adena Dern and I took him to the clinic at Winona Crossing. It's not serious, probably, but they wanted to take him up to Tallahassee for some tests."

"When he going to be back here?"

"Soon, I hope. He asked me to check on the store."

"You be in there tomorrow, the Coke man coming?"

"That's right. I'm Dana. Are you Trudy?" The woman nodded, suspicious still, so Dana held out her arm and dangled the key. "See? I've got the key."

Trudy waved this off. "You going to sell coffee to the Al-Anon?"

"Yes, Folgers, wholesale. The price is marked on the can."

This satisfied her abruptly. "I work sometime for Mr. Solly. I can come in nights and clean up if you want."

"Thank you, I will want that. And thanks for looking out for the store."

"I keep a eye."

"That's good of you."

"I keep a eye *out*."

She gave a peal of clear laughter that emboldened Dana to say, "You scared me to death. I wouldn't've wanted to mess with you." The laugh found a second wind, and everything fell into place. Not that there was anything Dana would have claimed to *recognize*—she did not have the same apparatus for judging a black face as a white—but considering the crochet and knit work in the back room, Adena's dismissal, Solly's defense, and that she herself had been sent here: Trudy was Solly's woman and Cassius's no-doubt-exiled aunt.

"I had to go up to Lake Stonybrook on a custody case," Phoebe said, "which took me past Shanksville. The field is green again, but they've fenced it off from the tourist crowds. You should see the stuff they've dumped there. It's Princess Di of the boondocks; it's teddy-bear landfill. The stink of wilting flowers is enough to choke you. They've got Port-o-lets set up, and guys who'll sell you a photo op and a rhinestone flag for your lapel."

Dana carried the cell phone around the store while she listened, tidying the magazine rack and the potato chips. Fritos, Lay's, Doritos, Funyuns, SunChips, Ruffles, Tostitos, Cape Cod. In Kabul, Hamid Karzai had sworn in several new vice presidents to gain control over wayward warlords. In Arizona, an Apache firefighter had been arrested for setting the fire he hired on to fight. The peanut cans looked greasy. Does grease osmose through tin?

"And in the meantime, a hit-and-run SUV half a county over crashed into an Amish buggy and killed two kids. The Somerset coroner said, 'The human race is a funny apparatus.'"

"Amen," Dana said, a little hollowly. Southern Pennsylvania seemed at least as far away as Kabul or Show Low, Arizona. It was also surprising how much disorder a dozen ordinary women could make in the ordinary task of morning shopping. The boxes needed lining up, the cans replenishing, the vegetables picked over and rearranged. A bag of rice had broken (Mahatma, like the one under Solly's head), and she'd need to sweep it up before the school bus arrived. But that required both hands.

"So how's it going with you? Have you heard from the, whatsit, niece?"

"Adena. Ex-niece-in-law, I make it. Not a word. I looked up the hospital in Tallahassee and got through to his nurse's station, and they said they'd be keeping him at least till Wednesday."

"God, Dana, that makes more than a week. How'd you get yourself into it?"

"You might well ask." It was Friday, and in fact she had seen neither Adena, her daughter, nor Trudy, although when she arrived in the morning the floor would be mopped, the counter tidied—Trudy the shoemaker's elves, she thought. And Adena had called to apologize. Bernadette had a doctor's appointment and then a swim meet, but she'd be sure to be in on Saturday. Adena was voluble and grateful and energetic, so it was impossible to mind. At first Dana thought she'd open just as Solly had asked, a couple of hours in the morning, a couple in the afternoon, and in between she'd swim or read, drive over to the island. But while she fiddled with the merchandise or balanced the ledger—paid out, taken in—the lunch hour dribbled away. And just as she was closing another delivery would arrive.

She said, "It's actually a pretty smooth operation. Interesting. The delivery guys know the stock, and they count it and figure out what I need. I don't have to *order* anything. A big gas tanker comes and tops up the tank for the pumps. The fishing salesman is the biggest kick. Got an MBA at Georgia but couldn't stand the office life. I sell Greedy Gut lures and Piscator baby shrimp rigs—is that expanding my range, or what?"

"Are you pulling some good-girl number?"

"It's only for a week or so. It's not so bad."

"It was one thing doing volunteer work when your husband was a senator. I hope you're getting paid."

"Yeah, well. That was not discussed."

"I'm serious, Dana, you're somebody who can get yourself taken advantage of. You spent twelve years with Graham, and what did you have to show?"

"I know. I know. It's only for a week. And I'm right here when Cassius calls."

She knew Phoebe would sigh, exasperated, and Phoebe, exasperated, sighed.

10

THE WOMEN WERE FRIENDLY and noisy, inspected the labels for calories, pinched fruit, complained of prices, counted their change. *How ya doin,* they said to her, *How do, How ah ya, How's it going, You doin' okay?* Which, so many times a day repeated, reminded her that people are often not okay, that anxiety is not an invention of the century, that the fundamental news has to do with pain, fear, sadness, or the mere and lucky lack thereof.

They showed her where the Baggies and the lighter fluid were kept and asked after Solly as if she had a right to know how he was. Most had either a child or a cell phone hung on one jeans pocket. One had a squarish mutt disciplined to sit on the porch at a respectful distance from the door. One had a cane. Little by little, overhearing or asking, she picked up names. April looked twelve but was probably twenty, scalped into a ponytail, the toddler in the stroller primped and pressed. Sarah wore low-backed tops to flaunt the scar across her spine. Flora and Evian were inseparable, one tall, one broad, one burgundy and one high yellow. Jessie used safety pins where her buttons were missing, so her pale belly flesh showed in the gaps, which made Emma flex her nose, which made Lou Ann ask piously after Jessie's kids. Marion was always tired, always in the same pair of dog-chewed pink rubber flip-flops. Parthinia flashed every day a new animal print on her callipygian form.

The after-school crowd had a different mood range, shy to sulky, mischievous to larcenous. With them, Dana was on probation. They peppered her with claims of "what Mr. Solly do." Nobody volunteered a name. She couldn't see the far aisle from the till, and assumed there was a certain amount of pilfering going on. Still, it was threatless. She may have lost a few Almond Joys. Nobody pulled a gun or walked off with the cash drawer. She scored a minor goal on Friday afternoon when, ringing up a bag of Utz Salt 'n Vinegar, she said after a departing sidesaddle cap, "I'll just count the stock and let you settle up with Mr. Solomon, shall I?" The boy sauntered on out but his companion snickered, and the nymphet flashed a grin over the potato chips. "He a bad one. You tell Mr. Solly."

But Saturday was chaos, a gabble of men and women and teenagers all at once. It took her till midmorning to realize that everyone had payday money, and some of the tourists wandered in as well. The gas pumps throbbed like a pair of hearts. The frozen bait went by the bucket. She sold out of the St. Pete *Times* ("Afghan Women Fear Violence and Repression") and the *County Chronicle* ("Hollywood Rebels Prefer Triumph Motorcycle"). She ran short of Rolling Rock. A boy she hadn't seen before, hair wet and pimple scars along his jaw, swore Solly never carded him, and how was he to know he'd need his license? She gave in, which discouraged her, and when a woman in a hairnet counted out fifty cents too little, Dana snapped at her. The woman pulled a face and put back a jar of peanut butter. It was too late to let it go. The door banged and Dana was flooded with the knowledge that this whole venture might be empty error, a delaying tactic like the hutch (which had at least the virtue of steadiness and solitude). She would last till Wednesday. If Cassius hadn't contacted her by then (*if* was her thought by now), she would push off west.

About eleven she was hugely relieved to see Adena plow through the screen door, emitting energy from her neon-green top, in her wake a tall girl like a yacht being towed by a tug.

"Oh, gawd, I'm sorry we left you so long. Are you coping?"

"Just about."

"Well, here's my Bernadette to lend a hand."

Her Bernadette may have acknowledged this, with a rouged and kohl-blackened blink. She was slender, statue still, blond roots showing where her hair was caught up like a bunch of blue chives sprouting from her crown. She had a purple rhinestone through one nostril and another through the navel on display between her chopped top and cutoff shorts. A double-chain tattoo encircled her upper arm, interrupted by a circle around a five-point star. She had a black chiffon scarf threaded through her belt loops, adrift down the backs of her thighs.

Adena said, "I promised Solly I'd run in and see him in Tallahassee, though Saturday is big in the real-estate trade, and Hancock is squirrelly about it, but what can you do? " She grimaced at the overflowing cash drawer, waggled a hand and said under her breath, "Better stash some under the counter. Solly does." Dana nodded. Adena turned and gave Bernadette a hug. "Do just what Mizz Cleveland tells you honey. Hear? I'll be back about four."

Bernadette wound her head slowly on its stalk, a seabird looking out to the horizon. In spite of the getup, she was drop-dead gorgeous. She had that luminous butterscotch-flavored skin that is meted out exclusively to sixteen-year-old girls. Her heart-shaped face was cruelly punctured with moist blue eyes in their kohl surrounds, her lips perpetually parted, as if they had been really bee-stung and it would hurt to close them.

"Hi," she said.

Adena, scattering hellos and haste at the customers, all of whom seemed to know her, apologized again — "Is there anything I should tell Solly?"

"I don't know. These bills have come, but I guess they'll wait till Wednesday."

"Better take 'em along in case. I'll tell him what a terrific job you're doing. Bye, sweetie. Thank you, Dana! I don't know what we'd do without you."

She was gone. Bernadette stood on one foot, planted. "What shall I do?" she asked, the word lingering in adolescent threnody.

What shall I doo? What shall I doo? The scent of sweet musk drifted off of her.

"First thing, I think, fill the Coke rack. Do you know where the spares are, in the back?"

Bernadette looked vaguely stricken but said, "Where the TV is?"

"Right. Put them in the back of each row and leave the cold ones toward the front, yeah?"

"Uh-huh." She moved off in resistant, limpid loops, like toffee being worked on a machine. A few minutes later Dana saw her shoving warm cans in the front of each refrigerator row.

"I'm Wiccan," said Bernadette.

"As in, a witch?"

"I'm not a witch yet."

"Like a novice, then?"

"Uh. We do a year and a day of training. I'm doing it online."

"Ah."

"At the College of the Sacred Moon."

They'd hit an early-afternoon lull. Dana had made fresh coffee, and Bernadette played with the plastic teat of a pint bottle of Zephyrhills water. Push, pull. Her tenderly formed toes, nails lavender with tiny black decals, pumped the rhythm on her sandals. Push, pull, push, pull.

"Most people think witches are evil," she revealed.

"I think you're right." Dana stepped out to check the mailbox, brought in a fistful of bills, industry newsletters, catalogs. She sorted them on the counter while Bernadette talked, her voice a mumble at once grudging, high, and sweet.

"And they think a male witch is a warlock."

"That's not right?"

"A male witch is a witch. *Warlock* is just a smear, like calling somebody *nigger.* It's, like, bigotry."

"I see."

Hartsfield Distribution, Verabon Home Dairy. Under the bills was a picture postcard of a fireworks display: *Centennial Olympic Park, Atlanta. Fourth of July Celebration.*

"Is Wicca the same as Goth?" Dana asked.

"It's got nothing to do with Goth." Bernadette managed to be both scathing and listless. "Goth is a lifestyle. Wicca is a *religion*."

Dana turned the card over. It was addressed to *Mrs. Trudy Lewis, c/o Sollys Corner, Pelican Bay, FL*. Her heart plummeted to her feet and stayed there tingling at her soles.

"Witches don't wear anything special. At least, anything to do with being witches."

She knew the handwriting because these were the very words she knew it in: *Sollys Corner, Pelican Bay, Highway 98*. The *P* was made from bottom to top, its long loop prone. The *S* and the *C* leaned over farther than the lower case, so they canopied the littler letters. *Solly's* was missing its apostrophe.

"I mean, brooms are for cleaning up!" Bernadette declared. "Not flying around in the sky!"

In the message space:

Dear Aunt Trudy

Happy Independence Day

Cassius

She turned it over again. Fireworks bloomed on the picture side, red and yellow and blue, bursting in air against plumes of ochre smoke. Instinctively she clutched the picture against her chest. She turned it back to the message.

Happy Independence Day.

"Mizz Cleveland?"

Dana perceived she'd missed a joke. She laughed, *ha ha*. Bernadette tipped back her long neck and drank from the water bottle. "There are bad witches," she conceded, "but that's like saying there are bad Presbyterians."

"Uh-huh."

"Those ones put hate on people, contrary to the Rule of Three."

Dana said, "Tell you what, we'll probably have a rush in a little while. Why don't you go on back and watch TV until it starts?"

"Okay . . ." Bernadette spelled indifference in the roll of her shoulders but instantly disappeared.

Happy Independence Day. She remembered very well. Well, she remembered partly. They were talking about her lighter. She said it was a symbol. He said, "Run that one by me." This sentence she remembered exactly because it was in his signature tone: deference/irony, throaty, low. *You'll have to run that one* by *me.* "The flag," she'd said. And he'd said, "Like fireworks on the Fourth of July," and she'd said, "Exactly." And she'd spelled out a *symbol of independence.* Hadn't she? Wasn't that it? And wasn't this a message encoded for her, Dana? What could *independence* mean but that he was getting free?

On the other hand, what would be the point? Why not write her directly? Surely he could slip a postcard in a mailbox without getting caught at it. And what was she supposed to do with the information (anger starting here; still in her prickling soles) if she couldn't call him? It was slim pickings, nearly three weeks after she'd left Georgia, with a threatening letter from his wife in her paperback and no word from him to go on. What made him think she'd still be here? What made him think—it was pure fluke—she'd see the card?

On the other hand, how likely was it that a full-grown black man in the Deep South would just happen to send Fourth of July greetings to an aunt? Didn't that seem bizarre? Did it suggest some impediment, even some danger she didn't know about?

The rush of customers came, and Dana fumbled through it, her mind elsewhere, her math a little damaged, Bernadette of dwindling use. By the time Adena arrived—nearer closing time than four, Bernadette back at the TV with a supper of cheddar puffs and Gatorade, watching reruns of *Saved by the Bell*—Dana had half a plan for ambushing Trudy.

"I'm so sorry!" Adena said. "The traffic was chockablock on 319. They're widening Thomasville, and I had to go up to the Wal-Mart to get Solly a pair of pajamas b'cause he can't stand those hospital gowns. Grouse and whine! He thinks nobody has anything better to do than fetch for him. He even asked if *you* were coming up tomorrow."

"Me?"

"Just ignore it."

"Is he okay?"

"The truth is he's grieving for Bucky, but of course—men of that generation!—he can't admit it, so it's all disguised as fretting about the store, how the stock'll go bad, the customers will take off elsewhere. As if they could. The only thing keeps this place solvent is the men go off to Lhamon Mill in the cars, and the women can't get to anyplace else on weekdays."

"I'd thought of that."

"Apparently they are going to release him Wednesday."

"Good."

"He's not wrong about the food—Kool-Aid Jell-O and coagulated gravy, *gagh*. I should've thought to take him some fruit. The nurses fuss over him, though. He used to be a charmer, you might not think."

"I *could* go up there."

"Jeez, no way. Take Sunday off."

Adena leaned over the counter, glowing with exertion. Her top had the hue and shine of a Granny Smith. She smelled of something sharper, sweeter, than Bernadette. *Obsession,* Dana thought. Phoebe used to wear it.

"Listen." Adena hesitated, tapped the counter with her keys, half laughed with a clearing of the throat. "I dunno if you've noticed. Solly sort of helps me out. With Bernadette's expenses, mainly, because Bucky was so . . ." She shrugged and crimped her nose.

"Yeah, I did see that in the ledger."

"He's a contrary old soul in a lot of ways, stubborn! My god, but you won't meet anybody more freehanded. He's a sweetie underneath."

"I don't think he hides it all that well."

"His sweetie side?" Adena laughed. "Yeah, but he's got his quirks. For instance, see—he's always strict about paying things before the end of the month. To keep the books 'symmetrical,' he likes to say. And this month, with Bucky's funeral, well, he knew I needed extra."

A little shiver of alarm. A flicker of resistance. What expenses did a divorcée of four years have for her ex's funeral? Still, that was being cynical. God knows Graham's rite had cost a bundle. Adena probably made the arrangements for the old man.

"How much did he want me to give you?"

"A thousand, he said. But, look, if that makes you uncomfortable . . ."

"No, no. In cash?"

"He always writes it in the ledger."

That was so. Dana reached under the counter, where she had stuck a cracker tin, and counted out a thousand dollars in twenties. What surprised—astonished—her, was not that she should be giving somebody else's cash away, but that a country store like this took in enough on a Saturday that there was still a pile of twenties, tens, fives, a wad of dollars like the stash in a heist.

"Be sure you write it down," said Adena, scrupulous, "or the register won't tally."

Trudy gave nothing away. It was pulling teeth to talk to her. They sat in the ex-porch room with the jalousies shut, Trudy clumped on a straight chair wearing a T-shirt with a flamingo in flight across her shackled bosom, Dana trying to perch on the edge of the sofa that sucked her backward. She was insanely self-conscious. Bernadette had smashed all the afghans and cushions into a backrest at one end, which if Trudy had done the crochet work was probably an insult, but it would be small-minded to bring up Bernadette just to blame her, and Dana didn't want to straighten them in case it looked proprietary. Sofa cushion *agonistes*! Afghan-istan! She missed Phoebe.

"Mr. Solomon should be home on Wednesday."

"That'll be fine," said Trudy, placid.

"I might go up to see him in Tallahassee tomorrow."

"Uh-huh."

"Would you like to go?"

"Two things I don't do, hospital and funerals."

It had been easy enough to waylay her. Dana had waited in the hammock till Trudy showed up about nine and let herself in the shop, then she knocked and offered the postcard. Trudy thanked her, gave the message a quizzical frown, pocketed it, and set about her sweeping. Dana had suggested they sit and talk for a moment, which she was now on her way to regretting. Trudy showed none of the spirit she'd shown the other night—no swagger, no sense of humor—and none of the communal purpose either.

"I'm sure he'd be glad to see you."

"Mr. Solly know I don't do sickbed."

Still, she thought she saw a hesitation, perhaps a softening. "Adena thinks Mr. Solomon is grieving for his nephew, and that's why he's still sick. Do you think that could be?"

"He been grieving for that boy for twenty years."

"Was he a problem?"

"Not up to me who the problem is. You got to turn all that to Jesus."

Dana tried waiting. Trudy sat, her cheeks plum dark, plum smooth. She was at once square and rounded, like a vintage Buick. You could tell she was older than she looked without being able to say either how old she was or how old she looked. After a moment, she frowned, rocked forward on her thighs as if literally digging in her heels. "Just let the good Lord take it off you," she advised.

It was muggy in here, another of those ceiling fans scrambling another thirty thousand gallons of stale air. This Gulf summer weather—either the day got stickier as it went along, or else it was Dana who tolerated it less. She'd put on shorts after supper, but that only made her thighs cling to the leather. She adjusted one leg with a tearing sensation. This place needed new AC as well as a sanding. And a computerized register. The doors stuck. The toilet had to be jiggled after every flush.

"Well. Thank you for helping me out. Bernadette was in today, but she's not, you know—she's a teenager."

"That one!" Trudy said with a small explosion. "Somebody need to take that chile in *hand*."

This was promising. Dana pursued it. "She told me she was studying to be a witch."

"Devil don't need no magic to do his evil. Devil can get along with ordinary."

"You're right there."

"Devil play him a shell game you don't know where he be."

"You're absolutely right."

"You just gots to put your trust in the Lord."

Faith as conversational cul-de-sac. Trudy stared at the ceiling beams, her mouth pulled into a righteous moue. The light bounced off her close-curled cap, barely dusted with gray. Trudy knew many things that Dana needed to know: Whether Cassius was in the habit of sending cards. Whether he had ever visited her here. How Trudy came to Pelican Bay in the first place, how long she had been with Solly, whether her family (which meant Cassius's) had ostracized her for it, what form their anger took. Above all, how to get in touch with Cassius without sounding the alarm.

But all these things were off limits, subject to complicated rules of privacy. She couldn't so much as admit to having read the postcard without signaling trespass. To compliment the crochet work would have been to presume. The possibility occurred to her that when Solly was here Trudy slept upstairs. She wanted to say that she would not intrude on her routine, but there, too, to say so would be to intrude. No way she could open up herself unless Trudy cleared the ground. Well, she thought, this is the legacy, five generations later, of rape and the whip, of buying and selling human flesh: that two women with a network of mutual interests can't sit down together without feinting and concealment.

She gave up. She took up the assigned task of the managerial class. "I think Mr. Solomon gives you five hundred dollars at the end of the month. I'll go ahead and do that if you like."

"That'll be all right."

Dana tried, smiling, "I understand he likes to keep the books 'symmetrical.'"

"Tchss!" Another minor explosion, containing both laughter and contempt. But whither directed she had no idea.

11

THEY HAD SOLLY in a wing called Care Club, where the patients' cubicles fanned out around a central desk and everything was painted in a brash peach semigloss. The patients were mostly not in the rooms but clustered in the corridor, sagging in their wheelchairs like bags of dried beans on a shelf, a pair of them slapping cards on a table no bigger than a platter. One wizened woman sat at an upright piano in an alcove, pushing at the same bass note in no particular rhythm. A nurse strode from chair to chair with a tray of pill cups as if the briskness of her enterprise could compensate for the inertia of her charges. It didn't look like a hospital wing, Dana thought. It looked like long-term stuff.

John Solomon was in his bed, though, in one of the cubicles on the periphery. He was not alone. A tall, thin man sat jackknifed over a book, a concave, sallow face and colorless hair pulled back in a single dreadlock at his nape. When he saw Dana he began unfolding himself, a process of imperfectly meshed gears.

"Hi. I've been waiting for you," he said.

Dana made a disavowing gesture. Solly seemed to be dozing but his eyes opened a slit when she came up beside him. He wound his hand to urge her nearer. "I'll give you a thousand dollars if you can tell me who Hoyt Wilhelm is."

Dana set her bag of peaches on the nightstand. "I give up."

"Ha. Hoyt Wilhelm perfected the knuckleball. You might need to know that." He made a claw to demonstrate the position of the knuckleball.

The very tall man reached to offer her a hand. "I'm Perry Hoyt. Solly likes to remind me what I have to live up to." He wore disreputable skinny jeans and a blue work shirt with rolled-up sleeves. She'd seen his type on Sag Island, a cross between a nuclear physicist and a beach bum. He would drive a pickup with bumper stickers like *Save the Manatees* and *Smith & Wesson.*

"Hi. Dana Cleveland," she said, and turning back to Solly, "I was with Adena when we took you to the clinic."

The creases of the old man's face broke from vertical to horizontal. "I know who you are. You been *pinch-hitting* at the store." The claw turned into a fist to celebrate his pun. Perry Hoyt laughed. Solly punched the air, the far arm inert on the sheet. *Oh,* Dana thought. *It's true. He's had a stroke.*

But his speech was clear enough. And free of the trappings of crackerdom, the aloha shirt and dirty cap, his was a striking face: broad and open, arches of white brows like sea foam, the thin hair (washed by one of those Reeboked nurses out there) flowing across the pillow, and the eyes a shock of blue. It occurred to her not for the first time that human skin sloughs and ruckles without fail, but there's no certainty the eyes will age. These were still in possession of their intelligence, the mind inside ready to speculate or joke whether the body would cooperate or not. Her dad had had such eyes once, and then he lost the look. *The last time I saw him he had gone out.*

The old man grabbed for Dana's hand and said in an urgent whine, "Perry's come to give you power of attorney."

"What, me?"

"To pay the bills."

"But you'll be home on Wednesday."

He rolled the blue eyes, churned his head. "Runs in the family.

Drink gets some and stroke the rest. Both like to got me, but I whupped the other."

"I'm sure you'll be home soon."

"Once you start with these things, there's no end of 'em. These gals go cheer-bobbing around here, I'm not so dumb as that."

Hoyt said, "C'mon, Solly, it's a temporary measure."

Solly jiggled her hand. "You gotta keep a eye on the delivery men. They like to empty the truck on you, some more than others, and then you got a rummage sale on the shelves."

Dana said, "Mr. Solomon—you know, I'll have to move on soon."

"Long as you check the stock, easiest is to pay 'em out of the cash drawer and get 'em to sign. Then you don't have to bother with the checks."

Dana said, stalling, "I gave Adena and Trudy cash."

"That's right. You take care of Trudy, won't you?" He shuffled his feet under the blanket, tugged on her hand again.

"She sends her love," Dana hazarded.

Solly slit his eyes. "Dud-n't sound like 'er."

He and Hoyt wheezed a laugh together. Hoyt said, "It'd be a kindness, Ms. Cleveland. It would put his mind at rest."

"Perry is my lawyer," Solly said. "He don't look it, but that's why I picked him. That, and his daddy and I went way *way* back."

"Back to the Dark Ages," Hoyt said, and held out a paper to her.

"Surely it should be Adena," she said, heart sinking.

Solly squinted again and glanced furtively at one peach wall and the other. He lowered his voice so that she was aware of the one low piano note in the hall, struck again and again, again.

"She took my clippings," Solly said.

"What?"

"Adena clipped my toenails and took the parings."

Dana glanced at Hoyt, who shrugged with his eyebrows. Who knows with the old where misunderstanding ends and hallucination begins?

"She just took them to throw away," Dana suggested. But she also uncomfortably remembered Bernadette's aspirations as a witch. Would that involve fetishes, voodoo dolls? Would Adena think it good mothering, or maybe just amusing, to lend a hand to such a project?

"In a plastic bag," Solly said, nodding significance.

The crooked way he held his torso reminded her of the one time she saw her father in that flophouse of a nursing home in Glendale, when she was a junior at Pitt and had no money to do anything about it. It had been a hundred and four that day in Arizona. The sun blazed on the patio stones, but her dad was wearing a knit shawl. Dana had on a polyester shirt, and the sweat ran down her arm to make a shiny spot on the wheelchair tire. She had said, "It's nearly four, Dad. I'm going to have to get my plane." Dad said, "Oh, yes? What time is it?" Comical, of course.

"Took my toenails right enough," Solly said.

Hoyt held the paper out to her. "Just for a little while more, Ms. Cleveland. Till he gets back."

Oh, well, what harm? She'd never heard of *giving* anybody power of attorney as a trick. The pile of bills she'd handed Adena yesterday sat there on the nightstand. It'd cost her nothing but a half hour's time to write the checks.

Dana signed. Hoyt wrote his name in a crabbed hand under hers, folded one copy, and handed it to her.

"There's my phone number, if you have any questions."

"I'm going to have to move on soon," she said, to Hoyt this time. "I'll do what I can, but I can't keep the store open every day."

"Just what you can," said Hoyt. "Solly trusts you." He turned to the bed. "And he don't trust many."

Solly wheezed again, conveying neither one thing nor another.

She headed south under weather headed east. Just out of Tallahassee the rain fell as fat capsules that exploded one at a time on the windshield and flowed upward, gorging on each other. Individual drops hit the road with a force you could almost hear, and sent steam up from the seared asphalt. Undulating mirages appeared where heat met wet. Five miles farther on the rain quickened and drenched the glass, sheeting downward now. She couldn't see the length of a car in front of her. The shoulder disappeared. She kept her eye on the yellow line and fought, crawling, past the fairgrounds, then through one intersection with a palely blinking light, her wipers waving like a frantic flagman, flinging water to no purpose. She knew it was as dangerous to pull off the road as to inch along, but when she thought she saw some sort of structure through the scrim to her right she gave up and edged into what may have been someone's driveway or a side road or a peanut stand. She didn't know whether her lights would protect her from some other blinded driver or whether they would mimic the road and invite a crash. She turned off lights and motor and sat in a downpour like some cosmic car wash.

This lasted for half an hour by her watch; an eternity. She had her cell phone—to what purpose? There was no one she could call to stop a rain. It was hot, and the world outside a uniform deep gray. Sultry limbo. Her reflection hung ghostly in the window until it misted over with her breath. It was too noisy to call Phoebe or Adena, supposing the connection could be made. She didn't want to drain the battery with radio or air-conditioning. She sat and sweated and listened to the rain, no recorded voice, music, television, phone, print, sign, or image demanding her attention, just the plummeting cave that surrounded her, the sounds of rain on metal, rain on gravel, rain on the road, trapped in a place that existed without reference to her.

There, forced back on her scant defenses, she saw that for a matter of days she had been running on two tracks, one busily trying to conduct a life, glean information, behave in a practical and quotidian way; the other based on longing, a figment that made her seek even a moment of stillness to think of Cassius. This was foolishness. He had sent her a message or else he had not. She knew where he was. She was merely marking time unless she went to him. To find out. To be done with it, if done with it is what she must be.

The rain feinted to the east. The curtain thinned and the road appeared. She cracked the windows, swiped at the windshield, started the car, and pulled back into the drizzle, which had disappeared by the time she reached Winona Crossing. The road steamed for another fifteen miles and then was dry. When she got to Snakebird Bay she had in her windows a perfect triptych of sundown: to the left the storm, still lowering, scudding east; before her a milky twilight over the Gulf, grays segueing into lavender and pink; to the west one of those extravagant sunsets that gilds every roof and tree, blazes orange and salmon, then plunges and takes daylight over the edge.

She fumbled her cell phone out and dialed Phoebe. She was ready to argue, over Phoebe's inevitable objections, that she must make a trip back to Georgia. But Phoebe surprised her and agreed. Phoebe opined that no man—never mind a black man—would in the natural order of things buy and write and stamp and send a Fourth of July card to an aunt.

"Go after him," Phoebe said. "Call the paper mill and set up a tour. You have to know one way or the other or you'll get stuck for life on that dingy coast."

"I can get Bernadette to mind the store."

"Fuck the store. It's not your problem. Don't be such a goody girl."

"Yeah, well." Along the coast the moon now glittered on the placid sea. "A funny thing, you know. For some reason, Solly doesn't trust Adena."

"She divorced his nephew. There's bound to be some family rancor."

"And yet she's the only one that seems to look after him."

"Welcome to the human flipping race. So what else is new?"

She called Adena and Adena surprised her, too, although she should have known Adena was a cornucopia of local information. She should have asked her about Trudy in the first place.

Yes, Trudy had a place of her own, a trailer long since paid for by Solly, and the land it sat on, too, out on the far edge of East Sink in a hummock full of gumbo-limbo and sea grapes and poisonwood and tamarind and paradise trees. A good acre, but not worth much on account of its position.

"But Trudy herself," said Dana. "How'd she get here?"

Oh, Trudy had been here for thirty years or more, a tester at Lhamon Paper for ten of those, till they computerized. She'd started out as a girl in Georgia somewhere . . .

"Atlantic Mills?"

Yeah, that sounded right, except it wasn't called that in the old days, it was independently owned then. Atlantic had bought it up as part of a huge expansion in the 90s. Anyway, the testers were always women, only not black women, even now. But Trudy had learned from some do-gooder in the mill that took her under her wing, and when Lhamon Mill ran short of testers, Trudy had come over from the coast. She worked out okay with the old-style stuff, stress test and liver test and old punch machines—till they upgraded with computers in '85. Then Trudy got laid off, and about the same time Solly's wife got sick and Trudy came to help out, and then the wife died, and she stayed on, and one thing led to another and another. Trudy shucked oysters now, at Henry's little canning operation, and she still cleaned up the store and kept Solly company till midnight, whatever keeping company could mean. Then she walked back to the far side of East Sink to her trailer.

"She's wilier than she looks," Adena said. "It suits her purpose to look dumb. She coulda moved in with Solly, but she's got her 'standing' to maintain, which means if nobody admits she's Solly's woman, she's respectable. That way she's got pretty well everything—a man who supports her, East Sink for a backup group, a paid-for house. *And* her independence."

"*Hmm.* Did her family disown her when she took up with him?"

"I don't know anything about her family, except they're not here."

"And they don't come to see her either."

"How would I know? I don't go butting in her trailer in East Sink."

Back at Pelican Bay Dana let herself into the store, took the checkbook out of the cash register, and sat in front of Solly's big TV. She stacked the bills and punched the remote. Martha Stewart was obstructing justice and would have to pay the piper. The fliers who'd bombed that wedding in Deh Rawud (two hundred dead, mainly women and children, mostly sleeping) were, however, not to blame. "They felt threatened," the spokesman said. Dana switched the channel and wrote checks on the coffee table while Jet Li rescued Bridget Fonda as a junkie hooker, and the two of them kicked Paris into little tiny pieces. *Kiss of the Dragon.* She fell asleep on the couch. Next morning she called Atlantic Mills and made an appointment to tour the Georgia plant. She was, she said, the widow of a Pennsylvania senator, interested in paper manufacture, doing volunteer research on recycling methods.

12

HER APPOINTMENT was for one o'clock, so she left before dawn and changed at a roadside rest stop, taking care to look the part: hair up in a French roll, a linen shift, slouchy shoulder bag, modest earrings, Lucite clipboard. Her face in the restroom mirror, tanned and tinted, remarkably aped a Pennsylvania widow on vacation in the South. But her fast-food brunch of muffin and tepid coffee sat shivering on her gut. She had left a sign saying the store would be closed on Friday and Saturday. She had told Adena only that she must visit a friend on the Atlantic coast, and the cost of this lie was that when Adena, volubly and cheerfully acquiescing, had added that Bernadette needed a hundred dollars for a swim meet—"Solly *always* pays it"—Dana hadn't the moxie either to argue or to put her off. If Solly hadn't wanted her to spend his money, he shouldn't have loaded her with power of attorney. She noted it down in the ledger and left the hundred behind in cash.

The pink-cheeked guard at the gatehouse of Atlantic Mills showed not a glimmer of recognition. Good. He directed her away from the workers' lots to the curved drive leading toward administration, a wide arc with no purpose but to impress, since the land lay open on either side. At a distance to the west a riding mower was repeating the swing of the road in swaths, one laid left, one right, like velvet brushed with a hand. She peered across the expanse of grass, hoping to spot a guard in the process of doing his rounds. She crawled along, checking in the mirror for back entrances to the parking lot. On that side, toward the workers' cars, the plant sprawled in a cluster of buildings the size of airplane hangars, smoke sidewinding from the stacks and slithering into the cumulus.

The administration building was an imposing cube with a central tower scored vertically, very thirties, very conscious of its heft. Here she parked and mounted the steps to a lobby opening a dramatic four stories high. Shafts of glass block filled the space with light. She was knocked back on her heels to be facing, not the murky seascapes she'd imagined, but a David Hockney canvas about eight feet wide, one of the electric-blue California swimming pools, with a pensive boy in swim trunks and an ebullient palm in a yellow pot. A mezzanine three-quarters of the way around was hung with massive paintings and photographs. There was a bank of back-to-back couches and a reception desk, where she announced herself and was told that Mr. McGarvey would be down shortly.

She dawdled. Behind the reception area an open door led into a small room where she could see several television screens and the back of a balding white man in a swivel chair. He was dressed in khaki like the guard in the hut. She faked stretching her neck to see left and right, but there seemed to be nobody else inside.

"He'll be right *da-own,*" the pretty receptionist assured her.

So she walked among the artworks, chastened that she had not credited Cassius with recognizing valuable art. She spotted a Louise Bourgeois bas-relief of a pink hand and a Laurie Lipton pencil drawing of a demented child, but most were unfamiliar as well as eclectic, risky, spectacularly good. Somebody with a keen eye had gone to a lot of trouble, not to mention staggering expense. There was a woman seated at the far end of the couch facing the Hockney, but when Dana nodded to acknowledge her, she realized she'd greeted a polymer replicant, one of those Dwayne Hansen sculptures perfected to the last wrinkle, dressed in aqua polyester, clutching a plastic purse.

"Mizz Ullman?"

McGarvey—"Do call me Gavin"—had a hard hat in each hand, but was otherwise quasiformal in shirt and tie.

"I understand you're interested in our recycling program."

"I confess to being an amateur."

"The best kind."

He was an aquiline man with a lustrous mop of graying hair and an air of sophistication that surprised her. He had lax and leathered skin, a little weariness around the jowls, eyes both wary and sad—spaniel eyes. She was glad of the linen sheath and the French roll.

"This collection is amazing!"

McGarvey acknowledged this with a hint of having heard it many times before. He handed her a hat. "It was an obsession of our former CEO. Abel Croft—affectionately known as Alpha Charlie—the only remaining member of the founding family, and he left it on more or less permanent loan when Atlantic bought him out. Would you like a coffee? No? Then I propose we tour first and talk later on."

He led her into a wire-covered walkway leading to a mountain of pine logs with a crane poised over it. He put on his hard hat, and she twisted hers, trying to decide which was the front. McGarvey sauntered ahead, chin strap dangling. "Alpha Charlie started it as demonstration of what paper did for art, but then it became an obsession. As you're interested in recycling, you might observe that some paper is worth preserving in and of itself."

"I did an MA in art history," Dana blurted, and was instantly ashamed of the impulse to credential.

"Is that a fact. Well, you must see our Picasso drawings. We keep them in the tearoom for those of a"—he raised a suggestive eyebrow—"an aesthetic turn of mind. Here, now, we'll start at the barking drum. Hang on to these earplugs and put them in when we go inside."

If she'd known what she was in for, Dana would have chosen sturdy shoes. For more than two hours McGarvey marched her up ramps and across bridges in her stack-heeled sandals, past open furnaces and deafening rollers, around water pits, over sawdust piles and gritty cement floors. The barking drum was a massive cylinder that swallowed whole tree trunks and chewed at their circumference until the dark skin was shed. Then some of the logs were diverted into jigged-stone grinders that grated them like so much cheese. Others went into a chipper with knives in a pattern of spokes on a wheel.

Everywhere McGarvey was greeted with friendly deference and returned the greetings easily. He didn't sweat. He lectured in a practiced combination of mime and shouting, taking her pen from time to time to add something to the page on her clipboard. He reminded her of certain senators whose power was a natural outgrowth of having been boys both handsome and on the honor roll, the ones who had never had to scramble or fall back on wit, for whom every encounter was a potential score, for whom friendliness was an overflow of self.

Block-long mesh conveyor belts sized the chips, sent the sawdust into the furnace to fuel the cooking, and blew the smaller chips into the digesters, over one of which they paused on a walkway built expressly for this view. Below them the tank of acid bubbled, as big around as a small house, extending three stories down to the cement floor.

"The digesters cook the lignin loose," McGarvey said. "That's the glue that holds the wood fibers together."

On a spindly ladder down the side of the vast cauldron, two men climbed catlike, and on a platform around its top two others prowled; white men in khaki shirts, black men in overalls. No one, McGarvey pointed out, was allowed on the rim except the three or four who oversaw each of these huge vats. "That's where the sulfur smell comes from—it's a sulfite process."

The power of the operation was staggering, the stench itself a kind of power. Dana imagined Bucky Solomon as a younger Solly, bulky, in a mesh cap, toppling from the walk into that gurgling stew. *The acrid liquid comes toward you. Your arms flail to no effect. All your life you've swallowed into your lungs the smell that now swallows you . . .*

Dana said close to his ear, "I've been vacationing on the Gulf. I heard that at one of the mills there, a man fell in the vat."

"Over at Lhamon. Yes, it's a terrible thing." His breath tickled. "We get blamed—and fined—for safety violations every time that happens. But from what I understand, that 'accident' was ambiguous, to say the least."

"You're saying suicide?"

"Something like that. Have you ever been drunk enough to be clumsy and reckless at the same time?"

"Enough to see what you mean."

"Of course we all have our troubled people. We employ eight hundred times three shifts at this plant. But even a huge corporation like Atlantic likes to think of itself as a family. Family is an attitude."

"I know. Some call it paternalism."

McGarvey had the grace to laugh. He had the grace—if that was the right word—to touch her elbow lightly, courtly, a touch meaning *touché*. He led her into the relative quiet of a low-ceilinged passage. "The lignin washes out down there. We'll purify the rinse water, reduce the chemicals for fuel, and use the water to rinse again. When you think of recycling, you mean used paper, but that's very small potatoes. We recycle the water, recycle the chemicals, fire the furnaces with our own waste."

"Impressive," Dana said for the tenth or dozenth time.

"First thing you'll see inside is the bleaching vats, and after that the beater room. When we pound the pulp, the water drains slower, but it helps the fibers mesh; the speed of draining is called the *freeness*. Watch your step."

At every stage she was looking for Cassius, never mind that she knew he was not inside. Some of these people might be his family—this stoker a brother, that chipper guard a cousin. But while she ran a furtive eye over the faces of the men, she asked competent questions, reacted appreciatively, broadcast health. It was natural to be with McGarvey. She *knew* him. And in some sense she was also operating on the source of power that fed the machines that dwarfed and dazzled her.

"Put the plugs in now. It's a safety rule."

The earplugs had the effect not of deadening the noise but of adding to it the interior sloshing of her body, the crunch of her joints in the thundering sheds. The machine in the third of these ran at least a city block, its near bed—they had entered on the walkway at the height of second floor—pouring forth a foam of diluted pulp onto endless belts of mesh and felt, which ran then through steaming rollers. McGarvey waved at the hard-hatted foreman, who grinned and saluted and mouthed his name. McGarvey pointed to the rectangle from which the pulp emerged, and wrote on her page:

stuff box
head box
slurry
slice

She descended after him to the vibrating concrete floor. Along the length of the machine into the distance of the shed, a system of sign language was being passed from man to man, one worker on the walkway poking a thumb toward the bill of his cap, another on the floor pressing his palms downward at knee height. The computer operator under the stuff box fanned three fingers in front of his cock and was thumbs-upped from the machine like some pitcher/catcher pair on a vertical baseball diamond. The slurry let fall a constant chemical rain as it passed on a wide mesh over thirty-foot rollers. McGarvey wrote:

breast roll
stretch roll
couch roll
suction box
king roll
queen roll
sweat dryer

She mouthed, "You must be kidding." McGarvey let his mouth wind in a mischievous grin, and added at the bottom of the page: *The sign language is even better.*

What was now recognizable as wet brown paper fed onto felt and threaded between steam-heated cylinders on a massive mangle. The shed, like an overheated hangar, pulsed with wet and stench and roar. She felt the power through the soles of her shoes. Piston and roller and slice, barker and grinder—everything was full of thrust and thunder. What would such force do but advertise its danger to itself?

The paper, squeezed flat now, heated dry, was wound onto spools, castrated into stubby rolls, and shunted off to the next station to be cut into box lengths. They descended into the basement, where stokers fed a dozen boilers with open flames; compressors and vacuum pumps competed for heat and noise; then up two flights to a control room where a dial-laden wall mimicked a space station out of some slightly dated fantasy. Two more city-block machines for heavy stock. More furnaces, more paper phalluses. At some point the role had taken over, she was half charmed by McGarvey, half forgot why she was here. Her feet hurt; she was worn down by the drumming noise and the impact of what McGarvey must surely know was too much information.

The tour ended in a little office called the Testing Lab. They removed the earplugs. A young white woman looked up from her microscope with an irritated smile. She wore square glasses and a shiny tan uniform that squared the space between breast and hip. She began her spiel with an official-tour smoothness that didn't quite cover her cranky mood: "Paper quality is a complicated matter. There are so many variables and so many *kinds* of quality. You want blotting paper to absorb and meat wrap not to, perfect writing paper makes terrible table napkins, and so forth." Dana scribbled while she talked, trying to imagine taciturn Trudy in this role: *caliper, densometer, glarimeter, tackiness.* The woman's ugly uniform made a *shush*ing sound everywhere it brushed her skin. *Pop test, gloss test, freeness, penetration, stress test, bursting strength.*

"I thought you'd like our language," McGarvey smiled, "being a cultivated person."

The woman gestured toward a device where a sheet of brown paper was clamped between two vises. On the sag between rested a bloody lump a little bigger than her hand. "That's the liver test," she said. "We need to know how long it takes the blood to drip through produce carton." She wiped a manicured finger in a spot. "All this is computerized by now. But McGarvey wants to keep the liver test. He's sentimental." A glance passed between them, coy.

McGarvey said to Dana, "I'm feeling sentimental about food right now. How about you?"

Back in administration the door of the guard room was now closed, and she couldn't think of a tactful way to ask about it, especially as McGarvey steered her efficiently toward the elevator. They stopped by his office to get his jacket, and only when Dana saw the plaque on the door did she realize that her guide was President and CEO. He led along a gallery—"Notice Picasso's amorous bulls; we have eight of them"—but scarcely gave her time to look, though she held back, correcting, "Aren't they minotaurs? I know this suite . . ." The etchings blurred by, the Pans with their pipes, the acquiescing nudes, the champagne-quaffing bull-headed lovers with their tails and human toes. McGarvey ushered her into a private dining room, a royal-blue carpet and a plateglass window that displayed the plant and the ocean but kept the smell more or less at bay. He commanded with an inclination of his silver head a snack of rock lobster, cress, and hearts of palm. These were delivered by a black hand that set them noiselessly on the spotless cloth. Dana kept her eyes down. She was ravenous.

"You've given me your whole day," she said, conventionally but also unsettled at the success of her deception.

"Well," McGarvey poured the wine. "You are interesting and my days are dull." He smiled with his spaniel eyes, to say this was the rueful truth. "I'm enormously gratified by your interest. Paper is easy to sell—the country consumes all we can manufacture—but it's taken very much for granted, yet civilization could not function without it." Dana murmured, agreeing, remembering the paper storm from the towers. McGarvey said, "I didn't believe you at first, you know. That your interest was 'amateur.' I thought you might be a plainclothes."

"A what?"

"An inspector."

"I assure you, not!"

"I'm glad. You're a breath of fresh air. I'd hate to have found out you were the devil in disguise."

"On the contrary, I'm very impressed."

"Good. Let me impress you further." And he set about to do this. He was both smooth and warm. He flirted tastefully. He described at considerable length the housing plan for the mill's two thousand workers, the school subsidies, the community centers, the town meetings, the equal-opportunity seniority. "It's a very happy workforce," he averred. "Every aspect of life revolves around the mill—churches, bars, schools, family. It's hard to understand if you haven't experienced it. I know when I first came from New York, it seemed like some nineteenth-century 'utopia,' New Harmony or Saltaire. But Atlantic is more hands-off than that. We try to be enlightened in a twenty-first-century sort of way, set up the programs and let the people run them."

"And racial clashes?"

"We let the people run those, too. You'd be surprised how few there are."

Over coffee and petits fours he became anecdotal. "As regards living and breathing paper . . ." He laughed, apologized for the stench. He and his wife had a cottage in the Smokies, he confessed. "Sometimes I get up there, I'm gulping in pure mountain air, and I open my briefcase—the whole mill comes pouring out!"

"Do you get used to it?"

"To the smell? You do. On the other hand." Gavin McGarvey inclined his silver mop and gave her a wry smile. "I grew up in Manhattan. Does one ever get used to the rural life?" He tipped a bottle of Hennessey to the snifters that had miraculously appeared. He offered Dana one and lifted the other. "To snobbery," he said.

Dana said, "*Salud.*"

13

SHE DROVE AWAY from administration and detoured onto a side road that carried her back around the digesters. For nearly an hour she wandered the mill grounds, left at one crossroads, right the next, then doubling back, hoping to cross paths with Cassius on his rounds. She didn't even encounter the groundsman she had seen this morning. There were wooded areas, though, plenty of places to tuck the car between scrub pines and wait till six. She let her hair down, opened the windows, and lay on the backseat. Heat and exhaustion buzzed around her eyes. The smell of paper making had settled into incipient nausea. She kept seeing McGarvey's handsome head, his earnest savoir faire. Had she met him in any other context, she would certainly have found him attractive. It was her falsity that made her read him now as false. She couldn't sleep and couldn't stay long in the hot car, so she walked around among the scrub, took off her shoes, and rubbed her sore feet. The uneven ground put her in mind of the precarious walkway around the digester vat, the stinking turmoil of the sulfur. Bucky Solomon who fell or jumped. The people in the two boiling towers who had chosen to jump instead of burn. She felt she had done a penance of waiting in the past three weeks, but she waited, letting herself turn on the air conditioner from time to time, but stingily, not to use up the battery.

At five-thirty she drove to the back entrance of the parking lots and began to wind her way among the rows of cars. They were of every make and year, but the lots didn't seem to be segregated according to status. She drove zigzagging through the first lot and the second. She set her vision for faded blue, saw what she was looking for at least a dozen times, but it always turned out to be a Ford, an old Datsun, a Dodge. No Wedgwood Pontiac. She snaked through the last lot keeping her tinted windows up, because men were starting to feed in from the plant. She began to doubt her eyes, to think she'd misread make or color. She wound through the first lot again, the second, third. His car wasn't here. She had played all this game for nothing! Now the rows were full of men and a few women, calling to each other, fanning the doors, tossing in their gear. Some of the cars were making for the exit. She pulled off toward the fork where the three roads converged, thinking that she could spot Cassius's Grand Am when it passed the barrier, but as she drew alongside a rusty four-door Chevy, the khaki-uniformed man opening the back door turned, and Cassius looked straight at her. She breathed relief. He kept on turning, no sign of recognition, and folded himself in. A stocky black man, shouting a greeting to someone else over the top of the car, dropped in the driver's seat and started up.

She was not mistaken; it was Cassius. He had snubbed her. No. He had not seen her through her tinted windows. Had not recognized her car because he wasn't expecting to see it here. She pulled in behind the Chevy and willed Cassius to turn around, but the three roads fed toward the fork, where the drivers politely braided themselves into place, so that by the time she passed the barrier, she was three cars behind. She gripped the wheel, assessing her chances to pass on the mill road, knowing that this would make her conspicuous.

But she was lucky. At the highway, the two cars in front of her turned left, and she was behind the Chevy again, headed north. She waited for a clear stretch and gunned, slipping into the passing lane, pulling level and then hanging there as long as she dared before moving ahead, back in lane. She waited for another clear stretch and then let her foot off the gas to make the Chevy pass her. It did, and the front-seat passenger threw her a "woman driver" grimace. Cassius, in the backseat, did not look up.

She was relentless. She would have rammed them if it came to that. Up ahead, the Chevy turned inland at an intersection with a Stuckey's Texaco and pulled past the gas pumps to the shop. She pulled in, too. She stopped at the far end of the parking row and hopped out. The men were slower. By the time Cassius unfolded himself to follow his companions into the store, Dana was leaning, ankles crossed, against her car.

He looked up and his face registered an amazement so pure it made *her* gasp. Not amazement merely, but also terror. She must have seemed supernaturally, perhaps demonically, to have appeared. But that lasted only a second. Then he shook his head in the you-just-know-how-to-do-everything way, signaled her with a firm splat of his hand to get back in her car, and followed his friends into the store. Five minutes later they came out without him. They drove off. Dana waited. A few minutes more. Cassius swung out with a couple of Ice Cream Crunch bars in his hand, strolled to her passenger door, and opened it. He handed her an ice-cream bar.

"How you doin', lady? Drive."

Not to Jekyll Island, but south toward Jacksonville, to an anonymous-looking Ramada on the beach, where she registered and he stayed behind the tinted windows, then came up the back stairs from the parking lot. She got it, now, more or less. At least she would not ask him out for a swim. They fell speechlessly into bed and made love in the smell of sweat and pulp and lignin, with a fierceness wholly unlike the first day, a driving need. They showered and ordered room service, and he hid in the bathroom until it came. They ate as they had fucked, famished, steak and potatoes and salad and beer and inferior pie. He shook his head. "You had lunch with Boss McGarvey! This lady come after me is something else."

She found herself gripping his hand, his arm, saying to herself, *I am with him. I am touching him.* She demanded, "What's wrong with your car?"

"Nothing big. A gasket. I can get it back tomorrow."

"You've had a hard time at home."

"Don't you worry. It'll pass over."

"What happened? How did they know where I was?"

"I went to shower, Luther went through my pockets. Dumb! — I shoulda figured on that." Sly smile. "I was some distracted."

"And he called Isobel?"

"Shit, he call out the God patrol."

"What does that mean?"

"Family business, don't you worry. It'll pass over."

Only now she asked, "Did you send that postcard to Trudy so I would see it?"

"I thought to send it."

"Did you think I would come here?"

"I don't know. I figured to send it."

His look, his manner, were as vague as the words. She couldn't read them, but sensed it would be better not to press. A little later she asked, "Why didn't you call me?" And the look on his face then was of a patient teacher with a slow, exasperating pupil.

"From where my family at, up to the Sheraton on Jekyll Island . . . ?"

"You could have called from somewhere else."

"Where is that?"

She dropped it, though not gracefully. It was her belief (not heretofore tested in black rural Georgia) that anybody could get hold of anybody in the world if they really wanted to. He could have called from the Stuckey's. He could have asked, or if necessary tricked, a friend into using his phone. Look how she had tricked Atlantic Mills!

So the sourness of the world seeped in, and yet it was small seepage in the love that enveloped them. After midnight she pulled out the shorts and top she had worn from Florida; he put his wrinkled uniform back on. They drove to a deserted public beach and sat in the car watching the moonlight on the surf. She touched his knee, his forearm. *Be here, be here.* They talked again about his dream of travel. They played at plans that they would carry on along the coast, take in New Orleans, Texas, California.

But she had stopped altogether playing. She had begun to imagine him in Pelican Bay in an idyll of their own making. Security is needed everywhere (this is what her logic amounted to), and with Solly and Trudy's help, they could find a way to live on the hinge between West Sink and East Sink.

She asked, "Can you leave here for a while?"

"I'm'a call in sick tomorrow, stay with you."

"No, but I mean, get away from here. So you can think through what it is you want to do."

"You don't know nothing 'bout black families. I'm going to smarten you up."

"Okay."

"I'm one of seven brothers and sisters, right?"

"Yes."

"How many fathers does that make?"

"I don't know."

Six, it turned out. Two marriages, and the one long-term relationship (Cassius and one of his brothers from that one), the rest from one-night stands.

She said, "The world has caught up, Cassius. I'm not so different myself."

"Oh, yeah? How many babies you got?"

"I mean . . ."

"You don't mean nothin'. My mama knuckle down and raised us right. We what she got. And we turned out good enough. But my question: do I want *my* little girl to have no daddy?"

"I know that." Stung, she let the silence settle, then asked, "Will you go back to Isobel?"

He hid his face in his forearms crossed on the steering wheel. Anguished: "I *can't.* I don't know. This being with you, it throws me. I want us to last a *long* time."

"I do, too."

"I'll call in sick. I'll get my car and come back tomorrow night, for however long you be here."

"All right."

"Then, I don't know past this: Whatever happen, I will always love you. You can book it down."

"Whatever happens, I will always love you," she repeated. "You can book it down."

The window of that room didn't open. They kept the curtains closed, and the cheap AC unit chilled stale air. In the morning they were both uncomfortably polite. When breakfast came she tipped the black bellhop too little, was ashamed of it, and immediately resented that the man hiding in the bathroom earned even less than he. Cassius called in sick to work (though he would not take the phone in hand till she had his foreman on the line), and then was restless, which he labored to conceal. It wouldn't work to spend the day confined here, she saw, and saw that in fact he wanted to get away. She tore a scrap of paper from her notebook, writing nothing on it this time but the phone number and the number of the room, and he folded this down to spitball size and shoved it in the coin pocket of his pants.

"How will I get you home?"

"I been thinking 'bout that. My brother Antwan working construction near my mama's house. We'll find him and he'll cover for me. Then I can get my car."

"Do you want to go now?"

"Best, maybe. He knock off at three."

First, though, she took his hand and led him to the mirror, where his doubled darkness stood out against stark motel white. She said, "You're a beautiful man," and he said, with an edge, "How many black mens you know?"

"I didn't say you were a beautiful black man. I said you were a beautiful man."

But his question hit its target. The answer was, she was acquainted with some dozen or fifteen black men—a couple of congressmen, congressional aides, a mayor, a columnist. Most of them she barely knew well enough to call by name. Two or three had been in her house, none at Graham's funeral. She hid her face in his chest, swiping her cheeks against him to wipe off her ignorance.

Back again along the coastal highway, they took the same turn at Stuckey's. He had been nervous all morning, but at this juncture his mood took on a manic edge, and he pointed gleefully to the squat, grizzled man at the pump. "Listen up," he said, "that my uncle Clifford. Now, when you drop me, I want you come back here and gas up at the pump, and call him that. Clifford. Act like you know him. Say you a social worker or some such. You gonna confuse his ass!"

The energy of the joke filled up the car, and Dana vowed to do as she was told. They laughed down the asphalt state road, then a rutted county blacktop, then turned onto hard-packed sandy streets, row after row of identical bungalows. They snaked right and left looking for Antwan's truck, just as she had looked for Cassius's in the parking lots, though here she lost her bearings and didn't know how she could find her way out. Cassius's high spirits turned tense. A couple of times she grazed the shoulder and felt the soil give. It occurred to her that if they should get stuck in the sand in the middle of this ghetto, there might not be a way he could defend her.

At last he spotted a truck in front of a gutted house, and told her to drive around back. "Slow. Keep to the ruts." Her tires spun in the scored drive, and she felt panic rise, but behind the house a single man with a wheelbarrow set it down, pulled off his work gloves, and walked over to the car. Cassius heaved relief. He rolled the window down. "Antwan, brotha," he said slyly, "I want you meet my woman friend."

Antwan, younger than Cassius, lighter built and longer in the jaw, shook his head in the familiar way, shook her hand and said he was pleased to meet her. She had never been so pleased to meet anybody in her life. She had still not rid herself of the belief that, Isobel apart, his family must welcome her once they knew she really cared for Cassius. Meeting Antwan's friendliness simply pressed the template of her expectations.

"Cassius says you're all right," she said.

"And he say you *fine.*"

She was not too dense, though, to see that they were in a hurry to be rid of her. So she touched Cassius's hand lightly and said she would see him at nine or ten, and drove off, the two of them looking after her in the wavy heat. She backed, wheels spinning, down the drive, and was alone.

Mania is next to terror and terror is the only teacher. Down the rutted street, everything she had not understood unrolled and laid itself out in front of her clear as the shining dirt. The houses were stucco cracker boxes with slab porches and tar roofs slanted one direction, painted in dirty pastels, like a parody of suburbia, differentiated only by the configuration of trees or tires or wash lines in their yards. There was no one outdoors in the noon-white heat except a child banging a spoon on a tub in one of the sandy drives, who looked up with startled disbelief at her face in the open window, so that she wheeled it quickly up and then passed three people walking on the road with a sense of averted catastrophe. She was a displaced person, an alien in alien lands. Her own fear taught her what Cassius's had been, every hour he spent among the mansions and the beaches where pale toddlers upended buckets of golden sand. Why would he not meet her at the Sheraton, swim off the docks, telephone her room? Why not indeed! Her nerves were like the trailing threads of a sea anemone, twitching in the liquid of her flesh, her stomach sloshing, her heart slapping in its wet cavity.

The road was much longer than it had been in the other direction, elongated by her fear so that the corners of each house became sharp, the dust distinct on the oleanders, the black slice of highway in the distance a beacon that would represent release. And she saw, too, that she was wonderfully alive. She was enjoying herself! She recklessly wanted more, more defiance, more challenge, more! She hit the blacktop and swung left toward the county road, right toward the Stuckey's, and squealed in. She had made it. Of course—he had given her a task; he knew how a joke bred recklessness and recklessness adrenaline. She pulled to the pumps leaving tread and got out tall, shouldered, sure of herself. The grizzled man crossed toward the island, deferential, rag in overall pocket, a cartoon of himself as she was of herself.

"Hello, Clifford," she said. "Fill 'er up, please. How's the family?"

He lifted the hose but eyed her, suspicious. "You know me?"

"Clifford! Well, of course. You pulled me out of the sand last November, down at Jekyll, remember?"

He twisted her gas cap, stood for a beat with it held aloft. "Oh, yes," he said, frowning. "I do believe I remember now."

He had said it would be ten o'clock before he made it back, so she came back to the stuffy room to pamper herself again, dressed in a black halter and a long skirt of Indian batik, and took herself off to Jekyll Island's summer-stock production of *The King and I.* She sat in the bleachers under a warm sky while lovely college children played out their interracial romances against a backdrop of cardboard pagodas and potted palms. When the King of Siam appeared, sallow skinned and shaven skulled, his movements delicate and his tenor full, she was scarcely surprised to recognize the desk clerk from the Sheraton. That combination of imperiousness and desire to please—*of course.* He had only been acting, as she had. At intermission she slipped away and was back in her room shortly after nine-thirty. Waiting.

She could not explain why it didn't hurt this time. At first she thought he would call, and then she reminded herself that he would not risk a wire that ran through the Ramada switchboard to connect him to her. She waited for his knock. Her corridor ran toward a stairwell with vending machines and a window onto the parking lot. She filled her bucket with ice, went back for a Coke, then every half hour returned just to gaze out over the cars. There was no hurt in it. About one in the morning, she took off her pretty skirt and climbed into bed. She slept at once.

It was five by the bedside clock when she woke. For a minute she was disoriented, then the knowledge returned, that he had not come. Also the knowledge that he would come when and if he could. She worried for whatever he had gone through. She did not doubt his desire to be with her.

Her throat was dry in the artificial air, and the ice in her bucket had melted. She took her key and stepped into the corridor, walked barefoot down to the ice machine and stood in its raucous clatter looking over the parking lot again, at the silvery moonlight, wishing, but without hurt, that she would spot his Pontiac.

The corridor was dim. She was almost back to her door, key raised, when she realized that the door was dripping blood. Top to bottom, one side to the other of the frame, the stuff ran sluggish, drying in draped ridges. She stood for a moment numb. For a second her mind tumbled over itself and she thought: *he has been murdered.* She stretched out a finger to touch the viscous thickness, its soft give. She tasted it. Ketchup. Above the brass numbers, a finger had written BITCH in the red sludge, and below it 666, which she knew was the devil's number; a curse, a prophecy of death. She looked over her shoulder. The door across from hers was painted just the same, only there at eye level was written the one word, DIE.

She locked her door. She drank a glass of water. Her mind seemed to be very slow, but also methodical. She should call the police, of course. The Georgia sheriff's office. And tell them what? That she was having an affair with a black man, and his family disapproved? No, she was the interloper, the intruder. In her mind's eye three white youths appeared, the trio from the beach, but uniformed, armed. *Them damn niggers.*

She should call the front desk. And tell them . . . ? Why their property had been defiled?

She should get out. In the dark, down that corridor, into that parking lot?

In the end, she propped the door open with the ice bucket and washed both doors. She was cold in the air-conditioning so she pulled a T-shirt over her nightgown. She was not so much frightened as an automaton. She rinsed quantities of ketchup down the basin, her hands growing and glowing pink. When the doors were clear, she went back to sleep. This did not later not seem to make sense, but that is what she did. Escape, a survival mechanism. She could not leave till it was light, and she needed to have her wits about her.

Soon after dawn she woke, packed, and slipped down the stairs to the parking lot. It seemed important to sign her bill and establish that she was here, to be seen in case anything . . . in case of need. So she walked in a wide arc to the front entrance and the checkout desk. She was hyperalert to black faces in the lobby, the breakfast waiter in his bow tie, the maid behind the linen cart, the window washer whistling "Papa's Got a Brand New Bag." She paid with the credit card still in her married name. It frightened her to sign.

Heavy-footing it south to the Florida state line, at every junction she sighted back along the line of traffic feeding onto the four-lane, stomach clenched, not knowing what car she was looking for, nor any face except that it would be black. Once a blotchy Beetle accelerated on her right, feinting to pull even with her and then dropping back, and she half saw the shotgun lifted to the window before she registered the white kid with the water blaster, the yapping Shih Tzu, the fat mother driver in the straw hat.

No one was following her. It is unlikely anyone would have tried. The desired result for the Hustons of Georgia had been achieved. She was afraid, and she was fleeing. She had no spare consciousness to ask *where to?*

III
Stocktaking

14

In retrospect, summer 2002 would seem the fulcrum (later the "tipping point") between the "evildoers" and "Iraqi Freedom." In retrospect, certain words and phrases revealed their slippage. The "homeland" was subject to "security"; there appeared a number of "incentives" to do with "clear skies" and the "culture of life," the slowing of the "growth rate" promised a "soft landing." The "working man" was allowed to "keep more of his own money." The Immaculate Heart of Mary won first place in the elementary-school division of the Stock Market Game.

There may have been, among the Roves and Rumsfelds, a preemptive strike of invidious design. But outside of New York and Washington—and possibly Somerset County, Pennsylvania—people absorbed the "threat level" and went back to their quotidian concerns. If they didn't exactly agree to "make the pie higher," at least they seemed to concur, "the past is over."

Dana was one of these.

She woke in the dark in her rattling cabin, a fat burst of drumbeats crossing the roof. She lay disoriented, knowing where she was but not when. Her face was damp with the aftersweat of a dream she could not recall, its images dispersed to leave only this sour residue.

She heaved to a sitting position, slid her feet into her flip-flops and remembered: fleeing Georgia. She crossed to the door and opened it on a sky surrounded in black cloud like an overturned black bowl with the bottom cracked away, lurid light around the circumference of the hole. Lightning flashed, distant.

She remembered: she had come back in the middle of the afternoon and, seeing the women milling around Solly's porch, had driven past, turned in a dirt drive, and crept back over the pine needles to park behind the cabin. She had meant to load the car and keep on going. But she was exhausted. The thought of packing filled her with stupid dread. She had sneaked in and climbed under the covers in her clothes, hiding from the women as well as from the anxiety of the road.

Now rain had soaked the pine needles, which in the sudden flash she saw as ominous, straw spun into gold. She was certainly ripe for melodrama. She could certainly suppose the weather was set here for her benefit. In her breastbone, as if in the bone itself, she felt a stab of loss.

She could see the sea-sponge density of his flat-cut hair, the whorled lashes around eyes not black but the color of burnished brass. She could see the scant curled stubble on his chin, the moving muscle of his arms.

Could there be such honesty where there was so much misunderstanding? She might put it a kinder way: Could there be such misunderstanding where there was so much honesty? But no, the first is what she meant. The misunderstanding was not in doubt. The honesty, in retrospect, was questionable. She had thought she knew pretty much what there was to know about bigotry. She would never have expected love or logic to sway a family of angry whites. But somewhere in her had lurked the conviction that his family *must* want a pale, educated, loving partner for him. She hadn't conceived of equal-opportunity prejudice. Exactly as she had told Phoebe, Cassius was a good, kind man in a trap. And she had sprung the trap. She didn't know to what extent her ignorance was an excuse. She did know that Cassius had tried to teach her better. She did know that she had been put to the freeness test, the stress test, and had failed.

She took a step out, catching for balance on the slick tread. A sliver of moon caught in the puddles and the lightning cracked again. *You step out onto the balcony that is strewn with shoes, a slightly scuffed pair of Florsheim oxfords, Nike trainers, black business pumps neatly lined up side by side, a single red sandal overturned on its high heel. You don't look any farther down than your feet. It makes perfect sense to want your shoes off when you jump. The air, so brilliant-clear a half an hour ago, is muddied now. You bend to slip a finger in at the Achilles tendon . . .*

But that was fantasy belonging to another world, and over the winter months had grown rote with repetition. Nine-eleven seemed a millennium away. In any case it had little to do with her. What belonged to her was the tremor, sickly and discouraging, that reached down from the base of her spine to settle behind her knees. This, this internal whimper, is what people really have to contend with who don't know whether they are threatened, who don't know where the danger is.

She went to the kitchen and flipped on the light. In the center of one vinyl tile a cockroach lay on its back scrambling its legs in pitiful throes. The paper-towel roll was out, so she reached to the drawer where she kept paper napkins, and stuck a hand half in before she registered that something wasn't right. She drew the hand back with an intake of breath more like a yelp. Curled on a scrap of blue toweling was a possum not much bigger than her hand, a ball of fluff with a sharp rodent nose tucked into a bald rat tail, cute and faintly disgusting.

She stood stymied. Would it bite? Was it likely to be rabid? If she closed the drawer would it crawl out the way it came (from where)? If she left it open, would it jump to the floor (to run where)? The thing was absolutely still, little slit-eyes tight—oh, right: playing possum. She backed cautiously, reached behind her to pick up a plastic bucket from the corner and a dish towel that hung on the stove handle, and crept back. It hadn't moved. She lay the towel over it, picked it up in both hands (squashing the fur to the narrow ribs), and let it go in the pail.

Now the creature unwound and looked up, blinking its little rat eyes. Now it scratched at the plastic in an exploratory way, showing no particular prowess. Now she had a teenage vermin in a bucket in a thunderstorm. What next?

Gingerly, she spread the towel back over the pail and lifted it by the handle. Holding it at arm's length she stepped out the kitchen door, down onto the wet pine straw in her flip-flops, across under the drizzle to the edge of the pine grove, where she set it down. She removed the cloth. The bead-eyes caught a glint of moonlight, quizzically, fastened on her. Then the possum curled back into a ball and assumed the position of its kind.

"Go on, *go.*" She tipped the pail over with a toe, stepped back and willed the idiot creature to run away. Nothing. Her hair was starting to drip, so she left the bucket where it was and sprinted back to the cabin. She peered into the open drawer, established that it was empty now, took one paper napkin to dab at her hair and another to pick up the dead cockroach, and flushed both napkins and cockroach down the john. She peed and flushed again. She turned out the light.

But now there were possible possums in every corner of the room, in every scratch and rattle, the hissing of the rain, the clunk of the ball cock shutting off, the sighing of damp pine walls. She knew it was nonsense, but her hackles rose. The genuine fear she had felt in Georgia took this debased phantom form, and—*the human race is a funny apparatus*—she could neither sleep nor stay in the dark.

There was still the option of packing and leaving. She decided to do that. But when she pulled a shirt off one hanger and another clattered to the floor, she jumped back with her heart in her throat. "Oh, for christ's sweet sake." She grabbed a rain jacket and her keys and determined to finish the night on Solly's couch, where the house was rodent proofed and the foundation plugged against nocturnals.

She glanced into the wet trees, wondering where the local bats hid in the rain. She had never tried the back door, but it would save her thirty yards, so she took the chance. And she was lucky; the key fit, and let her into the hall between the staircase and the shop. She felt safer here. She edged her way to the counter, and past it to the door of the living room.

Which was ajar. Silhouetted against the jalousies, Trudy sat on the couch looking not out but at the floor in front of her. She had her arms wrapped around one of the crocheted cushions. She sat stock-still, still as the possum. She gave no sign that she had seen Dana, but on the contrary, with terrible concentration began to rock over the cushion, over the spot she stared at on the floor. She made no noise, but her rocking and (now Dana's eyes had adjusted to interior dark) her open mouth had the rhythm of keening, the rictus of grief.

Dana stood undecided. Her fear had evaporated entirely. She hadn't, though, lost the sense that she might bumble into something that was not her business. Trudy keened, wordless. Dana waited, wanting neither to startle her nor to go. It went on for a stretch of time, till Dana felt slightly dizzy with her own immobility. Her back hurt. She took a step back, reached for the counter and accidentally clanked the keys against it. Trudy did not break her trance. The very steadiness of her rocking suggested, not just whatever trouble she was feeling, but that she might be in trouble of some mental sort. Hallucinating? Disassociating?

"Trudy?" Dana said. "Trudy?" She stepped into the room and said it a third time before Trudy looked up over her cushion, unsurprised, rocking, her mouth still rigid in the perfect oval of Munch's *Scream.*

"What is it, Trudy? Can I help?"

A clock chimed somewhere upstairs, and it occurred to Dana that it must be an electric clock to be running all these weeks with Solly gone, though it seemed odd for the old man to own an electric chime. Maybe Trudy went up and wound it every night. With the thought of Solly she connected the dots.

"Trudy, is it Solly?"

Trudy rocking said, "He *gone.*"

Dana crossed to the couch, slipped out of her wet sandals, and sat. "Oh, Trudy. I'm so sorry. What happened?"

"The stroke got him."

"How do you know? Did Adena tell you?"

"She don't tell me nothing!" Venom brought back a degree of animation to her broad face. "I learn it from the shuckers after he been gone half a day."

"I'm so sorry." Dana tentatively set a hand on Trudy's shoulder, which was accepted. She patted awkwardly. She said, "He told me he expected it, but I thought he was just downhearted." Funny; *downhearted* was not a word she used. But it seemed exact. "When I went to see him he told me strokes ran in the family."

"I didn't *go.*" Trudy's shoulders heaved and the tears started now, but angrily.

"You couldn't know."

"Mr. Solly *know* I don't do hospitals!" The anger was familiar, an obstacle thrown down in the way of pain. She had felt it toward Graham—*But I was ready to divorce you!*—that rage that, whatever form it takes, is the first bequest of the dead. She slipped her arm farther around Trudy's shoulder. She knew Trudy would allow it. How did she know that?

"Solly wouldn't have expected you to come."

"I told him time again I don't say no hospital good-byes."

She knew because she had wanted Phoebe's arm around her, Harriet Honeycutt's, whatever arm was handy, however sullied with mixed emotion she herself had been. Dana, clumsily still, pulled Trudy to her with a little bouncing motion, and Trudy leaned against her sighing, and the cushion somersaulted to the floor, and the rain drummed on the shingles, and they sat in the archetypal posture of the bereaved and the comforter.

Except, of course, it was more complicated. Forty-eight hours ago Dana had been in bed with Trudy's nephew. That affair was why she had come to Pelican Bay, which she had not admitted though she'd had several weeks to do so, and this was no time to be intruding a confession. Trudy's sister and the sister's family were murderously inclined, and perhaps in pursuit of her. They could be here right now, pulling up outside this very minute. She had every intention of getting out of Dodge—but how could she do that now and abandon Trudy in her grief? Besides, Solly had given her power of attorney, and if she split without saying good-bye, she would be suspected of absconding even if all the money was accounted for. And was Cassius safe? And what about her own loss? When would there be time for that?

Trudy's back against her forearm mingled their damp through the cotton blouse, just as her skin and Cassius's had manufactured heat between them. Cassius's genes were in this damp. She hugged Trudy to her. "It's all right, Trudy."

"Solly know he wasn't coming back. That's why he got you looking after the store."

Dana remembered vaguely that Solly had told her to look after Trudy, too. She hadn't then and didn't now consider it a very solemn obligation. Solly would certainly have left Trudy enough to live on. Besides, what could she do besides offer this shoulder (this *shoulder work*) of ordinary consolation?

In the end it was Trudy who spent what was left of the night on the couch. Dana pulled an afghan over her and sat till her breathing slowed, the heavy bosom rising steadily. Dana thought first she would go upstairs and find another bed to lie down on. But when she reached the landing—a beveled mirror flecked with rust, a pretty little gateleg table, a candle in a brass dish—she turned downstairs again. It wasn't that she feared a ghost (tonight's quota of irrational funk had been spent on possums) but that Solly wasn't dead *enough*. She'd feel like a trespasser invading his private space.

In any case she was awake. The only thing she could think to do was to slip back in the shop and check the stock. The store had been closed three days, so there were milk and yogurt out-of-date. Half the sliced turkey and four bolognas needed to be bagged and trashed. There was a pile of mail to sort and consequently bills to pay. She'd been surprised by how much the little store took in, but when she subtracted what was owed, the profit was minuscule, alarming. She'd lost Solly more than half a week's take, considering the Saturday rush; she'd missed six deliveries and the pest-control man.

She stood at the till in her day-old clothes to write the checks. Standing there she thought of Solly, whom she hadn't really got to know, but who had a full history in this spot, a whole life story mostly lived on his feet on these oak boards. She knew only this much: born here on the Gulf, married, wanted kids but didn't have them, lost his wife, had an understanding with Trudy but didn't live with her, loved a nephew that he lost in ambiguous circumstances, died.

She had liked him. Thought him funny and good-natured and intermittently wise. She totted amounts into the ledger so that when she left she'd at least leave things up-to-date. It was busywork, but absorbing enough that she was still there at seven when the first women rapped on the glass: April with her ponytail and her stroller, Parthinia in her wraparound leopard top. Dana went to close the door on Trudy before she opened up, but Trudy was gone, the cushions plumped, the afghan folded on the couch.

15

PHOEBE SAID, "Why are you still there, then? I don't get it."

"If they were coming after me, they'd be here by now, wouldn't they?"

"You're still looking for him to show up and sweep you off on a white horse—excuse me—black horse."

"I don't know. Maybe staying put is my 'war on terror.'"

"Jesus, what does that *mean*?"

"It was a joke."

"You use that language and it starts to sound like it does mean something. 'Ethnic cleansing,' 'family values'? Did you see Cheney is in Wyoming playing cowboy? Promising to oust Hussein? I'm not kidding, they're going to invade Iraq."

"They wouldn't, Phoebe."

"I'll lay you odds. 'Regime change.' Don't you read the papers anymore?"

"This is the South, remember? It's not part of the world."

"Is that a joke?"

"Yeah."

"Ha ha. Get out of there."

"Soon. But I've gotta go. I've got a customer."

Phoebe was right. It wasn't logical or even sane. It was a fault in her, this inertia. Look how long she'd hung around Somerset doing nothing but sanding a kitchen hutch while the bills piled up. No doubt it had to do with her staccato childhood, the abrupt departures, the constant moves. No sooner had they settled in a town and she'd made one friend good enough for a playdate than they were off again.

While she was thinking this—dreading the road west, those dank motels—she was selling turkey breast and sandwich bread, adjusting things on the shelves, feeding the cash can under the counter. Also alert to unfamiliar cars at the pump outside. She should have said to Phoebe: *It's not just me. This is what people do.*

You descend the steps into the subway, turn the corner that always smells of piss, slide your eyes right and left for abandoned packages. You pull out the token you've already stuck in your pocket; on guard, aware. You have six stops into Times Square and three more north on the IRT, checking out the ones with backpacks, briefcases, beards, swarthy skin. It could be a bomb, it could be gas. You're always operating on this undercurrent, but what's the alternative? They call it courage but it's also comforting. The danger is in the routine, but the routine is what steadies you. You do this every day, regardless. What else should you do?

The women arrived earlier than usual and stayed longer. Dana knew more of them now—Mrs. Usvedt with her nose narrow as a pine shim and a way of holding it flared that spoke of superior ancestry, Milly Allanson with her bunions, Maria Elena de la Iglesia who called her mother every day to verify the ingestion of Pravachol. She knew which of their dogs would lie docile on the porch and which would whine for entry. She knew some of their troubles, scandals, and feuds: that Sarah's husband was a mean drunk, that Parthinia's sister had filched away her man, that Jessie had a son in Chattahoochee hospital for the criminally insane. These departures from the ideal were no different from those Dana had known in Bobbindale Heights, except that here they involved more stubble and less bling.

This morning the women were in elegiac mood, recalling how

Solly used to set up the fireworks before the laws were changed, and how Mrs. Solly came from Birmingham and taught piano to all the kids, and how they worried about Solly, who seemed so lost when Mrs. Solly died. Sarah said, "He wasn't saved," and Mrs. Usvedt said, "He wasn't a churchgoer," and this sounded like competition rather than accord. Then a silence fell in which Trudy's name was not mentioned and was therefore loud—or at least that's what Dana heard, to whom they spoke commiseratingly, as if she were ex officio in mourning.

By the same token, standing in his spot behind the register, Dana was assumed to know more than she did. It was supposed that she'd been with Solly these past days—"his last three days in the land of the living," Jessie said—and no matter how many times she repeated, "I was away visiting a friend on the coast. I know less than you do," the rumor would cross the threshold, and Sarah or Flora or Mrs. Moomis would come in asking did he suffer or was he able to say anything at the end.

So it was a relief when Adena arrived, although Adena was not in good shape. "Oh, Flora, Milly, Marion"—she fell into the arms of each in turn. Her coiffure was clumped into mats and brambles. Her face was bloodless under the tan, her eyes at once swollen and pinched, uncontrollably seeping. "I wasn't ready. I can't take it in." She wore cutoffs and a heather T-shirt that showed the sweat under her arms and down her spine. "He was *so good* to us in the rough times—that time Bucky took off for four days?—Solly took us over to Panama City and put Bernadette on the water slides." She pushed at her forelock and crumbled a Kleenex at her mouth. "And you know how he never left the store if he could help it. He was wonderful, wonderful." She glanced vaguely toward Dana. A wave of blame passed over her face, like wind on grass, so fleetingly that Dana couldn't have said whether it registered in her mouth or around her eyes. "And now he died and *his store wasn't even open!*" There was either sweat at her cleavage or else the tears had fallen there. Dana remembered the equanimity with which Adena had faced her ex's death and had the ratty thought that the T-shirt was chosen for this reason.

"It was bad timing," Dana said, with no clear idea what she meant apart from an insincere acceptance of guilt. She, Dana, was a touch disheveled herself, playing substitute store clerk in the smudged pants and shirt she'd put on yesterday morning, last century, in the Jacksonville Beach Ramada Inn.

"He was barely seventy. I was nowhere near prepared . . ." Adena clung to Mrs. Moomis's huggable amplitude and sobbed, a sort of guttural howling—there was no mistaking the genuineness of her distress. It was just a different style from Dana's. Or a different style from Trudy's. It was grieving à la Greece or the Middle East, a way of plumbing the depths of it in order to get it out.

"He was *fine* on Saturday. He ate an Enchirito and a Nachos Supreme I brought him. And then all of a sudden Sunday . . ." The women gathered around, rubbing her arm, making soothing noises.

Adena looked up again at Dana, this time with an uncertain smile, said, "I'm so glad you're back," and wiped her eyes, and turned to envelop her. "Oh, god, I'm glad you're back. I'm so glad you're here."

Caught off guard in Adena's hug, Dana felt a swift, hard failure of sympathy. Yet Adena had cared for the old man while he berated her. She was allowed a cliché or two. None of us can say exactly what we mean in the face of death. This reasoning skittered through her mind. But her gut said: *claptrap.* She gently disengaged herself. "Well, but you know, I was planning to head out west."

"Oh, Dana, *don't* leave me now. There's the funeral to arrange, and it's high season at work, and there's no *way* I can keep the store open, too."

The women agreed, murmuring, "Solly would have wanted it." They would have supported any claim Adena made just then, but it was also true that most of them couldn't get to the IGA at Winona Crossing or the Food Mart on Sag Island except on weekends.

"We can't *do* without you," Adena said, and someone murmured, "It's the god's truth."

She felt herself relenting. Who else had a use for her? It was true, if the Hustons were coming after her, they'd have been here by now. "The trouble is," she objected, "a possum got in the cabin last night, and it freaked me out."

"Sleep here! You can sleep upstairs," Adena offered.

"If you going to live in paradise . . . ," Milly said.

And Flora finished the local doxology, ". . . you got to expect a few snakes," and all the women laughed, commiserating.

"What you need," put in Mrs. Usvedt, "is the Zebrowski boy. What's his name?"

"Herbie," said Flora.

"Herbie Zebrowski. I've got his number. He can put you right."

"It's no time at all," Adena lamented, "since I was burying Bucky, and now . . ."

Her eyes filled, and as if they knew their exit cue the women one by one departed, leaving Dana and Adena alone except for Maria Elena on the pay phone, saying, "No, Mama, that's the pink one. You just take one of those."

Adena put her elbows on the counter and her head in her hands. She hiccupped softly. "I'll send Bernadette to help you. I don't know how she's going to cope. I'll have to get her into counseling."

This was a surprise. "Was she close to Solly?"

"Very, *very* close. Like two peas in a pod." Dana registered that the idiom meant "identical," which could not be said of Solly in his leathern skin and Bernadette in her nubile shine. What was the matter with her? Why was she being such a bitch?

"Her daddy, and then Solly. It's too much for her. You have no idea how vulnerable she is."

"I'll stay till the funeral," Dana said. "That's all I can really promise."

"Just till we figure out what to do about the store. You're an incredible friend. You're a love, a friend in need. I really owe you."

Dana stubbed her tongue on a reply to this, letting a silence fall into which Maria Elena, a fist on her cocked hip, said, "Just put it in your *mouth,* Mama! Have you got the water?"

"Is what you'll want to do is," said Herbie Zebrowski, "I'll give it a good spray with the hose underneath so's any of 'em left in there'll clear on out. Then I'll go under on my wheely board and shoot some expansion sealant up in the joists. Prob'ly Shur-Fome, yeah?"

Herbie was six-foot-something, something-upper-teen, parlous thin and pale. He looked that tantalizing kind of familiar that meant she'd seen him before but couldn't put him in any context. Tattoos rolled over the bones of his forearm. He arrived in a pickup with a long-faced, mole-colored hound who bounded from the passenger seat, eyes hungering after his master's every move.

"Dudley Do-Right," Herbie introduced, and Dana said, "How-do, Dudley?"

"Then I got me a coupla humane traps we can leave inside a coupla days, and you're all set. You'll want a one-inch chicken wire around the base, and pin it, like, in the grass roots. And then trellis skirting is what I'd recommend for the look of it, to cover the wire."

Dana said. "Do you think maybe it's overkill?"

"Ma'am?"

"A lot of trouble to go to."

"No, ma'am, them things can be rabid."

"They do bite, then."

"They're scareder of you than you are of them, but they'll bite if you get up in their territory."

"How do they know it's their territory? That one was in my kitchen."

"Yes'm. But then I guess it was theirs before there was a kitchen on it. Anyways, you gonna rent the place, you can't have nobody waking up wiping a possum off their blankets."

"That's true." She didn't point out that she was the renter, not the landlord. Instead she cleared her stuff out into Solly's living room for the duration—slung her clothes over her arm and rolled her suitcase full of books, bathroom supplies, new shrimp pot, the Jekyll Island candles; hauled them through the back door and unloaded them around the room. She felt better here. She restacked the boxes so she could use the kitchen, which was old but serviceable, like the cabin's. Then, thinking it might be hurtful to Trudy to find her clothes dumped on a chair, she went upstairs after all to reconnoiter.

There were two generous, even huge, rooms under open beams, one with a fireplace and a sofa as well as a brass bed, the other with a worn set of dining chairs and an upright piano. She guessed that once upon a time this had been a kitchen (there were pipes protruding from the floor beside the piano), before Mr. Solly closed in the porch and Mrs. Solly took this for her music room. The piano was "pickled" or "honey-glazed," painted white and daubed with varnish, a renovation style that belonged to the forties and fifties, which meant the piano was old back then. A brass plate above the keys said IVERS & POND. A tentative finger produced a mournful twang. In the piano bench she found a stack of sheet music, "Blue Moon," and "The Battle Hymn of the Republic," and "Bach Melodies." There was a cupboard (the pantry once, maybe) with nothing inside but a full-length mirror—a mahogany oval swinging on a stand. Lovely. She pulled it out into the room on its squeaking wheels. The cupboard would do for her temporary closet. The room was otherwise bare—therefore not a shrine—but not made use of either, not refurbished or refinished, not expecting anyone.

Whereas the bedroom to which she returned had a patina of human passage: a calico quilt neatly smoothed, the floorboards worn, dime-store frames chipped around their photos, the slippers with their broken backs lined up beside the bed. The fireplace was stacked with wood. On the sofa were piles of *St. Petersburg Times* and a splayed copy of *Newsweek* suggesting an article half read. In the little bookcase next to it sat Dickens and the Bible, histories of the Civil War and civil rights. There was the chiming clock (electric after all) on a walnut chest, and a scattering of shells, but nothing you couldn't pick up any day on Sag Island beach, nothing of meaning to anyone who had not in fact picked them up. There was no dust on these objects but they were scuffed with use to a look of dustiness. She felt a pang of loss for the ineffable that lived in the husks of things. For Solly, whose belongings had been animated by their owner and, like his worn and unremarkable body, were garbage now.

Dana picked up a Kodachrome of a wedding couple: Adena in lace, flipped-up hair, and a glittering grin, and—no doubt of it—Bucky Solomon, blond with wide-set blue eyes in an open face.

Like Solly as a young man; like Bernadette if you saw her sans camouflage and piercings. Dana looked up from the photograph, out the dormer window, and was amazed to find that at this height you could see over the grass, the road, the palmettos beside the docks, over the bay to the tip of Sag Island and out to sea. Out over the crown of the world. She looked out and said good-bye to John Solomon, whom she hadn't known. And to Graham, whom she hadn't loved. And always to Chloe. And perhaps to Cassius.

The next day she made a pot of bay-scallop pasta and went down to offer some to Herbie Zebrowski, under the cabin on his "wheely board" while Dudley Do-Right guarded the grass at his heels. Herbie followed her up to the shop, and Dudley followed him, standing at the bottom of the steps with his hindquarters whipping back and forth until he was given permission to come in, then flopping obediently on the floorboards. Herbie ate at the counter while Dana closed up and restocked the shelves.

"I'm 'a fix the far side of your gutters if that's okay. You got leaves built up in there'll make the roaches breed."

"I guess that would be okay. I don't know what Mr. Solomon would do."

"Oh, Solly'd'a done it himself, only he was getting old." Forking the pasta with one hand while slugging from a Coke can in the other, he pointed out, "This here cash register's a antique."

"You're right there."

"Is what you need is a POS system—that means point-of-sale, a Nurit or a PC Express with a spectra-physics scanner. And a scale. Then you'd get your stock check and pay your bills automatic. It'd save you bigtime."

"I guess Solly liked the old method."

"Oh, I know. I was only saying."

"It's not my store. I'm just helping out."

"I do that sometimes, down at the 7-Eleven near the bridge, yeah? My bro-in-law owns it."

"Oh, yes."

"That's where I seen you."

She remembered now—that first night, when everyone had disappeared because of Bucky Solomon's "accident." It was Herbie's pale height she'd recognized, and the tattoos. She remembered now the dog at his feet. She remembered that he'd seemed laughably incompetent, whereas his work on the cabin was neat and thorough. "You've got a better memory than I do."

"Nah, you stick out because you're a Nor'easter. That's what Solly called the tourists. Only you don't have a accent like you had then."

Dana laughed. "I moved around a lot when I was a kid. I think I developed a habit of picking up the local dialect."

"Uh-huh," said Herbie, and rubbed the concavity where his belly might have been. "I better set the traps b'fore the sun goes down." He upended the can to his mouth and *plunk*ed it on the counter with a solid whack, at which Dudley shook himself and rose. "Coke is the absolute perfect corporation," Herbie declared.

"Oh?"

"Well, first off they started out makin' their soda out of cocaine, did you know that?"

"I'd heard it."

"And then they invented advertising, yeah? And they took the cocaine out and put caffeine in instead. Then later they took the sugar out, and then they took the caffeine back out, and the more they took out the more they sold, and by the end they was selling flavored water in near about every country in the world."

"And now they've taken out the flavoring, and they're selling tap water for three times the price of Coke."

"Yeah, well, there you are, yeah?"

"It's American genius," Dana said.

16

If Bucky Solomon's death had caused a local shudder, John Solomon's shook Pelican Bay to its foundation. He was a pillar of this boondock. He was not himself a joiner, but his store had been more of a social center than the Elks. He was not markedly generous; all the same he'd been known to run a tab during a hurricane or a strike, and nobody ever starved for lack of Spam. And of course he'd been here forever. There were some who'd bought their first Dubble Bubble at Solly's Corner who now depended on it for Depends.

In fact it could be said (no, it couldn't be said, but it could be briefly thought) that the hundreds who hadn't shown up for Senator Ullman's funeral showed up for shopkeeper Solomon's memorial. The service was held on Sag Island in the ballroom of the Swashbuckler Inn, which, if it hardly mollified the Christians, at least offended the denominations equally. The room was decked out in an ecumenical gathering of dining and folding, canvas and plastic chairs, a plain pine table with the tin urn of Solly's already-cremated ashes, and a blown-up snapshot of him squinting under the visor of his cap. The table was draped with boughs of slash pine between pots of mangrove, which made the outlying semicircle of hothouse lilies and gladiola sprays look vaguely vulgar.

They were all there, the Usvedts and the Moomises, April with Lee Annie in the stroller, Flora and Evian, Jessie, Maria Elena, fishermen who were familiar to Dana from Saturdays, a flock of schoolchildren fluffed or cornrowed, tall Herbie in a Sunday button-down, Solly's lawyer taller still with the dreadlock trailing down his back, a dozen AME dignitaries in their suits, a dozen Hells Angels in their leather, two young men, unknown to her, in T-shirts that said "Real Men Fear Jesus." Adena, in a black linen pantsuit, hugged each as they arrived, comforting and accepting comfort. Bernadette hung back to one side, gorgeously pouting (sorrowful? sullen? shy?), hair blond to her ears and blue from thence to her shoulders, balancing on espadrilles with four inches of rope sole. Her body made a single narrow scoop of some black fabric with the same luster as her skin. Herbie Zebrowski hovered in her wake, with Dudley Do-Right following after.

The locals, dressed in direct inversion to their means—wealthy Sag Islanders in shorts and Sink Street folks turned out in beflowered hats and stockings—one after another stood and told Solly stories. The men dwelt on his youthful indiscretions, his cantankerous oddity. April and Parthinia and Mrs. Usvedt waxed more sentimental, recalling Solly's knack for kids, and Mrs. Solly's spreading of music through a generation of them. Little Henry (of Henry's Café & Cannery) recalled how Solly was addicted to sour-ball candy and Almond Joys, and eloquently opined that *sour* and *joy* would do for his epitaph. Geraldine Loos from Pensacola, mahogany cleavage straining at turquoise spandex, belted "Amazing Grace" and "Wanna Go Home," and the crowd raised its voice to the brass-and-plastic chandelier.

Trudy was not there. Nor had she appeared at Solly's since the night she'd slept on the couch. Therefore, Wednesday afternoon, when Bernadette showed up for two hours' worth of languid clerking, Dana had driven across East Sink to check on her. Down the dirt streets, past swinging tires and swept sand plots, Dana was bemused that she suffered not one iota of the danger she'd felt in Cassius's neighborhood. There were personal reasons for this—she was not on a guilty errand, she knew most of the women, nobody demonstrably wished her ill. But also, though the sides of Sink Street might be divided by race, it occurred to her that they were equally bound by hardship. Was this so? That, contrary to popular belief, geography and minimum wage enforced a degree of tolerance?

She found Trudy's double-wide in a shady hummock ringed with crooked shrubs, so thickly intertwined that Dana thought of Sleeping Beauty in her ring of thorns. Trudy was awake, though, no longer keening but wearing her protective sullenness, hair bound back with a bandana tied on the nape of her neck. She invited Dana in and gestured grudgingly toward the kitchen, so Dana quickly said she couldn't stay. Trudy perched on a hard chair while Dana sat on the sprung couch in front of a coffee table that held a sewing basket and a bedraggled pink Christmas tree on a music box. Trudy suffered the small talk, the condolences, but when Dana suggested that they go together to the memorial, her whole thick torso rolled with rejection.

"Mr. Solly know I don't do funerals."

"Well, you regretted not going to the hospital, so I thought this once . . ."

"Solly be looking down, he think I was some kind of crazy to be in that fuss. I just stay here and cook for the folk."

"If you're sure."

"I give it up to Jesus."

"Yeah . . ."

"I give it *up* to the good Lord's *care.*"

Outside a dog barked, and then another farther off. As if in overreaction, a plane cracked through with a sonic boom. The tinsel arms of the little Christmas tree trembled. "Well. I want you to know you're always welcome at the house."

Trudy glinted. "What she's going to do with the store?"

"I don't know, Trudy. I'm just staying on while she decides."

"*Hmph.* You be there next week I'll come clean in the evenings."

"That's fine, but it's not the point. You can come whenever you like, it's not that I want you to clean up."

Trudy put a broad hand on each knee and leaned into them as if to rise, a gesture of dismissal. "Mr. Solly like me to keep it," she said. So Dana left.

Now in the ballroom of the Swashbuckler Inn, Geraldine Loos lifted her resonant bosom on the final chorus:

Wanna go home, lemme go home,
Wanna go ho-o-o-ome where I belong . . .

And the mourners joined in with gospel force:

Home! Home! Ho-o-o-ome!

Mrs. Loos swept up an armload of gladiola from a basket and carried them down the aisle to the double doors. Adena followed her with the urn, which was a maroon-painted tin the size and shape of a Saltine box. One by one the people in the front rows, men, women, and children, denuded the table of its fronds, the baskets of their flowers, and promenaded toward the sun. Dana joined the flow of the crowd out the doors, across the deck, down the wooden walkway to the beach, where they spread out two hundredfold along the sand.

Home. Home. Ho-o-o-o-ome . . .

It was a spectacular summer day, in the upper eighties—balmy for late July—and so dry that the gulf breeze struck a chill on cheeks and arms. Pennsylvania had spread an equally blue sky last year for Graham's rite, but—there, then—it was marred by the catastrophic smoke, whereas here there were only the little Disney puffs of cumulus. The crowd mingled in ragged rows along the beachfront, black and white, and Dana was sorry again that Trudy's squeamishness or scruples had kept her from seeing this. She imagined how she and Trudy and Cassius might be standing here together. Why not?

Ho-o-o-ome . . . !

A fresh sea smell rose from the beach. At the water's edge, Adena shifted the cracker tin of ashes to one hand and slipped a finger into her ankle strap, abandoned her high heels to the sand, and waded out into the shallow surf. And then, amazingly, one after another the locals followed her. The gospel singer with her armload of gladiola pushed in against the waves, Maria Elena in a navy dress, April lifting Lee Annie in a wide arc, Bernadette tottering on her rope soles. A pair of kindergartners, hand in hand, their full skirts parachuting on the froth, followed a youth in cargo shorts whose flip-flops rose and floated.

Some took a flower stalk, some a handful of ashes that Adena poured.

Home, home, h-o-o-o-ome.

They launched the flowers and strewed the ashes, which bobbed on the retreating tide. Shoes were strung along the sand. There were a couple of dozen in the water now, thigh deep in a trough near the shore but climbing to the shallows on a sandbar farther out, damp darkening their clothes, looking not like a funeral but like a communal baptism in some painting Dana could not quite bring to mind. Dudley leaped in after Herbie, snapping at the foam. Bernadette fed Solly to the swells with a flicking gesture like someone making piecrust, her mouth in motion around its incipient pout. Dana had an odd moment in which she imagined that Bernadette was flicking Solly's toenail parings instead of ashes. Then Adena spotted her and beckoned with a full-arm gesture. Dana raised her palms to demur.

"Better go on out."

Solly's lawyer was at her side, dreadlock damp and trousers rolled. Her memory stumbled on his name. Something to do with baseball, old-time. Ruth? DiMaggio?

"Perry Hoyt," he supplied. "We met in the hospital."

"Of course. I remember."

"I think you should join in."

"Do you?"

Adena, radiant in the descending sun, reached toward her with the dusty mouth of the cracker tin. Perry Hoyt put a hand lightly under her elbow. "Yah. Come on. And I'd like to talk to you."

"Now?"

"No, not now, after."

After, she warmed a pot of bouillabaisse on the old Hotpoint at Solly's Corner and brought Perry Hoyt a bowl of it at the coffee table. His jeans and her dirndl still showed high-water marks, and she felt she ought to make some sort of hospitable offer about this, but she couldn't think what (go up and look for a pair of Solly's pants? give him a towel?) so she did nothing, and doing nothing for him, felt obligated to remain in her wet skirt. She sat with her bowl on her knees, sandy damp around her thighs. Hoyt had brought in his scuffed briefcase, which he fingered where it sat on the floor. She knew that he would have some business to do with the power of attorney. She resolved to dispatch it with minimum effort.

But Hoyt behaved oddly. He'd waved away the Chablis and poured seltzer in his wineglass, and now he displayed an interest, palpably phony, in the glass itself—which she'd found at the back of the cupboard and which was in fact quite old and fine. Palpably phony, though: he turned the stem and peered frowning at the etched design and through the bowl as if looking for the vintage hue. Then he spread himself back against the couch, swirling the fizzy water at arm's length. He had an uncoordinated, knees-and-elbows kind of body, which would have been comic if it wasn't for his also-visible angst. He lounged with the effort of somebody trying to lounge. He said, "I don't know you well," and looked up under his pale lashes and she thought, *Oh my god; a come-on?* She was startled and a little charmed and not an iota turned on. Poor baby!

He said, "How—how do you like it here?"

She said, "I like it fine, but all the same I'm sort of impatient to get things in order and head on west." She thought this was hint enough, but Hoyt didn't seem to take the hint. He pursed his lips and looked over her head, as if out the window at a wall that had no window.

He said, "How are you g-getting on in the store?"

She wondered if she would have to say, *I'm spoken for,* or—what did one say?—*I'm committed, I'm in a relationship*—none of which would be true, except that longing for Cassius suddenly whacked her over the lungs. She said, stuttering like Hoyt, "It's a b-balancing act—no, it's a holding action. I can't see how Solly managed it alone year after year."

He nodded profoundly. He swirled the seltzer, examined it. Short of breath, Dana plunged, "Of course there's a lot that needs to be done, uh, if you were really going to make a go of it. The place is pretty ramshackle, down to the plumbing and electric. It'll be a big job for Adena—unless she sells it, which I expect she will; she said something about it, back when we first took Solly in."

"Uh-huh, uh-huh," said Hoyt, and she felt sorry for him, really, but—what was he, forty? Forty-five? What a backward—redneck, even—approach for a grown, educated man. He spooned a few mouthfuls of bouillabaisse, then looked up with a shrugging grin. His long and normally sallow face was pink with sunburn. "Are you sitting down?"

It took a second to recognize this as a joke. She said approximately, "Uhn."

He said, "Solly has left you Solly's Corner."

". . . What?"

"The store, the house, about forty-five acres."

"Me?"

"It took me kind of by surprise as well."

Standing in the sea just now, in the trough between the shore and the sandbar, she had been caught by an undertow just strong enough to slide the sand out from under her feet, and for a long second had shifted and stumbled. Now it was her mind that fought for purchase.

"I don't understand. Didn't you write the will for him?"

"Oh, yeah. And rewrote it, too."

"When?"

"In the hospital, that week after you were there."

Dana said, "It's not possible."

"Maybe, but it's legal."

"What about Adena? What about Trudy?"

"Oh, he left them the money. About fifty thousand each; they'll be all right."

It struck her sideways that fifty thousand was about what Graham had left *her*. "Hoyt—Perry, he was demented."

Now that his news was out, Hoyt sprawled more at ease, picked up his bowl and slurped from it, set it solidly down. "I don't know. He seemed very clear. His doctor thought he was a character, but, you know, stone-cold sane. He and the head nurse witnessed the will. But you won't need them to testify."

"To what?"

"If it should be contested."

"Hoyt, I don't want the store. I'll just hand it over to Adena. I know he was pissed off at her, but—didn't he have other relatives?"

"No. The brother, Bucky's father, he passed a few years ago. There was a sister, a spinster—I'm sorry for the word but I don't know a better one—she was much older, and dead, too."

"Which makes Bernadette his next of kin."

"The grandniece, yeah."

"Then I'll give it to Bernadette."

"You can do that if you want. But you'll have to, sort of, *have* it before you can give it away. I mean, it's all a trust, it can be executed pretty fast as these things go, but . . ."

"Hoyt, he was not in his right mind, he was senile." She didn't quite believe this, but it was the closest she had to sense.

Hoyt contemplated the surface of his fizzy water, then downed it. "There's plenty that would say so," he declared. "But it doesn't matter. In Florida you can give your fortune to feral cats if you want, long as you have testamentary capacity."

"Which means?"

"Which means that you know what a will is while you're making one, and know your *objects of natural affection.*"

"Which means?"

"Which means, as long as you're aware who'd be in line for it, your relatives and such, you can give it to the beach bums or the Society for the Prevention of Sodomy. There is such a thing, by the way. I ran into it on the 'net the other day."

"Then the law is crazy."

Looking vastly disburdened, Hoyt braided his fingers and stretched, knuckles cracking. Then reached for his briefcase. "Wouldn't be the first time."

17

NO USE PRETENDING it didn't change her view of things. Of Solly's things. Almost at once she began mentally sanding floors, putting up shelves, double glazing. Anyone with half an eye could see the possibilities. Install stained glass in the transom, rip out the kitchen and do an island in Corian or slate; extend a deck outside toward the ancient oak.

Ridiculous.

She went upstairs, indulging the fantasy for the moment: her fireplace, her four-poster, her view of the sea. She smoothed the contours of her lovely old log-pattern quilt. Ridiculous. The old man had made his deathbed wish out of spite, and to take advantage of it would be her very definition of corruption: greed for a windfall at somebody else's expense. No way. She flipped on the light in what she assumed had been the music room and fingered the pickled paint of the old piano. A blister collapsed under her touch. She played a one-octave scale (middle C was about all she knew how to find) and the notes came out sour—a melodramatic, sinister twang that made her laugh. She slipped a fingernail under the paint bubble and pulled away a strip all the way down to the ledge that would hold the sheet music. Along the edges of the gash the paint had lifted so that she could reach the fingernail under and pull again. It was flat paint over varnish, a sloppy way of going about things, even if it had mostly lasted for fifty years. The loose paint was obsessively inviting. Inch by inch, she lifted and pulled until she had made a dark island in the honey glaze.

And was appalled. What was she thinking? She didn't even play the piano, her childhood travels never having stopped long enough for lessons. The thing was, though, her vandalism had uncovered, under a crackling of dark varnish, a burled walnut surface fabulously cut and opened flat so that the two sides of the veneer mirrored each other across the center seam. They made an owl's face, swirls of grain around the eyes and coming to a beak over middle C, over the little brass plate, Ivers & Pond. She'd also come to the end of the easy lifting. Now at the perimeter of the bald spot she scratched to no purpose; the paint stuck fast. Only on an edge of the case just above the keyboard did she succeed in chipping another inch away—and counted fourteen hardwood ply.

There were carved emblems in the corners, scorings on the upright, intricate jig work on the music stand. An impossible job of restoring—or "renovating," as Phoebe had it. She'd never do it. Instead, she found a dust pan and brush and carefully cleaned up every flake and scrape of evidence. She closed down her fantasy and, turning to the mahogany swinging mirror she'd taken out of the closet a week ago, hoisted it downstairs in her embrace, feeling the back of each footstep with her heel and sliding her weight against the wall. She carried it into the shop and set it in the candy aisle at the farthest end from the cash register. She checked the vantage, angled it so she had a view around the corner from her perch. That would work, an in-store guard against pilfering children. She took a strip of adding-machine paper, printed *Homeland Security* on it in felt-tip, taped it in a loop, and hung it rakish on the mirror.

Then, after watching a serial killer get nabbed by a forensics expert in a push-up bra, she made her bed on the couch, a transient still.

But Monday morning was an uneasy snare of half misunderstandings and half concealments. The women were given to aposiopesis and lifts of pitch suggesting curiosity. "He seemed so lively. Who'd've thought . . ." "It goes to show you can never . . ." "That Solly, some character, eh?" Dana was brought two condolence casseroles, a sausage lasagna from Sarah of West Sink, of the halter tops and the knife scar across her spine; and later salt pork and red beans from Parthinia of East Sink—callipygian Parthinia in her leopard print. To Sarah she said the conventional, "It wasn't necessary," juggled the warm Pyrex and wondered whether she should make a return gift of the links and pasta that had surely come from here. To Parthinia she said, "Oh, really, you should take it to Trudy," at which Parthinia's perfectly plucked half circle of left eyebrow raised—scandalized? offended?—before she snorted, "Trudy the best cook in town already."

Dana took the pot, murmured something, and deposited it in her kitchen fridge. She was a klutz this morning, jumpy with the fear that Adena would show up. And sure enough—Parthinia still fingering the okra, the Doritos man restocking, a couple of kids considering investment in Tootsie Pops—Adena sailed in at noon, bringing with her the energy of a spare generator. She was lithe in a tank dress, still funereally black but with a splash of oriental brilliance—scarlet peony, turquoise carp.

"Sweetie, I just came by to see if you're all right. Do you need anything? It's madness, I don't know how I'm going to cope, ten days behind at work and still cards to write, people to thank. Hancock's been a honey, but she's got an agency to run. I'm just going to take this PowerBar, okay? I know I promised you Bernadette but she's impossible! At this stage I don't know what's broken heart and what's just teenage, the way she mopes around. I need to get her an appointment but I have to go into Panama City today, Tallahassee tomorrow, it's mad. Can you cope till next week, and I'll get by to clear things out? I promise."

Dana, grateful not to get a word in edgeways, said, "I'm fine." And Adena was out the door, curls churning, into her car and halfway down the road.

In any case, it was not her place to deliver the legal shock. Hoyt would write both Trudy and Adena, but such letters wouldn't arrive until Wednesday at the earliest. She dared not think how Adena would take Solly's betrayal. For the moment it was her dishonesty toward Trudy that seemed unsustainable. When the store was empty she hung the Be Right Back sign on the screen and stepped down toward the cabin, where Herbie Zebrowski was tacking chicken wire over the new gutters, and for no reason connected with this sight, it hit her that she'd got the matter backward. Her position had always been more or less false. Now it stank of bad faith.

"Hiya," Herbie said from the ladder. Dudley yawned.

Why did she assume the store belonged to Adena? Adena was — or Bernadette was — the nearest thing to a relative Solly had. But Trudy was the nearest thing to a wife. If she'd been his wife in fact, if there hadn't been a dragline of racism down here in the Gulf that kept them from solemnizing — what, eighteen years? — cohabitation, then wouldn't Trudy be — what had Hoyt said? — his "natural object of affection"?

"Sump'n wrong?" Herbie tacked a cove edge to the roof and stowed his hammer.

"Sorry. Trying to think of seven things at once." Maybe Solly hadn't left the store to her out of spite, but in a simple dilemma about whether it should go to his woman or his family. And if so then he'd sloughed the decision off to her, Dana, the same way he'd commandeered her to run the store. The sun hit Herbie's face with a particularly reddening ray. "You should wear a hat," she said sharply.

Herbie grinned. "'S what my sister says. But I get red under a hat just the same."

"Herbie, could you watch the store, half an hour at most? I need to go over to Henry's."

"I was goin' to tell you, I wouldn't mind watching it sometimes; give you a break. If it's all right, I'm planning to mend those back steps, and I could do one and the other."

"Well, but what about your brother-in-law? Don't you have to work for him?"

"Oh, no, ma'am, he's sold up."

"Sold up how?"

"To them developers from Pascagoula. My sister's been after him to move up to Marietta with my other sister, and they got the waterfront, y'know, where the 7-Eleven is, and this guy made him a offer he can't refuse."

"I see." She was a little alarmed in case Herbie assumed she could go on hiring him indefinitely at fifteen dollars an hour. But then, for the time being the Solly's Corner cash take was hers, wasn't it? It's not as if she was spending it on shoes. She walked Herbie back to the store, gave him minimal instructions, and started on foot for the highway, a distance only a wimp would drive.

Henry's Café & Cannery sat on pylons half out over the bay, the restaurant to the right, with tables where you could slip your shrimp shells through a flap in the windowsill and watch the seagulls fight the fish for them. At the left was the fresh-fish store, behind that the shucking shed, and yet farther left the vats and bottle belt of the canning operation. The whole place was about the size and glamour of four garages, and now at two in the afternoon both restaurant and store were empty except for Henry, standing behind the stalls of iced shrimp, small and wiry, wearing a baseball cap that had his name embroidered in Old English flourish. He greeted her with a hint of the mourning deference she was used to now. He wiped his hands on his apron.

"You doin' okay?"

"I'm fine. Henry, I need to talk to Trudy. Would that be all right?"

He shoved aside the warped flap of plywood that served as a door to the shucking shed. "Yes'm. She may be out back."

She faced him as she passed through. "How is Trudy?"

"Well, I don't know. It's hard to tell with Trudy." He wheezed a laugh and let the door fall to, closing her in the hot smell of fish and bleach, layers of the one succeeding the other day after day for fifty years. Inside, a dozen women black and white sat around a metal table ten-feet square, their elbows inside the rim and their fingers flipping crab detritus toward the center drain. They called it a shucking table but at this time of year there were no oysters being harvested, just shrimp and crab, small meat in a punishing solidity of shell. Eight or ten hours a day they sat in the reek of fish and bleach, shucking, shelling, gutting. Flora, Lou Ann, and Marion hailed her. Trudy was on break, they said. Just out back on the dock checking her lines.

Henry's dock led sixty or eighty feet into the bay, weathered gray and warped by salt damp, railings here and there repaired with newer two-by-fours the greenish tinge of pressure treating. This dock wasn't part of Henry's operation — shrimpers docked with the catch every morning before dawn — but rather a private sideline of the shuckers, especially Trudy, who was known to be the keenest rod fisher on Pelican Bay. Every ten feet along the railing a plastic tube had been screwed into the floor, and a rod handle was wedged in the tube up to the reel, its line dragging either side into the shallow bay. Trudy sat on a bench halfway out, knees spread to anchor with her forearm a foot-long flounder. She was intent, and Dana strolled up quietly, leaned against the railing, then felt the uprights give and thought better of it. The bay lapped midnight blue seven miles out to the tip of Sag Island, and from there stretched mirror surfaced to infinity. The fish on Trudy's lap was silver, too, periodically shuddering its tail as she delicately turned and tugged the hook, turned and tugged, coaxing the barb out with as small a tear as possible. Dana did not mistake this care for kindness. The less damage to the fish the longer its dying would be delayed, and that much fresher it would be in the eating. Her hook retrieved, Trudy opened a worn polystyrene cooler and dropped the flounder onto the ice, on top of a catfish, and maybe a whiting.

"Pretty good catch," said Dana.

Trudy shrugged — it was impossible to tell whether she had known Dana was there, whether she was surprised to see her, or cared. She might have taken a vow never to be surprised. And yet. The word *blanched* came oddly to mind, and Dana thought of the fact that blanching was done by scalding, and that a grief-blank face was not so much made pale as scalded rigid.

"Trudy, I need your help."

"I be over."

"No, not that kind of help. But several kinds. I think—you may not want to do this, but if you do—I think you should have first pick of Solly's things."

Trudy wagged her head noncommittally over her line, crimping a weight between broad thumb and finger. She reached into the cooler for a shrimp and threaded the hook expertly lengthwise into the curve of the shrimp's body before she asked, "Mizz Adena say so?"

"It's nothing to do with her."

Trudy glanced up, scarcely raising her head, the purposely skeptical look of someone peering over glasses.

"I need to talk to you," Dana said.

"What kind of talk?"

"All right, I'll tell you. Solly has left the store to me."

"Uh-huh."

Getting to her feet was a kind of shrug. The casting of the line was a getting-rid-of. Trudy had a good arm. The bait and weight arced far into the sea, sun sparkling on the line. Her back to Dana, she rooted the rod into the plastic sleeve, adjusted the reel.

"Do you know why he would have done that? Shouldn't he have left it to Adena? Or to you?"

"What I be doing with it?"

"Running it? I don't know."

"How long you think the white folk be buying they eggs at a old black woman store?"

"I don't know."

"It was Solly's to do like he pleased. Maybe he thought you to keep it up."

"I can't. Trudy, I'm serious. I need to know what to do."

"Uh-huh."

The impassivity was beyond placid, more deliberate than grief. Dana wanted to shake her. She took a bite of breath. "And that's not all. Your nephew Cassius."

"What about Cassius?"

"I know him."

"Well, that ain't no news."

"You know about that?"

"He send me word 'bout the time you arrive: look after his friend that rent the cabin."

"Why didn't you tell me?"

"You didn't name Cassius to me."

That was true. Dana registered the fish smell off the sea, backed by a sulfurous waft from Lhamon Paper. She felt faintly queasy. But she pushed on. "He's in trouble with his family over me. They chased me out of Georgia."

Trudy turned her back and grasped a rope hanging off the rail. She hand-over-handed it out of the water till a crab trap surfaced, its metal mesh noisily shedding water. She peered in. It was empty but for a chunk of bloody fish.

"I come over to Solly's place," she said stubbornly, "I usually come after dark."

"Oh, for god's sake, Trudy, Solly's gone. Nobody can gossip about you coming to see *me.*"

Trudy let the trap splash back into the lapping waves, took a chunk of ice from the deck, and washed her hands with it as if it were a cake of soap, until it disappeared entirely. She passed Dana walking back toward the shucking shed, wiping her hands on her skirt. "I get finish here about seven," she conceded.

By evening she had softened somewhat, stowed her bag of fish and ice in Solly's fridge, accepted a last bowl of the bouillabaisse, and listened to Dana's account, first, of Perry Hoyt's revelation, and then of her history with Cassius, the latter story somewhat edited for sexual content but with the violence of the daubed doors intact. Trudy said little, seemed neither shocked nor — what did Dana expect, charmed? — but was willing to look as well as listen; willing, it seemed, to meet Dana's eyes.

"That might could be Luther ketchuping doors. I don't know Cassius's wife."

"Do you think they're likely to follow me?"

"You going to stay?"

"Not *stay.* But if I stay until the will is settled, will I be safe?"

"Ain't nobody safe. You mean will that bunch come after you, I'm 'clined to doubt. They mightily tough in they own yard, but they don't go far. They ain't come here in eighteen years."

"Since you've been with Solly."

"*Mmm.* Cassius was not much past a chile last time I saw him." She squinted at Dana. "Is he set to come after you?"

"I don't know. How could he?"

"Well, if he don't come after you, they won't. But you settled to wait and find out, ain't you?"

"I don't know."

Later Trudy followed Dana upstairs and opened this cupboard, that drawer, with a sure familiarity that told Dana anything she might have asked about her life with Solly. Dana's impulse had been that Trudy would want some mementos, but Trudy retreated again behind that face of numb detachment, and seemed mainly concerned with the utility of things.

"I know some can make use of this," she would say from time to time.

Dana brought up trash bags and empty cartons from the store, and Trudy filled them, matching the seams of Solly's trousers, smoothing them with the flat of her palms, spreading his shirts on the bed and folding them into store-neat rectangles. She uncurled pairs of socks and flipped a fist into each to check the heels, the toes, sorting them into a box for distribution or a bag for trash. Dana asked if she wanted help, but she did not. Dana asked if she would like to be alone but this was answered laconically, "I want you to see all what I take."

Insulted, Dana did not answer. She sat on the couch aware of the soup lying under her diaphragm. She didn't miss her after-supper cigarette. Trudy's abstracted movements were familiar. Uncannily so. Dana saw herself less than a year ago, stuffing china into boxes, dragging suits across the backseat of the car. This methodical erasure of the dead was work that fell to women.

There was of course much less to get rid of from a country storekeeper's bedroom than from the bourgeois warehouse of a bored marriage. But that was not the difference. Trudy slipped her fingers into Solly's slippers, pressed with the heels of her hands on their broken backs, rubbed them down her thighs, and placed them carefully aside. The difference was not the quantity or the shine of stuff, but that Trudy had earned her grief. Dana was deeply envious of that numb mourning, its integrity. And then, as so many times during even the part of the day spent behind the shop counter, she was flooded with loss herself. Loss amorphous, loss aggregate. It came as liquefaction at the base of her spine, a mimicry of desire. *You settled to wait and find out, ain't you?*

It was late. She was tired to death of Pelican Bay, a life not her own, a featureless future into which she could not quite draw the energy to escape. She looked at Trudy's neat piles and remembered how Cassius had folded her clothes. She didn't know — there had not been time to learn — whether they could have loved in this daily, sock-worshipping way.

18

WAITING AGAIN. Waiting for Adena to call or show up in the whirl of whatever hurt or fury she might bring. Waiting for any sign that the Hustons were in pursuit. Waiting for some word from Cassius, or, lacking word, her own capacity to give up on it.

None of these things happened. Trudy continued to come in the evenings all week (after dark, however), methodically emptying cupboards, boxing rummage, sorting trash. Herbie rebuilt the back steps and installed a fan in the crawl space to minimize wet rot. Phoebe sent an impenetrable pile of briefs on "testamentary capacity."

Phoebe. Must be right again, though it was her own fault. She was the one who'd introduced the phantom of the horse. Phoebe was immune to love since her divorce. She had flings but she didn't have relationships. She viewed the opposite gender as a diversified portfolio: friendship, confidences, giggles, sex—you wouldn't risk your assets on a single stock.

Anyway, the horse, neither white nor black but the muscled color of Cassius's skin—was that called *bay* on a horse?—appeared against her will, Cassius bareback, in cutoffs, denim vest; horse and man fused into a gleaming centaur galloping along the Sag Island surf. She lay on the couch in the heat, flushed through her whole body with the humming image of it, desire she had never felt as an adult, but reborn out of half-remembered songs and films, hyper lit, forbidden; the midlife resurrection of some ineluctable adolescent yearning.

In the first week of August, Tropical Storm Bertha formed just east of the Mississippi mouth, meandered over southern Louisiana and back into the Gulf. Briefly, it picked up speed. Business also sharply picked up at Solly's Corner. Dana ran out of candles, Sterno, charcoal, and masking tape. There was some talk of evacuating Sag Island. Dana asked Herbie if she should tape her windows, but Herbie shrugged. "Time enough if she gets up to strength." Hurricane strength, he meant. And in fact Bertha swiped at the panhandle, wimped into south Texas, and fell apart, though not until she had taken one life in the high surf off Pensacola.

"We live in the land of near misses, that's a fact," said Mrs. Usvedt.

"Dumb-ass surfers," Sarah said.

One morning Dana woke at six and, brushing her teeth at the kitchen sink, saw a car stop just beyond the drive-in to the gas pumps. A hard horizontal rain was lashing them, the last gasp of Bertha, downgraded to a depression. The car was an old tank of a sedan, maybe even a V-8, Cadillac or Olds, dusty blue. Her heart stopped because it was the color of Cassius's car, but it was nothing like the shape of Cassius's Pontiac. It pulled ahead ten feet or so. It backed. The rain hammered its wide roof. It started a clumsy maneuver to turn around in the narrow road when it could easily have pulled into Solly's drive. By the time it crept toward the highway at ten miles an hour, her heart was beating as hard as the rain. The Hustons? Someone casing the joint? But the next clear evening the car came back and a polite old man with grizzled sideburns helped Trudy load the boxes for East Sink.

The next afternoon Herbie brought over a "Nurit point-of-sale cash register with a spectra-physics scanner" that his brother-in-law was selling "practically out-of-the-box, super cheap." Dana resisted briefly, but in the end reasoned that whatever modernized the store would have Adena's approval and make it more salable, too. Herbie installed the computer beside the old brass cash register (which instantly took on the cachet of an antique) and bolted it down, explaining that in the old days thieves would grab the cash, whereas with these new lightweights, they'd make off with the whole thing underarm. He was right about its simplicity; he taught her the basic use of it in an afternoon.

Every evening she asked Trudy if she'd had a letter from Perry Hoyt, but none came, and by Friday morning her nerves were not amused. She stood on the store's front porch with the *Tallahassee Democrat,* skimming the In Brief items, her first cigarette making her queasy. Maybe it was time to give it up again. Kim Jong-Il, she read, had ordered seven thousand sparrows slaughtered for the down to make his duvet. Governor Jeb Bush ("Baby Bush," the locals called him, some fondly and some not) had complained of "soft bigotry" against "people of faith." In Brunswick, Georgia, Atlantic Mills had announced the closing of its operation at a loss to the area of two thousand jobs.

She read this again. It gave a tentative closing date of October first. The land had been acquired for development by Speculum Properties, Inc., of Weehawken, New Jersey. The art collection of the plant's previous owner, eccentric benefactor Abel Croft, was to be dispersed by the family to various museums. Where two thousand employees would be dispersed it did not say.

It was three weeks to the day since she'd sat over lobster and Hennessey with Gavin McGarvey while he praised the recycling schemes and the utopian worker conditions of Atlantic Mills. She had liked him, flirted with him. She had thought him, by contrast with her image of the typical CEO, capable of playfulness and nuance. Nuance indeed. There was no possibility he hadn't known that the mill was to close.

Whole ghettos, whole generations whose lives were bound up in the making of paper, who had never lived in air free of that sulfur stench, would be thrown into unemployment, dumped into cities or other mill towns. What would happen to Cassius? Which of the

Huston family chipper guards and stokers might try to sign on at Lhamon Paper? How many would be jobless? Recycled into poverty? And how had Gavin McGarvey and his confreres upped the ante on her own next move?

The paper folded and refolded on the counter to display, like a talisman of change, the paragraph "In Brief," the sick lift in her stomach compounded of rage and hope, she stood still running the tape loop through her mind (Cassius was a security guard, not a mill hand, so he wasn't dependent on the paper trade, but would that make it harder or easier to find work near home? Forced to make a fundamental life change in any case, would it make it easier to break away?)—when she looked up from the counter to see Herbie hovering, Coke in hand, popping the door to the cold-drinks case. The rubber gusset made a sucking sound.

"You got a minute?"

"Sure. What's up?"

"Well, I was thinking. My sister and them are headed up to Marietta Sunday. It means—like, I'll have a get a place of my own or either go up with them."

"Oh, I'm sorry. I hadn't thought."

"Is what I was thinking is, if you're not going back to the cabin, I could trade you work for rent. I got some saved so I won't need much else. And we could see to the roof."

Truth was, she'd meant to move back into the cabin a week ago. The floor was possum proofed, the crawl space had a fresh lattice skirting, the gutters were running clean. Here she still slept on the couch because, even if she had by fluke and the belligerence of an old man inherited, it was not her place.

On the other hand. If Herbie worked eight hours a day five days a week times fifteen dollars that would be six hundred a week. The rent on the cabin would pay for nearly half. The rest she could make up out of what Solly had paid to Trudy and Adena. Couldn't she? She'd check with Hoyt whether they could start drawing on their bequests. Herbie could make repairs, help out when it was busy, and sometimes let her get away to swim and sun—the all-but-forgotten purposes of littoral paradise. Why not?

"If it suits you," Herbie said.

She said, "Why not?"

It was after eleven when Adena called. Dana was upstairs settling her underwear into the emptied drawers. She knew it was Adena, had been expecting the call ever since Trudy came by at nine with a letter from Perry Hoyt. There was no phone upstairs, and she made her way deliberately down to the living room, letting it ring, knowing that Adena knew there was no upstairs phone.

"Hello?"

A swallowed silence. A gulp for breath. "Dana? I guess you've heard from Perry . . ." You could hear the raw throat, the engorged sinuses, the flushed nasal septum of a good long cry.

"Yeah," Dana said. "Adena, listen . . ." Had McGarvey felt like this, guilty for having known what it wasn't his to divulge?

"Solly was crazy, you know. I'm not the first one to find that out the hard way."

"I don't want the store."

"He's been off for a long time. I didn't like to say so. When I think of the past five years . . ."

"I know you looked after him . . ."

"Vindictive old devil. Haven't you known people, strangers think they're the cat's meow, and they're a tyrant to their own families?"

"Yes, I have. Have you talked to Hoyt? Apparently it's not as easy as saying I don't want it, because it doesn't default to anybody. I have to *get* it to give it back. So just tell me what you want, and I'll do it. Do you want to put it on the market?"

There was a pause at the other end while Adena blew her nose and Dana studied the kindergarten handprints on the rock-candy jar. She swallowed. "I know Solly hurt you . . ."

"It was meant to hurt me."

"He was old and sick."

"It runs in the family. Bucky was just the same."

"I know what you mean," said Dana, who didn't, quite.

"One time Bucky and I were feuding. I can't remember what it was about—you can never remember what it was about, can you?

He started asking this secretary from the front office down to the canteen for lunch. Big girl, she was, lots of leg and hair, lots of bone. She'd come down to eat with the men and then Bucky would go around asking the guys please if they didn't mind just not to let on this girl had been there. Lola her name was — Lulu — something. So naturally the first thing they'd do is go home and tell their wives. They loved it. Their wives loved it. It got back to me inside a week. I laid into Bucky, and he stonewalled and turned around and did the same thing the next week, and it'd get back to me, and so forth. So this goes on for a few weeks, Bucky showing up later every night, till I'm steaming out my ears, and I go over to Pensacola to get a piece of this Lola, or Lulu. Had to sweet-talk a floor boss to get her address, drove over there one night about half past midnight. She comes to the door in her skivvies, her 'partner' right behind her, butch as a beanbag. Laugh! They thought they'd die."

"Did Bucky know?"

Adena let out a plosive breath. "That she was lesbo? That was his whole point. That's what I'm *telling* you."

A memory of Graham surfaced: a fortnight in Hawaii, jubilantly planned, which had begun in the five-star bedroom with Graham sending back a coddled egg. An egg! And it had gone downhill from there. She'd said, martyrish, "It makes me uncomfortable to have people waiting on me." And he, lofty: "I can understand that, with your background." And all the celestial cliffs, the divine hibiscus, the cerulean sea — all were dragged over the psychic mudflats because he couldn't stomach a teaspoonful of undercooked albumen and she couldn't forgive him for it.

But Adena did not seem to play by the rules of girl talk, tit for tat, *I understand you because I have felt the same.*

"That doesn't sound like Solly, though."

"What?"

"Wanting to humiliate someone."

Adena hiccupped. "Solly resented me since long before the divorce. We call old people cranky and stubborn when they're just malicious. Look how he used you. Look how he used poor Perry."

Even if a friendship had not developed between them, this ought to be a happy business. That was the agenda: Dana would announce her generosity and Adena her gratitude, and together they would avert injustice, countering the forces of pique and greed. Wasn't that the agenda? Outside under a streetlight a towhead boy of ten or so was teasing a pair of feral cats. He tore minute pellets of something and landed them a foot nearer on each toss. When the cats prowled within a couple of yards he would charge, juking left and right. His hair was brutally shorn, his wide-leg trousers hung stiff from hip to ankle, a style so pervasive that he might be the son of a local fisher or a preppie down from New York.

"Listen, Adena. I don't want the place. I agree with you. It should have gone to you. So you can have it."

As if she had suddenly caught up, or waked up, Adena plunged forward. "Oh, god. Oh, god, that's so . . . that's so . . . you're such a good *person,* Dana."

Dana grasped at this. "I think you're right about a lot of things. That sign—I don't know that the tree has to come down, but it could be trimmed. Herbie Zebrowski can repaint the sign. And there could be another one at the highway."

"Uh-huh . . ."

"And you were right about selling beach stuff. Weekends, we get a lot of tourists. In fact, we ought to be open seven days a week."

Adena hummed in the back of her throat. "You don't have to stick around for this. Perry can do it all by fax."

"But the better shape the store's in, the more you'll get for it."

"People always think that, but—you know, they put in a pool or redo the kitchen—and then they don't make back their outlay."

"But surely it's a question . . ."

"I can send Bernadette to help you."

"I don't think she likes it here."

"It'll be good for her."

"You don't need to, really."

"But *I will.* And listen," Adena said, "I'll get over this week to clear out Solly's things."

Dana fumbled. Guilty-when-innocent was her stance. The years of being the new girl in the school, the one who arrived in the middle of term, the stringy one with the hippy mom. It had left her with this legacy of never quite knowing, never guessing right, where the power was, who was the lead girl, who the gossip, who the sneak. "Trudy has already cleared it out."

"Cleared out what?"

"Solly's things."

"Trudy has!?"

"She loved him, you know." Dana heard chair legs rasp against a floor. The air at the end of the phone took a few surflike lifts and crashes, and then the sobs came, rising, diminishing. "You've accomplished a *lot*."

Dana said, "Get a good night's rest and we'll talk soon."

She set down the old receiver, closed the shop door, picked up a stray T-shirt and belt from the living room, mounted toward the beveled mirror on the landing. Trudy had deep dusted everything with some stuff that left a waxy scent. The cupboards were emptied, the drawers wiped out. In the gilded twenties frame Dana's face, overlaid with flecks of rust, looked lean and tired. Her hair was nearly down to her shoulder blades.

She said to her reflection, "You're doing the right thing. Absolutely." Then she went back down, took a metal spatula from the kitchen, went back up and attacked the piano with long, digging scoops. Top, back, sides, front, piano bench, she sheered off the pickling wherever it would yield. The paint chips flew. Lucky that the wood was sturdy and the varnish weak.

She stood back. Surveyed the field. A piano in battle rags, long gouges in its yellowed paint, scars in the glazing, the floor a field of trampled snow. She let the spatula fall and went to Solly's bed.

19

IN SOME PLACES September is already autumn. On the Gulf it is a sour dishrag, wrung at four or five every afternoon onto the tourist-excavated sand, which it leaves pocked with giant drops and crosshatched with the rush of gulls. On Pelican Bay the miasma of paper manufacture hangs at eye level, and everybody's eyes sting either with that or with *Gymnodinium breve,* red tide, the threat of which sends the oyster dredgers into dour and sometimes apocalyptic mode. At Solly's Corner the two rush hours were double rushed because school had started and the mothers of toddlers stopped by on the way to and from the bus. By Labor Day Herbie had trimmed the twisted pine and repainted the Solly's Corner sign in bright yellow and deep blue ("Morton Salt colors," he said. "Proved to be eye-catchy.") — with such immediate success that the weekenders on their way to Sag Island and Sea Oat Dunes spilled in for flip-flops and salted nuts and four kinds of imported beer. The ancient air conditioner wheezed and all but capitulated. Dana kept the fans running, but the coolers sweated and the chocolate sagged.

Herbie said, "Man, if you put in a new AC you'd save half what you pay to keep the freezer going," and Dana shrugged, agreeing.

Tropical Storms Edouard and Gustav sidled up the Atlantic Coast; their sister Fay twisted around the Gulf from Apalachicola to Palacio, missing Pelican Bay entirely but for a few squalls and minor squalor.

The anniversaries came around: September 6, the day she had come into the living room and felt the pulse in Graham's neck (at the time she thought: the way you check fruit for ripeness; *ripeness is all*) and had called the paramedics, but he was gone. September 11, the day she and Phoebe took a limousine to the funeral, ignorant of how vast a cremation was in progress not only in New York and at the Pentagon but in the smoke they passed beyond the Shanksville farmhouse. This anniversary was observed by the Bushes ("Big Bushes" as opposed to "Baby Bush") with a quick round of wreath-laying ceremonies, and on Sag Island with a candlelight vigil that several teenagers crassly took as occasion to use up fireworks left-over from the Fourth.

At Solly's Corner the women *tsk*ed and *hmm*ed about that day, but except for Marion Attles's grandson in Afghanistan, it didn't seem to have changed them much. It was impossible to know, really. Just as it would have been impossible to guess, a year ago, that, here, now, is where she'd be.

She had a staff of three. Herbie moved into the cabin with Dudley Do-Right, equally ready to patch the roof or man the till. Trudy stole in at night to tidy up and stock the shelves. Bernadette, true to her mother's word, began showing up regularly after school and Saturdays in a new used fire-engine-red Camaro whose fenders she lovingly caressed with her black manicure. For a while Dana mistrusted the advent of this third reinforcement, then she was bemused by it, and then, when Bernadette waved away her wages—"Just keep track, it goes to Mom"—she figured out that the Camaro had been advanced as a bribe. Which probably meant Bernadette was set here to spy.

That Herbie was in love with Bernadette put him, no doubt, among a pack of several dozen. Still, the bleak, mute swagger of it, the amateur attempt at indifference, was endearing to Dana, conscious of her own romantic failings. Herbie dogged Bernadette's footsteps the same way Dudley dogged his own. He would invent late-afternoon repairs that brought him into the shop when Bernadette was there. He would wash down the pumps on Saturdays, peripherally buffing up her car. Then, metamorphosing from handyman to geek, he would join Dana at the till to teach her in Bernadette's earshot the finer points of computer accountancy. If Bernadette bent to scratch Dudley behind his long hound ears, Herbie would beam and swell as if she'd done something clever.

Bernadette did not notice, but then she noticed little. She could place items on a shelf or in a plastic bag; she could work the register and count out change. No one would think to ask more of her. She'd had the blue ends of her hair cut off, leaving three inches of natural platinum that she glazed and corkscrewed into spikes around her milkmaid eyes. She wore fingerless black lace gloves and miniskirts with plastic boots. She wore vestigial bits of trailing crepe or hung a chain from her navel ring to the belt loops of her jeans. She was a walking experiment in the sartorial grotesque, each oddment of which made her more exquisite. She had the languid, sleep-eyed look of chosen ignorance and the sleepwalking gait of latent sex. It would be hard to posit a more open invitation to the world. But she was unaware of it, being totally absorbed in a ketchup spot that had somehow attached itself to the hem of her midriff top, or a patch of sunlight on her enameled toes.

One afternoon she blinked at Herbie's forearm and asked, "What's that?"

Herbie stretched his arm out on the counter, preening, if Herbie could be said to preen. He had taken to brushing his hair upward from both sides so it formed a quiff like a barely cresting brown wave on top of his head. The thing on his arm seemed to be a rectangle within a rectangle, the acid green-black peculiar to injected ink, with a couple of doughnut holes and a few vertical strips of skin showing through.

"That's a space heater," he said proudly.

"A spa-ace heater," Bernadette affirmed.

"Why a space heater?" Dana wanted to know. "As opposed to an eagle or a rose?"

"Or a devil," suggested Bernadette.

"Nobody else *had* a space heater." Herbie swiped the far hand up his arm, lifting the sleeve of his T-shirt to expose his biceps. In fact, he did have both an eagle and a rose tacking back and forth above the tattoo in question. And in fact he did have (all that roofing and hammering) a considerable if pallid biceps, which he clenched to make the eagle ripple.

Dana laughed appreciatively. "But what makes your generation so fond of tattoos? Are you punishing the flesh?"

Bernadette took up eagerly, "It's how you *express* yourself. It's how you show your *individuality.*"

This was the first time Bernadette had ever praised Herbie, or seemed to praise him. His face flamed, and she, suddenly also awkward, rubbed the back of her hand down her skirt, fingers clawed.

Since her talk with Adena, Dana was feeling itchy, querulous, inclined to tears. Maybe it was the heavy weather or else she was still just making heavy weather of her limbo, marking time. Food sat lumpen on her stomach. Her energy came in fits and starts. When she lay in bed at night she invoked the phantom piles of clothing, the scant things Cassius had folded on the bureau at Jekyll Island, the stacks of Solly's old shirts and trousers Trudy had set on this quilt where she lay. She invited these images to her mind's eye because she could no longer picture Cassius. His face was fixed and fragmented at once, no more alive than snapshots in an album: his forehead at this angle in such and such a light, his dark hand placed so on her thigh. She could not be sure she would recognize him if he walked into Solly's Corner.

Be here, be here.

You can book it down.

You know how to do everything, don't you?

Phoebe said, "You have to get past it. It's just the nature of infatuation." Phoebe said, "Your heart gets captured and your mind goes to sleep. Feelings change; that's what feelings do. You'll wake up one morning and say: *what was all that about?*" But this did not convince her. It only made her itchy, querulous, inclined to tears.

On impulse one afternoon she invited Herbie upstairs to look at the piano. She had cleaned up the debris again, and she made no reference to how it had got in this awful state, just said it was a shame and asked if he thought it could be stripped.

Herbie fingered the ravaged honey glaze. "Weh-yeah, sure. You'll want a Strip-A-Way number seven that sorta sucks the paint and varnish up. You hood it, like, with a plastic sheet, to keep it soft. I can do it if you want me to, no sweat."

"Wouldn't it need to be outside?"

"Naw, this stuff they got now is envir'nmental friendly. You want goggles and gloves, maybe the windows open and a fan."

So Herbie went off to Panama City to buy Strip-A-Way and goggles while Dana paved the floor with old issues of the *Democrat*. According to Herbie she'd made a lot of work for herself when she stripped the hutch. You didn't want to sand, because the surface had been prepared before it was varnished the first time. The idea was to soften and wipe away the old coats without roughing up the wood.

And in fact the piano was denuded and revealed with amazing speed. Herbie worked at it mornings, Dana dealing in the evening with the fiddly bits, carved corners, grooving, the cutouts of the music stand. The stripper absorbed the pickling and the varnish to form a dirty cottage cheese, which they lifted off with the shirts Trudy had thought too disreputable to give away. They worked from top to bottom, and the burled walnut appeared as if peeled out of a husk. It was a warmer color than the oak had been, paler, its striations fine and flat. It gave off a luster. Dana had a sense of larval transformation, of freeing a creature that it would only take a decent pianist to set in flight. She herself could not play, of course. But it occurred to her that frog princes and tree nymphs came from some deep identification with the bursting of a cocoon. People saw it happen in the insect world, mythologized it, and anyone could feel the force of the idea: entrapment and rebirth.

She admitted this turn of mind to Phoebe on the phone, but Phoebe said, "What interests *me* is how hyped you get about laundry and old furniture. I'm not putting you down! It's interesting. It's the real 'eternal feminine,' maybe, taking care of people, taking care of things. Whereas men manufacture things that are meant to self-destruct, and take people with them."

But next day, thinking they were nearly done, Herbie peeled the tape off the keys and frowned at lines of greenish grit on the adhesive. He poked hard at a few discordant notes. "D'you see any dust puff up between the keys?"

"Maybe a little. What is it?" Dana asked.

"Looks to me like there's Paris green in there. Arsenic trioxide? They used it a lot b'cause we've got so many borers in this damp. But I wouldn't keep it around the house."

"Can we vacuum it out?"

"Naw. I need to take the front off and wipe it down."

"How do you know about all this stuff, Herbie?"

"I guess you learn it growing up."

"Not most people."

"Well, my dad was a builder—houses and boats and all."

Knowing how to dismantle a piano was another matter, but Herbie studied up on the Web, and next day he removed the hinges of the lid over the keys and unscrewed the front panel, revealing the felted hammers and their intricate striking mechanism. The powder lay in wavy lines like bright green dust. Together Dana and Herbie, gloved and masked, dampened rags and threaded them under the action levers, gingerly pulling them through the width of the piano, plopping them in a plastic bag.

"If it's this dangerous, how come they didn't know it?"

"Beats me. My dad—he did roofs all his life down here, and he always said that was a bunch o' hooey about asbestos. But then he got lymphoma, so I guess—I dunno."

Dana wondered if Mrs. Solly had likewise put herself in harm's way—year after year bending over these keys teaching Bach melodies to bucktoothed kids, puffs of arsenic trioxide rising alike from the right notes and the wrong.

Herbie said, "I'm'a take the pedal case off, too. Better safe than sorry, yeah?"

So he carefully unscrewed the lower case, and they lifted it off, tilting it forward to reveal the iron frame, the strings, the bass and treble belly bridges. They hoisted it carefully against the wall and peered into the raw case. In the space underneath, the emerald powder lay lightly on the soft and damper pedals, on the pedal boards, and on the carcass of a four-foot garden snake.

Herbie whistled.

Dana remembered, "If y' gonna live in Paradise . . ."

Green over green, the snake stretched as straight as a rope deliberately laid. It was delicately scaled, dry, perfect, even its black eye preserved from insects by the lethal powder that had killed it. Herbie poked it with his gloved finger, and a section of the skin flaked and disintegrated, as brittle as the carapace of a caryatid.

So much for transformation. Herbie touched the thing again, and again its scales broke apart and fell to dust in the poison dust, revealing this time an inch or two of the vertebrae, still intact. And suddenly, ineluctably, Chloe was in her mind. Chloe in her coffin, the evanescence of dust and death. Tears vaulted to her eyes.

"It's nothing to be scared of . . . ," Herbie said, but trailed off, seeing that "scared of" was not the point. "Hey," he said.

They scooped the snake out in sections with a spatula (the same one she'd attacked the piano with in the first place), dragged their damp rags through, and bound spatula and all into the plastic bag.

"You'll need to get it tuned," he pointed out.

Saturday morning she placed the Monday orders with the Produce Collective and Appleyard Dairy, signed for the gas fill-up from the tanker, and served the bait-and-beer crowd and the kids with their burning allowances. So it was noon before she left Bernadette in the store and took the mail back to her living room for a coffee break.

The postcard was on top. It showed a montage of Talladega National Forest: waterfalls, Odum Trail, a white-tailed deer, a topiary of Smoky Bear. The postmark was Tupelo, Mississippi. It was addressed as before to *Trudy Lewis c/o Sollys Corner.* It said: *Traveling with K. She is OK. Hoping to see DC. Love, C.*

She fingered the cryptic initials: *K, OK, DC, C.* She set it on the coffee table. Carefully, as it might be blown glass. She sorted through the rest of the bills and circulars. The shudder in her viscera was dangerously close to anger. *Traveling with K.* could only mean his daughter—Kenisha, wasn't it? Which meant that he had kidnapped her? Or that they were on a holiday? *DC* meant either District of Columbia or Dana Cleveland. But traveling from Alabama to Missisipi, he'd be going the wrong direction for either one. Was it intended as a code? A reassurance he would eventually show up? How could you know?

She turned the card over and over, set it down. He hadn't been able (willing?) to tell her whether the earlier postcard was meant for her, so there was no way to know whether this one was. It might be very clever or it might be an accident or it might be clever and he not realize it.

He offered her too little, at intervals too great. He had told her she was ignorant of black ways, and she was. This was genuine, rock-bottom ethnic *difference.* He did not trust telephones and treated all plans as contingent. He was honest but he was not given to explain. Well, that was male, partly, but it was male overlaid with a lifetime's wariness. How could she pledge fidelity to layers of hidden motive, alien indirection, unnecessary feint-and-parry? She only needed him to come out with it.

She endured the afternoon, the evening news (*"Saddam says anyone who attacks Iraq will die in 'disgraceful failure'"*), a sandwich of mayo and Virginia ham (sell-by date: tomorrow), a debate between a professor of astronomy and a born-again senator regarding the imminent likelihood of the Rapture, and a fitful fifteen minutes' nap until she heard the key in the back door.

"Trudy? Can you come in here a minute?"

Trudy, already broom in hand, set the broom against the door, hung a rag on it, complained of September, established that she was fine, that Dana was fine, and sat. It would be untrue to say that they had grown easy with each other. The opposite: unease had lent their dealings a formality that had become ritual, as if they had over these few weeks acquired the mutual deference that she and Cassius had adopted instinctively. So Dana knew that Trudy would accept a coffee and a cookie, preferably chocolate chip, but not wine or beer or any kind of cheese; that to suggest she need not clean would insult her and deny her purpose; that she would likewise disdain to be paid because "Solly done took care of it," and to accept money from Dana would diminish both his status and hers. She was a widow, not a maid. Her rights to this house and store consisted of maintaining her position in it, which included caretaking but also the right to an opinion. Her knowledge of Solly was her claim on him, and that he had known his mind when he left the store to Dana was the article of faith proving her superior to Adena. Trudy in her turn understood that to recommend Jesus would be found tiresome, and that she might nevertheless sometimes choose to be tiresome in this way. She knew that Dana would invite her to stay and watch some kinds of trash TV but not others (which Trudy might prefer), and that Dana would strangely take it as a compliment if Trudy picked up her crochet hook and an afghan square. Moreover, Dana knew approximately that Trudy knew these things, and vice versa. They had learned each other in fits and starts, mostly by the clumsy vernacular of body language.

So they turned it over together, Odum Trail and Smoky Bear, the Mississippi postmark, the ambiguity of "hope to see DC." Trudy did not know any better than Dana what Cassius meant them to think he meant. Code? Kidnap? Why was he on the road?

"Did he usually send you cards?"

"Oh, sometime, long time ago."

"Did Cassius ever stay in the cabin?"

"Yeah, one time he was maybe fourteen, fifteen. That was after I got laid off up at Lhamon. Mrs. Solly was still alive, and they aksed me in to clean because she was sickening. I had me a room at Big Emma's over East Sink, not room enough to swing a cat. The cabin was just built then, and Mr. Solly said if my folk wanted they could stay and he wouldn't charge 'em nothing. Cassius"—here she gave a bellow of a laugh—"he be still losing his baby fat—one day a hard man, all cool, and the next day some little bitty boy chile scooping minnows in the Gulf."

This was both the longest speech she had heard from Trudy and the first time she had heard her laugh since the night they met over the gas pumps. "Trudy," she said, "have you heard anything about the mill closing in Georgia?"

"Yeah-um, they talking about it over at Henry's this afternoon. Some them at the mill worrying will the floor workers come looking after jobs. But I don't see that. Lhamon got to know they got a riot on their hands, they just turn out they own workers for a new bunch ain't no better."

"Do you think Cassius' family might come looking for work there?"

"I'n't know nothing about them."

"Are you in touch with anybody?"

"I hear from my cousin Charlene around Christmastime."

"Could you call her? Would she know if Cassius has left? Or if he's taken Kenisha?"

Trudy was as wary of this notion as Cassius himself would have been. Her square body hunched in on itself. "I *could* call . . . ," she said doubtfully.

"But?"

"My sister' folk cut me off. I don't like to ask nothing 'bout them."

"But would you? Please?"

Trudy may have acquiesced. It was hard to tell. She bent her head in half a nod, turned it half a shake, deepened the sullen lines around her mouth, but bent to the basket on the floor at the end of the couch.

20

HANNA DEVELOPED as a tropical depression, meandered south of Pelican Bay, and made landfall near the Alabama-Mississippi border. Hurricane Isidore hit the coast of the Yucatán Peninsula, then moved north as a tropical storm to Louisiana, where four people drowned. Josephine and Kyle, remarkable for being a record seventh and eighth named September storms, kept to the Atlantic. Half a season had made Dana blasé about Weather Channel melodrama, but she'd also learned to be prepared. The shelves were stocked with water, batteries, and coals; she'd added rakes, rope, and rainbow-cased transistor radios, which became an item of choice for the middle-school contingent. Herbie's enthusiasm for improvement snowballed—or, considering the weather, gathered steam.

"You know what I could do, yeah? I could rent a sander, and I figure if we started on a Saturday when you close, I could strip the floors in the shop and get 'em polyurethaned two coats in time to open Monday morning."

"Do you think?"

"I could find out what it would cost to put in a new AC. Something high-tech, easy on the BTUs, you know?"

There was more. If you were installing AC anyway, you could do an extension off the east wall to store the spare stock and get it out of the living room. That'd mean you could do a kitchen island and a dining space. And a deck outside, said Dana.

Who, like the tropical depressions, changed tack more than once. She still swung between internal turbulence and malaise, and one moment she'd get caught up in Herbie's hype and blow on past him, then she'd get practical and try to wind him down. They came to an agreement that, like the piano, a refurbishing would have to begin at the top. Roof check and roof repair, first, and then the ceilings spackled and painted white. That could not be too expensive, Dana thought, and meanwhile it cost nothing to check out the AC. If you looked at it plainly, it was up to her what she spent on Solly's Corner. She was making the property more valuable, which would benefit Adena no matter what she said, and honor Solly's trust in her as well, since the one thing certain was that he'd cared about the place. If she dipped into her own money, she surely had the right to recover it when the store was sold. She'd be sure (hiring Perry Hoyt if necessary) that she was reimbursed.

So Herbie spent the dog days of September slantwise on the shingles, and Dana pored over fixture catalogs, neither quite committing to the project nor rejecting it. Either way it was a welcome distraction. Trudy had called her cousin Charlene, whose husband worked at Atlantic Mills. It was true about the closing. Her family was moving up the coast. Maybe to Pennsylvania; Atlantic was expanding some other mills. And yes, it was true that Cassius had left with his daughter. The whole Huston family was up in arms. Luther had filed a kidnap charge and the police had a warrant out.

This last Trudy did not believe. "You just settle now, and wait to see does Cassius get here. Because I knowed that Luther coming up, and he ain't gone to no *po*-lice."

Adena sailed in at noon in a shift of nubby turquoise with cutout embroidery. She enfolded Dana in the odor of hot J'adore. She laughed and unwrapped a Ferrero Rocher chocolate from the jar beside the register.

"I hoped I'd catch you alone. You know, with Solly's death and all, I never got the August payment, and it's time for the September one."

Dana said, "I understood from Perry you were getting an allowance from the bequest."

"Oh! That's different, isn't it? A different, um, *pot*. And you know, expenses are ferocious right now. Bernadette needs beaucoup new clothes. Well, you've seen the way she gets herself up, and at Emerson High everything is competition!"

"Trouble is, profits are pretty thin right now, with the repairs."

"What repairs?" When Adena focused, her whole body snapped into place. That seagrass wave of anger passed across her face.

"Nothing major, nothing that won't get back its outlay. Come on up, I'll show you how Herbie's fixed the ceilings between the beams."

Adena took the stairs ahead of her, scarcely glancing at the ceiling, its cracks plastered over, its color fresh. At the sight of the piano she laid a hand on her clavicle and let drop her mouth. "Oh!" She slid her fingers over the surface, now French-waxed to a buttery glow. "Winifred's pia-a-a-no," she said. Dana did not remember ever hearing Mrs. Solly's first name before. "Oh, I *learned* on this thing. Oh, god. It used to be white."

"Honey glazed."

Adena wilted sideways onto the bench and lifted the cover. She spread and arched her fingers over the keys in a convincing look of imminent concert, and let them fall hard on the first bars of "A Mighty Fortress Is Our God." The force of her playing shook the old floorboards and carried her on through the off-key twanging of the first few lines.

> . . . *Our helper He amid the flood of mortal ills prevailing.*

Adena belted in an alto fortissimo. Her small hands, amazingly muscled, pounded surely on the unsure notes. She played as she talked, all out there, nothing held back. Herbie appeared in the doorway with a spackling knife.

> *For still our ancient foe doth seek to work us woe;*
> *His craft and power are great, and armed with cruel hate . . .*

Here Adena's emotion got the better of her, and she trailed off, spread her arms, bent and embraced the keyboard to all its length. Minor-key vibrations hung in the air.

"I didn't know you played," Dana said resentfully.

Adena lifted her head and stroked the music stand, eyes misty, mouth brave. "You didn't have it *tuned*!" Herbie and Dana glanced at each other in a swallowing way. They had peeled the husk from this piano. They had scoured it of poison and a snake. They were proud of it, and possessive. But a piano is to play.

"Winifred *promised* me this piano."

Herbie said, "*Solly* didn't play."

Adena sighed, "Poor Solly. Couldn't bear to part with it."

This made no sense at all. Dana had an intimation—not the first—of Adena's power, peculiar because unearned. She was pretty, she was voluble, she was persistent, she was smart—but no more any of those things than a lot of the women in West Sink who lived on minimum wage or couldn't find a job. What Adena had (how had she come by it?) was amazing self-esteem. She was empowered. She was entitled. These were attributes to admire. A feminist's feminist. So why should Dana grudge a piano she couldn't herself play?

They left it that Herbie would look into how to get the piano down the stairs. Adena would check into tuners in Pensacola. Adena was "thrilled." She was "dazzled" by the work they'd done refinishing. She was *really grateful* for the check Dana wrote to help out Bernadette. She was almost out the shop door when she turned and leaned against the jamb.

"Oh, yeah, if you see some guys poking around the woods tomorrow, don't freak out. They're just appraisers down from Lempicke and Zetti."

"Appraisers of what?"

"*You* know. The land. Perry *told* you."

"You're going to sell the woods?"

"Duh, Dana!" Adena forked her fingers through her hair, which was unbound today. "Lempicke and Zetti are the real deal." Then, abruptly, she pitched herself upright. Shrugged. "Not that they're prob'ly interested, little patch of marsh and palmetto bugs. But I just didn't want to freak you out."

Too late.

Dana closed up at seven as usual, and as she often did, she sprayed herself with Cutters and headed through the rough grass toward the woods. She straddled a fallen pine whose disinterred roots rose to frame one side of her view. The days were shortening now, so beyond the roots and the road, beyond the puny skyline of Pelican Bay, beyond the bridge to Sag Island and the far western reach of the sea, the reliable wonder was already in the works. Wisps of cirrus dashed above the horizon. A mammoth disc of red-hot copper slipped from cloud to cloud, seeming to hesitate, to elongate sideways as it descended—flinching from the sea, where it would be put out with a cosmic hiss. You were supposed to avoid looking at this even with sunglasses on, but that was impossible. Like an alp, a volcano, a canyon, it impelled the eye with its size and implacable rhythm. *How small are you? How brief? What does it matter what you desire?*

She sat until the spectacle disappeared, then wandered in twilight as she often did to stretch her store-punished legs. The woods were pine and mangrove, myrtle, palmetto and the occasional cypress, the soft ground dipping here and there deep enough to outline an algae-covered pond, or simply sloughing into swamp grass so you were ankle deep before you knew it. She thought of this plot as "the woods." She had known in some part of her brain that it was Solly's big backyard, but she hadn't consciously registered it as belonging to anyone in particular, let alone as the forty-five acres Hoyt said fell to her.

The land fronted the highway for five hundred feet or so, then stretched back behind West Sink so that the whole tract formed a fat-footed *L* with Solly's Corner at the farthest reach of the foot. Spanish bayonet and prickly pear, nicker bean and bloodberry, yucca—the land had a barbed and defended air. Several acres inland the marsh was skirted by a path that looped beyond the houses and met up with Devil's Sink. West Sink towheads often came to catch polliwogs in the ponds, and from East Sink the black kids came the long way round to do the same. Two of these stood on the far side of the pond now, one with a bamboo pole, among saltbush, pokeberry, and a mud turtle sunning on a cypress knee. All three creatures misjudged her. The boys turned and ran; the turtle plopped into the water and disappeared into the cypress stain.

"It's all right!" she called. Too late. She had already freaked them out.

She remembered her father's joke about "a swamp I could sell you," but of course by now the wetlands had become prime real estate all around Florida. Filled, they supported malls and mansions, they turned into beaches and luxury hotels, spas where you could get your nails done for two hundred dollars an hour.

She could see it. It made perfect sense. The beaches around here were all built up or bought up. "Second tier" and "third tier" houses on Sag Island were selling for half a million even if they didn't have a view. On Solly's land Lempicke & Zetti, "real deal" developers, could do McMansions right across the road from water, and others on stilts that could look over them to the bay. Or they could build a tract facing inward on itself, around this pond, say; incorporate Solly's Corner as a curiosity. Or tear it down. West Sink would eventually be eaten up and the owners become rich. They would wall off East Sink at first so as to keep a supply of minimum wagers, but eventually the regentrification would take in that side, too, and the grandchildren of the people who now came in to buy hot dogs and Dr. Scholl's would take a profit and move inland.

This pond, no more than twenty feet across, had a narrow beach of black silt from the fertile land to the north, mixed with the backwash of pearly sand, so it was both dark and shining. The brackish water, cypress stained, winked in the last of the pink sky through the pines. Here and there little clusters of gnats moved as one cloudlike creature. Invisible in the undergrowth and underground there lay whole towns of rodent and insect, reptile and crustacean life, coexisting in territory nevertheless excavated and defended. Those, too, would move inland or die off.

To be at the edge of water brought memories of the edge of water. The fountain where her father floated paper. A slow red river in Tennessee. A pebbled stream in the desert. The lake in Montana paved with pastel shale where her mother, always "of two minds" about whether to wade or nap, joined them for once, laughing and bucking as she splashed. The beach at Jekyll Island where Cassius edged his vest up the sand. The boardwalk into the sea where she had swum alone while he slept above her. These memories came not in sequence but layered in her, the texture of life as a transient. Images of impermanence, images of loss. She fished a cigarette out of her pocket and put it back again.

She went to the house and called Phoebe.

"She's going to sell the whole caboodle."

"Uh-huh."

"They'll put in a Winn-Dixie or a Wal-Mart, but they won't put the money into the town, they'll take it back to the shareholders. They'll buy out the fishing industry and hide fish farms behind the boutiques."

"So?"

"I thought I was taking hold by heading down here on my own. But look at me—I'm waiting for one man who won't speak his mind and pinned here by another, some old geezer, stuck between his—I don't even know what—generosity, or spite?—and a flake with a stronger claim than me."

"So what are you going to do?"

"I'm going to tell Herbie to get the AC guy out." Phoebe laughed. "At least I can make it hard for them to bulldoze the store."

"Don't spend too much of your own money."

"And I'm sending back your lighter."

"No shit. Did you give up again?"

"It doesn't agree with me—makes me queasy in the morning." There was an arrhythmic pause. The floodlight outside the jalousies came on and lit up the oak. She waited. Phoebe always had something useful or provocative to say, some angle she hadn't thought of. "What?"

"When was your last period?"

"Oh, I've been off schedule ever since Graham died. Honestly, I told you. We were careful."

"How careful?"

"Very. Absolutely. Do not complicate my head."

But of course it was not quite true. There was that first fierce time when she chased the Chevy from Atlantic Mills. Cassius had taken the back stairs of the Ramada three steps at a time.

Phoebe said, "If you're sure."

Dana said, "Not to worry."

It was after eight. But there was a late-night drugstore at Winona Crossing.

21

WHAT NEXT?

The black man showed up on a Friday. She saw him first in the rough beside the highway and mistook him for one of the Lempicke & Zetti guys, but those had worn long pants and carried clipboards. This one had a khaki shorts outfit and the bulk of a linebacker viewed from the far end of the field. Then Jessie demanded her attention complaining about the rise in the price of Jif, and after that it was the 10 A.M. upchuck, regular as clockwork, for which she had to run upstairs because the downstairs john was in use again. Herbie said they should replumb and build on a men's and a women's, or else with this many customers who'd been on the road since Sopchoppy or Panacea, they'd overwhelm the septic tank, and then where would they be?

The next time she saw the man it was toddler-and-primary hour, the aisles clogged with hand-me-down strollers and six-year-olds at the candy jars, and he had his back to her, taking, it seemed, a leisurely inventory of her soft-drinks selection. He had a blunt shaved head over which the dark skin looked as if it had been jerked tight, the excess settling in folds around his nape. He moseyed to the snacks and then the canned-goods aisle (marking time, she thought, a little sliver of wariness tracking up her spine) till the kid crowd cleared out. People she didn't know came into the store every day, but there was something both random and purposeful in the way this one moved, browsing labels, putting the boxes back, not really looking to buy. She was glad Herbie was in the stairwell putting a second coat of antique white on the walls. She studied an order blank, watching the man at the periphery of her vision as he ambled to the counter with his small selection, and she looked up in an effort at offhand.

"Afternoon," he said, a genuine basso mellowing up from his viscera. He was over six feet and thick as a truck. The khaki shirt had a spate of pockets on its hind and fore tails—pockets pleated, zippered, Velcroed, buttoned, webbed, double sided, double stitched.

"Good afternoon. Will that be it?"

"Yes, ma'am." He scooped a wallet from his hip and fingered out a few dollar bills, the fingers fat as Jimmy Dean links but moving sensuously, precisely, as if the feel of the money was delicious to them. "Though there is some information you might could give me if you would be so kind."

Her stomach clenched—no, it was her *womb* that clenched, a hard knot in her groin with little radiating tentacles of fear like an anemone. She rang up the bill and cocked her head, noncommittal.

"I wonder do you know a Mrs. Trudy Lewis—a colored lady; she would be getting on in years." He spoke in a soft boom, letting you know how much power the voice held in check; courtliness as a second language.

"Oh, yes. Ms. Lewis works for us sometimes," Dana said, the "us" just slightly emphasized and the "sometimes" deliberately vague, as a woman might say, "My husband will be home any minute." Either the basso of his voice or that note in hers had brought half of Herbie's head around the door frame. "She's not here now, but I could get a message to her."

The man smiled unctuously. She met his eyes and—it was a shock but no surprise—they were that luminous, metal-filings bronze of Cassius's eyes. There was a little spasm in her neck as her hackles rose. She knew it was Luther—although he had never been described to her and, apart from the eyes and the molasses-dark skin, looked nothing like Cassius — knew it by the sham politesse and the use of "colored lady," a term that would have embarrassed her mother and now concealed contempt.

"That would be verruh kind, verruh kind. Do you know when she's likely to be here?"

"I'm not sure. Ms. Lewis pretty much makes her own schedule," Dana said, at which Herbie drew his chin in, quizzical. Trudy came six nights a week, regular as the morning barf.

"You don't happen to know where she resides?"

"Sorry," Dana lied, smiling brilliantly.

He returned the smile, only the top row of his teeth appearing. "Thank you. Ah'll just take my chance and wait for her here."

He carried his Fritos out to the front porch, where Dana had put a couple of rocking chairs, and sat fanning himself with a *Homes & Land,* nursing his Mountain Dew. Dudley, in a favorite shady spot, rolled over and exposed his belly to be scratched.

Herbie asked, "Who is he, though?"

"Just somebody wanting Trudy."

Trudy was across the highway shucking shrimp at Henry's as usual, but Dana wasn't going to send the stranger there without warning her. There was no way she could get to Henry's herself without passing down Sink Street in full view. She could send Herbie, but what form would the warning take, without embroiling Herbie in more information than she was ready for him to have?

So she waited while the big man sat in the hot shade, and the sun relinquished the apex of its arc, and the lunch eaters at Henry's drove away, and the next time she looked out he was gone.

But by the time the school bus stopped at the corner he was back again, pulling into the pumps in a Yukon SUV half a dozen years old or so — a sort of incandescent khaki color, so stuffed to the window tops that she thought of him sitting on it like a suitcase to close the hatch. He'd acquired a camouflage hat he held by the brim and patted against his thigh. He came in and paid for the gas — Herbie had finished painting and was at the till — chose a candy bar, poured a cup of coffee. Dana busied herself among the middle schoolers.

Out on the porch again the big man engaged Flora and Evian in conversation. Dana tried to read their gestures: his expansive, Evian wafting her hand in the direction of the road, probably telling him where Trudy was, Flora probably just flapping at a fly. But while the women came in for runner beans and small talk, he sat again. He rocked, took a sip of coffee, spoke to the hound in his dulcet profundo. His Snickers lay on its wrapper on the broad arm of the chair, chocolate melting and sagging—like the ketchup sagged on her door at the Ramada Inn.

He was playing her. He was letting her know he could squat on her territory.

She remembered being frightened when the fear felt good: driving down those streets of the Georgia ghetto, hidden behind the tinted windows of her honky-white Celica, in a neighborhood where it was an insolence to be drunk on sex and fierce with righteousness. She was scared then, but being scared had honed her, filled her with the joke: *how're you doing, Clifford?*

What if she went out now and said, "How you doing, Luther?" But there was no fun in this. She felt wobbly kneed, discouraged. She didn't want to deal with it.

Was that what Cassius felt?

You check into cheap motels, park in some space not visible from the highway, put down the blinds. The little girl is fretful, bored with the long drive, hungry, lonely for her mom. You have to placate her at the same time as you hide, day after day. You turn on the TV to the cartoons, check through the blinds, tell her to stay right there, you'll go and get her a plate of fries . . .

The shuckers knocked off at five on Fridays, so when four-thirty came and he was still on her porch, Dana went back to the living room, out of earshot, and called Henry's—apologetic because Henry didn't encourage calls to his employees.

"That's awright, Mizz Cleveland, I'll go get her." People deferred to her more these days. Did they know about Solly's will? This room faced away from the porch, so she couldn't tell if Luther was still there, but she felt invaded, not any wall or door secure.

"Trudy. I wanted to let you know—there's somebody here asking for you, and I think it's Luther. He doesn't know where you live and I didn't tell him. I thought you might want not to go past Solly's on your way home."

"How I'm going to do that?"

"I don't know. Cross through somebody's yard or something?"

There was a dismissive puff. "I guess I can handle Luther." A pause; then, an afterthought: "Don't you worry. I be there the usual time."

Dana went upstairs and positioned herself at the bedroom window that gave on to Sink Street. A little after five, sure enough, Trudy trudged up from the highway toward her turnoff and after a minute the SUV pulled after her, then stopped so that it blocked Dana's view of all but Trudy's grizzled head.

Which did not pause. The big car jerked forward, stop-and-go, while Trudy kept a dogged pace. After a time the car dropped back and crept after her up the street, five miles an hour, while Trudy slung her handbag over her shoulder and hunched forth, as if hauling the SUV in her dusty wake.

There was not much but junk to eat this late in the week (she cooked on Sundays), and this worried her. She should have hot meals, yellow vegetables, natural calcium and niacin. She made a turkey sandwich and ate it standing at the sink. She'd let Bernadette close up. Herbie had taken off early for Panama City to buy Spar urethane ("Like they use on boats, yeah?—practically indestructible"), and would be back by seven with three friends, a sander, and a dolly in his pickup truck. They had to get the piano down the stairs before tomorrow night, because this was the weekend Herbie would refinish the upstairs floors. Next weekend they'd clear out the shelves and do the store. She'd thought she was up for it, but now her energy had flagged. She peeled a mango and ate that over the sink, too. She lay down on the couch and tried to rest.

Phoebe was "supportive." Phoebe would back her up whatever she decided. Because if you're pro-choice, then you have to give lip service, at least, to *choice*. Back in the eighties they'd marched together carrying placards for abortion rights. But *rights* was one thing; single-parenting a biracial child was something else. Phoebe said if Dana decided to have it, she could come back to Pennsylvania. Phoebe would set her up and see her through it. Phoebe said.

It was kind of her. Heroic, even, because she clearly thought Dana was deranged. Phoebe had all kinds of virtues—wit, sense, heart—but imagination was not her forte. She couldn't see it from where Dana sat, thirty-nine years old, having lost one child (the tiny palm appeared, the cruel lie of its lifeline scored aslant down the pale skin), carrying a second pregnancy that was almost bound to be the last, with the considerable advantage of having been begot in love. Dana hoped Cassius would arrive and own his fatherhood, but if he didn't, she could no more consign this flesh to suction than she could send Chloe to the flames. It was not a question of rights, or even right. It was what she *could*.

But how much could she? Daylong malaise, incipient nausea, a hodgepodge of secrets and obligations she had willfully incurred, a windfall she meant to refuse, and a future less certain than when she left Somerset. And now this Luther.

She had two weeks to make up her mind.

She needed calm, focus, a clear reckoning of what mattered. Instead of which, here were the truck, the dolly, Adena, and three spare boys—Herbie directing the operation while Adena stood at the bottom of the stairs flinging plaudits in all directions.

"I marvel at you, Dana, I really do. You're a person of so many talents—every time I turn around, you're dishing up some absolute surprise! And Herbie, well you've brought him along, haven't you? Even Bernadette says so, and you may have noticed Bernadette doesn't go throwing that many bouquets. I'm telling you, that girl is driving me insane. I can't keep a candle in the place, goes off with my salt! All for some silly ritual, I don't know what girls *want*—well, she wants a 'chakra wand' for her birthday, $69.95, I swear to god. What is *chakra,* I ask her? All she knows is, it's got chakra *stones.* Oh, look at it, will you? Who'd have thought you could uncover such a gorgeous piece under all that gunk? If only Winifred could see it! And Herbie says you're going to perform the same magic on the floors. It's a waste of your skills, really. I'll tell you what you ought to do. I've got a couple of fixer-uppers you could flip for twenty thousand. Net. *Each.* I'm not kidding. Let me know if you're interested."

Her voice strained after the high notes, slightly out of tune, while Herbie's friends grunted the dolly down one step at a time, the great box shuddering, and Adena put her hands up in mock fear of the descending tonnage. Dana sighed. She had thought this banal woman would be her friend.

"He come preachifying at me—he ain't no more Christian than them over at West Sink. He say *bygones* this and *bygones* that, I say, Luther, time for that has done gone *by.* Eighteen years not a sorry word out the whole family, now I tell him Solly is gone, he think to come in and use my toilet."

Dana had to laugh. "I wish I was as tough as you are."

"Tough nothing, I'm telling you. He going to get mighty tired living out his sport u-*ti*lity."

According to Trudy, Luther had no idea who Dana was. On the contrary, he and the family assumed that Cassius had taken off with his white woman (called "white" or "fancy" interchangeably). They thought he and the woman were traveling together with Kenisha, and Luther's theory was that his fancy woman would tire of it. When she dumped him and Cassius ran out of money, this theory ran, he would come to Trudy. Luther was going to wait him out.

"He say it bad enough, the family breaking up, Antwan staying in Georgia for the new construction and most of the rest going up to Pennsylvania. I just look at him. He talk to *me* about family breaking *up*?"

"Why Pennsylvania?"

"Atlantic Mills got jobs up there."

"Why does he think Cassius will come to you?"

"He don't say so, but he think because I was friend to Mr. Solly, we two of a kind."

"Two honky lovers."

"Yes'm."

"Who does he think *I* am, then?"

"Who he's going to think you are? Some woman run the store. Some kin to Solly. He don't care."

"He doesn't know my name?"

"I don't know about that. He call Cassius's woman names I don't want to say."

Well, that made sense. The note she still kept in her paperback (but would hide tonight) was addressed to *Miss Dana, Villa Starfish.* If Isobel had known more of her name than that, she would have used it. The second time, Dana had written down nothing but the phone number of a motel, the number of a room. Even if they had somehow got to the registration desk, her credit card was in the name of Ullman, whereas here she was known as Cleveland. There was almost no chance, unless the name *Dana* struck a bell, that Luther had any idea who she was.

She was reassured. Eventually she slept, though so late that she woke with the sun at an alarming angle across the bed, and was somewhat chastened to find Herbie had already opened up. Even Bernadette was parking her Camaro, dawdling up the steps in several layers of gauze and knit that still managed to display square feet of flesh.

"God, it's *hot,*" Bernadette complained. Herbie murmured condolences, though it was not as hot as usual in here, in spite of a crowd of Saturday bait and ice seekers. Bernadette stowed her Guatemalan rucksack thing, extracting the paperback *Astral Spells for the Modern Witch,* which as usual she set on the counter and tapped three times.

Things looked better after a sleep-in. Tropical Storm Lili had veered off south, taking a slow jog along the north coast of Jamaica. Bernadette notwithstanding, the air was calm and promised a hint of fall. She remembered that Solly had said his favorite months were May and October. They would be hers, too. If she decided—if she decided to have the baby—it would come in the spring.

Luther was back, afoot, about eleven o'clock. The customers had cleared out some, and Bernadette was at the till. He loitered in the aisle as before: soft drinks, candy, canned goods. Half his broad back filled the oval mirror with its jaunty paper sign: Homeland Security. Dana ignored him, standing at the counter while she checked over the deliveries. She totted up yesterday's receipts and found a discrepancy. She kept her eyes on the sums, even when she heard the *thunk* of whatever single item he came to pay for. Added seven-twenty-one to eight-sixty.

Bernadette reached out and Dana caught in the corner of her eye a blur of red. She could no more control her gaze than the rise of hair on her arms. A bottle of ketchup. Thirty-two ounces. Super size.

She lifted her eyes to where the big man's smile divided his blunt face.

He said, "The Lord has blessed us with a glorious day, all praise to Him."

She nodded, curt.

Bernadette dragged the ketchup past the scanner. He smiled still, at Dana still, a smile mainly in the teeth. Then with a self-deprecatory bounce of his massive head, he said, "The Lord puts temptations in our path."

Bernadette said, "Yeah," and dropped the plastic bottle in a plastic bag.

Luther—he could do irony—bowed himself backward and turned out the door.

A man buys a bottle of ketchup. What could you possibly make of that?

IV
Restoration

22

PEOPLE HAVE GOOD REASONS to stay put in a hurricane. They don't want to abandon their pets. There's the threat of vandalism. They've already sat out six or seventeen or thirty-two storms and no harm done. If they left every time there was an advisory they'd spend all summer on the asphalt running out of gas and food in ninety degrees in a traffic jam. What could be worse? Anyway, where would they go?

She heard these arguments Sunday along Sag Island beach, and also in the Flaming Flamingo over deviled crab. She had slept not at all, or the little that seems not at all. First she'd helped Herbie stack the furniture in the upstairs bathroom, mattress in the tub, couch upended between john and sink, chairs and end tables in a precarious pileup. Then Herbie banished her and she lay on the downstairs sofa while the sander roared overhead, glad of the accident that he would be here all night, but starting up at nothing, getting up to check empty windows and locked doors. After four o'clock the smell of polyurethane, which she had always liked, spilled down the stairs into her burning lungs, her fragile stomach. When Herbie went back to the cabin to crash and wait for the first coat to dry, she drove to Sag Island and spread her towel on a grassy dune and fell asleep in a sunrise over Eden.

Not that this mini-evacuation could be called safe. The island was only seven miles away from Pelican Bay, if anyone had wanted to follow her.

Nor, as it was shaping up, was the island safe. Out there in the Caribbean, Lili was no longer a tropical squall but hurricane force and strengthening, headed north to Cuba. After that it would be back in the overwarm waters of the Gulf. Four days out it would hit somewhere along this coast, the cone of its possible landfall stretching from Texas to Florida and the meteorology mavens predicting a Category Three. If it hooked north, Sag Island could be ground zero.

She heard this first at the Sandpiper, a bar-and-doughnuts dive with one TV turned permanently to ESPN and the other to the weather. It was the favored topic among the bikers on the pool deck of the Swashbuckler Inn and among the vacationers clotted into community along the beach on an afternoon of paradisiacal calm and brilliance. Strangers volunteered incredulity to each other: *you wouldn't think there was a storm anywhere in the world.*

It was true. The water was as calm as a Constable pond. No, it was more complicated. Like a Turner seascape with some placid name, *Moonlight* or *Peace* or *Sun Setting Over a Lake,* the surface looked flat but its flatness was made up of particles of force and fire, molecules in riot. Here in her near view, individual grains of sand shot back the sun, droplets on her forearm came into focus as silver webs. Where the water met the shore it fluffed and roiled itself, and every time it sank, a thousand coquinas upended and drilled under. She waded in, and shoals of evanescent minnows fled. The seafloor underfoot was tiled with sand dollars, brittle but alive. Children scooped them up, quarter and cookie and saucer sized, the domed gray surface of each traced with a rope of star, each flat underside a teeming field of fat hairs waving microscopic algae toward the mouth. Rapt or squealing or in recoil, some of these children would thirty years hence recall (as she herself remembered a jar full of fireflies) the spooky pulsing of those hairs.

And she, too, back on her towel now, utterly still, was teeming. The skin where the sun hit sent the atoms racing (heat is speed by another name, scientists explained); the cells under her still-concave belly were dividing, differentiating, hungry to become a creature; the synapses in her brain snapped and struck: *If Luther, who has known Cassius all his life, thinks Cassius will come here, then there is the more reason to think he will. If Luther does not know who I am, then there is nothing to fear. If Trudy knows Luther . . . if Luther knows who I am . . . if I go and Cassius comes . . . if I stay and he does not . . . It's like an unsolvable algebra problem with a complicated pattern and no known terms: If X over hope has the value of Z plus risk, then what is Y to the nth divided by desire?*

At the Flaming Flamingo, where she had supper—its logo the bird in flight on burning wings—Lili was discussed with nostalgic reference to storms past. The Flamingo was Sag Island upscale, which meant avidly down-home. It was hung with nets and smelled of jalapeños and smoky mullet. The chairs were Wal-Mart plastic and the salt came in Corona bottles, but if you wanted your tonic with Bombay Sapphire they could oblige. Vacationers in Manolo Blahnik flip-flops sat on three sides of the dining deck, gazing through salt smear at the sea, while inside the locals congregated with the air-conditioning and the Weather Channel. Dana sat among them, feeling guilty toward Herbie, who would in any case be asleep again by now, the second coat drying in the upstairs rooms.

She ordered deviled crab, which the Flamingo concocted of pure claw meat, no bread, a sauce of cream and clam broth with a jazzy cayenne aftertaste. Flavor, like the sight of sea oats kowtowing to the dunes, seemed heightened and important. The sun in its decline flung flame-colored mirrors on the wet sand, in which long-beaked sandpipers, feeding on algae, seemed to peck at their reflections. She dallied over her food, delaying a return to Solly's and the decision she must make yet *again*.

"I won't evacuate for a voluntary," said the waitress beside the bar, "but a mandatory, well . . ." She pulled at the back hem of her shorts, exposed between the edges of a bibbed apron.

The old-timer in the beard and ball cap scoffed up at her. "Voluntary, mandatory, them ologists don't know what the danger is. No, sir. This is my home, I was born here, my kids was born here, the Lord can wash me out if he has a mind to, but I ain't going on my own."

"I was here for Opal, though," said a plump young matron, also in shorts. "We didn't get flooded but my memaw did. It was touch and go for her, up to her knees and the whatnot floating like a dinghy in the dining room."

"Opal was nothing," the man said. "You wasn't born for Eloise. That was seventeen foot of surge smacked right into Panama City. We boarded up and sat on the porch roof, handy for the mucking out."

"I don't know," Dana put herself into the conversation. "Does it make sense to take the risk?"

"You can't keep evacuating," said the waitress. "People don't have the funds."

"No, sir. Tape up or board up, and get yourself prayed up," advised the old man. "That's the three things you can do."

"And that ain't the beer talking," the matron laughed. "That's the friggin' truth."

Dana drove home while there was still twilight, past the River of Faith revival tent (*A New Take on God!*), past condos under construction like the skeletons of storks, still pondering why people stay when every instinct must say they're impotent, ignorant, at the mercy of catastrophe—worrying this conundrum because it might hold some clue for her—or, no, might substitute for choice, like a tossed coin. She circled the store, heart in throat, looking for ketchup on the doors, the porches, the windowsills. There was none. *Why do they stay?* She entered into the fresh tang of new finish, muted now. She wedged chairs under the doorknobs as she had seen people do in films, where it had seemed to serve some purpose, whereas these chair legs skidded easily inward when she pulled on the knobs. She gave it up, checked the locks, and mounted to the landing to peek at the bedroom, empty and spotless from the replastered ceilings down to the refurbished floors. *They stay because they can't think of anywhere they'd rather be.* No, that's not quite it either. She descended, opened the jalousies, turned on the TV. The Weather Channel carried an aerial view of the banana crop that Lili had flattened on Santa Lucia. On NBC a woman demonstrated how usefully the seats of her minivan collapsed to conceal her shopping spree. Dana flicked the outside lights on and the inside off, so the ancient oak flared dramatically. *They stay because they can't give up the illusion of control.*

Herbie was in at six A.M., enthusing about the floors. Upstairs he danced his eagerness to be praised, and she didn't have the heart to deny him. It was true, the place was fresh and lovely, light sliding along the grain. She crossed on bare tiptoes—"Don't worry, it's bone-dry"—the room that had been emptied of the piano. There were capped-off water pipes from the time when it had been a kitchen. You could put a basin there, like an old-fashioned bedroom, big enough to bathe a baby. Roller blinds to dim the afternoon sun. She leaned on the sill and gazed out over the woods.

From the direction of the pond a wisp of smoke arose, wafted to the level of the myrtles, made a hard turn inland, and dissipated in the breeze. "Look." She pictured the two boys she had last seen there—a stick fire to boil a pot? the cruel killing of a turtle too small for soup?—when there came from the same spot a winking light, small and harsh, like someone sending code. "Has somebody got a fire out there?"

"Yeah, I seen that yesterday. It's that new guy is camping on your land. I reckon he's got him a trap, and he's roasting squirrel."

"Oh, no."

"Squirrel is good eating."

"I don't want him camping there. What's that light?"

"Dunno, looks like a mirror. He must be shaving."

"I don't like it."

"No'm, you'll want to run him off, or otherwise you'll have hippies and all kinda trash camping out."

"How do I accomplish that?"

"I reckon Lili will do it for you."

But Herbie was not really interested. He had other urgencies, getting the sander back to Panama City before they charged him extra, and "I was thinking we should have some four-by-eight ply in case we need to board up. Sandbags wouldn't hurt. I could get some spare in case folk want to buy 'em."

"Do you think we should evacuate?"

"Oh, no, ma'am, not at Solly's. This is just about the strongest place on the Bay. Solly used to let the trailer people stay when there was a 'cane."

"Stay how?"

"Oh, they'd just party as long as it was blowing. You can't sleep. Trudy and Marion and them, the Allansons. Trudy'll know."

"You think I should have them in as well."

"That's up to you. All depends where this Lili goes—prob'ly off in Texas somewhere—but I tell you, even if she does, we're north and east of the eye, and that's where the weather is. I'd rather not be out in the cabin my ownself, if you don't mind."

"No, of course. I'd be grateful to have you here."

Was that a decision? There wasn't time to consider. Business was brisk in gas, batteries, and bottled water. It had been a weekend full of event, and gossip flared. Harry Moomis was up in Tallahassee getting a stent put in. Sarah's man had come in drunk on Saturday night, and the cops were called. One of the Adams boys was caught in Pensacola with crystal meth. Beer, chips, and salsa sold like game day. When Herbie got back with plywood and sandbags, those went, too. He'd taken it upon himself to stock up at Home Depot, retail price, and argued that Solly's deserved a ten-percent markup for delivery. Dana vetoed this as price gouging, and Herbie sulked a little. But when Bernadette came in and he gave her the candles he'd saved back for her, she lavished on him a smile of pre-Raphaelite vacuity, and he cheered up again.

"Winds of at least seventy-four miles an hour over the western tip of Cuba will likely gather strength over the Gulf in the early hours . . ." Dana kept one of the rainbow-colored transistors on the counter. Conditions were expected to deteriorate on the coast through Wednesday, and engineers were already monitoring water levels against the threat of flood. "Hurricanes is like football," the director of emergency management was heard to say. "It starts the scrimmage in July, but there's no real game till you get into September."

Luther made no appearance, though next morning Dana saw again the rise of smoke and the wink of what Herbie said was a shaving mirror. Dapper dude, Luther, with his smoke and mirrors in a swamp.

"That's him," Trudy agreed, "can't make no mistake. Luther got a head like a *thumb*."

"But if he doesn't know who I am, why is he there?"

"Luther think to catch Cassius here where they stayed when they was boys."

"I don't know, Trudy."

"Don't you worry. Luther fixing to pull out when the weather hit. He stubborn, but he ain't stupid."

Beyond Hurricane Alley other storms were brewing and duly dropped on the porch as bundles of the *Democrat*. U.N. Chief Inspector Hans Blix and the Iraqi military hacked out an agreement for renewed inspections. The French accused the U.S. of imperialism. Congress gave Big Bush authority to go to war.

"Up on the Hill," said Phoebe, "as per usual, the monkeys run amuck. Did you see the African bishops are ripping up the Methodist Church?"

"We sold Christianity to the heathens and it's coming around to bite us in the ass. Good thing irony is dead."

"Now watch us convert the Middle East to democracy."

But for those three days, goodwill settled over Solly's Corner. Henry's and Lhamon Paper closed down Tuesday noon, and the mill workers and shuckers crowded in for supplies. Mutual trust hung in the pheromones. They stayed longer, laughed louder, hugged more freely. Advice was more vigorously given and more enthusiastically received. *Take care. Be safe, now. I'll be thinkin' about you, darlin'. You need some help with the sandbags, I'll send Daniel over, hear?* Clyde Usvedt paid for Maria Elena de la Iglesia's flashlight batteries. A high school girl balancing a chemistry book on her head squatted, to general applause, to retrieve a Salt 'n' Vinegar bag dropped by a toddler. Those in cars drove gallons of bottled water to the bungalows of those afoot.

Community came to Dana in the scent of fresh thermoplastic floors. She knew that most of these people, forced into long-term intimacy, would arrive at irritation and disillusion, in some cases at contempt and small-claims court. What they expressed in the few square yards of splintery oak on which they shuffled in their sneakers, flip-flops, mules, stilettos, wedges, half soles, Pumas, and bare feet was no more than a promise conditional upon outside threat. You could see it as superficial but you could also see it as fundamental. *People stay because in danger anxiety takes the form of love.*

And she felt fine. Did she feel fine? Was that possible? It was too early for the morning sickness to have subsided—that should happen at four months and this was barely three—but it seemed to have subsided. Each morning she waited for it, but it did not come. Her eyes in the mirror were bright. Her hair shone.

23

By Wednesday afternoon the air was as thick as jellyfish. One pass of the storm's outer bands had brought pine boughs down and gravel rattling against the pumps. Now it was merely raining again, a sallow, sodden wall.

"Can you see the SUV?"

Trudy, peering through the jalousies, shook her head. "Can't be sure. I think he still there."

Exasperated, Dana said, "What's the *matter* with him?"

But Trudy burst back with great bitterness, *"How I'm supposed to know?"* and punished a strip of window glass with her dish towel. "I ain't pass two dozen words with him since he come here."

She turned on her heel, back to the kitchen where, all afternoon, she had cooked for the first time since Solly died: fried chicken, red beans, gumbo that could be heated on Sterno cans if the power went out. Abashed, Dana watched her reach for implements that might or might not be where she expected them. Trudy had never complained of having been usurped. But she must feel it.

"I don't blame *you* . . ."

"I ain't pass two dozen words with his sorry self since they cut me off in '84." She hoisted a gumbo pot, clattering it on the burner. "He want to be playing games in the soaker, that's his lookout."

"I know." Anything Dana said risked another blunder. So she stood planted awkwardly in front of the television set, where Lili slow-churned like ice cream over the whole of the Gulf of Mexico.

The weather woman had olive skin and a voice rich with gravitas. "The eye is expected west of New Orleans but the wind speed is strongest a hundred miles east of the center, with gusts clocked at a hundred and twenty-five knots. Watches have been posted from Apalachicola to the Texas border."

Outside, tufts of pine needles fell on the glass slats like a rain of whisk brooms. It seemed strange to have these technological updates hour after hour, these diagrammed and detailed warnings of when and from which direction and in what strength the crisis would arrive: a Category Four, over warm open water at the moment, due here between eight and ten P.M. All day there had been a measured ascent of tension, played out in mundane tasks. They'd had time to fill the sandbags, muck out the drainage trench, stack ice bags in the fridges in case of outage.

Not least among oddities was that Dana appeared to be giving a party, the first since before that bleak winter day Graham was diagnosed. Under her apprehension about the storm, about Luther, she could track the hostess angst, familiar but disused, that seemed to reside in her esophagus. She brought down extra chairs. She broke open packets of blue-corn nachos. She denuded the big backyard hibiscus of its blooms—the tempest would slash and bedraggle them anyway—and a double dozen of them burgeoned, flamed, and flounced from a copper jug on the coffee table. She remembered standing in the "turret" with a clipboard taking down one of Graham's endless invitation lists, writing the names of people whose deep pockets or local-circuit celebrity made them valuable in his eyes—people, on the whole, whose self-esteem amounted to a pathology. She remembered saying, "One of these days I'm going to throw a party, and the principle of invitation will be *people I want to see.*"

She closed up at five, and they gathered in the living room: Dana, Herbie, Dudley Do-Right, and Bernadette—Bernadette because, as Herbie reported, "She don't want to stay with her mother's dorky realtor buddies in P City—they'll just get drunk and hit on her"—and the rest of them, including Trudy, trailer dwellers from the Sinks.

There was board-skinny April in her ponytail, stationing little Lee Annie's stroller at one end of the chairs, Milly Allanson rolling Tork's wheelchair toward the other. Milly, a generation younger than her husband, carried her hugeness carefully between gelatinous arms as she maneuvered him into place. Flora and Evian, both tall and ample, one mahogany, one golden oak, commandeered the sofa. Flora was the more vivid of the two, from her bosom-hugging flowered dress to her foghorn laugh, while Evian, Toklas to her Stein, kept up a hum of affirmatives: "Uh-huh, ya'm, *mmm,*" as the small talk stuttered into place.

"Get that wheel, honey. Give it a tug up, will ya?"

"Sit, Lee Annie! I can't undo it if you wiggle."

"Um-hm."

"I seen it like this a hundred times. You think it's norther and it comes around and slaps you from the east."

"Yes, Lord."

Lee Annie squirted free of the stroller and butted her blond curls into the sofa under which Dudley cowered. Marion, dumpy, the hue of steeped chamomile, slung her plastic tote on a chair and shed the water from her flip-flops by rocking her full weight on them. "Ain't nothing," she averred, and did not elaborate.

That comprised the expected eleven. Then—just when everyone had settled, the Weather Channel running a loop of brave reporters in yellow slickers and Milly unveiling from the vicinity of the wheelchair's axle two six-packs (coals to Newcastle)—there, suddenly, was Adena tapping on the glass. She waved. Herbie went to the back door to let her in.

"I just couldn't *make* myself drive all the way to Panama City when I knew you all were going to be at Solly's!" She flapped at the yoke of her silver trench coat, spattering the nachos. "Sweetheart." She bent to brush a kiss across Bernadette's crown, but Bernadette, positioning a ring of candles on the floor, only glanced up at her mother, faintly scowling. "Tork!" Adena said. "It's like old times, isn't it? Remember when Bucky and Solly had the arm-wrestling tournament? In the *dark*?"

"That Bucky," said Tork.

"Man could put away some beer," Marion remembered.

"But Tork here could take the both of them!"

Herbie brought a chair while Adena shed her coat and embraced the air between her outstretched arms. "We must've been twenty that time—wasn't it Opal? Or was it Kate? Dana, what can I do to help? Put me to work and lemme work off these nerves! God, I've been pushed to the limit getting the renters off the island."

So in the space of a minute Dana, still stung with remorse at displacing Trudy, found the ownership of the party lifted from her. Adena, handing round the forks, passing out napkins—"Honey, where do you want these cashews?"—managed in the guise of subservience to take control. Trudy stationed herself behind the gumbo, and Dana found herself, too, obediently backed into that space. She thought of cats spraying the same territory, one after the other.

Adena lifted Lee Annie from where she had plunked down on the floor beside Bernadette. "Whoop-a-dadie!" she said, and redeposited the child. "It won't be the same without Solly." And then, to Dana in particular, with a note of plaintive challenge, "It won't be the *same.*"

Dana nodded vaguely and busied herself with the chicken wings.

"Woman ain't been here fo' hurricane in years," Trudy muttered, face like a stone.

Adena wheeled, gleaming. "What's that, Trudy?"

Trudy did not miss a beat. "I say we best eat while we got the electric."

They ate. The dusk sky took on an emerald stain never before seen in its spectrum. It glowed like a translucent dome. Dudley let out a muted, mournful howl, and Herbie consoled him, and an unsettling stillness fell, silence stripped even of the inevitable undersound, leaf and cricket and surf and footfall. From the highway, not a sound. From the Gulf, the road, the houses, nothing. Sound negative, into which their voices dropped like metal splinters. The Dark Lady of the Weather Channel resumed her dire narrative. "Officials have confirmed four deaths in landslides on St. Vincent, another four in Jamaica including a child of three, and a further four in the floods of Haiti."

"Devil like him a dozen," Trudy did the math.

"Child of three." April wagged her ponytail mournfully.

"Mm-hm, mm-hm."

Bernadette refused food and lit her candles, saying things like, "Blessèd be this circle of flame," and "I call on the spirit of the goddess from whom we come," persisting, blank faced while Adena rolled her eyes. Lee Annie—TV-savvy toddlers always zero in on beauty—latched on to Bernadette's limp patchwork hem and dogged her every move. Bernadette suffered this. "I light this candle and ask protection from the spirit of earth, so mote it be."

"Motherhood is a global conspiracy," Adena comically confided.

"Yah, mm, hm."

"Amen."

Tork had perked up when she arrived, and now he entertained them with storm stories from the past while the dome darkened and the wind began to whip again. Tork was a handsome ruin of an old salt, face ruckled, crosshatched, caved in between the bones. His legs had been destroyed by some wasting disease but his upper body still bulged with muscle. Milly babied him in a matter-of-fact way, listening distractedly (*been there, heard that*) while she anticipated his need for a glass, a bib, a spoon. There was a kind of heroism about the way she steered her enormous body with no fuss, especially while Tork aimed his anecdotes mainly at Adena.

"Time I got caught in a squall off Shell Point," he said. "I was in cargo then, out to Sag Island before the bridge was built. You remember that."

"I'll say."

"We most remember," Flora said.

"An' that's a fact."

"Every damn nail and potato had to be brought out by boat. Well, this time, at the last minute they shoved a crate in the stern. It was looking ugly off south and I figured I better get docked by dark."

"Uh, huh, yas," warned Evian.

They left the TV on low, and could plot the hurricane's counterclockwise pattern as it thrashed against the windows and overhead. The irony was that as the cone on the screen narrowed and veered west toward Texas, as Pelican Bay fell outside the danger zone entirely, as Dark Lady canceled the hurricane watch for the panhandle and they lost the brief celebrity of danger, the storm rose in ferocity around them. The wind swelled from strings to brass to timpani. The sound of wood snapping was followed by a penetrating smell of pine. Branches thudded on the roof or crashed in the woods, and Dudley whimpered from the shelter of the couch. When a lightning flash hit just beyond the live oak tree, Lee Annie screamed, and when that brought her a rush of coddling, she continued to do so at every strike. Tork raised his voice, arm wrestling with the thunder.

"Time I got into the middle of the bay, that ole surf was suckin' and poundin', lift me clean out the water and slam me like a hammerhead. They tell you your life passes afore your eyes, it's the god's truth. Passes just like a fil-um. I fought her across, come into a lump of shadow I thought was the Sag Island docks, all's a sudden I feel a hot breath on my neck. Panting. I'm not one for ghosts. But I tell ya, the hackles rise up, I could feel every hair on my neck kinda tremblin' in that hot air."

Tork paused for effect and upended his beer into his mouth. The last of the six-packs, Dana noted. The wind was in a tantrum now, palmetto fronds slapping the siding like wet towels. Bernadette sprinkled salt around her candles and intoned, "Elements of power, protect us in our dangerous hour, so mote it be." The lights flickered. Lee Annie screamed.

"What happened?" Flora asked—of Tork, pretending indifference to the storm.

Herbie said, "It's time we get to th'interior."

"Oh," said Tork, piqued at having his punch line interrupted. "It was a pit bull, goddam crate had busted open."

They were held in place a moment longer by an eerie groaning from beyond the windows, a sound neither mechanical nor animal but something like the amplified whine of either. A strobe light pulsed across a bank of cloud and backlit the slow descent of an ancient pine. It rocked at an angle for a moment, hung suspended over the power line, and fell, describing a ninety-foot arc that laid it with an ear-hurting crack across the yard. The lights went out. The television gulped dead. Bernadette's candles became puny footlights making little glow-pools on the shabby planks.

"Now," Herbie said.

Dana picked up one of the candles to lead toward the inner hallway. As she gained the door there was a roar of wind and a series of cracking sounds across the dark: *Whack, whack, whack.* Near or far? Impossible to tell. *Whack! Whack!* Tork said into the blackness, "That's a water spout. The island will be deaded out."

Bernadette said, a little hysterically, "I call on thee in the time of lightning and the powers of flame, that thou shouldst protect this circle from harm, so mote it be."

Adena, stumbling over something from the sound of it, said, "Oh, Bern, for chrissake give it a rest, will you?"

Lee Annie wailed.

Dana, Trudy close behind her, entered the store, braided her way between the aisles, achieved the counter, and set down her little light, fumbling for the matches and the storm candles she had set here earlier. She could hear the squeak of Tork's wheelchair at the door, feel the press of the others waiting. Her diaphragm fluttered as if it were spreading wings over the fragile embryo. The porch joists rattled and drummed. Before she could strike a match, a bolt of lightning struck and blared its brightness across the porch, the drive, the gas pumps, and the roof of the sparkling khaki SUV. Silhouetted in the flash, linebacker broad in the window of the shop door, Luther's hulk.

"Ah-ahh!" Trudy drew in a startled breath. Dana fumbled toward a match and struck it but forgot to tilt it, and it snuffed out. Clumsy fingered, she lit another. The thunder crashed, and hard on its heels another lightning strike. *"Shit!"* The monstrous lump of him appeared, backlit with conflagration. There flashed across her inner eye the ridges of coagulating ketchup on the door, and the number

scribbled with a fingtertip: *666*. Dark fell again. Luther pounded on the frame as the thunder pounded: the hurricane demanding entry. Dana got the candle lit and turned to Trudy, whose features were screwed up in pain—brow clenched, cheeks high, mouth straitened; a face for a pietà. Dana held the candle up between them.

"He *family,*" Trudy pleaded.

Dana stood for the moment stupefied. Then—as once when, a teenager, she had been caught with a shoplifted mascara; as once when her car had swerved and she saw the brick wall coming at her; as once when the nurse reached out to take Chloe away—she capitulated. The bird in her belly landed. She could feel the round weight of its body settling on her bowels. Giving up was a relief.

"Let him in. Here. Take this light."

She lit half a dozen of the heavy hurricane candles in their sturdy sconces. She kept her back to the door, the grating of the bolt, the flurry of lukewarm wind. She carried a pair of candles across to the waiting bunch, and they made for the stairwell and inner hallway at the safe heart of the house. Only when they were crowded into that space did she say, "This is Trudy's nephew," and turn to him with a rictus of welcome. He held her eyes. He bowed, a sweep of one massive hand, the other pressing his diaphragm. Then, in that booming basso that could hold no more humility than a sieve, he said, "Thank you for taking pity on a foolish man."

She nodded and retreated to the stairs. He intruded his shaved head into the hallway. He said at large, "The Lord has opened the heavens with a mighty hand."

"Ahh-men," said Evian.

And Flora, "You know that's right."

The storm was long. It bullied them hour after hour with its limited percussive repertoire: thunder, wind, lightning, rain. Trees fell. Unseen debris scoured by in yard and road. Lee Annie crawled up the stair treads and bumped down them on her padded rump and screamed.

Clamped into that dark stairwell no wider than an elevator, they arranged and rearranged themselves in tiers, two stair steps per, with Tork against the john wall and Milly on a stool beside him, Dudley coiled into the space between her feet. Luther, martyr, stood the whole time leaning against the frame of the arch into the store. The others took turns at the relief of sitting on one of two canvas chairs also wedged in that meager rectangle. Herbie somehow affixed sconces to the banisters, which gave them a tunnel of wavering light.

Dana stationed herself at a middle step above the others, the dark behind her, forked bolts illuminating Luther though the back-door glass. Sometimes in that flash his head was turned her way and sometimes not. Sometimes she thought the metallic glint of his eyes sought her out. Sometimes he addressed the floor beyond his folded hands.

"We *give thanks,* oh God, for this rending of the skies. We are Your poor creatures in the valley of the shadow, and *Thine* is the power and the glory forever and ever!"

Bernadette meanwhile segregated herself and arranged her ring of tapers on the shop counter. Between the skirt perched on her hip bones and the chopped black T-shirt, her midriff was exposed at just the height of the candle flame, so the jewel of her belly ring caught fire. She turned and swayed. From time to time in the intervals of Luther's apostrophes, she raised her voice, "I light this candle that represents me, all that I be," or "Elements of Power, protect us in our desperate hour, so mote it be." Herbie paced between her and the stairwell, nervous because she was too near the window and because he lacked authority to scold her for it. Dudley paced after Herbie only with his eyes.

"Even so, Lord God Almighty, true and righteous are Thy judgments." Luther kept his face turned to the lightning. "For all nations have drunk of the wine of Thy wrath."

"Amen."

After a time Milly made to buy more beer, so Dana offered up the contents of the cold-drinks fridge, though she could see that Tork, and probably Millie, and possibly Marion, would be pie-eyed by morning. When Millie hoisted Tork into the john they performed a pantomime of deafness.

Now Flora asked questions of Luther, who settled into the door frame and denigrated any interesting reason he might have for being here. "Passing through, merely passing."

"He visiting from Georgia coast," Trudy claimed, resentful now that she had saved him.

Luther contradicted her, "Just a stop along the way." He added mournfully, "My family is in transit from the state of Georgia to the state of Pennsylvania," as if *state* referred to a mode of being rather than geography. Did he lift his eyes to Dana as he said this? There was a murmur of condolence. When Flora persisted, he fulminated on the closing of Atlantic Mills and the dispersing of the workforce. His voice, a sonorous octave below Cassius's, reverberated up the stairs even in a murmur. "People going through a spiritual hurricane right now. There are brothers out of work, who have been *put* out of work, and there are sisters forced from their homes and children going 'out their supper." Luther had a belly with impressive range. When he stood erect his shirt hung hollow from his barrel chest; but when he relaxed or bent, his buttons strained, and bits of flesh emerged in the gaps. He waxed eloquent in terms that Dana hadn't heard since poli sci, that harked back to the Cold War, in the rhythms of the baptistry. "A paper mill, I can tell you, is a propagator of *forgery.* A paper mill is a *counter*-feiting operation." Could he have known that she spent the day with Gavin McGarvey? "These are robber bosses make paper in order to manufacture paper *money,* and the money manufactures further im-*aginary* money, and so on, and on, to feed the coffers of the ruling class."

"Speak it, brother."

"Know that's right."

Dana sat halfway up the stairs, her ass numb on the hard treads, hovering between exhaustion and suspicion while he gave florid voice to opinions she resented precisely because she shared them. Trudy sat straight backed, looking at her hands, hooked into each other in her lap, a posture of deliberate self-containment. All other eyes were on this new demagogue who mainly addressed the *sisters.* If this was a territorial contest over these splintered boards, then Luther was top dog.

"They do not *care* for the labor of the working man, they do not *care* for their own promises to the working man. They do not *care* if the land is ravaged in their exploitation of his honest labor."

"Lord have mercy."

Nobody was inclined to contradict him. Each of them had somehow suffered, or known people who had suffered, by being beholden for their living to papermaking. Besides, from Dana's grudging point of view, what he described, minus its scourging rhetoric, was much the way Gavin McGarvey had explained Atlantic's profits.

The hours dragged on, alarm taking turns with enervation and unease. The AC had of course gone out with the electricity, and of course they dared not open a window, so the air grew close and smelled cloyingly of polyurethane and sweat and hound. The women fanned themselves with copies of the *County Register.* Dana kept the little transistor on her lap so she could track the progress of the storm, but the news was west of them by now, Lili first threatening New Orleans and then passing still farther west. Nevertheless, if they once or twice decided they might return to the living room, a limb would whack the roof in reprimand, and they would settle back into their sardine tin. They all became blear eyed, and tempers flared without warning or consequence. Dana sat cauterized top and bottom, fighting a grainy sensation behind her eyes, musing on the passing preciousness of sleep. When Luther had clearly established his verbal supremacy, and Tork had pulled out a few more tales of naval heroism, and Adena had reasserted her rights as a native hurricane survivor, they tried singing camp songs, and then hymns, and then *"Ninety-nine bottles of beer on the wall . . ."* while Lee Annie, exhausted and hyper, danced in place between Marion's legs. By the time they got down to *sixty-four bottles of beer on the wall,* Dana conceded that the freezer food was lost, so she directed Herbie to open up the ice-cream case. They gorged on sloppy Creamsicles, Wall's Cornettos, and Häagen Dazs. Herbie shared a Klondike bar with Dudley.

Even Bernadette joined them for the ice cream, perching on the bottom step, taking dark Dove miniatures between her black nails and tucking limp patchwork around her ankles. Luther, who had not appeared to take any notice of her (but he noticed more than he seemed to, Dana thought), bent to her in his pompous undertone.

"Take care before you call upon the powers."

"Umm," said Bernadette.

"It's a fearsome thing to play in *that* toy box."

Bernadette smashed a delicate morsel with her tongue. "Oh, uh, umm. It's just some spells."

"The Devil takes small steps," Luther declared.

"It's nothing to do with him. That's all just *prejudice.*"

Herbie hovered.

Adena said with a defensive laugh, "She's going through a phase."

Luther licked the last seaweed extract from a Creamsicle stick and Evian handed him a roll of paper towels. And Dana thought: *the South,* where voodoo has been passed on to the body-pierced offspring of the aspiring class, while Jesus takes up residence with the ghetto deacons.

The wind seemed to have died for good now, and Tork was nodding off on Millie's ponderous shoulder flesh. Lee Annie, though, had revived on a sugar high. She thumped up the stairs and shrieked down. "Look! Mom! Mama! Look at me!" While April indulged her, "You are the best. You are the princess, the gorgeous one," which made the black women shake their heads, mouths tight.

"Uh-uh-*uh,*" said Evian.

From Trudy, "Take that chile in *hand.*"

Dana suggested, "I'll bring down some pillows and we can make a bed for her."

"We can try it," April said doubtfully.

As Dana mounted, Adena scrambled after her. Dana took up cushions from the bedroom couch, an armful of pillows from the bed.

"Who *is* he?" Adena whispered.

"Can you take this? Trudy's nephew, like I said." The bed was ineluctably inviting. She shook her head to clear it and peered out to where the tip of Sag Island usually marked the way out to sea. The horizon had disappeared in blackness. It was all pitch-nothing. Tork must have been right, a tornado had taken out the utility poles and the island was "deaded out."

"Has he been nosing around the property?"

"He's been camping. I wouldn't call it *nosing.*"

"I don't put it past Trudy for a minute."

"What do you mean?"

"Don't give me that. Sniffing out if she has some claim."

"Why would she do that?"

"Why!?"

Dana folded the quilt around the pillows. "She's seventy. What would she want with it?"

"*Achh!* You are so naive."

"I asked if she wants the store. She doesn't. She doesn't think people would come here if she did."

"So *naive.* If she doesn't want the land, what is her nephew doing here, with his car stuffed to the gills?"

"He's moving up to Pennsylvania. *Really.* The Georgia mill is closing down." She enjoyed a moment's contempt of Adena, who painted Luther's motives in the coloration of her own. Though Dana had so lately been doing exactly that.

24

Karst is the name given to the limestone substrata of Florida. The porous carbonate is furrowed and pitted, pocked and cracked. Like a sponge it swells with the underground rivers it lets pass. Like a honeycomb it retains its form partly thanks to the liquid in its walls. The fullness of water upholds the fragile bridge of sand and clay on which people build, into which they dig their foundations, pipes, pumps, drains, ditches, sewers, and reservoirs.

Rainwater, slightly acid from decaying plants, absorbing carbon dioxide from the runoff of industry and farms, seeps into the bedrock, percolates through and nibbles at the cavities. Over time the limestone pores erode, dissolving into larger voids. Here and there the mantle gives. A weekend gardener might buy a fifty-pound bag of potting soil to fill a depression in her backyard and find that she needs another a few days later. A suburban father might undertake to bury the family dog and find the grave's sides caving underfoot. The process makes for hummocky topography, annoyance, and occasional catastrophe.

In February in the subtropics, a heavy rain followed by a period of sun adorns the world with blossom. The same seesaw pattern of wet and dry repeated in June produces a mosquito plague. Contrarily, in autumn, if a drought is followed by a flood, the karst can shatter and the fragile overburden then collapse. The subterranean river gulps down a quarter acre of surface soil. It happens rarely, and it's only news in the still rarer instance that some person or edifice was on the deflated ground—now called a *sink.*

They came out into a morning scoured and scattered. The sun was out on wet bark, a sparkling new sponge of pine needles, puddles in the pitted road. Dogs released from the loud night plowed their noses through churned soil, Dudley bouncingly among them. Branches lay like pick-up sticks. Here and there a mighty pine was down, exposing its shallow root pan as an eight-foot disk of snarl. Everything smelled of fresh dirt and pine. The birds were going mad with relief and joy. On both sides of the road there sounded already, near and far, the hacking of axes and the whine of power saws. Every soul gave thanks to God and Black & Decker.

"We dodged the bullet again this time."

"Surely did."

Now there was plenty of traffic back and forth across Sink Street as neighbors black and white dipped into each other's yards to help drag an oak limb or uncover a drain. A jungle gym had been overturned by a Yield sign blown out of god-knows-where. The waterspout that had plunged Sag Island in darkness had crossed the bay as a plain twister and snapped a path through the pines as if they were candy canes. The houses were mercifully spared, though half a tree went down on Frank Sutter's Silverado, and a piece of the Usvedts' roof had peeled across to bash in the hood of Darren Washington's newly leased Dodge Ram. Fathers stood guard over downed power lines until the county crews would arrive. The refugees from Solly's Corner had all snatched some bit of sleep (April, Lee Annie, and Dana ended in the upstairs bed, Trudy on the couch beside them), and they were, if not rested, nevertheless adrenaline-awake. Adena took off to reconnoiter the damage to Sag Island. Herbie volunteered to go back and man the store, and Dudley followed him at a martyred trudge, but the rest of them worked their way up Sink

Street, pausing to help tug a stoop free of debris and accept a cup of coffee brewed on a grill.

"Any word when we'll get the juice back on?"

"Everything in the freezer's lost. I'm'a grill up the lot. Y'all are invited."

"Mizz Dana, are you all out of bottled water?"

"Dodged another one for sure."

"There's eight dead in Luzianna, 'cording to Emergency."

Some stopped for a break, plaid-shirted men holding tree saws like rifles at ease, women bare armed but gloved for pulling branches, kids with puddle-muddied feet. Flora and Evian linked arms. Lee Annie sat now placid in her stroller. A little crowd gathered around Luther, for no reason except that he had *presence*—not exactly that he was a stranger, nor the strangeness of his draped neck and domed head, nor his bull-fiddle voice, but all of those and, more, the eddies of magnetic air he stirred with his churchly gestures, the sucking in of his belly, the Demosthenic choices of vocabulary. He identified himself as Trudy's nephew—"just passing through"—and took with a courtly bow their condolences for having picked "this unpropitious time." He lifted his arm and lowered his eyes in the posture of benediction, and not only the Baptists Flora, Evian, and Marion, but also Catholic Clyde Usvedt and Episcopalian Mary Moomis and atheist Dana and Bernadette the witch for no discernible reason bowed their heads.

"Lord, we have watched this night the terrible beauty of Your power," Luther said. "We have watched the heavens rent and we have watched the heavens healed. We step out into this new dawn with our hearts full of awe at Your majesty, and full of gratitude that we have been spared."

This was not all that far from what Dana was feeling at the moment, though Trudy whispered, "Always be needing the spotlight. Always was."

Luther drew breath to go on but was halted by a call of "Mizz Trudy! Mizz Trudy!" Down the street wheeled Samson Adams, known as Sams, recently turned twelve, making time on his secondhand Mongoose Mountain. "Mizzuz Trudy!" He took a pothole deeper than it looked, flinging water and hanging for a second before his front wheel thudded. He braked and squealed, tires spitting mud, and skidded sideways into the little crowd. "You house is *gone*!"

Small for a sink but bigger than a pond, the hole was an irregular oblong sixty feet across, at least that deep, still shifting silt and clods down its sheer sides. The john end of Trudy's double-wide had broken off and was submerged, upended, just the blasted window glass visible below the tea-dark water. On the far side of the hole the rest hung half in, half out, tipped on the tangle of vegetation that surrounded it as if the roots were holding it from falling. That may have been the case. A hunk of road had been swallowed, and a hundred-and-fifty-year-old live oak sucked down upright. The townspeople looked down on its topmost branches, several million leaves still quaking like green minnows.

"I was standing right there, Mizz Trudy. Wasn't nothin could be done for it."

"I woke up to it, ground shook like a dynamite!"

"And sound like a big old bathtub drain."

Trudy burst into wails, writhing between Flora and Evian, who held her back from diving in. Luther said, "Mysterious are His ways," but when there was no echo of affirmative he shut up like the rest of them, and after that Trudy stood stoic, or numb. The whole of Pelican Bay was gathered, near neighbors having come on foot as soon as they heard the news, and those from more than a mile away arriving in trucks and coupes stuffed full as a circus trick. They stood at a distance from the unsteady edge, leaning forward but backpedaling every time a miniature avalanche crumbled down the side. Dana put her arm around Trudy and with the other hand wiped her sleep-starved eyes. She had seen these people at the water's edge before, at Solly's funeral, but there they braved the surf in defiant elegy. Now they stood in their shorts and tank tops, their jeans and tees, hollow-eyed and hunched like souls waiting to cross the River Styx. She among them. Bits of useless learning floated in her mind: a Burne-Jones oil painting of the waiting shades, Dante's "muddied people in the slough," "the souls of those whom anger stupefied." She remembered that Styx was the river of hate and circled Hades nine times. Why nine times? Why the river of hate? More awesome to realize that a river flows underground at all. That it can open up any time. You ready an army and the attack comes by domestic air. You dodge a tempest and *terra* gapes.

Dana relinquished Trudy into the hugs of others. *If there's anything we can do. Honey, now, we get you through this.* Sams Adams, basking in double celebrity because his brother had last week been arraigned on a meth charge and today he had been chosen messenger, danced close to the edge, pointing out the flotsam, a piece of pipe, a box of Kleenex drifting in a vortex.

A man with a tree saw dangling from his hand admonished, "Sams, get back from there! You don't want to be making the six o'clock news."

"There a moccasin!" Sams alleged.

"Ain't no moccasin in a new sink, Sams. Git back from the edge."

A youth in a do-rag agreed, "That'll be a cypress knee. Come 'way from there."

"Ain't no knee. Be a snake for sure."

Scolding, the neighbors looked where he pointed. They followed the angle of his arm, where, sure enough, the alleged root bobbed and disappeared. It reemerged three feet on and dipped slithering between the treetop and the drowned trailer.

"Told you so!"

Within seconds, car trunks banged open, truck doors swung and slammed, at least four pistols and two rifles were aimed and blasted. The snake fled underwater.

"By the branch there! No, by the roots!"

"Git that mother!"

Bullets pocked the water. Some broke divots from the bank.

"Jesus!" said Dana under her breath, more alarmed by the firepower than the snake or the sink itself. But by that time the sheriff's patrol was arriving, five squad cars one after another. On the side of each car it said, *Trust, Loyalty, Commitment.* The guns disappeared the way they had come. Trunks and truck doors slammed.

The cops ordered vehicles out of the vicinity and cordoned off the sinkhole, and everyone obediently backed up, schooled by prime time in the authority of plastic tape. Two fire trucks pulled in, and the firemen circled the sinkhole checking that everyone was accounted for. This took a while, since some had evacuated before the hurricane and a few (Harry Moomis getting that stent in Tallahassee) were just away. A utilities crew arrived, no more than capping live wires for the moment because they had a dozen towns to get up and running. By noon an engineer from Water Management and a state geologist were poking the ground with iron rods to test its stability. Then there were reporters from Tallahassee and Winona Crossing and three TV camera crews, including one from as far away as Jacksonville, who set up shop on the ground declared more or less stable by the engineers.

Haggard—no one, including the cops and the repair guys on their cherry pickers, had slept last night—the town stood staring on into afternoon, into the dark water, half scared and half impressed with themselves to be on the periphery of such a drama. The locals said for the cameras the things that locals say for cameras—*like a movie; out of the blue; I was standing right in that spot there* . . . One of the cameramen lingered on Bernadette's spiked hair and belly ring, but all she could think to say was, "Like, rilly, what a *bum*mer." Luther on the other hand was dexterous dealing with the media. "Just when we think we have weathered the storm, the abyss appears at our feet," he told the local ABC affiliate. "People are feeling a sinkhole in their hearts right now. But this is a generous community. These are individuals who take a stranger in. And they will rally for their sister." Once again this was more or less what Dana had been feeling, though the sacramental language made her wince. Luther added it was a "miracle" he happened to be here visiting his aunt, and that the reporters "would most surely comprehend" if she didn't want to speak for the cameras.

The broken end of the trailer shifted—and dropped for all intents and purposes out of sight—whereas the living room and kitchen hung there in their bed of mangrove shrubs. The news cameras caught a few great shots that none of them would see because the electricity was out. One of the engineers told Trudy, "If you can find a tow trucker with guts enough," half her home might be pulled out and some of her belongings saved, though the structure would be "compromised." The land, of course, was gone. He said they "might inject grout and clay to halt the degradation," but, "anything you put in to plug it would collapse it all the worse."

Trudy, after her initial outburst, behaved with exemplary lack of fuss, though she kept a grip on Dana's arm that would leave a mark.

Luther spread general consolation. Some thought he had been sent by FEMA, and he didn't disabuse them. "All of us are sent," Luther contended, and the good folk of Pelican Bay could not quarrel with that.

"I feel He must have had a purpose in sending me here," Luther said, and set his tea mug gently on the coffee table. Green tea he drank. Surprising. But why was it surprising? Would it have been surprising if a white preacher or politico asked for green tea? It was surprising how delicately he could move his kielbasa fingers when it suited his purpose. And he did have purpose—you had to give him that.

"The ways of our Lord are mysterious but they are not altogether hidden from us. Sometimes we mistake our plan for His, and sometimes our eyes must be opened by storm and rupture, our hearts must be opened by the rending of our hearts."

She wasn't so ready to grant him the rent heart.

Six o'clock Sunday and they finally had electricity. Sag Island had been connected almost at once on generators trucked in for the purpose, but Pelican Bay was full of minimum wage and minimum leverage, so they'd had to make do. There had been block parties to use up everyone's refrigerator goods. A lot of warm beer had been drunk. The dogs had feasted on the scraps. Dana and Herbie scrambled to save what they could and give the rest away, cancel fresh-food orders and double up on the canned goods, keep open late and Sunday. Trudy, after three nights upstairs in the spare room on a borrowed blow-up mattress, had gone back to stay with Flora and Evian for the duration; and Luther now moved comfortably from East Sink house to house, having established himself as a kind of itinerant philanthropist.

His voice, which he never raised, seemed to emanate from the floors, resonate with the jalousies. "As is probably known to you, I haven't seen my aunt for many years, and that the confluence of events put me on her doorstep in her time of need—well, He works in a mysterious way."

Bullshit, of course. The "confluence of events" had put Luther on Trudy's doorstep to trap Cassius. And after that? Take his little girl away? Force him back into a marriage that couldn't work? Whip Dana's "bony ass"? All that was known to her for sure was that Trudy had chased Luther off her doorstep.

Dana was no longer physically afraid of him. Like an offscreen monster, he had been un-demonized by his appearance. Now it was more complicated. The fear had been replaced by a deep, amorphous mistrust, mixed with tiresome self-scrutiny. She wondered whether she would have found the same diction so irritating from a white man. *Yes.* She resented that she must ask herself these questions.

"I'll be frank with you—though perhaps this is already known to you. I grew up in a family that had no father."

Dana bobbled her head ambiguously. Known to her how? There might have been no father, but she happened to know that there had been a series of "uncles." Did he mean to lead her into revealing what she knew? Or was it just one of those oratorical repetitions of no significance? She'd lied about not knowing where Trudy lived—he would have realized that. If Luther knew her part in the "confluence of events," he was either clumsily concealing it or more deftly laying hints. She was out of her depth trying to guess which.

"My mother and her sister Trudy were verruh close. When Aunt Trudy took us to church she would carry in her purse little pink mints, little pink wintergreen mints to amuse us restless children. I was verruh small, I could not often understand the message of the preacher, but I could understand the mints. And to this day the message of the Lord carries for me a refreshing whiff of wintergreen."

He chuckled nostalgically, patting the arm of the sofa where one of Trudy's afghans lay and smiling with beautiful eyes in that unhappily formed head. She was touched, and resented being touched, and resented that she must soften to him a little and begrudge that little. She could see Trudy portioning out mints to quiet the children, could imagine Cassius, plump, squirming on the pew. She could not explain why Luther ended up as this boondock Sharpton and Cassius ended up as Cassius: funny, ironic, loving.

"I remember standing in my mama's living room while the two sisters, Trudy and Margaret, took apart old sweaters, sweaters from the trash, sweaters with holes in the elbows and coming apart at the hem. And they would pick at a thread and unravel these sweaters and roll the yarn into a ball. And they would knit this salvaged yarn into afghan squares, cutting out the bad parts and tying the yarn underneath so they could knit them into shawls to cover our beds in winter. Perhaps this is already known to you."

Not wanting to meet those Cassius eyes, she looked into space, and the space she looked into held the Blake drawing on the wall, all evil browns and blues and naked flesh, three gnarled figures in the mouth of a cave, the setting sun showing through the clouds behind. In the foreground a bearded man and a young woman knelt chained together back-to-back, behind them a youth folded into himself in apathy and grief. She knew the caption well now, though she'd meant to look it up and failed to get around to it. *Visions of the Daughters of Albion.* Underneath that it said, *The Eye sees more than the Heart knows.* Curious. You'd think it would be the other way around.

"There came to be a quarrel between my mother and her sister. Misunderstanding came between them, and they grew angry, and they grew estranged. To be frank with you, a silence came between them that lasted many years."

"To be frank with you" was a favorite trope with Graham on the stump, always followed by a lie: "hope of the future," "accountability in government," et cetera. One would never follow "to be frank with you" with an uncomfortable frankness. Would never say, for example: *To be frank with you, Luther, I am carrying your brother's child. Perhaps that is already known to you.*

"I have heard it said that the falling away of the land is a signal of God's displeasure. I do not believe it. I do not believe in a vengeful God, but a healing God."

"No," Dana said. "It would make you wonder, wouldn't it, if He picked an old woman to punish."

Luther chuckled—not sweetly this time. She had broken his euphonius flow. He sipped his tea. Set it down as delicately as bone china, though it was an ironstone mug. "I have walked among the people here in your little town. I have talked to them as they went about the business of cleaning up after the storm. I have seen their industry and I have seen their generosity, I have seen them sharing food and heat and light. I have seen them solacing their sister whose home was lost in the terrible collapse."

"Salt of the earth," Dana agreed, and then remembering Solly added, "and some pepper, too." Luther raised his eyebrows and fixed her with a benign look. *Oh, god. Salt and pepper.* "I mean, some of them are eccentric. Feisty . . ."

"Yes, indeed." He splayed his fingers ruminatively on his knees. He took a breath that flexed his diaphragm. "Nor is it only the people on the east side of the road who have given of their pittance. I have crossed over and been welcomed into the homes of the white folk of this community, even as you have welcomed me into yours."

She waved this off and immediately felt her gesture to be stingy. She could do nothing right in front of this Luther, nothing authentic. Nor could she be certain where he was coming from, though she had a pretty fair idea where he was going. For the truth was that, apart from his rhetoric, she couldn't fault him. He'd capitalized on the brief publicity of the sink in ways no one else in Pelican Bay would have thought of. In a matter of days he'd organized the local women to take up collections at their churches. He'd launched an appeal with an interview in the *Tallahassee Democrat.* He'd contacted the black owner of a trailer franchise in Panama City who'd agreed, in exchange for widespread acknowledgment, to provide a "manufactured home" at cost. This should have made her admire him, whereas in fact it made her sulk. She envied his easy acceptance by the town. And yet they had accepted her in the same way.

"I have seen with my own eyes your care for my aunt, and those of us who had the good fortune to shelter in your home in the hurricane know the extent of your generosity."

"Thank you." Dana said. "It's not a matter . . ."

"Be assured I am not asking you for money. I would take my aunt back to her family if she so desired, but she has made her home here now for many years, and she is loath to break ties with her friends of long standing." He hesitated for a moment after this renovation of the facts. His Adam's apple did a slow, froglike bob. "I hear from some in the community that you have the good fortune to be Mr. Solomon's heir."

She was not surprised he had learned this, though she wondered who the "some" might be. Adena would be unlikely to spread the rumor and so give Dana's claim legitimacy. Trudy was close-mouthed as a matter of principle, and Herbie did not gossip. Bernadette was an innocent in the Blakian sense of *clueless*. More likely the gossip traveled on hints and guesses, which have a disconcerting rate of accuracy. Dana said, "And you want me to donate the land for Trudy's trailer."

Luther's eyes lit. He had tight-curled eyelashes like a girl. Like Cassius. He murmured, "You anticipate me."

"Your information isn't entirely accurate," she heard herself say archly. She'd always picked up the local lingo when she was a kid. A way of fitting in. "Mr. Solomon's niece is the actual proprietor of the land. But I don't see why she wouldn't be amenable." She lifted the teapot so that he would turn down a refill and know enough to leave. "To be frank with you, I can't see any problem."

25

It might not have been the best idea to go straight to Sag Island. She hadn't ever caught up with the lost night's sleep, and her mind still skittered, lighting now on this, now that. But she wanted to have this one thing settled. Tomorrow the real-estate market would crank up again, and it was hard to get Adena's attention once she was in selling mode.

October was back in its glory, the air over the bridge soft, the water winking. The necklace of sand on the bay side reflected a full moon. Tamarack and oleander seemed to throw up burnt paper scraps: bats greeting the young evening, as inevitable over this piece of earth as the snakes in the undergrowth.

It occurred to her as odd that she'd never been invited where she was now headed, but then Adena came so often to the mainland, and had no doubt formed a one-way habit over years with Solly. Dana knew the address and had passed the house several times on her way to the beach. It was a Cape Cod bungalow in the "third tier"—that is, two streets back from the Gulf—built straight on the sandlot in a time before the regulations required stilt construction, and clad before vinyl siding had conquered the whole shoreline of America. Its aqua clapboard was in need of paint. It had a wide veranda, a forecourt of scrub grass, and a walkway with a latticed arch. She pulled up behind Bernadette's Camaro just as the gate of this arch flapped open and Bernadette flew out, face streaming, features bunched and knotted under the jaundiced streetlamp. She raced blindly past, flip-flops sounding on the verge, breath keening through her nose. She ripped open her car door and flung back toward the house, "You killed him! And now you want to kill me!"

Dana would have fled then, but Adena was already at the gate, drink in hand, her mouth wide in incipient yell. "Bern-a-*dette*!" She saw Dana and pulled back, a chin-doubling, exaggerated double take, laughed, lifted her glass. "Oh, lordy, you caught us. Welcome to teenage tantrums one-o-one." The Camaro spluttered into life and lurched away.

"I'm sorry. I can come back later."

"No, no, no. Couldn't be a better time. I could do with a chance to rant, I've been on the receiving end all afternoon." She stepped back and performed a theatrical bow that ended in a catch for balance, and Dana realized she was drunk. Not seriously so, not falling-down-pissed, just a little ruddy, a little sloppy. Her hair was tousled, her white shirt tied at the midriff over a pair of white capris streaked with mud or sauce or blood. *You killed him.* The classic roasting of the pet rabbit, maybe?

"I never saw her like that. Will she be all right?"

"Oh, yeah. Come on in." Adena beckoned as if winding a ball of yarn. "You gotta make allowances, though, we're in a cyclone here." She clattered up the path. "I see her that way a *lot*." She shoved the door open and turned again to Dana. "Seriously, y'know, since the hurricane I haven't had a goddam minute to tidy up. It's a dis*aster*."

"Shit, I don't care," said Dana, but was nevertheless impressed with the morass of goods and chattels that met her gaze. The couch was piled with towels and underwear, the floor with plastic bags, the table on a dais with cereal boxes, the sink in the open kitchen beyond with dishes. Stacks of real-estate brochures, forms, files, and manila envelopes covered the end tables and a credenza. A computer was open on a coffee table spilling with more of the same. It had the look of a long-accreted habitat rather than recent crisis. On one side of the dais or platform that served as a dining room stood the piano, rising from the detritus rich with gloss, a dozen dead plants on its upright top. On its keyboard lid a coffee cup, a paisley garment of some kind, and a tuxedo cat, recumbent but awake.

"Christ, you know?" Adena said panning the room. "It's awful, ain't it? You don't see it until somebody else does. Want a Harvey Wallbanger?'

"Sure. What's a Harvey Wallbanger?"

"A sort of a tarted-up vodka orange. You'll like it. Just lemme . . ." She whipped a few pieces of clothing from the couch and a chair, disappeared beyond a door and reappeared at once. "Where'd I put my glass? Gilbey's okay? You're not supposed to like it, but just call me trash." She giggled. She dug in the cupboard for a glass and set about the making of the drinks. Dana stepped up on the platform to pet the cat, who rose to her fingers, writhed deliciously, turned, and hissed. Stacked against the near side of the piano, three feet high, was a pile of brightly colored boutique bags—stapled or ribbon tied, as if bought but never opened. Dana ran her fingers sentimentally over the owl-face pattern in the wood of the piano. The cat bumped her fingers.

"Do you get much chance to play?"

"God, I meant to call you about that. I've been so busy. No, I tell a lie, I put off calling you, I felt so bad. The tuner came, you know? It can't be fixed; the sounding board is cracked. And not only can't it be tuned, it's actually *dangerous,* he said. The board's under a gazillion pounds of pressure."

"Dangerous how?"

"It could explode."

"I never heard of that."

"Uh-huh. And after all your gorgeous work. I feel just *terrible.* But what can you do? Shit happens, right?"

"Right." Resentment simmered in her. An exploding piano? Didn't sound quite credible, but then, what did she know? The cat insisted against her fingers. Dana relented and stroked. "What's her name?"

"What? Oh, *his.* That's Horse. Bernadette blackmail, from back during the divorce. She wanted a pony, naturally—well, she was twelve years old. They all want a horse at twelve. I told her this was the best I could manage. Now she'd trade him in a heartbeat—'cause he's not black enough for a *familiar.* Throw something off and take a seat."

"What's she upset about?"

"Oh, nothing. *No-thing.* It's the seventeen-year-old job description. You have to announce the end of the world at least once a week. Speaking of the end of the world—I haven't got over to see your sinkhole yet, the rentals have been crazy. Wouldn't you think people would know what's meant by an act of God? *No, you don't get reimbursed for a mandatory evacuation.* Criminently. How is everybody coping over there?"

"Okay, considering. We've got power back. Trudy rolls with the punches and gives Jesus all the credit. We found a tow trucker 'with guts enough' to pull her house out, and she's salvaged quite a lot. That's actually why I came to see you."

"Poor Trudy. She's always been a right old complainer. Now she's got something to complain about."

"Mm." This seemed a particularly inept description of Trudy. "Listen." Dana accepted the drink and sipped it. It was herbal and oversweet—vodka, orange, vanilla, but more complicated. Anise, maybe? "Trudy has insurance, it turns out. I was looking through Solly's old papers to find out what coverage we had for the store, and there was a policy he took out in her name. Paid through the year, so it's just as well it happened now instead of January. State Farm sent the adjuster out, and they'll do the value of a replacement. But naturally they don't cover the land. *What, land?* They never heard of such a thing."

"Insurance companies. Don't get me started. Do you want some nuts or something?"

Dana shook her head. "But Luther—you know, Trudy's nephew that was there that night?—he's got the churches donating to replace her furniture."

"Uh-huh." Adena made a nest of the towels on the couch and

wiggled in, slipping her flats off and tucking her feet back under her thighs. She rolled her glass against her cheek. "If god didn't want us to have Harvey Wallbangers, he wouldn't have made Galliano." She performed a delicious sigh and threw her head back on the couch. Horse leaped and settled against her thigh. "Now, Bucky, you could never get him to drink anything with a liqueur in it. Your real alcoholic doesn't like the taste of sugar, did you know that? Of course Bucky drank mainly Bud, but you could set any rotgut in front of him long as it wasn't sweet, any snake poison, any moonshine, and he'd slug it down the same as the beer. By the six-pack, I mean. Bernadette doesn't like to hear that! I don't mean to go on about him, but, poor Bern — loses him, and then Solly so soon after, her whole world comes falling down. I think that's why she was so upset about the sinkhole. Don't you?"

"Was she?" For the first time Dana saw Adena's logorrhea not as excess of candor but as the verbal equivalent of the chaos on her floor. Random flinging of whatever came to hand. Poor Adena — who emerged every morning with her makeup impeccably in place, scarf cunningly knotted, color-coordinated sling backs over a pedicure. Dana took a breath and plunged. "Luther suggested giving Trudy a plot off of Solly's land."

"He did, did he?"

"I'd already thought of it, actually. The section along the highway next to the store is high and dry, and the utilities would be easy to connect. I could give her permission to put the trailer there right away — they call them 'manufactured homes,' naturally — and then when all the paperwork is done, you could make it official."

Adena, head lolling, rolled it back and forth in time with the syllables: "Da-na, Da-na, Je-sus." She toasted with her glass. "What did I tell you he was after?!"

"I know. But it was hardly Luther who caused the sinkhole. I don't like him either, I think he's creepy, but — I can't see he's getting anything out of this himself, unless it's 'laying up treasures in heaven.' No, I take that back. He's one of those people who gets off on being the good guy."

"And you? Don't you get off on being a good guy?"

There followed a silence with a sting in it. Then Adena combed at her hair with her fingers, rolled her eyes. *"Didn't cause the sinkhole,* but he knows how to make use of it, doesn't he? Not Trudy's kin for nothing."

"It's really nothing to do with him," Dana said hotly. "It's just simple, an acre—half an acre if you like. She's lost the ground she *lived* on."

"Yes, well, I'm really sorry. But it isn't simple—or not the way you think. Anyway, that land is in *West* Sink. How do you think the Moomises and the Usvedts will take to having an old black woman on their side of the road?"

"Jesus, that'd be pretty stupid. They live closer to each other as it is."

"Just wait till they start talking about *property values,* which they will. You think I'm the only one around here that keeps an eye on the market, just give another think."

"This is the twenty-first century, for god's sake. Keeping her out would be illegal, for a start . . ."

"What are you going to do, take West Sink to court? Naw, you're in over your head there. Everybody's all nice and concerned and touchy-feely for the moment while the sinkhole's fresh. But—an old black woman in a trailer—have you read about the haggling over the towers in New York, over who's owed what? That's the twenty-first century in spades. Excuse my French."

Maybe Adena was drunker than she'd seemed. "She was Solly's *wife,*" Dana said. "Tell West Sink that's the way it is, they'll take your word for it. You know they will. Just do it while the honeymoon is still in progress."

"Mmm." Adena seemed to consider the primacy of her word. Now she sat up, put her glass down carefully, her far hand flat for balance on the table. Her face took on the efficient-businesswoman mode, except that she wobbled slightly. "And what do you think Lempicke and Zetti are going to say? *Oh, we lose an acre of highway access? No problem.* I don't think so. No, Dana. The deal is for the whole packet."

"What deal?"

"The whole enchilada. Not forty-five acres minus a chunk right in the middle of the front where there happens to be an old black woman in a house trailer."

"What deal is that?"

"Wait till you see what they're gonna do. Primo quality, I mean *primo,* kid you not. Two hundred and eighty units, houses and high-rise and time-share mixed in with stores. Neo-eclectic. Two pools, exercise room, sauna, hot tub, it's the cat's *meow.*" She stroked the cat's tuxedo front. "Isn't it Horse-ums? Mexican tile. Beaucoup balconies. Corian shower stalls. Wait till you see!"

Dana's breath snagged in her diaphragm. "The will isn't settled yet," she said evenly. "We aren't even sure all Solly's hospital bills have been paid. There can't be any deal to sell the land."

"Contingent." Adena lofted her hand and twirled it: *poof.*

"It's contingent on my signing it over to you."

Adena giggled, mocked a pout. "Oh. You want a cut now?"

"No, I don't want a cut. I want you to give an acre to Trudy Lewis."

"No."

"Tell you what," Dana said. "I'll sign over forty-four acres to you. The other one will be my 'cut.'"

Adena hiccupped softly. "Seriously. This. Is. Going to. Happen. Don't get in the way of it." She let her jaw drop, widened her eyes. "I'll tell you what. I *will* cut you in. Seriously, it's only fair. I'll give you five percent. Like an agent's fee. It'll knock your socks off how much that comes to!" She downed her drink.

Dana sat forward and pressed her fingertips into her nape, slid them up to the base of her skull. She couldn't tell from Adena's tone how much of this was vodka, how much play, and how much threat.

She said, "Then I'll keep it."

She intended to say this, it's not as if she "heard herself saying it" and was surprised. But, saying it, her heart knocked so hard she thought she felt the baby kick, which was not possible, not yet. Her eyes held the pattern of a cushion on the floor, primitive birds worked in the weave, some flying one way and some another. She felt herself suspended for a moment in their wayward flight.

Adena scoffed. "You don't want it. You told me you didn't want it."

"I've changed my mind."

"You won't get the same deal, don't think you will. They'll steal you blind. I'm a pro. You're better off taking me up on my offer."

"I'm not selling it. I'm going to keep it."

"What, as a swamp?"

"As a wetland, yes."

"And be a shopkeeper for the rest of your life?"

"I don't know. Maybe I will."

"What a load of crap." Adena stood abruptly, lost her balance, retrieved it with the hand on the coffee table, and leaned toward Dana with teeth bared, and a steely gaze so theatrically intended to be a steely gaze that Dana suppressed a laugh. "You're out of your depth, *Mizz* Dana. I will take you to court so fast . . ."

"To court! For what?"

"We'll see what a judge has to say about your puny claim."

"The will is good," Dana said, surprised. And remembered, "The doctor will testify Solly was compos mentis."

"Compos-my-ass." Adena stood unsteadily and folded her arms. "I've got his toenails!"

This time Dana did laugh. The technology of medicine contained many marvels, but she didn't think there was any sanity test for toenail clippings. "Why don't you sober up, Adena?" She set down her glass, picked up her keys, and picked her way through the debris. "We'll talk again. But Trudy *will* have a piece of ground for her home."

All across the bay she tested the thick and plosive sound of the word: *shopkeeper.* She saw the address in Cassius's hand on the cover of her paperback: *Sollys Corner, Highway 98. Pelican Bay, Florida.* She said aloud, "What have I done?"

But the store/house rose in ramshackle welcome among the pines, the upstairs window lit by a reflection of the moon. She pulled into the familiar patch of pine straw between the back door and the cabin, then swerved to miss the Camaro, which was parked with its nose snub against Herbie's door.

Well, well.

Freezers and refrigerators had to be wiped down with baking soda, the floor dried with a fan heater where there were leaks or spills. The cases restocked, which meant dealing with a dozen deliverymen: beer, soft drinks, ice cream, dairy, bakery, sundries, electrical, farmer's market, eggs and cheese. The insurance adjuster. Dig out the orders and bills for what she'd lost to the storm. Find some credible evidence (how do you come by that?) as to how much rotting or souring stuff she'd thrown away. Phoebe was pressing her to get back online, but there wasn't time to go out and buy a laptop. She expected a call from Adena, and in the clear light of day half expected a postbinge apology, but no such call came. Bernadette seemed preoccupied, but that was not unusual. If you asked whether she was okay, she smiled in her absent, beatific way. "No problem." Herbie was anxiously in love, part mooning calf, part nurse. The sanding of the downstairs floors had been indefinitely postponed.

Tuesday Dana was alone in the store — she and Herbie had made out a rotation to keep open seven days a week — when a couple strolled in, recognizable as tourists by his guaybera shirt, her linen capris. They made for the refrigerator cases, the woman dawdled over the display of rope sandals while the man, a six-pack of bottled water in one hand, rounded the aisle to study the Slim Jims display. That brought him facing her. With a pleasant shock she recognized Gavin McGarvey. Leathered jowls, spaniel eyes, a thick and unruly mop of silver hair. He picked out a bag of Planters cashews and a Mountain Man turkey jerky with the same deliberative style he'd displayed on the catwalk of Atlantic Mills. The executive goes slumming. Mrs. McGarvey — as silver haired as he but more impeccably coiffed, a former beauty by the set of her cheekbones — came to him, said something in his ear. He bent his head, deferring. Dana waited amused, embarrassed, wondering what she'd say. *Just helping out. Researching recycling in small-town retail.* Would he have the grace to be embarrassed, too, at how he'd lauded an enterprise already on the block?

He set his things on the counter. Dana said, "Will that be all?"

"Yeah. No—thanks—a pack of Marlboro Lights."

"Flip top or soft?"

"Flip top."

He glanced up, smiled on auto-pilot, reached for his wallet. She rang up the water, the sandals, the nuts and jerky, the cigarettes. He handed her a fifty. She said, "Is traffic heavy out there today?"

Which forced him to look at her. "Not very."

"There are still a lot of people coming back from the evacuation."

"There are?" Now he angled his lustrous head, quizzical, and looked her full in the eyes. Off to her left Mrs. McGarvey sauntered out the door. He said, "I thought that was last week."

She counted the change into his hand. "People are slow around here sometimes."

He nodded, arched his lip, which could have been a sneer, but was not, was just a question mark of the mouth. He smiled, rote. "Thanks a lot." He took his bag and followed his wife outside.

She lay in the bed that had been Solly's, propped on the pillows that had been Solly's, looking out over Sag Island to the watery rounding of the world. Lights edged the narrow strip at the island's eastern reach. Beyond that the lamps of the shrimp boats dotted the black sea so that it was as if the stars began on land and continued in an upward arc through the water to the sky. *Let there be light.* It was more beautiful than any view she caught as a girl on the backseat of a Malibu trying to fix one image of the fleeting world.

It was too early to feel the baby but she listened for it with an inner ear, to the pumping of her blood, the traverse of oxygen, nutrients, trace minerals, vitamins—the engine of this creature not yet viable but alive. Her longing for Cassius had become a dull ache that ran under the surface of all things. In the real world, what you don't expect arrives from the direction you least expect it. In place of Cassius, Luther comes.

She worked at accepting, now, that Cassius would not come for her. She told herself that it was, like the loss of Chloe, a necessary ache. As Chloe's enchanting particularity had gradually dwindled to a few details (toenails, palm, iris, mole), so her memory of Cassius was now reduced to a handful of snapshots: ironic glance, sly, crooked smile, pallor of her hand against his thigh. And even as Chloe and Cassius lost definition in her mind, this new-made tadpole invisibly went on acquiring its particulate and particular self.

She was awed at the infinite convergence of chance that went into the creation of exactly this live thing. It was the butterfly effect in reverse, not a butterfly flapping its wings on one side of the world to cause a tempest on the other, but a cataclysm of events that must fall randomly into place in order to produce the identity of one ordinary soul. It's not a question of whether we *have* free will, but that our will is so minuscule beside the forces of history and chance that bring us to the point of choice. Look how many deaths had coincided that this particular infant might be born: Chloe's death, which revealed the shambles of her marriage; Graham's death, which kept her when she meant to go; the three thousand deaths of nine-eleven, which immobilized her for half a year. The mother of some unknown security guard for whose sake Cassius had exchanged shifts; Bucky Solomon, who would have been heir to this spot, looking out this window, if he had not died instead. And Solly, who for reasons still not understood had chosen her. It was not a mystery but a web of mysteries that she was here: hand on belly, pillows, window, sea, stars.

26

SHE FISHED WITH TRUDY on the dock, learning to curl the hook through the shape of the shrimp's body, to let the thumb trigger go at the apex of the cast, to dance the line left and right as she reeled it in. She was a novice at this, though she remembered river fishing with her father, he in hip boots balancing on slimy rocks while she lay reading on the bank, lazily glancing at her bobbin from time to time.

Trudy, like her father, fished impassive and intent. Trudy walked the dock in rubber clogs the color of wet moss, from trap to pipe-rooted line and line to trap, squatting at the cooler to pick up a chip of ice that she turned between her hands until it had melted into nothing, casting with the heft of her whole body behind the arc of the bait, dropping to a stool as if suddenly depleted, only to start up again.

Everyone in the town agreed that Trudy was remarkable—unruffled, doggedly drying and sorting the contents retrieved from her ruined home. But Dana saw this seeming serenity in a different light. On the dock her pacing had the rhythm of fetish or obsession. She was losing weight. It didn't show in her stolid body, but the globe of her face had dented like a deflated basketball. The contours of jaw and cheek appeared, hollows under her lusterless eyes.

What Dana believed was that, for Trudy, the void had opened up with Solly's death. That the land collapsed was no more than punctuation. Not that Trudy thought in metaphors. No. Solly died. The land he bought for her was sucked away. One confirmed the other. That was that.

Henry had given Trudy the week off—a sort of compassionate leave that was, Dana thought, not necessarily a kindness. Normal routine might have brought her quicker back to normalcy. But there was no doubt that fishing was Trudy's therapy, and she spent her days on Henry's dock twenty yards from the job of which she had been relieved.

"Your redfish and bluefish, ladyfish, come 'round this skinny water here," Trudy pronounced. "You want big fish, tuna or grouper or snapper, you need a boat out deep."

She seemed glad enough of Dana's company (instructed her, laughed at her gaffes, affirmed her rare catch), at least insofar as you could read Trudy, who espoused reticence as a way of life. What must it have been like, evenings with Solly—that sunny and loquacious man, and Trudy as backboard, buffer, muffler, straight man, judge—that she should be so palpably grief stricken at his loss?

Now Trudy concentrated on bait and trap, but from time to time she bestowed information of a kind, and friendship of a kind. She had not forgiven Luther, and that he had appeared just now was harder for her than it was for Dana. He was a reminder of the family who had spurned her, he whose unctuous help she must now accept because she needed it, and because her community would see her as ungrateful if she did not. "He find a way to put me in his debt, make him all puff and proud. He love to hear everybody tell how I should be proud, how he so fine."

"You have to admit he's done a lot."

"I admit it. I surely do admit it. I surely thank him. Now I be pleased if he go on up north with the family."

"Can you convince him to?"

"Maybe can, maybe cain't. I be thinking on it."

Trudy continued to insist that Luther didn't know who Dana was, in any connection other than part-time employer. More enlightening—real information—was that Luther had no intention of forcing Cassius and the child back to Isobel.

"I never met that woman. But she batty-haywire, Luther say. She come in my sister's house and smash up the TV. They crank up the car and she rise up in the headlights like a haunt." And this was apparently not new behavior, but long-standing trouble for the family. Isobel had burned Cassius's clothes, slashed his tires, threatened him with a kitchen knife. "That woman ain't right, Luther say, she talk so cold and do so hot."

Cassius had specified none of these things to Dana, no fires, knives, or vandalism, only "terrible fights" in the generic. Male pride, it would have been, that kept him from those details. Whereas for her part Dana had assumed that all but Cassius and Antwan were parties to her terrorizing. She had not counted on insurgencies among the Huston factions.

"What does Luther want with Cassius, then?"

"Want him to drop his fancy woman, come up to Pennsylvania with the family, let Margaret and all them help to raise up that chile."

Like every idea of Luther's this seemed feasible, even reasonable, at the same time as it insulted her. Why was she not adequate to *raise up that chile*? Why should a grandmother do a better job than she?

Often they fished for half an hour without a catch, sometimes in the earthy sea smells of weed and salt, or when the wind turned, in the infernal stench of the paper mill. Either way, there was no sound but the lapping at the dock, the intermittent whistling of a cast. One day the water was abruptly clogged with silver, as if giant coins were being spun alongside the dock. Then they began to leap, silver slivers taller than they were wide, shimmering parabolas. Dana fumbled to bait her hook, but Trudy stayed her arm. "Angelfish ain't got meat enough to make a soup. Lord give 'em a purpose to be pretty only."

Another afternoon a flock of small tufted birds lit in a tamarind, so numerous that the branches bounced. Each bird cocked its crest and called one harsh note. Each black tail was brightly edged as if dipped in yellow paint.

"Waxwing," Trudy said. They fished for another twenty minutes while the birds continued their laconic chat. Then Trudy ventured, in the grudging tone that might augur self-revelation, "I aksed the preacher at AME."

Dana waited.

"They say we reunited in heaven. But if Solly and Mrs. Solly going to reunite, will I go back to where I was taking care of Mrs. Solly? Or back before I know them?" She frowned at this mystery. "Reverend say there some things hard to trust but you got to do it in the Lord."

"But that didn't answer your question."

"No."

One waxwing took off, and then the whole flock followed, as if slung upward in a net. Dana used the untangling of a knot to cover her hesitation. "You know I don't believe in it, don't you, Trudy?"

"Mr. Solly didn't believe neither. Jesus going to let that sin go by."

"Well, then, the way I understand it, in heaven all our hatred and anger and jealousy will be—I was going to say burned away—but not burned, just gone. So Solly will love you. But Mrs. Solly will be fine with that. And you won't mind that he's also still with her."

Trudy considered this, shook her head. "It's hard."

"It's hard," Dana admitted.

"Reverend say everything in time won't be in time, it be all at once. Time come from the devil, he say, a game he play." She shook her head again, once, twice, three times. "You got to trust."

A while later, settled on her usual stool, tugging the hook from a whiting's mouth, Trudy mused, "Then my sister Margaret going to forgive me for going with Solly, ain't she?"

"So far as I understand it."

"But I don't want her to. I throw her 'giveness *back*." She tugged the hook free. The force of her judgment informed her arm. The fish flew overhand twenty feet out into the water. "And I don't forgive *her.* And I don't want to. And I don't want to *want to.*"

Still, it was another day before Dana got up the courage to tell what she had come to tell. It was, unusually, a cloudy afternoon, the water dull, the week of "compassionate leave" almost gone by. And she had taken advantage of Herbie's good nature by spending so much time away from the store. She sat on a bench and hooked her elbow over the railing, having learned by now how to make it support her without crashing into the bay. Trudy pulled a trap, extracted a pair of midnight-blue crabs, and installed them in the cooler with a satisfied grunt.

"Trudy, did you know I'm pregnant?"

Trudy put the lid on the cooler, crabs scrabbling noisily inside. "I seen the signs." She fixed Dana with a stern look. "You been for the amnio?"

This was not the question Dana expected. Her first reaction was to laugh. "Yes. I went up to Tallahassee. The baby's *fine.*" But Trudy held her scolding gaze, then dropped her eyes and superfluously resettled the cooler lid. She held her head awry. Her hands fumbled at each other—and Trudy's hands were never less than nimble. Dana blurted a guess. "Trudy? Were you ever pregnant?"

Trudy flapped a hand at the question, stretched her head, frowning, as if against a stiff neck. She pressed her palms together between her knees. She was wearing a wide-brimmed calico hat today, which made no sense since there was no sun to speak of, but Trudy had her own sartorial reasoning. It was cool enough for both of them to be wearing sleeves in the middle of afternoon. Trudy pressed her hands between her calves down to the ankles, then straightened up and said without looking at Dana, "Mrs. Solly was a long time dying."

Dana said nothing. And little by little, letting frequent silence fall, repeatedly rubbing her hands between her legs and leaning into them as if keening, Trudy rewarded her patience by describing those days of Mrs. Solly's long-time dying. How Solly sat by Mrs. Solly's bed hour after hour. How he went downstairs to sit in the big chair and cry. How he walked like a ghost, forgot to mind the store, forgot to eat or sleep. How Trudy cared for Mrs. Solly's food and medicine, changing the sheets from under her, spooning the broth three times a day. Turning her pillows, rubbing her feet. It went on day after day, month after month. Solly got thin, and Trudy began cooking for him as well. Looking after the clothes he no longer cared about. Tidying the store at night, the house by day. And then one night he was weeping in the downstairs chair, and she put herself in front of him, standing against his knees, offering herself as a wailing wall. He put his arms around her hips and sobbed into her belly. Trudy put her arms around his head and bade him shush.

"That was a good man, knowed how to love. I always thought I would do like that for him, like he done for her, weep his passing. I didn't know he'd die in no time at all." She bit her thumb and lifted it from her mouth with a little flip, a shrug from the wrist only. She glanced at Dana. "Yeah, I got with child," she said. "Early on, too early on."

"You didn't have the baby."

"How I'm going to have that baby? What he's going to do, that may be his wife is still alive when time for the baby come, or if she not long in the ground, what he's going to do, 'knowledge me and that chile?"

"Oh, Trudy. What did you do?"

"I went to my sister but she turn me out, so I went to my cousin Charlene and she help me deal."

"I'm so sorry."

"Anyway, the devil know how to lay his hand. That baby was no good. I was near on fifty then. I had the amnio test, and they told me that baby was a Down."

"Oh, Trudy. How did Solly take it?"

Trudy looked up, shocked. "I tell Solly nothing! I com ome, he was nearer dead than Mrs. Solly, and with thinking, too t I didn't care but to run out on him." Her face had been lax w emembering, but now the crescent shadows under her eyes tight again, her full mouth bitter. "All while I was gone Ade ne over hassling at him. She come to him all carrying on ucky couldn't do her right. She drank with Solly. She know how to drink, she egg him on, even though she be all the time crying that Bucky drink too much."

"And you never told Solly about the pregnancy?"

"How that's going to help anything?"

"That was hard for you."

"You best believe it." Trudy drew one foot out of a clog, set it on her knee, and pressed her thumbs into the pink flesh of her sole. "It was Solly told *me,* all about that Adena. She mess his head up sum'n fierce. He never did touch a drink again after that night."

Dana noticed it was the male of the quartet whose wounds were salved, while Winifred Solomon went on with her dying, and Adena went back to Bucky, and Trudy carried the burden of the secret. "I don't know how you could keep that in for so many years."

The crab trap had been idle all this time, unbaited on the dock. Now Trudy picked up her knife and carved a bloody slab of mullet flesh. She jerked the hook through it. "Don't nobody get all they want," she said.

27

TAKING STOCK AGAIN. She stood for the time being in the pervasive mood of loss, mostly behind the counter of a small-town Florida-coast general store, not-waiting for Cassius, not doing much of anything else, letting what would happen happen.

What next?

Adena called.

Bernadette had two suspicious moles on her thigh, which was not especially surprising because her skin was naturally so pale and how could she avoid the sun growing up on Sag Island? Bucky was just the same, supposed to wear a hat though he almost never did and the Pensacola doctor who did the biopsy said Bernadette's moles needed to be removed but the insurance wouldn't pay even though the condition was precancerous because by some bureaucratic blooper or sleight of hand they, the insurance, those assholes, considered it elective surgery. Adena needed a thousand dollars.

She was urgent, friendly, confiding, and confident. She made no reference to Dana's Sunday-night intrusion, and her tone so thoroughly excluded reference to their quarrel that she must have forgotten it. Isn't that how a blackout works? You seem to be purposeful and quasi-reasonable while you're drinking but you do and say outrageous things that you don't remember afterward?

Dana said, "The estate is in a sort of limbo now. You're getting payments on the bequest, aren't you, but . . . uh, the principle . . ."

"It's not in probate is it? The will was legal?"

Caught off balance, Dana began to waver. She'd always said Solly owed Adena, and if Adena didn't even remember Sunday night . . . *Don't you get off on being a good guy?* "Listen. I can send you the thousand dollars, but I want you to understand, about the land . . ."

"You're a brick. I'm forever grateful. Insurance companies! And, listen, Dana, I want you to know you can count on me to stick up for you."

"Stick up for me how?"

"You know—if there's anybody bad-mouthing you about Solly, an old man on his last legs like that."

On the TV screen a drawbridge parted to let a steamship pass, accompanied by a voice: *What can a drawbridge teach us about brokerage firms?* Dana felt herself to be living in a major disconnect. "I know it seems unjust to you," she said, "even vindictive, because you looked after him for so long. We can talk about it, nothing's written in stone—except, whatever else, I'm turning over an acre to Trudy." At the far end of the wire, a plosive silence. Dana said gently, "You know if Solly was alive that's what he'd do."

"*Phh!* You don't know shit about what Solly would do. Solly would do what he damn well pleased, vindictive ain't the half of it, grudging, penny-pinching joker that he was. Just see how your *written in stone* and your *whatever else* hold up under cross-examination."

"Under what?" Dana thought: We watch too much television.

"Don't think they won't look into it. Don't be surprised if they have you up for elder abuse. Or extortion. I saw the way you sidewinded him. He was always a fool for a pretty girl."

This was so off the mark that she wondered if Adena was truly deranged. And yet hadn't Adena always cheerfully talked this way about Solly, about Bucky? About Bernadette, when it came to that?

Phoebe called.

"Did you see the Army Fifth Corps and the Marines Something-Force moved their HQ to Kuwait?"

"I saw."

"What I want to know is, how come it was the Sydney newspaper that got the scoop? Isn't Australia a ways from the Middle East?"

"They're going to attack, aren't they?"

"It's déjà vu to the nth degree. I swear to god, when it was Reagan in the Oval I thought we had it bad, but now it's Bonzo. Hey? Are you okay?"

"Okay. I've had a crazy call from Adena Solomon. She's talking about taking me to court for the land I said I was going to give her."

"How come?"

"I told you about going over there—I think she was drunker than I thought."

"Don't give her any money."

"I didn't, but she's asking for another thousand. Some skin operation for Bernadette—and that doesn't make sense either. Did you ever hear of elective surgery for precancer?"

"Don't give her a penny. Call your redneck geek."

"Who?"

"Your lawyer."

"Oh, Perry. I never thought of myself as somebody with a lawyer. But I will if she keeps it up."

"I'm not kidding."

Tork and Milly Allanson, Harry and Mary Moomis, Clyde (but not Selma) Usvedt came to call. They didn't come to shop, because Mary had a handbag over her arm and Milly a belt that circled her girth like the equator line on a globe. Tork's hair was slicked back. Clyde wore a woodsman plaid either new or ironed. They waited on the porch, rocking, fanning, Tork agitating his wheelchair wheel until the after-school crowd thinned. Then they came inside and dawdled till the last kid left. Dana spread her arms on the counter top and leaned, a stance that felt in her sinews like some posture out of the Old West.

"To what do I owe . . . ?"

"Well, now," said Tork, "we thought to speak with you about the situation."

"You mean Trudy's situation."

"Yes, ma'am, and how that affects the neighborhood."

"Good," Dana said. "Fire away."

And they fired, the friendliest fire imaginable. Milly thought it was marvelous how the churches and the neighborhood had rallied. Mary opined what a fine man Luther seemed to be. Clyde thought Trudy must be proud of him, his energy, his organizational skills—and the man could talk! Harry could understand why Dana would want to be part of such an effort. Milly and Tork had reason to know—anent the hurricane—how willing Dana was to help the community.

But had she realized?—this was Tork, who seemed to have been made central spokesman—"Now, all Solly's land that he's left you—and nobody's saying it isn't yours fair and square—but did you reckon that it's all in West Sink?"

Milly put in, "We've had our way of doing things time out of mind, here in Pelican Bay, and *good* relations . . ."

Dana recognized Milly's smiley face, Tork's reassuring forward tilt. *Déjà vu.* She might have been standing in the garage of that bungalow that had seemed at the time a step up the social scale, in Logan, Utah (wasn't it?), listening to Mom fumblingly explain why Camilla or Clotilda's eight-year-old daughter would not really find it suitable to come every Wednesday afternoon.

"I appreciate your coming to me," Dana said. "I'm trying to do what Solly would have done. Trudy was his wife for eighteen years."

Milly cast her eyes down and shuffled. Tork bothered the wheels of his chair back and forth. "Common law," he conceded merely.

Clyde Usvedt pulled up with a jerk. "Solly didn't rub our noses in it." (But why hadn't Selma Usvedt come? Maybe she was breaking rank?)

"There's some *concern,*" Tork said, "about a trailer up front on the highway."

"I agree. We should think about building her a proper house. I'll have Herbie look into it. Of course, Trudy has more right to the land than I have."

"Solly wanted *you* to have it." This was Mary.

"Trouble is," said Harry, "is the *property* values . . ."

"Are you planning to sell up, then?"

"Ma'am?"

"The property values—they only matter if you're going to sell. Because that's an alternative. I can turn the whole thing over to Adena and she'll make a deal with a developer. Did she tell you that?" The blank faces suggested that she had not. "And then the property values will go through the roof, probably, in East and West Sink both. Trudy can sell her sink! And we can all move inland on the profits."

"Well, now, wait a minute . . ."

"We're not talking about selling up."

"I only want to do what's right. I do know Solly would have given Trudy a place to live out of his own land. So I can stay here and keep the store, and do what he'd have done, or I can let it go to the developers. Talk it over. Let me know what's best for you."

Adena called.

"Hi, Dana, how's it going? Bernadette says you never said a word about that check, which I would really appreciate pronto, these doctors think they can get blood out of a stone, I swear."

"About that . . ."

"And I was wondering if you'd got Trudy squared away for land somehow. I know there's a fund for her. I was thinking I could pledge a contribution for when my bequest comes through."

"I don't get what . . ."

"I was down there chatting with Harry Moomis—you know he had an operation so I came around to call. Fabulous what they can do these days. He's up and around, chipper as a chickadee. Fabulous. Anyway, he told me Trudy's nephew has set up this fund."

"I told you about it."

"Did you? That family is cunning! Don't let them pull the wool. Anyway. I asked Harry shouldn't FEMA be dealing with it, but Harry says you'd have to get it declared a federal disaster, and one sinkhole does *not* qualify! So I was thinking about a pledge. But I do need that advance I mentioned, because Bernadette . . ."

"I'm giving an acre to Trudy."

Midsentence, Adena stopped. Her breathing quickened, but her words came like extruded clay. "What. A. Jerk. You. Are. You know that? You're a fucking blue-state jerk. Come down out of the frozen North, Nanook of the Con Job. Lemme tell you something. I know people in the ju-di-cial system of Florida. Judge Norquist is a friend of my family three generations back . . ."

"I'm hanging up now, Adena."

"Don't you fucking hang up on me. Don't you . . ."

Luther, at Trudy's instigation, came to call.

Waiting for him, Trudy sat foursquare on the bulbous couch, stabbing and notching a length of pale yarn. Trudy used sullenness as protective coloring, but beyond the hurt she would not show was a layer of grit of which she herself was probably unaware. Solly must have seen it in her, what it had taken, born into that ambitious but rigid family, to be the first black female paper tester in a white-owned mill, to leave the family for that advancement, live alone in another town, only to be pushed out of her job by a computer. And then to alienate her family with her choice of lover—no wonder she went around turtled in a carapace.

Now she turned a corner on her square, hooking the yellow wool to itself. "I know Luther out of money, and he got a job waiting," she said. "He supposed to get to it by November. He just need prying loose."

"He's got a preaching job up there?"

"Luther? He a chipper guard."

"I thought he was a preacher."

"Lawd, no, that just his *way.* Oh, he teach Sunday school sometime. He run the raffle every chance he get."

Bemused, Dana retreated upstairs — this was Trudy's show — and watched from the bedroom window as Luther arrived in the usual bellicose shirt and shorts — but freshly ironed, the labor no doubt (all those pockets!) of some benefactress in East Sink. He crossed to the porch with a tentative gait unusual with him, and Dana was reminded of the callers in Bobbindale after Graham's death, not sure what they were here for except for a show of obligation. His voice, however, ascended the stairs as confident as ever — "We have seen nothing but beautiful weather since the night He troubled the waters" — ever the barometer of God's mood.

She waited upstairs long enough for them to settle to their cake and tea, then descended one step at a time, avoiding the treads most likely to creak or whine. She stationed herself by the refrigerator cases, where she could appear to be busy if the need arose, but from where, between the frame and the door, she could see a narrow slice of living room, an edge of Trudy's arm, and a strip of Luther's face taking in half a nose, a quarter of an eye. Trudy's arm moved up and down in the narrow gap, crocheting, flaunting that she was at home.

From snippets of distorted sound, mainly from Luther, Dana gathered that they stayed civil regarding the hurricane, the sinkhole, and the neighborliness of the neighborhood.

". . . humble before His ways . . ."

". . . don't speak of judgment . . ."

". . . in Miss Flora's care . . ."

But then of a sudden the volume on their talk turned up, and she heard something from Trudy about how Luther was here to "ambush" his brother Cassius. Then, "You know he only trying to be a father best way he can. Sisters not going to take *that* for Christian charity, uh-uh. All that *admiring* going to take a turn." And not only was Trudy threatening to expose him, but — Dana now realized she'd been hearing it for some time — Luther, his voice as full in range and depth as always, had dropped the grandiloquence. He was talking Trudy's language while she berated him like a child.

"Luther, you born for a fool," Trudy said at this new pitch. "Cassius ain't traveling with no woman. He ain't seen that woman since you all run her off in Georgia."

"You know this for a fact?"

"I know it."

"How do you come to know it?"

"Ain't your business how I know it. I know it because the knowledge come to me."

"You mean by magic?"

"How you take *me* for the fool? By the U.S. mail, by the postman sack. You are the sorriest chile . . ."

"If you have a letter from Cassius, show me."

"I show you the toe of my boot. Now listen here. You done good and I thank you for it. I 'preciate your help. But you also been trespassing on my Solly's land. Me and the sisters can handle it from here. You take yourself enough money out the pro-ceeds to fill up your tank and buy what all you need. You fold up your belongings and set 'em in your Utility, and get on up North where you need to be."

"You promise me Cassius ain't with no woman."

"Swear by Jesus and hope to die."

"I'm going to leave you the address where you can find Margaret. Promise me if Cassius show up, you'll tell him the family waiting to have him back."

"I'll tell him."

"Swear."

"I said I'll tell him!"

Perry called.

He'd hoped it wasn't going to come to this. He didn't really understand it, but he'd had a letter from Orville Gordimer—a good ol' boy, had worked with Perry's father at the Capitol back in the day—that Adena Solomon was bringing a challenge to the will. Hadn't Dana intended to hand everything over to her anyway?

Dana said it was complicated. She guessed she'd better come and see him.

Perry said she maybe she'd better. "The challenge is on testamentary capacity. Which just means Solly would have to have known what a will is, what he owned, who his family was—'natural objects of affection' in the legal term. Essentially, the law is to protect old people from gold diggers."

"I never for a moment . . ."

"I know. I was there. But I don't know how they're going to prove he was demented. The law is lenient. The bar for proof is very high. There's one precedent where this old guy was convinced his daughters were witches, but the judge said so many upstanding citizens believed in witches that he couldn't be called incompetent on that account."

"It's Bernadette who believes in witches."

"All the same, if Gordimer took the case, they must have something up their sleeves."

Phoebe called.

Phoebe picked and poked at elements of the goings-on. She asked questions and then asked them another way. It was her job. Hadn't Adena complained that Bucky "couldn't get it up"? Now she'd made a "contingent" sale of the land to a developer? And she needed money for some procedure not insured? And Mrs. Solly never had any kids, but Trudy had an abortion in Georgia eighteen years ago? During which time Mrs. Solly was dying, and Adena got Solly drunk? And Solly was bitter enough to make an heir of a perfect stranger? And Adena had clipped Solly's toenails and taken them away with her? And, just to be clear about this part, Bernadette needed some kind of "biopsy" that was not insured?

Phoebe said, "Sweetie, they're not thinking *capacity* in the sense of *sane.* She's going to try and prove he didn't have the *information.*"

"What information?"

"Bernadette is Solly's daughter."

28

LUTHER GASSED UP and picked out half a dozen bottles of Snapple, a block of cheddar, Triscuits, two apples, and an Almond Joy. He waved off the offer of a plastic bag and punched these down into his canvas tote. He paid in cash, mostly ones. Dana wished him a pleasant trip. He hesitated, then jutted forth his mighty hand and thanked her for her kindness to his aunt.

She took the hand. "No, I thank *you* for *your* kindness to her," she said officiously.

His other hand came to enfold hers. "We are all precious in God's sight, but sometimes the task of Christian charity falls to strangers."

Dana nodded, her hand trapped between the soft pads of lion paws. "It's no hardship doing favors for a friend," she said.

One by one the cats mark their territory.

She retrieved her hand and turned, purposeful, to count the cigarettes. When she heard the door tinkle and sigh to, she flushed with relief and exhaustion very like victory.

But when Herbie called her out onto the back porch, where he had set the polyurethane in preparation for the downstairs floor, she was met with murk and mess. One of the cans was tipped over on its side, the thick glaze hardening in a delta that flowed down the steps and into the roots of a wild magnolia. *Had been* tipped, or merely *had* tipped? A possum or raccoon, a clumsy kid, deliberate vandalism?

Dudley danced toward the step and away, yapping at the smell. Herbie rolled his shoulders to the tops of his ears, repeatedly, as against an ache he could not reach. "That was a half-used one," he said. "I swear I hammered that lid on good. What kind of bozo would go around spilling poly'thane?"

Luther was her first thought, but it wasn't Luther's style, and nothing suggested that it was, apart from the draped ridges of the stuff hardening (no other message, no *Bitch, DIE*). The murdered magnolia was browning in the ruined earth.

"Who'd do such a numb-nuts thing?" Herbie wanted to know. "I was just gearing up again."

Not Tork or the Moomises or Usvedts, surely? More likely someone who would know the frozen flow of it would intimidate her? She remembered Cassius: *What good is a fence around forty thousand acres? Anybody with a mind to get in will get in.* And she realized that, whether such quotidian mysteries were solved or not, every time she felt threatened or apprehensive or merely mistreated, she would think of Isobel Huston and half expect her to appear, even though she had never met the woman and had no firsthand image of her except a schoolteacherish snapshot and a schoolgirl hand. Even now she could see those careful round loops on the *o*'s and *l*'s. And 666.

She told Herbie to take the day off. The floors would wait another week, she said. "Just leave it. Go get Bernadette and take her for a swim, why don't you?" She blamed herself for working him long hours, and mainly at clerking when he wanted to be renovating. Or at least, he'd always wanted that before. Now it was not so certain. Bernadette's Camaro could sometimes be seen parked next to the cabin until late, but if Herbie's devotion had finally impressed her, he did not seem to be having much joy of it. Bernadette herself did not come in to work.

"Herbie, is she all right?"

"She's just hassling with her mother." But he avoided her eyes.

"Do you know what about?"

"It'll work out." But his face said this optimism had a funny taste.

"If I can help . . ." But he was eager to be off, and she let him go.

It was another long day, tense, hard on her back and legs. Profits were up since Herbie had refurbished the sign, but the stock was still down from the hurricane, and delivery schedules still discombobulated. She turned back to her conundrum: The more determined Adena was to get Solly's estate, the more determined Dana was to fight her for it. Perry said that Trudy's testimony would be crucial. But suppose after all Solly didn't know Bernadette was his daughter? Suppose Trudy herself didn't know? In any case Trudy came from an ethic of discretion. If she wouldn't do hospitals, how likely was it that she would go to court? Yet if she did not testify and so prove Solly's will in order, Trudy might end up with no place to live.

Late in the afternoon April and Sarah came in, voluble and gossipy: the Adams boy got probation, he'd better thank his lucky stars; the National Guard was being mobilized, including two from East Sink and one from West. "Mo Washington's going up to Georgia for combat training," Sarah said. "And he's forty-five if he's a day."

When they brought their goods to the register, April volunteered, "Don't think everybody feels like the Moomises, you know. Let Mizz Lewis have a place to put her trailer. Geez."

Sarah leaned toward her, conspiratorial, "You think things are split East Sink–West Sink. But I can tell ya', there's just as much disagreement male-female, if you know what I mean."

"Don't think Selma Usvedt comes down on the same side as Clyde," April specified.

"Thanks. I wondered about that."

"And lemme tell you something, there's some is very satisfied it's you in here and not Adena Solomon, native to Sag Island she may be."

"Thanks."

"Just because the kittens are born in the oven," Sarah added, "don't make 'em biscuits."

"Thank you," Dana said again.

She closed up at seven and set about making gumbo, trying to emulate the Flamingo's mix of spices. While it simmered she stood lost in contemplation of the Blake watercolor. *Visions of the Daughters of Albion;* she had bought a copy of the poem in Tallahassee when she went up for the amniocentesis. This was Blake's prophecy of America. The two chained figures were young Oothoon and the slaver Bromion, who raped her on her way to meet her lover. In the picture the rapist was as firmly chained to his victim as she to him, hoary haired, his eyes and his mouth wide with horror. It was she who still struggled against her bonds. The abolitionist-lover sat contorted into himself in shame, prototype of knee-jerk liberals to come. Through the louring clouds hung a sphere too red for a moon and too matte for sun.

In this painting Oothoon was blond and bright. But one of the illustrations in the little book represented her not as a woman but as a captive African, hands bound behind him, body arched. That long ago, the poet-artist had been prescient to equate the subjugated women, slaves, and the exploited American plains.

The phone rang. "Did you ask Trudy?"

"Phoebe, how can I?"

"I've been thinking about Solly. He couldn't leave it all to Trudy, and leave her to fend off Adena. So he picked a stranger, a ballsy Northerner, someone he thought would fight."

Toward the back of the room, at the farthest jalousies, Dana thought a shadow passed. She wrapped the phone cord around her hand. "Not so ballsy as it turns out."

"You're just in the muddled part. The law is a process, not much fun while it's going on, but if you're in the right, it's worth . . ."

"Wait," Dana said.

"What?"

"I heard something." She pulled on the phone cord and strained to listen beyond the gulls, the owls.

"What is it? Are you there?"

"Yes. No, nothing I guess."

"You're just jumpy."

"Of course I'm jumpy. Just because I'm jumpy doesn't mean they're not after me."

Phoebe laughed. "Gird up your loins, girl. Fight the good fight."

But she was full of dread, and when she hung up she had a hollow space where her guts should be. You're pregnant, alone, in a legal muddle, and your best friend is a thousand miles away, and you're more embroiled in local politics than a senator's wife from Pennsylvania . . . She took a bowl of gumbo to the coffee table and turned on the TV, but the new season lineup was showing a strange dichotomy: all entertainment was either supernatural or else a cockroach-eating contest, the latter known as "reality." This reminded her of Phoebe's mantra, "Nothing is real and everything's for sale," which reminded her of Phoebe, which reminded her that she felt very much alone. She decided to turn in. But first she had to bag the shrimp shells and take out the trash or it would stink by morning.

She scraped the shells into a bread bag, closed it with a twist tie, put that in a plastic Baggie, dropped that in the trash, lifted the kitchen liner out of its bin and knotted it at the top. There. A handful of shrimp shells in three layers of nonbiodegradable plastic when you could toss them on the pine straw and they'd be gone by morning having contributed to the food chain via possums, gulls, and/or raccoons. All of which scavengers would then gather round your doorstep demanding to be fed and housed. Discouraged by the trivial thwartedness of things, she hoisted the bag out the back door and, avoiding the puddled varnish on the steps, dropped it in the bin. She tested the security of the lid, and turned, and he was there.

He was backlit by the streetlight, haloing his nappy hair, which had been cropped back close to his head, so that the fear of a stranger came first, and then lifting hope, before the heart stop of recognition. She had so often pictured him here when he was not here — at the back door, or beside the hammock that had gone down in the hurricane, or by the holly bush, or in the road—and then had to unpicture him on account of his not being there—that it was simple fact that at first she did not believe her eyes. She had one hand on the trash-can lid. The other rose to her hair. She became absurdly aware of her body, every plane and bend of it, the left foot with the weight on the toe, the other planted on the walk, her hip canted to the right, and the right shoulder lowered where her hand was raised. The hand smelling of shrimp. He on the other hand squarely faced her. His arms reached out a yard apart: a peace posture: *Here I am.* The signal of surrender: *I have no weapon. You may approach.*

An hour hence they would laugh at how long they stood thus frozen, but for the moment neither breathed. A squirrel or a bat squeaked in the top branches of the floodlit oak. An owl or a bat flapped. The surf whispered out in the bay. *Sh. Sh. Sh.*

She broke first. "Cassius?"

When he moved, his arms were so arranged that he need only step toward her and he was around her. The softness of his skin. The solidity of him. Bulk, bulwark, blackness. Harbor, haven, home. There came to her mind the image of Trudy standing against Solly's knees, offering herself while he wept. And it was this image that brought the tears. She clung, hand over hand across his broad back while she sobbed. *Be here, be here, be here, be here, be here.*

"Sh. Sh. Girl."

He crept the Pontiac forward onto the pine needles behind the store, where it wouldn't be visible from the road. He said, wry, "I race here after a hurricane to see if you all right, and *damn* if I don't find Luther hanging round your door." He handed her a duffel bag and opened the back door to slide Kenisha out. The little girl mumbled in her sleep but didn't wake. Her legs flopped over his arm, one brown foot bare, one sandal on. Her hair was inexpertly cornrowed, each tail clamped in a small barrette, her hands curled against her chest, her face ecstatically relaxed in sleep. The streetlight elongated the shadow of her curly lashes. Cassius shifted his grip and the girl rolled herself into him, nuzzling, catching at his shirt, sighing and settling. He bent his cheek against her hair and stood a moment to make sure. It seemed to Dana that among the wonders she had seen along this coast, none was quite so full of wonder as this — statistically anomalous — bond between this father and his sleeping child. Her life unfurled at her feet: two children, two loving parents, Solly's store. It was all vouchsafed, it had all been willed to her. She opened the door and followed them up the stairs.

He lay Kenisha on the mattress that had (everything falls into place) been borrowed for Trudy after the hurricane, and he slipped off the sandal and pulled the cover over her, and they waited hand in hand till they were certain she still slept. Then they edged out, left the door ajar, and Dana led Cassius to the room with the view, to the bed in which she had longed for him so many nights while she looked out over the tip of Sag Island and out to sea. They were hesitant to touch each other, each as if the other was breakable. They laughed at this, and were afraid. Her index finger on the mole on his shoulder, his fingers taking the measure of her jaw. They exchanged stories, hers of Solly and Trudy and the store, the inheritance, the sinkhole. He told her of travel and hardship, running out of money, worrying about Kenisha, finding a day care or a sitter sometimes so he could earn a little, trying to comfort the girl among all the changes, longing to dare to come here. She told him about Luther, the plan that Cassius should join the family in Pennsylvania. He said, "Luther's right about one thing. I can't do it on my own. I need you." She noticed that he had, after all, tried it on his own, but she pushed that thought out of mind. He'd been afraid that the family would find him here, but still more worried about her well-being in the hurricane — hadn't he implicitly explained that? In any case she pushed it out of mind, and they said deliciously hackneyed things and shook their heads to admit their inadequacy. *I can't believe you're here. I've so wanted you. I couldn't be sure. You can book it down. I love you. Be here, be here.*

They made love not with the fierceness of their second encounter but with the tremulousness of the first. He painted her into being, skin and plane and curve and bone. When he touched her belly she caught his hand and held it there. Then let it go. She wouldn't tell him yet. She had been given everything piecemeal, but for him it was too much at once. Instead she pressed the hand to her mons veneris and arched her body against his.

When he fell asleep she continued awake looking into the familiar dark, the moon on the sea, her mind skittering between the sweep of wonder and frivolously precise plans. Chloe would have been almost Kenisha's age. Tomorrow she would open Kenisha's hand and trace the lifeline on her palm. She would teach her stability and gentleness; she would teach her gumbo and bouillabaisse. She would learn to cornrow. Bernadette would paint Kenisha's toenails. Trudy would be in Kenisha's life and she in Trudy's—a restitution, a partial mending. There would be plenty of space in the music room for two children for a couple of years. Later they could build on a modest wing as Herbie had advised, a bedroom for one child and a storeroom for keeping the extra stock. They would hang a new tire from the oak tree, or a pretty fretwork swing. They would build a tree house in the woods on the path between Trudy's new acre and Solly's Corner. Gradually Cassius would lose his wariness and she her self-consciousness. Trudy and Herbie and Bernadette would be their extended family. Among them they would knit Pelican Bay into a coalition, they would crochet it into a goddam blanket.

29

MORNING WAS A different matter, as morning tends to be.

Kenisha woke at five with a penetrating wail. Cassius slipped out of bed at once, into his briefs and jeans, was across the hall before Dana was oriented or awake. The girl's snuffling cries gradually subsided under his soothing. Dana put on her clothes, peed, brushed her hair and teeth, and pushed into the room preparing a light smile of introduction. The two of them were propped across the bed against the wall, the girl still whimpering in his lap, chewing on the corner of a baby blanket. When she saw Dana she flinched and hid against his chest. Cassius made a face: *what-can-you-do,* a shrug of one hand, and a low-key, "A little later."

She nodded and backed out—smiling, but disappointed. She went downstairs, although it was too early to make breakfast and she hadn't slept enough. She curled on the couch to wait for them. She was still awake when the timer cut out on the floodlight outside, but asleep when Herbie unlocked the back door.

"Herbie?"

His long face ashen, he came into the living room, balanced on the edge of a chair and, like Trudy on the dock, folded his hands between his knees.

"Could you go and talk to her? She's—I dunno, I dunno what to say to her. She's taken something."

"What do you mean, *taken something*?!"

"No, I don't mean—I don't *know*. She's messed up."

"Open up the store and I'll relieve you when I can. Is she in the cabin?"

"Yeah."

"Herbie, I have guests upstairs. A nephew of Trudy's."

"Trudy's nephew?"

"No, *another* nephew. And his little girl. I'll explain later. If they come down, just tell them—tell them to make themselves at home."

She raced out the back door and across the dew-damp pine straw, past Dudley head-on-paws in patient vigil for his master. It was almost November, and almost cold this morning. The door was open, and Bernadette huddled on the wicker couch in a cocoon of blankets, wearing a white chemise like the heroine in a bodice ripper. The platinum spikes of her hair were bent askew at every angle, her heavy kohl-and-mascara eye job melting down her cheeks. Like Kenisha, Bernadette turned away, hid her face against the wall, but this time Dana stood her ground.

"Bernadette. What have you taken?"

"What!" Bernadette whipped around and flapped her studded tongue. She rolled her eyes in exasperation. "One Ativan. *Je*-sus. Whatever. Not enough to calm anybody's nerves." As if in demonstration, her shoulders began to shake, and she huddled further into the mess of blankets.

"Is that all? Are you sure? Are you cold?"

"Oh, yes, I'm very cold! Ask my mother! She'll tell you I'm the coldest person ever born. Cold as a witch's tit!" She forced a laugh.

"Please, Bernadette."

"Believe me, if I take pills you'll know it!"

"Dear. Be quiet." Dana wrung her hands; only a moment to decide. "I think I know what's upsetting you."

"Sure you do! Every-stinking-body in the world is going to know. He was my *father. Bucky* was my father! He raised me since before I was born!"

"Of course he was your father. Nobody can take that away from you."

"Oh no? Take away! Take everything away! I heard them quarreling about Solly the night before Daddy, Bucky, he, he, he, he, he . . ." She could not say it. Whichever word it was, *died, jumped, fell,* she wiped it away with a jerk of her arm. "But I didn't know what it was about. I didn't know it was going to kill him! Oh, she killed him, she didn't care." Dana reached out to stroke her, but she jackknifed into her cocoon. "Solly! He was so *o-o-old.*" She drew the word out in a contemptuous wail. She dug her black fingernails along her arm. "I'm unclean. I can't get clean!"

"Sweetheart. Please calm down."

"He lived with that old woman, a, a, a, *shucker* and a *maid.* He fucked her!"

"Bernadette, it's not Trudy's fault. It's hardly fair . . ." But she remembered that Trudy had nothing but contempt for this girl whose existence must be bitterness to her. And she heard the euphemisms: *unclean, shucker, maid.*

"My mother says I have to testify! And every-fucking-body in the world will know."

"Testify to what?"

"That Solly didn't know he was my father. Never acted like it. Never called me anything but my name, never said I, I, I, I . . ." She threw back the blankets and then grabbed at them again, coiled them around her. "I must have done something terrible to bring down the Rule of Three! But I don't know what! I never did anything one-third as bad as this."

"Bernadette. You don't have to testify to anything. We'll settle it between us. Our quarrel has nothing to do with you."

"She'll make me." Petulant, which was nearer her usual mode, Bernadette wiped her face, great swaths of kohl on the blanket, smears of foundation on her chemise. Tattooed, punctured, matted, bleary, pale, snot- and makeup-smudged—loveliness emanated from her. An early Picasso. *Seated Harlequin, Harlequin with Folded Hands.* No, no, you can't take that away.

Cassius was standing at the jalousies, Kenisha strangling one of his knees. Fully awake now, the girl held her head down and turned away, stabbing glances in Dana's vicinity.

Cassius said, "Kenisha, this is Dana," which had the effect of making Kenisha hide behind his thigh. Cassius shrugged, apologetic. "She's shy." Dana said how nice to meet her and she bet some bacon would be a treat.

It must have been bewildering to him, the disrupted routine, both the disruption and the routine. Dana sent Herbie back to Bernadette. She told Flora to come back later and flipped the door sign to Closed. She called Henry and asked him to tell Trudy that Cassius was here — which message Henry received with reduced compassion. She felt ostentatiously efficient, half seeing herself through Cassius's eyes, busily familiar and at home while he and the girl stood alien.

She set about making breakfast and now felt she was trying to look busy, whereas in fact her hands worked automatically while her head skipped like a stone from one to another of the things she should be taking care of. The store needed to be open. Bernadette needed to be seen by someone, but that was not Dana's business, and phoning Adena would make matters worse. Perry would be calling any moment to lay out strategy. Neither Trudy nor Bernadette should be involved, and the whole matter of the will could be swept aside or shunted into the future except that her future with Cassius was tied up with it. Cassius stood, outside of this anxiety but ill at ease, in the very space where Luther had sparred with her. Classically beautiful where Luther had been strangely formed, loving where his brother had been both pompous and threatening. It was superstition to think the *space* was spoiled.

Cassius meanwhile worked at placating Kenisha. Look at the pretty tree. Look at the tire swing. He'd brought her blankie down, did she want it? What a big television. Would she like cartoons? Look, here was a blankie just like the one Granmama made her, only brown and yellow instead of pink and white. He asked Dana if it was all right if he turned on the television set, and Dana said, "Of course," and he said, "Look here, *The Powerpuff Girls,*" but when he left her on the couch she ran after him and grappled his thigh.

Dana said, "Never mind."

Cassius said, "A little later."

Kenisha said nothing but looked fury and alarm. She was wearing a skirt in bold stripes and a T-shirt with the requisite princess, cartoon eyes and yellow hair. When the girl thought Dana wasn't looking she would stand slightly swayback, arms akimbo, palpably asserting *self,* and Dana ached simultaneously to sweep her up and cuddle her, to win her over, and to restrain those resentful limbs. Cassius stooped slightly, putting his tall body in relation to his daughter or else bowed under the effort of it.

Dana set the table for three. She said, "Would you like to help?" She put the bacon and scrambled eggs on the table. She put the orange juice on the table. She said, "Do you like orange juice?" She fetched the toast from the toaster and put it on the table. She called brightly, "Come and eat!"

She sat at one end, Cassius's and Kenisha's plates flanking hers. Cassius smiled and took his chair—how awkwardly, by contrast with their time alone, in the one-legged scrape of it, the paper napkin spread on his knees. But Kenisha would not have this arrangement, would sit in Cassius's lap, where she clamped her face into his chest. Cassius said, "You *love* bacon, baby." Kenisha ate the bacon, curling in to press the greasy crumbs against his shirt.

Dana and Cassius smiled at each other over her head. Dana said, "She's had so many changes to get used to."

He said, "You know that's right. Sometimes we did three states in a week."

Kenisha put her hand hard against his mouth. "Don't talk!"

He took her out to the tire swing while Dana cleared the dishes, but the tire swing had not been used in years, and when Cassius lifted Kenisha in, the rotted rubber made a streak across her skirt. You could hear her shrieking through the jalousies. Cassius took her upstairs, brought her down again in fresh green trousers.

Dana said, "My, what pretty capri pants. That color is called apple green." The stupidity of her words made her sick. Kenisha understood exactly their stupidity. She said, "Not pants!" and smashed her face in her father's groin.

Cassius said, "Kenisha, Mizz Dana is a friend of mine. I want you to be nice to her. Go and shake the lady's hand. Give her a hug." Kenisha garroted his thigh.

He cakewalked across the room, carrying the girl on his leg with each left step. He said, "Now. Give Miss Dana a hug. *Now.*"

Kenisha strained at his hand, pulling backward. "Don't talk to her!"

Dana said, "Let it go. Why don't you let her watch TV?"

She busied herself. It seemed out of kilter to have closed the store only to stand here drying the skillet. She never dried the skillet. The two of them, Cassius and Kenisha, sat on the couch for *Scooby Doo.* Through the *Teletubbies.* While *Atomic Betty* foiled Maximus's plan to spread biochemical poison over the world, and returned in time to weed her mother's garden.

Trudy let herself in the shop door, peeked around the door frame and let out a whoop. She held Cassius's two hands, surveying him at arm's length. "When you grow up to be such a man?" She knelt before the girl. "How come you let him grow up to be such a *fine* man?" The tension in the room lowered by a few degrees. Kenisha, one foot on each side of her father's foot, stuck her face to the side of his thigh, copper eyes fastened on Trudy.

Who chided her, "He s'posed to be a little bitty chile!"

"Uh-uh!" The mischief she had seen in Kenisha's photo came into her eyes.

Trudy stood and walked away. She picked up the baby blanket. "Whose is this here? I didn't make this blanket here."

Kenisha's hand bolted out.

"Shall I take me this blanket here?" Trudy wondered.

Kenisha said, fierce, "You got my blankie!"

"That a sure pretty blanket. You want it back? I give it to you for a hug."

Kenisha darted forth, whipped the blanket from Trudy's hand, performed a perfunctory hug, and scampered back to her father. She shoved the blanket into her mouth and hung on to his leg.

For days some version of this scenario was replayed. Around Dana the girl remained intractable, jealous, and afraid. Bernadette came crying, raging from a confrontation with her mother, Herbie talked her down, they managed a few hours in the store. Kenisha ran from the room whenever Dana entered it, slamming out the jalousies, the hall, the shop, leaving the doors wide, running until Cassius caught up with her. Dana would say, "Honey, don't leave the door open, because you know an animal might come in." Kenisha would flinch and put her hands over her head, insultingly, melodramatically, as if to ward off a blow. If Cassius and Dana began a conversation, Kenisha would boldly enough push the flat of her hand across his mouth — "Don't talk!" But she could not sleep unless her father stayed with her, and he, enervated and exhausted, sometimes fell asleep beside her, leaving Dana as jealous and petulant as the child.

Kenisha, however, gave in to Trudy's cleverer advances, and Trudy took her for walks in the woods, even sometimes managed to put her down for her nap. Relieved and grateful, Dana was also wounded and ashamed.

One afternoon when Cassius was at the pump, Kenisha appeared at the shop door, combative, sullen. Still, there she was. Borrowing a page from Trudy's book, Dana squatted in the candy aisle in Kenisha's sight, cocked her head and frowned. "What's that you say? Go on, Kenisha doesn't want a Butterfinger. What? No, she doesn't want a Tootsie Roll either!" Dana dusted the rack. Kenisha stared through the screen, giving no quarter, so Dana stood and walked toward the counter, turned sharply back. "Well, I declare!" she said in imitation of Trudy, "you M&M's are a noisy bunch! I know you-all want Kenisha, but Kenisha doesn't want to come in here!"

The screen door creaked. Kenisha took a few steps in. "I like a M&M," she said. She slid one bare foot along the floor in the direction of the candy aisle. Dana returned there and squatted, cocked her head again, and affected a falsetto. "Please, *please,* let us go with Kenisha! Please, Miss Dana!" At the angle her head was now, she could see that the second tier of candy boxes was askew. She lifted them forward, straightening the row. Kenisha said, "I like M&M's!"

Under the boxes, tucked at the back of the rack where she would have to run into it eventually, sat the half-used bottle of ketchup. Heinz sixty-four ounces. Supersized. It was open and propped tilted, so that a turd of ketchup spilled browning on the floor below.

"I *do* like those candies!" Kenisha stood at the end of the aisle, defiant. Dana slipped the bottle behind her (as if it would mean anything to the girl). "Do you? Well, I guess you have to come over here to get them."

Kenisha slid one grudging foot along the floor. She performed a little stamp to show how much against her will this was. Confused and disheartened—when had Luther left the bottle here? That last day, when they were sparring with compliments?—Dana held out the bag and Kenisha leaned hard into the next step. Then she belted a widemouthed accusatory scream.

"What?"

Cassius was in through the slamming screen. "What happened?"

Kenisha rolled on the floor holding her foot.

"Oh, it's those damn old boards. She's got a splinter." Dana backed to the counter pocketing the candy bag, stupidly hiding the ketchup bottle now from Cassius. "I've got a tweezer right back here." He lifted Kenisha to the counter and held her down while Dana took hard hold of the foot and fished for a quarter-inch sliver in the ball, Kenisha howling and kicking against her hand.

"Got it! One evil splinter down!" She held it up for their inspection at the tweezer end. Cassius said, "Good for you." Kenisha fought and bawled. Dana spilled hydrogen peroxide liberally on the thrashing foot, the counter, the telephone, and the *Democrat.* She pulled the M&M's out of her pocket.

"There you go."

Kenisha made slits of her eyes but snatched the candy. Cassius shrugged: apology, capitulation, irony. Dana tossed the ketchup bottle in the garbage bin and went to wipe the dried ketchup off the floor.

She said to Phoebe: "It's a myth that kids and dogs are good judges of character. It's not true. I'm a friendly. I wish her every sort of good. I want to mother her. She won't give me a chance."

Phoebe said, "She's afraid of white people."

Dana, despairing, said, "I know."

Nights when Kenisha was finally asleep, they made love hungrily. *"Girl,"* he said. His hunger seemed in direct opposition to how difficult Kenisha had been, as if to reestablish and prove his priorities. He knew Kenisha was difficult. She knew this was a grief for him. They promised each other the child's will would soften over time. She would get used to the three of them together. She would learn to accept Dana, even love her. They turned to each other to seal such promises in flesh.

He had taken to calling her *girl,* and she had liked it. It excited her. There was desire in it, and pride, and possession by which she was not threatened. But now she found herself absurdly, pettily, troubled by it. She wanted to be acknowledged as the woman. Kenisha was the girl.

She did not mention this, although they talked for hours. Or they talked *around*. She recounted the dramas of the Sinks, he told stories of life on the road. They rehearsed their early days together as if there had been many more of them than in fact there had, perhaps reminiscing as a way of delaying plans. She sketched their future lightly—the luck that they had this option, how Trudy could be given purpose, how Kenisha could grow up among children black and white. Sometimes he encouraged her. When she said, "Of course it's possible Isobel will follow us here," he scoffed, his accent thickening at the mention of his wife. "Isobel don't budge out her own backyard. She won't go to Jax 'fear she get 'taminated." But another time she said, "We can give Kenisha a little brother," and he fended her off with the flat of his palms. "Hold on, girl! One step at a time."

So instead she gave him a detailed account of the mill as she had toured it, surprising him with the terms she'd learned from McGarvey: *breast roll, couch roll, king roll, sweat dryer, liver test.* "That's right," he laughed. "You got it." But he was bitter about the mill. "Ain't nobody told in advance. Pink slip in the pay envelope and off you go. There's many that's hurting."

"That's what Luther said."

While Kenisha napped, or when she was away with Trudy, there were intimations of what their life might be. Cassius understood that for Trudy's sake she couldn't leave with the will unsettled. She understood that he would need some time to be at ease here. With Herbie preoccupied and Bernadette no use at all, Cassius fell into rhythm with her in the store, though he wouldn't front the desk, only stocked and bagged as he had all those years ago in Georgia, pumped the gas, sparred with the deliverymen, flirted with Flora and Evian. He smiled his sly smile over being "Trudy's other nephew" and accepted Parnithias's chiding that, "Trudy surely trucking in the men." There may have been a time or two that Dana caught someone—a woman, black or white—with a calculating look, as in: *What is the setup here?* But on the whole the regulars responded friendly enough when she introduced Cassius, and greeted him easily when they returned.

Cassius's physical presence was so powerful to her that whatever section of the shop he occupied held gravitational force. Others could feel it surely—his gentle, offhand authority. When he stood under the fluorescent strip of the refrigerator cases, she looked for the highlight on his cheekbones and was cast back to the moment that, now, she thought of as the first moment she had loved him. She half forgot the moment had another meaning.

But once, recalling some excess of Isobel's, Cassius said, "If I had any, we'd be in Alaska now." She knew the "any" stood for "any balls." She didn't know who "we" were—the three of them, or two, and if so which two? She said insincerely, "If you want, you could go on west and I'll join you when the will is settled," and he very satisfactorily replied, "You know I won't do that. We in it together now." And she had faith that if she was patient, loving, *perfect*—he would recognize this salt Gulf reach of the world as home. Then she would tell him they were already a family.

One night when they got up in the early hours for a snack, she found him standing in front of the Blake etching, intent. She loved the shape of his head, the long, lax angle of his jaw, and she watched him watching the tortured rapist Bromion, the struggling Oothoon.

"Do you like it?"

He shrugged. "I've seen better."

"Up at Atlantic."

"Um-hm, yeah."

She opened her mouth to hold forth on Blake's prophecy, but he said, "You want art, I got a present for you."

"What do you mean?"

"Come on out here. I'll show you art."

She thought this was foreplay and was ready to play, but he pulled her toward the back door with some determination. Led her to the Pontiac and popped its faded trunk. There he pulled out swimming rings, shoes, a pair of coats, a doll stroller with a brown plastic baby doll.

"What is it?"

"Wait and see."

He stacked the welter on the ground and set the spare tire beside it, swept leaves and sand aside with the back of his hand. She took up the doll and cuddled it, stroking its plastic hair. He lifted the rubber mat and retrieved from the wheel well a square package in brown paper tied with string.

"Got a present for you," he said aggressively. She shook her head: *no idea*. He set the package on the bumper and removed its wrapping. Inside was a baroque gilt frame with a line drawing that it took only a second to recognize: a reclining Minotaur, raising his glass, attended by a limp-eyed, toga-wearing maiden—one of the Picasso etchings from the Atlantic dining room.

"Cassius! That's . . ." She shed the doll down into its stroller.

He barked a laugh. "Uh-huh, a felony!"

"No doubt! Is it real?"

"*Yas.* Now, you want to know how I come by it. You want to know did I steal for you."

"Did you?" Thrilled. Scandalized.

"Well, I found it, you might could say. Last coupla weeks at the mill they have these *art* shippers come around to pack. High-end motherfuckers in the packing bidniss. One day one of 'em takes these eight pictures off the wall, sets 'em on the carpet, and packs up a couple. Then he says, would I be so kind to keep an eye, he's got to piss. So he goes off down the hall. There's six of them waiting to be packed. I just slide one around the other side in a office already empty. When he come back he say nothing, packs up the five — Styrofoam, bubble wrap, in the crate all expert and pro. Goes on to some other part the building. Every day I check it, it still leaning on that office wall. Next time I'm on nights, I drive my car up the back way and stick it in."

"Stealing wheelbarrows."

"That's it, that's it."

Thrilled and scared. "You know we can't keep it."

"Ain't my problem. It yours now, girl."

"Cassius."

"Don't Cassius me. You the one so crazy about pictures." He wrapped the frame again and carried it up to slide under the bed.

30

TRUDY AND DANA tramped through the rough grass toward the highway, Trudy in the lead, whacking an oleander switch from side to side.

"I go down to the pond all the time," Dana said. "I never scared up worse than a skink."

"You lucky. They be rattlers in this grass here." Trudy whipped a hummock higher than the rest. "I take me a switch, same as I sleep with the carving knife under the rug."

They had left Cassius and Kenisha watching *Get a Clue* while Herbie, kept by the new domestic traffic from refinishing the floors, decided at least to varnish the counter after hours. Bernadette was napping in the cabin. "You got a circus," Trudy said of them.

The clocks had been turned back last weekend, so at seven the sun was down, leaving a flame-colored backdrop to the long, low skyline of Sag Island. An occasional car passed between them and the cannery. Dana lifted the hair off her neck and twisted it. "We'll mow around your house, or dig it up and plant a lawn."

"I ain't afraid a rattler. I just let 'em know I'm coming."

Four short stakes marked the corners of the site, their Day-Glo orange streamers lifting in a breeze off the bay. To one side a hedge of palmettos, on the other a tortured cedar behind which the sun would rise.

"What do you think? We can plant a screen of oleanders between you and the highway. They'll bring utilities straight across from the bayside, and Herbie can do a boardwalk to the store."

"Yeah-um," Trudy judged thoughtfully. "That be fine, now. Only you ain't got it yet."

Dana scuffed her sneaker side to side like Trudy's switch. "I have to ask you something—difficult. Personal."

"You ain't told Cassius you in the family way, have you?"

"Not yet. We have so much to work out. And Kenisha . . ."

"That young'un need somebody to take her in *hand*."

"I know. But it can't be me. She's still . . . not comfortable with me."

"Huh!" Trudy marked the understatement.

"I have to ask you about Bernadette."

"*She* a mess. Don't take no genius to see that."

"Do you know why?"

"I guess I do."

"Did Solly know? I mean, that she was . . ."

"Did Solly know!" The switch lifted and cut the air. "That Adena woman make his life a misery! If he didn't do this, she's going to tell Bucky, if he didn't do that, she's going to tell."

"She blackmailed him with Bernadette all those years?"

"Bucky the only family he had left. And Bucky in such a misery with the marriage he made. Solly couldn't—he *couldn't* let her take that away, his only chile. I told him, let her tell and devil take the hindmost. But he couldn't do it."

"And then they divorced." They were walking between the stakes now, flattening the grass in a wide perimeter. Trudy's switch swung like a metronome.

"Didn't make no difference. Adena still come at him after the divorce, if he didn't do this-and-so, she going to tell Bucky. It all the worse with the divorce. Bucky started up worse drinking, and she gonna drink along."

"And then one night she told him anyway."

"I don't know if she did or not."

"She must have. Bernadette heard them quarreling about Solly. And the next day Bucky was drunk on the catwalk. Bernadette thinks that's why he jumped."

"That like to kill Solly, too."

"Trudy—are you willing to testify to all that—that Solly knew Bernadette was his child?"

"I don't do court, huh-uh."

"If you just *say* you'll testify, I think we'll settle out of court and then Bernadette won't need to either. And if I own the store, I think Cassius and Kenisha will stay. If not . . . I don't know what we'll do, but I know I won't own this land to make it yours."

Trudy shook her head, maybe for refusal, maybe for the complexity of things. She used her switch to fret the orange tag on the survey post. "I do regret for the hurt to that sorry girl," she said.

They were nearly back at the store before they noticed the car beyond the pumps, and from the tire mounted on its rear Dana recognized Adena's little SUV.

"Let's go around the other way." Her impulse was to put herself between Cassius and the shop. But they were too late. She and Trudy entered through the stairwell. Herbie was backed against the wall next to the counter, quizzical alarm on his long face. Cassius stood at the refrigerator case with Kenisha locked around his leg.

"There you are." Adena faced them between the counter and the door, a paintbrush held absurdly before her like a pistol or bayonet. The can of polyurethane sat on newsprint on the floor, and a few strokes of varnish along the counter showed where Herbie had been interrupted. "Here you *all* are." The brush shook in the intensity of her grip, scattering drops of the gummy stuff on her linen clam diggers and the lower shelves. It came to Dana with a start that it had been *Adena* who spilled the polyurethane down the steps.

Dana said, "Herbie, go take care of Bernadette."

"You sure?"

"I'm sure." She was not afraid of Adena Solomon, tilting at Fritos. She said, "Adena, put down that brush." The sentence erupted in a familiar, cinematic rhythm: *Travis, put down that gun. Gentlemen, hold your fire.* Cassius might see the comedy. Adena certainly did not. Her flaccid weapon thrust before her, her eyes burned with elemental fury.

"I have to hand it to you," she said in a voice at once choked and shrill. "I didn't see your scheme."

"There is no scheme."

Trudy crossed and held a hand out to Kenisha. "Come on, honey-gal. I read you a story *up*stairs." Strangely, Kenisha did not object, but took the hand and mounted. More strangely, Adena only watched them go, with a tooth-gritted smile until they were out of sight. Cassius edged toward Dana.

"It's really funny, ain't it? It's a hoot," Adena said. "Nobody comes around to see Trudy in eighteen years, and all of a sudden here's the whole family. Nephews, kiddies, I don't know what all. Two great bucks nosing around."

"Nobody's *nosing around.* Cassius is *my* friend."

"Oh, wonder! Cassius is *your* friend. Why, sakes alive!" Adena bent and dipped the brush. It took her attention for a moment, the way the varnish ran back in the can and slowed. She counted the drips. "One, two, three, four . . . I do declare, Miss Dana, how I *do* believe that Cassius is your friend! When Clyde told me about *more* nephews, and little cute cornrowed girls! — I said, Clyde, Miss Dana was prob'ly their friend back when they-all hatched up this scheme to get my land. But was it Trudy's idea in the first place, or was it girlfriend's? I think *so.* And then the big bad brothers egged you on and here you came, renting the cabin all tourist and widow, Mizzus Fine Nor'easter Boo-hoo. But the question is, how did you work on Solly? You got him back to drinking? It was just so hot you *had to* take off your clothes?"

Dana shook with anger. "Was that how *you* did it?"

Cassius said, "Girl, *hush.*"

"Ah-ah-ah. You think I can't prove you *abused* him, but lemme tell you, lady, where there's fire, there'll be some smoke!" She laughed at her wit and dipped the brush again, swiping it up and down the sunglass rack. "All these years I waited!" Cassius stepped toward her and she swung around to fend him off. She lunged and painted a swath across the belly of his T-shirt. "Tarred with the same brush!" she laughed.

"None of that *means* anything," Dana said.

Cassius reached and caught Adena's arm, pried the brush from her fist.

"Go home now, Missuz."

Adena jerked her arm away. "I'll tell you what *means* something, you little slut. What *means* something is that Judge Norquist is a friend of mine. And he's going to sucker punch your clever scheming little ass . . ."

She lost her balance and set one hand on the edge of the gallon can. Fire in her eyes, she lifted it, heaving its contents upward in their direction. Cassius turned and put up a hand to shield his face. The stuff hung heavy, like a liquid tarp, then fell and shattered on the back of his head, the counter, the cans and packets, the aspirin and the dog food, the Greedy Gut lures and Piscator shrimp rigs, the floor, the Nurit PC scanner, Dana's sandaled feet. The tang of resin enveloped them. Adena flung the can at the counter, where it bounced and rattled to the floor. She said again, "Just watch me. I'm gonna break your lying ass."

"Is there any in your eyes?!" Dana held a washcloth over the sink and dumped white spirits into it. He shook his head, the stuff oozing in sluggish ridges down his nape. Like drying ketchup. She could have reached out a finger and written in it. He peeled off the T-shirt, shed the shorts on top of it, and kicked them toward the kitchen bin. Stood tense in his briefs. The air didn't so much stink as sting. He shied when she squeezed the cloth into his hair, then pressed back against her hand as she scrubbed the solvent in. "It's the only way," she said. He nodded, neck muscles flexed, hands in fists at his sides. All this time she had been waiting for Isobel to appear, waiting for Luther to attack, for the exotic threat from the unknown. She *knew* Adena. But in fact you never know when violence will erupt at your own front door. She poured more solvent into the rag and rubbed again. Again. Again. His neck and shoulders. *Shoulder work.*

She said, "Adena always judges other people's motives by her own. She's the one who's been scheming to get Solly's land. For eighteen years!"

He said, "She's crazier than Isobel."

"That's for sure."

She relaxed a little at this evidence of accord. But his back was burled and knotted against her fingers. The smells of resin and solvent made her nose run, and she wiped it with the back of her hand. She took a clean cloth and soaped it, soothed the stinging spirits with a circular motion on his back and neck. Again.

"I had enough crazy women in my life, I don't need to be called *buck.*"

"I know. But it isn't race with her. It's all about money."

"How you know what's race and what isn't? It ain't *racial* when Isobel come at me with a scissor, but I don't need to hang around, uh-*uh.*"

Dana stiffened. She said, so that he could contradict her, "You mean you don't need to hang around here."

"That's right. I don't need to be toting and lifting. I done my bag-boy time."

She took her hands from him, long enough for her shock to register. Then she rinsed the rag and applied it warm against his flesh again. He leaned against the counter and let her do this. After a while she said, "You own this store. As good as. It's yours by rights. Trudy was his *wife.* If she doesn't want it, it should come to you."

He said, "That's speechifying," and turned to face her. "He left it to you. If you don't want it, look like it belong to that Goth girl."

"I do want it. I want it to be *ours.*"

He took the cloth from her and swirled it over his face, rubbed it around his neck and down his chest. He turned on the tap and bent under it, shaking the water from his head.

"Cassius. Love. Be pragmatic. Think of it in pure economic terms. Where could we ever have something handed to us like this, where we could work together, live together, make a good living at it?"

Toweling his head with a dish towel, mocking: *"Economic terms!"*

"It's not the money, it's the *life*. It's a good life."

"I told you up front, my family all mouthing at me how I should make more. Do my duty, make a decent living. Shit. I want to be *out*side. I want to *go*. You was heading to California, I thought you to be my navigator. I never did want you for my fucking boss."

"Is that what you thought?! Navigator? Boss? Those are my options?"

"Seem like."

"Are you Kenisha now, that you think I wish you harm?"

"Don't use Kenisha!"

"Are you Isobel, then, all white people are out to get you?"

"How I'm s'posed to know what to think?" He rubbed at his chest and arms. Very like Bernadette: *I can't get clean*. "I lived in no more town than this. It's no kinda traveling for me to live on the white side of this town."

"My side."

"Your side."

"Have I ever . . . Cassius, have I ever . . . ?"

"I'm only telling you . . ." He took a breath, in dangerous territory. "I'm not interested to be Mister Dana."

She pushed past him, out into the room at a pace that would take her straight through the jalousies. Stopped short and turned, fists against her thighs. She could tell him, now. The words were pushing at her throat, her tongue. She could shame him, and he'd never dare accuse her that way again. *Waif attack*. And the fact itself of the pregnancy, the fact of the child, would be forever shackled to this first moment of hate between them. She wavered, wanting to say it, wanting to win, but afraid of the cost of winning this way. She dropped her eyes. "Mister Dana? Is that what you think you are?!"

"To all these folk around here, *yas, ma'am,* that's what I think." He flung the rag on the counter, but it sank limp and unconvincing. Unsure of himself as she was unsure: "You introduce me all smiles and girly, what do they think except: *That's her buck*."

"My god." Her viscera was liquid. "I thought we were together, equals, *in it together* is what you said!"

"Yeah, well, but sometime I think you like the shock. You always asking do I pack a gun, or was I in a gang when I was a kid."

"I never heard such bullshit."

"Why you think I stole that picture? Don't I know how to please you?"

She sank onto the linoleum, where the smell seemed thick. The unfairness of it sank with her. She couldn't catch her breath. Wasn't it unfair?

He was pacing now, voice raised now to give himself swagger. "You like it that I'm black. You like that I'm *dark* black. You proud of yourself to love a *dark* black man."

"Don't say that to me. You'll regret that you said that to me." But was it true? Was it true when they met—no, be clear: when *she* called *him*—benumbed by the falling towers, her little life stripped of significance, was it true she had needed this jolt to set herself back in motion? Never mind how it jolted him?

"And now you want me to settle down. Just like Isobel. You want me to work inside where the money is!"

"Whsht!" Trudy was in the doorway. "Don't you wake that chile! One crazy woman enough for one night."

Cassius dropped into a chair and held his head, bare torso, bare thighs, a black *Thinker.* Was it true?

"I'm going to Flora's now. You two hush. I seen the mess in there." She looked askance at Dana crumpled on the floor. "What you going to do?"

"I don't know, Trudy."

"What you going to tell the people?"

"I'll tell them we were attacked by vandals."

"Umph," Trudy said, an affirmative. "Don't wake that chile." And left.

Cassius sat head in hands, agitating his crown. "I said I'd never let her hear me shout again."

Dana elbowed herself awkwardly onto the sofa across from him, spent, small. She took several breaths of the air that was clearer now. She let him breathe as well, until she could match her breath to his. He continued to chafe his cropped head. "Cassius. We could do something here that's never been tried here. Across on Sag Island nobody looks twice at a mixed couple. They're rich, they live however they please, it'd be gauche for anybody to object. Racism is *uncool.* But here in Pelican Bay — these people have been so busy getting by till payday they don't know how to change. Even Solly, even Trudy — they didn't want to jettison the rules that kept them apart, not really. It was more comfortable to pretend. But you and I — if we run the store, side by side, equals, we raise Kenisha — and maybe other children? — raise them right, we can have what Solly and Trudy didn't. These are tough, honest people. They'll accept us, both sides of the road."

"I'm not looking to do no social work."

"*Don't* say that. It's *not* that."

"I want no pulpit. That be Luther's trip."

"I want to make a *home* with you."

"Seem like you already home."

"Cassius. Can't we be together? It's what you want. It's what I want."

"Not here. Not if we got to stay with you."

She leaned and let her hair fall over her hands. Dug her fingertips in her scalp. *Social work.* The store was a mess, the inheritance was a legal quagmire, Trudy had no home. She would not be leaving the campsite cleaner than she found it.

"Give me a few days. What will Trudy do?"

"She can come if she's a mind to."

"She won't."

He agitated his head. He was stone. "She got more friends than you do. She been here eighteen years without seeing me, and she never heard of you before a few months ago. She can deal."

Dana leaned over her crossed feet for balance, wrapped her arms around her head. She did not know if what they had said tonight could be unsaid or would follow them across the country on I-10. She did not know if, or how much of, what he said was true.

She hid her face in her arms. She said, "All right. I'll go with you."

• • •

The eye sees more than the heart knows. This riddle ran its Möbius strip through her brain when she tried to sleep. When she got up to take a swallow of ice water and lay back down, the chill backed up her esophagus and she saw herself as Herbie's carpenter's level, the bubble tipping back and forth from throat to stomach as it tried to find equilibrium.

At three she went downstairs, careful to avoid the creaking treads.

Phoebe said, "It's three in the morning."

Dana said, "I need to talk."

"Okay. Shoot."

She heard the flint of the lighter rasping, the intake of breath. At intervals all through her recitation she could hear the tap of the cigarette on the glass ashtray. "I don't know if he's right, or partly right. My grandmother was a bigot and my mother was a hypocrite. Maybe I haven't come any further than humbled and confused."

"Sounds like progress," Phoebe said lightly, and then let a silence fall. "All this time you've been in love, sweetie. Now you're in the world."

"I'm not any less in love because I'm in the world."

The cigarette tapped the glass. "Yes, you are. You thought love would take you out of history. But it can't do that. It's more complicated. You're not in a love *story* anymore, and that's always disappointing."

"I'm not disappointed."

"Yes you are. You're in a *store-owner* story, a *lawsuit* story. Just because you've decided to take on race, it doesn't mean you don't have to deal with all the other hassles. You're in a *pregnant* story, a *stepparent* story."

"Yeah. Well. Anyway." Dana pushed against a headache with her fingertips. "Anyway. I'll go with the love story."

"Almost everybody does. That's how I make my living," Phoebe said.

31

SHE PACKED A COOLER for the beach. Cassius sat on the couch with Kenisha in his lap, reading to her out of a *Barbie* magazine from the rack at the front of the store. He made princely faces, did the voices, wicked stepmother, falsetto sister. Kenisha stared rapt. Her hands lay lightly on her father's arms. What's wrong with this picture? Not a goddam thing, except that if Dana stepped into the frame, the spell would be broken and the angst descend.

Nevertheless, she packed a picnic cooler: homemade chicken nuggets, turkey sandwiches, apples, Twinkies, Coke, and beer—willfully in limbo from whatever needed her attention. Yesterday, Saturday, she and Herbie had cleaned up the store as well as they could and opened in the afternoon. Tomorrow she would call Perry Hoyt and hand the lawsuit over to him entirely. She would explain to Trudy, she would apologize to Herbie. But today they would go as a family to Sag Island.

They would go in her car. He would drive. She gave him the keys and he gathered up Kenisha's gear. Kenisha slammed out the back door, and Dana went back and closed it. She checked around the house and closed the jalousie door, which had been open all night, apparently. Cassius stood with his hand lightly on Kenisha's shoulder. Dana opened the back car door for her.

"No!" The girl slipped out of her father's grasp, circled to the driver's side, and climbed in. She clambered over the gearbox and plunked herself in the passenger seat.

Cassius opened the door. "C'mon, Kenisha, you sit in the back. Mizz Dana's going to ride up front with me."

Kenisha said nothing, glared, and adroitly fastened herself in the seat belt. Cassius reached across her to undo it. "In the back, baby. There you go."

"No!" Impressive fierceness buckled her little face. She hit at her father's hand and began to cry. Dana's muscles clenched for the confrontation.

But Cassius straightened up. "Maybe we best try another time."

"Oh." Dana stood a moment longer, then folded herself into the backseat. Belted herself in. She sat in the back just as she had for all those childhood years (but in her own car now), watching the world blur by in the blunted triangle of the window. Giving directions, *right at the highway, left to the bridge, left at this fork.* Trying to fix one image while the two up front sang along with somebody named Raffi on her tape deck. Reminding herself how extraordinary he was, what he had gone through to be with his daughter. How he had gone against *his* history that far. But what was she to do with the waves of resentment like nausea? What was it that Phoebe said about territoriality? *The bottom brain, the lizard part.*

They rode in silence for a while—the bay as bright as ever, the seagulls complaining at the wind—and then she said to Cassius, conscious of a violence, "We have an expression for it. 'Taking a backseat.'"

He said nothing. She read his silence clearly. It said: *Don't make me choose.*

At the apex of the bridge the Gulf spread out to infinity. Kenisha sang cheerfully, *"I like to eat, eat, eat apples and bananas."*

The Gulf showed them dolphins and kite surfing and as many starfish on the shore as there had been stars last night. Off the cape they saw five floating pelicans lift in formation, wheel and plunge, then in perfect unison bounce to the surface, point their beaks skyward and gulp their prey. "A chorus line," said Cassius. "The chorus of the food chain," Dana said. Cassius and Kenisha built a castle while Dana dug a moat at a discreet distance. But when Kenisha became absorbed in making a tunnel to the moat, Dana dared to dig from the other side, so that their sandy fingertips touched under the bridge. Kenisha laughed and, laughing, glanced up at Dana, though she withdrew her hand. Then Dana and Cassius sat on a towel and had a beer while Kenisha deigned to continue on her own, tiling the tower with coquina shells. None of the passersby paid particular attention to them, and they saw a few other couples in combinations of tan and sable. Dana was careful not to point this out.

Instead, she said of Kenisha, "It will just take time." He nodded. She smiled at him, shedding sand from her palm.

When they got back to the car, Cassius picked Kenisha up like a mannequin under his arm, opened the back door, and set her in. She clawed against him but he pressed her back, did up the belt. She yelled and beat her fists. He got in the driver's seat and Dana on the passenger's side. Kenisha screamed and twisted past the new construction on the inlet, past the River of Faith revival tent, over the long bridge across the bay. Then all at once she was asleep, lashes webbed with tears. They exchanged a smile.

You win. You get the front seat all the way across America, your reward for being the stepmother, the one who has bought the power. You sit in the front seat all the way from a truck stop in Lake Charles to a Hampton Inn in Dallas to a Seal Beach Motel 6. When you stop for gas you walk the aisles of the 7-Eleven, choosing dark chocolate, choosing Mounds with its chewy center, wiping your neck with a damp paper towel. When you stop for a week or a month, while he works at whatever will pay enough to propel you back along the road, you stay behind in "efficiency" apartments, entertaining a hostile toddler and a hungry newborn, making do. You wheel the stroller down cracked cement, boil macaroni in battered pots. When the girl is old enough, you teach her Monopoly. Your role is risk taker, you squander cash for real estate, blow on the dice, build hotels on Park Place. Do you take up tarot cards and homeopathy? Will you seek acupuncture and mud massage? Will you bolt some intolerable muggy night in Idaho?

They pulled in to Solly's and crept as usual over the pine straw behind the store. He lifted Kenisha out and carried her up the stairs while Dana dragged their gear, their beach treasures and detritus, off the seats, from the floor, the trunk. She carted it all inside. She poured herself a wine, taken by a petty selfishness that would not pour one wineglass more. She lay on the sofa and kicked off her shoes. Placed her hand over the secret greed of the tadpole self. She had not told him. She would have to tell him now. Tonight. The necessity turned in her mind, and she dozed away from it.

She waked startled at a shriek from upstairs, although Cassius was at the kitchen sink—or had been, because by the time she bolted upright he was on the stairs. She rose unsteadily, stomach churning, and hurried after him. He was by now a broad outline in the door of the music room, in the blue glow of the nightlight, across which, back and forth, a black scrap flitted, whirring. Cassius dodged across the room and snatched the frightened girl, pushed back past Dana and leaned against the landing wall behind her, Kenisha's head tucked under his protective hand.

The panicked bat swooped toward them and away, scratched against the glass of the ceiling fixture, banged a wing against the window, squeaked and caught for purchase on the empty curtain rod. They stayed a moment, adults and bat, figuring out what to do. Kenisha was heaving against Cassius, still emitting little sobbing shrieks.

"Take her downstairs," said Dana. "I'll deal with it." She closed the door.

"I'm not leaving you. What you going to do?"

Install hydraulics on the doors, she inanely thought, and raced down again, into the store, where she grabbed a net off the fishing-tackle display. Wachter landing net, the best she carried. She shed its tag on her way back upstairs. Cassius still stood against the wall, Kenisha's legs locked around him.

"What are you going to do?"

Dana gained the landing, opened the door in one sweep, and checked that the frightened bat was still grasping the curtain rod.

Hanging upside down now. Playing possum. She crossed in a crouch against the possibility that it would fly. Cassius said, "Dana, wait. Don't." But she was not going to wait. She was going to prove herself to him, to Kenisha. She raised the net and lifted it gingerly up over the rigid body. Bagged it. When the net brushed its flesh, the bat screamed and thrashed. It flung itself against the string, tangling wing and claws. Its small muscularity was startling, like the sudden force of a fighting fish. Now that she had it, its terror terrified her. But she held on, net and bat at arm's length. She opened the window with one hand and with the other threw the writhing mess out, net and all. Handle tumbled over netting and, midway down, the bat flew free. The net hit the pine straw with an insignificant *shh.*

She closed the window and turned, trembling. Cassius was wedged against the wall, Kenisha's legs still jackknifed around his waist. Her eyes were on Dana, wide with fear and blame. She pointed with a jabbing finger.

"She the devil! She the devil!"

What next? How foolishly we suppose we have earned respite, that because the car is totaled the pipes won't burst. Scarcely an hour later, Cassius was scarcely down the stairs, when they heard the siren pulling in from the highway west. *Sarah's man is drunk again,* Dana thought as the lights swept over them. Then, *Are they going to Herbie's?* But the lights curved on, and pulled between the gas pumps and the store. *The Picasso?* The door was hammered on. Cassius was back upstairs before she made it to the store. The patrolman on the porch was small and sinewy, his colorless hair sweated flat to his head by the hat he now turned in his hands.

"Mizz Dana Cleveland?"

"Yes?"

"You're wanted over on Sag Island, ma'am. A Herbie Zebrowski is asking for you."

"What's happened? Is anybody hurt?"

"No need for alarm, ma'am, the lady of the house is away, but there's a fire, and the daughter—the young lady needs you."

"Do I come with you?"

"Best you follow me, ma'am, if you're all right to drive."

"I'm fine. Just let me . . . get a sweater."

She took the stairs two at a time. He was crouching in Kenisha's room between her bed and the door, Herbie's crowbar in his hands.

"They're not after Kenisha, love. It's Bernadette. I think she's set fire to her mother's house."

"Don't go with them."

"I'll be back before dawn."

"Don't go. I can't be always waiting on you."

"Cassius." She circled him with her arms. She felt the tremors surfacing from deep inside his body, deeper than any place she had the capacity to touch. "You must see — if it weren't for me she'd never have found out Solly was her father. I can't walk out on her."

"And I can't be hanging where the *po*-lice in and out the house, *you must see.*" She saw — the irony turned sour, the hands on the crowbar held between them. He wrung the iron haft. "You walk now, I won't be here when you get back."

"What? Would you keep me with an ultimatum?"

"What else you offering *me*?"

She got it. The hall light gathered to a pinpoint on his brow, the hurt hammered in his brazen eye. She leant to kiss him as he shied.

She said, "Cassius, I must."

She touched his jaw with her fingertips and stood and descended the stairs and got in her Celica behind the tinted windows and pulled out after the officer, following the squad car's flat red eyes.

Trust, Loyalty, Commitment, it said on the side of the car.

They were never able to locate the tuner who said the piano could explode, though Adena insisted on this story, and Bernadette remembered he had been there. Every tuner and piano store they consulted in Pensacola, Panama City, or Tallahassee (an avid junior detective also called venues in Chicago and LA), said that such a thing was impossible. A Web site called Exploding Piano turned out to be a promotion for a concert of iconoclast composers.

It's true that the cast-iron frame of an upright is under forty thousand pounds of pressure, two hundred and thirty wires for eighty-eight keys, seven and a third octaves stretched from wrest pin to tuning peg, the bass notes overburdened with three strings to each note, the bass and treble bridges crossing each other in a giant *X*. But that's why it's made of cast iron, isn't it? The iron frame of this piano was bolted to a wrest block made of fourteen layers of maple wood with the grain of one veneer perpendicular to the next. It could burn, no question, but it could not explode.

The girl's motives were not clear either, and were somewhat fudged in the police report. She seemed "a kind of a flake" in the officer's unofficial assessment. She considered the piano "a bad influence" because it had belonged to "an enemy of her father." She admitted to "working a charm on it," though she apparently hadn't thought this through. About the actual operation she was surprisingly adroit. She waited until her mother was at a Realtors' conference in Jacksonville. She unscrewed the front of the case just as a piano tuner would, and wedged her candles in the striking mechanism. Six candles — she was clear on this — one each for "earth, air, sea, and fire," one for herself, and one for a Mrs. Solly, whom the girl had not actually known, but who "needed to get some peace." She sprinkled the felts with Indian oils called "Mystic Veil" and "Dragon's Blood," and waved over the piano a "chakra wand" which was a kind of baton with semiprecious stones. She chanted the following:

Bide the Witch's law we must,
In perfect love, in perfect trust,
Eight Words the Wiccan Rede fulfill:
An ye harm none, do what you will.

She was insistent on this, because she did not intend to harm anyone. She just thought "the Law of Three owed" her, and anyway "the piano was no good." She lit her candles and replaced the case. She thought the candles would clog the action and maybe the keys with wax. She thought, yes, it was possible the felts would catch, but she thought they would flame out, like incense. It was meant for a controlled burn.

Dana followed the little officer, right at the highway, left to the bridge, up over the water on a highway sustained in air by pillars deep in sand. It was not seven hours since she had done this route, though then she had been in the back and now she was in the driver's seat. She felt, not the control that figure of speech implies, but rather as if she were on an airplane in a wind-sheer drop. Her stomach left her. The bay below was winking in its accustomed watery way. Above the crescent of trees on the near side of the island, smoke hurled itself up over a dance of orange flames. The smoke was mole-colored against a raven sky.

For all practical purposes, what occurred could be reconstructed, though it defied several centuries of pianoforte engineering. The piano was old and the striking mechanism all but tinder. The felts caught first and then the hammer shanks, and the hammer rail the width of the piano scorched and sputtered. The damper-lifting lever, the tuning wrest, the tuning wedge—every intricate and precise component of every wooden part caught like brush and twigs. The Indian oils flared hot. The new varnish of the case melted and pooled in flame. The softwood brace went up. The strings—which are not strings but wire, steel, and steel bound with copper—began to snap with a sound like pistols firing (heard by the couple next door and four passersby on their way to the Flamingo); the fourteen-ply of hundred-year-old dry maple veneer seethed and peeled, and although by this time the treble strings were popping at machine-gun speed, against all odds and probabilities (*unless the witchcraft worked,* somebody said) the frame buckled and the piano shot its innards in all directions under forty thousand pounds of pressure. Hammers like flaming arrows, shrapnel of melting ivory. The welter of trash and cloth and paper in the room went up. Foam cushions shriveled.

Boutique bags smothered their contents in a shroud of smoke. The television exploded. The beveled mirror exploded. The lava lamp from QVC exploded.

The cat, Horse, bolted out the cat door and survived.

Herbie had Bernadette wrapped in one of those gray fire-department standard-tragedy-issue blankets, wrapped to her hollow eyes, red eyes. Her spikes of platinum hair, rising from her expression of uncomprehending horror, gave her the look of someone whose hair had turned white from fright. Dudley Do-Right padded back and forth in front of them, head cocked and whimpering in that doggy need to understand what he could not. The house was a tower of flame, collapsing now, sending out scraps of blackened paper like little bats.

"An ye harm none," Bernadette kept repeating, in self-defense, or perhaps as plea. "An ye harm none." Herbie had his arm around her. *"Sh,"* he said. *"Sh, sh, sh."*

The fireman who came to speak to them was very sad and very tired. You could see in his twisted smile the standard apology for bad news. He shook his head to Dana, as if to say: *these kids today.* He said he was sorry, they weren't going to be able to save anything. He said they had contacted the mother. He said Bernadette would have to make a statement, but she could do it tomorrow at the station. He wondered did she have a place to stay tonight.

Dana thought how everything falls into place. There would be an empty bed in the music room by now. She said, "I'll take her home."

It was nearly dawn by the time she could settle, Bernadette asleep upstairs on a knockout pill and the blow-up mattress, Herbie at last convinced to take Dudley back to the cabin and catch some z's. Dana pulled an afghan over her thighs—it was chilly at this hour, this deep into the year; she'd have to learn how to light the woodstove—and fingered a frilly sock of Kenisha's that seemed to be all they had left behind. That and the Picasso. Outside, the floodlight timer clicked off and the raddled oak trunk disappeared, to be followed at once by a gold edging of the upper branches as the sun came up. *Let there be light.* How different a simple tree seemed, lit from one direction and then another.

She had known that Cassius and Kenisha would be gone, and all the same she was struck numb. The events were in motion (the old blue Pontiac rolling on the asphalt of the journey west) before she had quite fitted herself to this version of events. It seemed imperative to take in her new estate. So she sat in a place she recognized as limbo, here in this room, where Solly had lived out his time, and she would live out her time, and Cassius would loom large in his absence, a persistent ghost.

"Do I want my little girl to have no daddy?" he had demanded. Now her child, his child, would have no daddy; a fact of life, a failure daily to be dealt with, an unchosen choice. She would not duck the issue: They had been decent, yes, and loving, yes. But she had supposed herself made of some altogether different stuff than her small-minded grandmother and her mother who was "torn," had supposed that Cassius could tear himself and Kenisha from Isobel and Luther and their willful kind; and that together they could leap past and out of sight of the myth of race.

Phoebe was right, history is in us, that's what history is. We only pretend we have the power to leave it in the past. Nor, if you choose eyes-wide-open to flout one taboo, are you given a pass on the other obstacles of desire: gender, money, the generations, jealousy.

"Cassius," she said aloud. She wrapped her arms around herself, taking the measure of her solitude. At that angle her reflection appeared in the blank television screen, distorted, foreshortened, moonfaced, skinny, knobby kneed. A squirrel laughed or scolded in the crotch of the live oak tree. The sunlight poured across its crown and dappled the pine straw on the ground. Her ground. She folded the afghan. It was time to open up the store.

EPILOGUE

Renovation

SPRING COMES to Pelican Bay in February. When there has been a wet Christmas, as there was this year, followed by a spell of sun, as there was this year, it arrives midmonth as an extravagance of azalea blossom. Trimmed or shaggy, planted or volunteer, in yards and roadways, pots and gullies, swamps and woods — bushes of no distinction, which have masqueraded all year as mere privet, fling the length of Sink Street a carpet of petals and a bower.

Up which Dana strides toward Devil's Sink, 2.6 miles there and back. The long hours behind the counter are hard on her back and legs, but she is prescribed no bed rest. Rather, she is told to walk. Her perspective afoot is different from that in the driver's seat. Apart from the colors of azaleas (*scarlet, fuchsia, fire, annatto, carmine, crimson, salmon, rose*) what she sees in her mind's eye is the pumping of the baby's heart, black and white, as it was on the computer screen. She pumps her arms. Muscles, lungs, and lymph respond, power her around the pond, in cahoots with her heart and liver to build new bones.

Remarkably, she has never had any fear for this baby's health. The amniocentesis says it's a hearty boy. It does not specify his color. The local women rag her for her belly now. "Whose is it?" they ask, and she says, "Mine." Some of them will be shocked, and Phoebe thinks it will be hard on the child, but Dana continues to believe it's time to breach the border between the Sinks. *"Sincerely,"* she says, to which Phoebe replies, "Sincerity is American shtick." But Phoebe will come for the birth, which is due on the twentieth of March. Insofar as numbers project a mood, this has a blooming, symmetrical sound: *oh-three, two-oh, two-oh-oh-three.* Unlike, for example, *nine-eleven,* which was full of sticks and stones.

The fire was ruled an accident, and whatever punishment Bernadette suffers is self-assigned. She and Adena do not speak, although Adena, having as a real estate broker cultivated good relations with her insurance company for twenty years, has done rather well out of it. She took her settlement, sold her charred double lot for a million-three, and opened her own agency up in the new Lhamon Mills Estates.

Bernadette lives in the cabin with Herbie, a statutory illegality, which for the moment is the best available brand of what she needs—Herbie's devoted, not to say abject, attention. Whether she will stay with Herbie is anybody's guess. If she doesn't, and Herbie needs her shoulder, Dana will be here.

Trudy's new double-wide is hooked up to power and plumbed, equidistant between the store, the highway, and the woods. Trudy has resigned from Henry's and will help raise the boy. From her cousin Charlene she knows that Cassius and the girl have joined his family in Pennsylvania, and that he works security for Atlantic Mills. She is skeptical about the keeping of long-term secrets, but as she rightly says, "I been schooled to keep my part." In any case she does not hear from Cassius, and Dana does not hear from him.

Dana has hired two part-time clerks, one from East Sink, one from West, and has started selling frozen casseroles from the best cooks of both sides. Horse the cat pads between the cabin and the store, killing chameleons, cowering from possums, ostentatiously ignoring Dudley Do-Right, who gives him right of way. The downstairs floors have been sanded. There's a sink in the baby's room, new cabinets in the kitchen, and a deck under construction between the jalousies and the tree. The oak hutch shipped down from Somerset fits perfectly between the kitchen and the fake Miró, on the other side from the Blake reproduction, which hangs across from the Picasso. If anyone asks, this last is a print she picked up in some antique store, but no one has asked, and probably no one will.

On Sag Island last month an exchange student from Tehran was beaten by a biker who will soon be acquitted of assault. The National Guard has been sent to Fort Jackson for desert-combat training. The Allansons and the Moomises continue to chafe against an old black woman living on their side of the road. The developers continue to set their sights on a piece of beach-view swamp, and eventually they will get it, some years before the ice cap melts and the coastlines of the world are whorled away.

Any sane person, Phoebe and Dana frequently agree, would conclude that we have learned nothing at all, that three hundred and fifty years after slavery began, the best we can do with each other is clubfooted and halting, the laws do not protect and the anger does not subside, the best willed are paralyzed with self-consciousness, while out in the world we are still turning people into commodities wherever a buck is to be made; and the posturing monkeys rule the earth, and bigotry filters down as always through the sieve of our ignorance. And the bleak shall inherit the earth. And the little anyone can do is so clearly too little too late that most of us don't bother but sit in front of the TV set that presents us with the paranormal, the gimmicky, and the rivers of spilled blood.

Notwithstanding, at Devil's Sink the world sets itself to breed and mend. The new sinkhole has been declared off limits by Water Management, but here the drakes are treading on the ducks, literally, web-footing them along the spine. One who yielded too early in the season scuttles her wobbly brood—fourteen of them—to the icy water. Dana tosses bread heels, which the adults scramble to steal from the chicks. The turtles in their sturdy armor spook and disappear. A white heron stands its ground under a willow, immobile on one crowbar leg, brilliantly ashimmer in its wintry white.

The children are all in school, but here and there on the dirt path a few mothers are pushing in their strollers infants still bundled to the eyes. Two women sit on a bench under the deformed oak tree, one grayhaired in a denim jacket, with square-framed glasses and a squashed cloth hat, the other in trousers and a cardigan, in her lap a plastic bag. They are seated a few feet apart, chatting easily. The one in the hat points out a pair of copulating ducks, and the two of them laugh and fling up a hand each, meaning: *I'm done with all that, thank god.* One of these women is older than the other by perhaps a dozen years. One is black and one is white.

A scent of wood smoke from the fireplaces and stoves of January still hangs about the Sinks. The dark water gives back Dana's suntanned face, hair lopped at the chin, regular and unremarkable features except for a mobile mouth, from which it would surprise anyone but Phoebe to hear an acerbic remark.

Dana is remembering a woman she met long ago at some fundraising dinner in Philadelphia. A historian and memoirist, she'd been to Latvia to research an account of her grandmother's life there at the turn of the century. The villagers were generous, flattered, eager to help. They wanted to tell her amazing things. But she was a historian and had no trouble imagining the extreme. She wanted to know what the ordinary felt like, how to pluck a hen, how the ice sounded cracking in the well, what they did with wet clogs in winter, the sundry smells of burning, the uses to which straw and grease were put. *There was the time the Lord Justice came!* they said. But why was he strange to them? What did he wear that was different from what they wore, so that they recognized him as a potentate? *There was a garroting in the barn!* But what did they do with their quotidian dead, how lay out a corpse, how commemorate, how mourn? Tyranny and murder are trifles to imagine, being everywhere the same.

Ain't nobody safe, says Trudy. *Ain't nobody gets all they want.*

Little by little, says Phoebe, *we come not very far.*

But here are two women, lower-middle-class, black and white, chatting on a bench at the edge of a Florida sink on a February Tuesday afternoon. Glory to our hippy mothers. Hosannah to our fathers who loved enterprise. Bless our errors. Shalom. Peace.

Acknowledgments

Parts of this novel appeared in slightly different form in *Iron Horse Literary Review* (Vol. 7, Nos. 1–2), *Prairie Schooner* (Vol. 82, No. 4; www.prairieschooner.org), and *Narrative Magazine* (www.narrativemagazine.com); my thanks to those magazines for permission to reprint.

For help in research, thanks are also due to the staffs of the Gilman Paper Mill in St. Mary's, Georgia, and the St. Joe Paper Mill in Port St. Joe, Florida — both unfortunately now defunct — and of Mashes Sand BP and general store at Panacea, Florida — thriving. The Florida Department of Environmental Protection was a font of information on sinkholes and the Gulf Coast karst. Timothy J. Warfel, attorney at law in Tallahassee, Florida, Joey Miller of Tallahassee, and Willie Hobbs of Virginia State University were all generous with their time and expertise, as was Anne Garee, program director of piano technology in the School of Music at Florida State University.